JANE STEELE

A CONFESSION

LYNDSAY FAYE

THORNDIKE PRESS
A part of Gale, Cengage Learning

GALE
CENGAGE Learning·

Farmington Hills, Mich • San Francisco • New York • Waterville, Maine
Meriden, Conn • Mason, Ohio • Chicago

LIBRARY OF CONGRESS CATALOGING-IN-PUBLICATION DATA

Names: Faye, Lyndsay, author.
Title: Jane Steele : a confession / by Lyndsay Faye.
Description: Large print edition. | Waterville, Maine : Thorndike Press, 2016. | © 2016 | Series: Thorndike Press large print reviewers' choice
Identifiers: LCCN 2016013158| ISBN 9781410490797 (hardcover) | ISBN 1410490793 (hardcover)
Subjects: LCSH: Women serial murderers—Fiction. | Interpersonal relations—Fiction. | Large type books. | GSAFD: Mystery fiction. | Black humor (Literature) | Romantic suspense fiction.
Classification: LCC PS3606.A96 J36 2016b | DDC 813/.6—dc23
LC record available at http://lccn.loc.gov/2016013158

Published in 2016 by arrangement with G.P. Putnam's Sons, an imprint of Penguin Publishing Group, a division of Penguin Random House LLC

Printed in Mexico
1 2 3 4 5 6 7 20 19 18 17 16

JANE STEELE

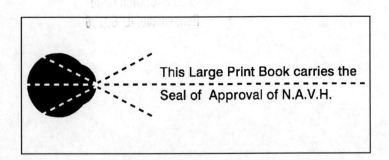

This book is humbly dedicated to Miss Eyre and Mr. Nickleby

"I am no bird; and no net ensnares me; I am a free human being with an independent will. . . ."

— *JANE EYRE*

How many species of creeping things, and how many birds hast Thou caused to fly!

— NANAK, founder of Sikhism, as quoted in *The Sikh Religion*

■ ■ ■ ■

VOLUME ONE

■ ■ ■ ■

ONE

"I wouldn't have her heart for anything. Say your prayers, Miss Eyre, when you are by yourself; for if you don't repent, something bad might be permitted to come down the chimney, and fetch you away."

Of all my many murders, committed for love and for better reasons, the first was the most important.

Already this project proves more difficult than I had ever imagined. Autobiographies depend upon truth; but I have been lying for such a very long, lonesome time.

"Jane, will you be my friend again?" Edwin Barbary had asked.

My cousin's lips were gnawed red, his skin gleaming with exertion and desire. When his fleshy mouth next moved, the merest croak emerged. He breathed precisely five more times, the fat folds of his belly shuddering against his torn waistcoat, and then he stilled like a depleted clockwork toy.

More of my homicides anon— the astute among you will desire to know why a dyed-in-the-wool villainess takes up pen and foolscap in the first place. I have been reading over and over again the most riveting book titled *Jane Eyre,* and the work inspires me to imitative acts. My new printing features a daring introduction by the author railing against the first edition's critics. I relate to this story almost as I would a friend or a lover — at times I want to breathe its entire alphabet into my lungs, and at others I should prefer to throw it across the room. Whoever heard of disembodied voices calling to *governesses,* of all people, as this Jane's do?

Hereby do I avow that I, Jane Steele, in all my days working as a governess, never once heard ethereal cries carried to me upon the brawny shoulders of the north wind; and had I done, I should have kept silent for fear of being labelled eccentric.

Faulting the work for its wild fancies seems petty, however, for there are marvellous moments within. I might myself once have written:

Why was I always suffering, always browbeaten, always accused, for ever condemned? Why could I never please? Why was it useless to try to win any one's favour?

I left such reflections behind me in childhood, at the bottom of the small ravine where my first cousin drew his final gurgling breaths. Yet I find myself pitying the strange, kindly Jane in the novel whose biography is so weirdly similar; she, too, was as welcome in her aunt's household as are church mice in the Communion larder, and was sent to a hell in the guise of a girls' school. That Jane was unfairly accused of wickedness, however, while I can no better answer my detractors than to thank them for their pains over stating the obvious.

It was the boarding school that taught me to act as a wolf in girl's clothing should: skulking, a greyer shadow within a grey landscape. It was London which formed me into a pale, wide-eyed creature with an errant laugh, a lust for life and for dirty vocabulary, and a knife in her pocket. It was Charles who changed everything, when I fell in love with him under the burdens of a false identity and a blighted conscience. The beginning of a memoir could be made in any of those places, but without my dear cousin, Edwin Barbary, none of the rest would have happened at all, so I hereby commence my account with the unembellished truth:

Reader, I murdered him.

I may always have been wicked, but I was not always universally loathed. For instance, I remember my mother asking me at five years old, "Are you hurt, *chérie*?"

Then as now, I owned a pallid complexion and listlessly curling hair the colour of hazelnut shells. Having just fallen flat on my face in the garden behind our cottage on the outskirts of Highgate House, I considered whether or not to cry. The strawberries I had gathered were crushed under my apron, painting me with sweet gore. I pored over the best stratagems to gain my mother's undivided attention perennially in those days — back when I believed I might be merely naughty, fit to be punished in the here and not the hereafter.

As it happened, my mother had been well all day. We had navigated no weeping, no laudanum, no gnawing at already-bleeding fingernails; she was teasing and coaxing, snatching my hand up as she wondered whether we might cover some biscuits with berries and fresh honey and host an im-

14

promptu picnic.

Therefore, I saw no need to cry. Instead, I stuck out my tongue at the offending root and gulped down the swelling at the back of my throat.

"I'm fine," I told her, "though my wrist is sore."

Smiling from where she sat on a quilted blanket beneath our cascading willow, she called, "Come here then, and let me see."

My mother was French. She spoke to me often in that language, and I found this flattering; she directed her native tongue at no one else unless she desired to illustrate their ignorance. She seemed to me unpredictable and glimmering as a butterfly, one worthy of being collected and displayed under glass. I was proud of her; I belonged to her. She noticed me when no one else bothered, and I could make her laugh when she could bear no one else.

Ma mère studied my wrist, brushed the specks of juice and flesh from my pinafore, and directed a dry look in my eyes.

"It is not very serious," she declared lightly in French. "Not even to a spun-sugar little girl."

"It hurts," I insisted, thinking, *It may have been better to cry after all.*

"Then it is most profoundly serious to

me," she proclaimed, again in French, and proceeded to kiss me until I was helpless with giggling.

"And I lost all the berries."

"But consider — there is no harm done. We shall go and gather more. After all, have you anything of consequence to do?"

The answer was no; there was nothing of consequence to do, as this garden party took place at midnight under a wan, watchful moon. Having spent my entire life in my mother's company, I thought nothing amiss herein, though I was vexed I had not seen the root which had tripped me. Surely other little girls donned lace-trimmed frocks and enjoyed picnics featuring trifle and tea cakes, sitting with their mothers under the jewel-strewn canopy of starlight, never dreaming of sleep until the cold dew threatened and we began to shiver.

Do they not? I would anxiously ask myself.

It is relevant that my beloved mother, Anne-Laure Steele, was detested throughout our familial estate, and for two sound reasons. First, as I mentioned, she was — tragically and irrevocably — French. Second, my mother was beautiful.

I do not mean beautiful in the conventional, insipid fashion; I mean that my mother was actually *beautiful,* bizarrely so, in the ghostly, wide-gazed sense. She possessed a determined square chin, a chin I share, so that she always looked stubborn even when meekness was selling at a premium. Her hair was dark with a brick-red sheen and her almond-shaped eyes were framed beneath by pretty caverns; her wrists had thin scars like pearlescent bracelets which I did not then understand.

At times she screamed under the indifferent moon in French for my dead father. At others she refused to budge from the bed until, groaning at the slanting afternoon light, she allowed our combined cook and housemaid, Agatha, to ply her with tea.

What's the matter, Mamma? I would ask softly. Now I am grown, I comprehend her answers far better than I did then.

Only that yesterday was so very, very long.

Only that my eyes are tired and nothing in the new novel I thought I'd like so well means as much to me as I imagined it would.

Only that I cannot think of a useful occupation, and when I do, the task daunts me, and so cannot attempt it anyhow, sweet one.

Never could I predict when her smile would blaze forth again, nor earn enough of the feathery kisses she would drop to my brow inexplicably — as if I was worthy of them for no reason at all.

In short, my mother and I — two friendly monsters — found each other lovely and hoped daily that others would find us so as well.

They did not.

I shall explain how I embarked upon a life of infamy, but first what my mother told me regarding my inheritance.

When I was six years old, my mother announced in French, in August, in the shade-dappled garden, "One day you will have everything, *chérie*, even the main house. It all belonged to your father and will always be yours — there are documents to this effect despite the fact inheritance for girls is always a highly complicated matter. Meanwhile, our cottage may be poor and plain, but you understand the many difficulties."

I did not fully understand the many difficulties, though I assumed my aunt and cousin, who lived in the estate proper, did so because they were haughty and wanted the entire pile of mossy stonework, complete with dour servants and tapestries hanging sombre as funeral shrouds, to themselves. Neither did I think our cottage, with its mullioned glass and its roaring fireplaces and its cheery bay windows, was either poor or plain. I did, however, understand particular difficulties, ones regarding how well we got on with our relations.

"You see the way your aunt looks at me — you know we cannot live at the main house. Here we are safe and warm and friendly and ourselves," she added fretfully, worrying at the cuticle upon her left thumb as her eyes pooled.

"Je déteste la maison principale," I announced.

Passing her my ever-ready kerchief, I dried her tears. I plucked wild sorrel to sprinkle over our fish supper and told everyone who would listen — which amounted only to my mother and frayed, friendly Agatha — *Let us always live just as we please, for I love you both.*

Such was not to be.

My aunt, Mrs. Patience Barbary — mother of Edwin Barbary — was, like my mother, a widow. She had been wed to Mr. Richard Barbary; Mr. Richard Barbary was the half brother of my own father, Jonathan Steele, whose claim to Highgate House was entire and never called into question in my presence. I presumed that our Barbary kinfolk resided with us due to financial necessity, as my aunt could not under any circumstances be accused of enjoying our company.

In fact, one of our visits to the main house, shortly after my ninth birthday, centred around just such a discussion.

"It is so very kind of you to have us for tea," Anne-Laure Steele said, her smile glinting subtly. "I have said often to Jane that she should better familiarise herself with the Steele estate — after all, she will live here when she is grown, and *mon Dieu,* to think what mismanagement could occur if she did not know its — I think, in English — intricacies?"

Aunt Patience was a sturdy woman wearing perennial mourning black, though she never otherwise appeared to regret her lack of spouse. Perhaps she was mourning something else entirely: her lost youth, for example, or the heathens in darkest Africa who perished in ignorance of Christ.

Certainly my uncle Richard was never mentioned nor seemed he much missed, which I found curious since his portraits were scattered throughout the house — a wedding watercolour from a friend in the drawing room, an oil study of a distinguished man of business in the library. Uncle Richard had owned a set of defined, almost pouting lips, an arched brow with a tuft of dark hair, and something rakish in his eyes made him seem more dashing than

I imagined "men of business" ought to look — ants all walking very fast with their heads down, a row of indistinguishable umbrellas. I thought, had I known him, I should have liked him. I wondered what possessed him to marry Aunt Patience, of all people.

Thankfully, Patience Barbary was blessed with a face ensuring that conjugal affronts would not happen twice, which did her tremendous credit — or at least, she always threw beauty in the teeth, as it were, of my own mamma, who smiled frigidly following such ripostes. Aunt Patience had a very wide frog's visage with a ruddy complexion and lips like a seam in stone-masonry.

"So much time passed in our great Empire." Aunt Patience sighed following my mother's uncertainty over vocabulary. "And despite that, such a terrible facility with our language. I ask you, is this a proper example to set for the — as you would have it — future mistress of Highgate House?"

"It might not be," my mother replied with snow lacing her tone, "but I am not often invited to practise your tongue."

"Oh!" my aunt mused. "That must be very vexing."

I yearned to leap to my mother's defence, but sat there helplessly dumb, for my aunt hated me only marginally less than she did my mother. After all, I was awkward and gangly, possessed only of my mamma's too-thin neck and too-thoughtful expressions. My eyes were likewise catlike — voluptuous, in truth — but the plainest of ordinary cedar browns in colour. My mother ought to have done better by me, I thought on occasion. Her own irids were a strange, distant topaz like shards of frozen honey.

I never blamed my father, Jonathan Steele, for my shortcomings. I never expected anything of him — not remembering him — and thus could not expect *more* of him.

"*Aimes-tu ton gâteau?*" my mother asked me next.

"*Ce n'est pas très bien, Maman.*"

Aunt Patience simmered beneath her widow's weeds; she supposed the French language a threat and, in retrospect, she may have been correct.

"*Pauvre petite,*"* my mother commiserated.

Mamma and Aunt Patience embarked upon a resounding and communicative silence, and I felt Cousin Edwin's eyes on me like a set of hot pinpricks; when the adults abandoned decorum in favour of

___

* Translation: "Do you like your cake?" "It isn't very good, Mamma." "Poor little dear."

spitting false compliments and heartfelt censures at each other, he launched his offensive.

"I've a new bow and arrows I should show you, Jane," he murmured.

For a child's tones, Edwin's were weirdly insinuating. The quick bloom of instinctual camaraderie always withered upon the instant I recalled what my cousin was actually *like*. Meanwhile, I wanted to test his new bow very much indeed — only sans Edwin or, better still, with a different Edwin altogether.

My cousin was four years my elder, thirteen at the time. Our relationship had always been peculiar, but as of 1837, it had begun to take on a darker cast. I do not mean only on his behalf — I alternately ignored and engaged him, and was brought to task for this capriciousness by every adult in our household. I let them assume me fickle rather than snobbish when actually I was both. Granted, I needed him; he was closer my own age than anyone, and he seemed nigh drowning for my attention when no one else save my mother noticed that I breathed their cast-off air.

Edwin, on the other hand, was what his mother considered a model child; he was brown-haired and red-faced and sheepdog simple. He chewed upon his bottom lip perennially, as if afraid it might go suddenly missing.

"Have you seen the new mare yet?" he inquired next. "We might take a drive in the trap tomorrow."

I maintained silence. On the last occasion we had shared a drive in the trap, the candied aroma of clover in our noses, Edwin had parted his trouser front and shown me the flesh resting like a grubworm within the cotton, asking whether I knew what it was used for. (I do now; I did not then.) Other than gaping dumbly as he returned the twitching apparatus to its confines, I elected to ignore the incident. Cousin Edwin was approximately as perspicacious as my collection of feathers, which made my own cleverness feel embarrassingly like cheating. It shamed me to disdain him so when he was my elder, and when the thick cords of childhood proximity knotted us so tightly to each other.

Just before arriving home, he had asked whether I wished to touch it next time we were in the woods, and I laughed myself insensible as his flushed face darkened to violet.

"You are a wicked thing to ignore your own kin so, Jane," Edwin persisted.

Kin, kin, kin was ever his anthem: as if we were more than related, as if we were *kindred.* When I failed to cooperate, he stared as if I were a puzzle to be solved. My dawning fear was that he might think I was *in fact* a puzzle — inanimate, insensible. Though I no longer presume to have a conscience, I have never once lacked feelings.

"But perhaps you are only glum. I know! Will you play a game with me after tea?"

Games were a favourite of my mother's, and of mine — and though I was wary of my cousin, I was not afraid of him. He adored me.

"What sort of game?"

"Trading secrets," he rasped. "I've loads and loads. Awful ones. You must have some of your own. It'll be a lark to exchange them."

Considering my stockpile of secrets, I found myself reluctant.

I tell Agatha every night I'll say my prayers, but ever since I skipped them and nothing happened six months ago, I don't.

I tried my mother's laudanum once because she said it made everything better, and I was ill and lied about it.

My kitten scratched me and I was so angry that I let it outside, and afterwards it never came home and I feel sick in my belly every time I imagine my kitten shivering in the dark, cold woods.

I did not want Edwin to know any of these things.

"Fiddle! You aren't sharp enough to know any secrets worth having," I scoffed instead, pushing crumbs around my plate.

Edwin was painfully aware of his own slowness, and hot blood crawled up his cheeks. I nearly apologised then and there, knowing it was what a good girl would do and feeling magnanimous, but then he rose from the table. The adults, still merrily loathing each other over the gilt rims of their teacups, paid us no mind.

"Of course I do," he growled under his breath. "For instance, are you ashamed that your mother is no better than a parasite?"

My mouth fell open as I gaped at my cousin.

"Oh, yes. Or don't you hear any gossip? Doesn't anyone come to visit you?"

This was a cruel blow. "You know that they don't. No one ever does."

"Why not, Jane? I've always wondered."

"Because we are kept like cattle on our own land!" I cried, smashing my fist heedlessly against a butter plate.

When the porcelain flew through the air

and shattered upon the hardwood, my cousin's face reflected stupid dismay. My mother's was equally startled, but approving; I had only been repeating something she slurred once during a very bad night indeed.

Aunt Patience's face practically split with the immensity of her delight, as it is no unpleasant thing when an enemy proves one's own point gratis.

"I invite you for tea and this is the way your . . . your *inexcusable* daughter behaves?" she protested shrilly. "I should beat the temper out of her if I were you, and lose no time about it. There is nothing like a stout piece of hickory for the prevention of unseemly habits."

My mother stood and smoothed her light cotton dress as if she had pressing obligations elsewhere. "My *inexcusable* daughter is bright and high-spirited."

"No, she is a coy little minx whose sly ways will lead her to a bad end if you fail to correct her."

"And what is your child?" Mrs. Steele hissed, throwing down her napkin. "An overfed dunce? Jane does not suffer by comparison, I assure you. We will not trouble you here again."

"You will not be *welcome* here again,"

Aunt Patience spat. "I must offer you my congratulations, Anne-Laure. To so completely cut yourself off from polite society, and then to offend the one person who graciously allows you to sit at the same table — what an extraordinary effort on your part. Very well, I shall oblige both our tastes. If you cannot control that harpy you call a daughter, do keep entirely to your residence in future. I certainly shall to mine."

My mother's defiance crumbled, leaving a wistful look. Aunt Patience's plodding nature would have been forgivable had she been clever or kind, I decided; but as she was common and gloating, I hated her and would hate her *forever.*

Mamma softly pulled her fingers into small fists.

"Please in future recall my daughter's rights, *all* of her rights, or you will regret it," Mrs. Steele ordered, giving the table a single nod.

She departed without a glance behind her. Mamma often stormed away so, however — ferocious exits were decidedly her style, so I remained to assess what damage we had wrought this time.

Aunt Patience, though purple and fairly vibrating with rage, managed to say, "Would you care for more cake, Edwin and Jane?"

28

"I goaded her, Mummy. I'm sorry for what I said before," Edwin added to me, his tooth clenching his lip. He wore a stiff collar that afternoon, I recall, above a brown waistcoat and maroon jacket, and his neck bulged obscenely from its confines.

"That's all right, Edwin. Thank you for tea, Aunt Patience." Like most children, I loathed nothing more than embarrassing myself, and the sight of the fragmented china was making me physically ill. I rose from the table. "I had better . . . Good-bye, then."

Aunt Patience's eyes burnt into me as I departed.

I went to the stables that evening, where I could visit the docile mares and peer into their soft liquid eyes, and I could stop thinking about my cousin. Thinking about Edwin was a private class in self-loathing: I hated myself for indulging his mulish attraction, yet it had been a tidal pull for me over years of reluctant camaraderie.

Flattery, I have found, is a great treat for those born innately selfish.

For the hundredth time, the thousandth time, I stood listening to soft whinnies like lullabies, pressing my cheek against sinewy necks; whether the horses at Highgate House liked me or my sugar cubes I have no notion, but they never glowered, nor warned me I teetered upon the hair-thin tightrope of eternal damnation. Smelling sweet hay and their rich, bristly coats always calmed me — and I calmed them in turn, for a particularly fidgety colt often stilled in my presence.

My thoughts drifted from the horses to the uses I might make of them. I day-dreamed of riding to an apple-blossom meadow where my mother and I should do nothing save eat and laugh; I envisioned charging into war, the heads of Aunt Patience and Edwin lying at my feet.

Mamma and I never took more than a light supper in the springtime, and following a departure as precipitous as the one she had just executed, I knew that she would lock herself away with her novels and tonics, and thus I stayed out until the wind began to nip through the slats in the great stable door and the horses' snuffles quieted under my caresses . . . never realising until the following day, in fact, that I had been left entirely, permanently alone.

The ominous liquorice aroma of spilt tincture of opium drenched our cottage when I arrived home at eight o'clock. I learnt my mother had retired to bed at seven, which was unfortunate timing, as I never saw her again. Our servant, Agatha, found her the next morning, still and cold in her bed, marble eyes directed at the window.

Two

What a consternation of soul was mine that dreary afternoon! How all my brain was in tumult, and all my heart in insurrection!

"You cannot attend," Aunt Patience explained in a strained drone for the third time. "You are far too hysterical to appear in pub —"

"Please, oh, please — I won't say a word, won't make a *sound*!"

"Gracious, child, show a little restraint!" my aunt cried. "Pray for her soul, and accept God's will. It is a hard thing to lose your mother so suddenly, but many others have lived to tell the tale."

I took the news that I would not be allowed at my mother's funeral precisely as well as I took the news of her inexplicable death. Skilful knives had carved the heart out of me, leaving me empty save for the sick, unsteady fear flickering in my bones telling me *alone, all alone.* I could not claw my way out of the horror of it. I screamed for my mother on the first day; sobbed for her on the second; and on the third, the day of her funeral, sat numbly in an armchair with my eyes pulsing hellfire red — that is, until my aunt Patience arrived. Being forbidden to attend Mamma's funeral felt as if I were spitting on her grave, and questions swarmed through my pate like worms through an apple.

What will they do with me now that she has gone? Assurances that I would always reside at Highgate House now seemed reliable as quicksand.

How did my mother come to die at all? She had taken a sudden bad turn, according to Agatha; Aunt Patience muttered of fits.

Why should I not see her put in the ground? Both agreed I should not be present, but neither would explain the reason.

I fell to my knees, tearing at my aunt's stiff black skirts.

"Don't bury Mamma without me there," I begged. "However much you might have hated her, hate me still, please don't do this. I won't survive it."

"Have you *no* control over your passions?" Aunt Patience's toad-like face was ashen. "I ask for your own sake, you unprincipled animal. You will come to a bad end if —"

"I don't *care* what end I come to, only let me —"

"That is a monstrous thing to say," she cried, and then slapped me across the cheek.

Falling sideways, gasping, I clutched at the place where my skin throbbed and my teeth rang. Her slap was painful, but her visible disgust far worse.

"I'm sorry," I whispered, reaching for her wrist with my other hand. "Please, just —"

My aunt recoiled, striding towards the hall. "The situation is a hard one, Jane, but what you ask is impossible. Try to calm yourself. God sends comfort to the meek and the chaste, whilst the passionate inflict agonies upon themselves."

Aunt Patience stopped — hand splayed on her broad belly, eyes frozen into hailstones.

"You are very like her, are you not," she whispered. "The bitter fruit of a poisonous tree."

The front door clicked shut.

Grief until then had bound me in spider's silk and drained me with her pinchers. Afterwards, however, I wanted to inflict exquisite agonies upon Aunt Patience; and had I been informed that a few weeks later,

I would serve her the deepest cut imaginable, I am not certain that I would not have smiled.

Morbidity has always been a close companion of mine. Hours were spent meditating on my lost kitten and all the ways it could have (must have) died because of my inflamed temper. My late father was the source of infinite questions — was my slender, sloping nose like his since it was not like my mother's? After Mamma died, however, I thought of nothing save her lonesomeness under the earth; and when I did think of her in paradise, I next thought, *but they'll never allow me into heaven, and so I still will never see her again.*

There are doubtless worse hobbies than meditating upon your dead mother, but nobody has ever suggested one to me.

Agatha knelt with me in the garret a week after the funeral, because I wanted to go through my mother's trunk. For seven days, life had been a sickening seesaw between fear that calamity would befall me and the desire calamity would take me already and have done with it. Now I wanted to touch Mamma's gowns and her gloves and her letters, as if I might combine them in a spell to summon her; even today, if witchcraft existed by means of toadstools and tinkers' thumbs to bring her back, I should do so in an instant.

"Well, 'ere we are," Agatha said in her broad rasp as she drew out an iron key.

Our servant, Agatha, who trudged about with wisps of blond hair falling in her squinting eyes, spoke entirely in platitudes. She was my sole comfort throughout that hellish week; hot broth mixed with sherry and soothing pats on the cheek are greatly cheering, even to juvenile she-devils.

The lock clicked open and I surged to plunder the trunk's contents. We had a pair of tapers, but the light was dim and ghostly, and when my seeking fingers struck lace, I hardly knew what I held.

"Ah, what 'ave we 'ere?" Agatha rumbled from my right.

"Mamma's summer parasol," I recognised as I lifted it.

"Aye, Miss Jane, and what a parasol."

There was no refuting this, so I drew out more relics — cracked men's reading spectacles, a fawn carryall. We went on until I was so sated with untrimmed hats and books of pressed flowers that I scarce noted I held a pair of empty laudanum bottles.

Agatha placidly took them away. "Now, Miss Jane, them's in the past, them is, over and emptied, so you just put 'em clean out o' yer mind."

I supposed Agatha meant Mamma was no longer ill, so I nodded. Diving into the trunk once more, I emerged with a lock of nut-brown hair very like mine woven into a small lover's knot and pressed under silver-framed glass. I had seen it before, when it sat on Mamma's mantelpiece, but it had long since vanished.

"This was my father's. Were they married long before he died, Agatha?"

"Not as long as yer mum would've liked, poor dear."

"Cousin Edwin told me she was no better than a parasite," I whispered.

"Now, Miss Jane," Agatha growled kindly, "there's sorts as you can trust to speak plain, and there's sorts as will say whatso-ever suits. And if those two kinds o' folks were only obvious, wi' signs or marks o' Cain or the like, a heap o' trouble would be saved."

A worm of guilt stirred in my gut. I had lied to her that very morning, when I said I would take buttered porridge and then dumped it by the pond so as not to worry her.

Lying has always come as easy for me as breathing.

"Did my father prefer living at the cottage too?"

"Bless you, he never lived 'ere after marrying yer mum. They met in Paris, where Mr. Steele dun banking — I figure he preferred being wheresoever she was."

My head fell upon her burly shoulder. Agatha smelt of lye and the mutton she had been stewing, and just when I was too exhausted to contemplate getting my weakened legs under me and leaving the darkening garret, I pulled something I had never seen before from the trunk.

It was a letter — one in my mother's elegant Parisian script with its bold downstrokes like a battle standard being planted. It read:

Rue M——,
2nd Arrondissement,
SUNDAY

Dear Mr. Sneeves,

Pardon, *s'il vous plait,* for my writing in haste, but I can hardly shift a muscle for the grief now oppressing me: my J—— has expired finally. The doctors could do nothing, and I am desolate. Doubtless your legal efforts upon my behalf and that of my daughter have been heroic, but in the absence of my husband, I must confirm our complete readiness for relocation to Highgate House. *Si ce n'est pas indiscret,* as my beloved J—— was ever a faithful client of yours, I request an immediate audience, for every second may prove invaluable. And please return this letter with your reply, as I live in horror our plans will be anticipated by those who would prevent us.

> *Veuillez agréer mes salutations*
> *empressées,*
> Mrs. Anne-Laure Steele

At first I had imagined that the letter was two pages, but it was kept together with the reply in a crabbed male English hand:

Rue du R——,
1st Arrondissement,
SUNDAY

Chère Mme. S——,
My most heartfelt condolences upon behalf of the firm. Mr. S—— was a highly valued patron of Sneeves, Swansea, and Turner. I await your arrival and assure you that the documents have already been drawn up to the late la-

mented Mr. S——'s satisfaction.

Humbly,
Cyrus Sneeves, Esq.

I could only understand that these documents referred to my eventual ownership of Highgate House; puzzled, I passed them to Agatha, who carefully folded both letters together again and returned them to the trunk.

"Well, that weren't what I'd been expecting." Agatha's squinting eyes narrowed further.

"My mother wrote that when my father died?"

"A wise hen always sees her chicks are looked after. Now, there's pickled 'erring and toast to be had. Your mother's things seem to 'earten you, and this trunk will be 'ere tomorrow, and the day after that."

Agatha was again strictly correct, but mistaken in her accidental assumption that *I* would be present.

"Did you ever meet my father, Agatha?" I questioned as she shut the trunk and heaved herself upright.

"Why, bless your 'eart, Miss Steele, what a question." Agatha tsked fondly and trudged downstairs.

Infants own memories, perhaps, but by

the time I was nine, hazy visions of Jonathan Steele were locked away like mementoes in a safe to which I knew not the combination. The bread crumbs I had gathered into his portrait scarce made a crust, let alone a meal.

Your father was un homme magnifique, *and his eyes were the brown of sweet chocolate just as yours are, and he never stopped thinking of ways to make us safe,* from my mother.

'E was as good a man as any, and no worse than some, from Agatha.

Don't speak of him, for God's sake, from Aunt Patience.

Now I knew he was a banker in Paris with an English solicitor friend my mother trusted; I imagined Jonathan Steele a positive hero of finance with sweeping moustaches, who had rescued my mother from penury with a flourish of his fancifully enormous pen.

"How did he meet Mamma?" I called from the top of the creaking garret stairs.

"You'll use up all your chatter and be clean out o' words, and then 'owever shall we pass the time, Miss Jane?" Agatha chided, beckoning.

I wondered over the unsettling notion of words running dry. My footsteps as I fol-

41

lowed her made no more sound than the virtuous dead, fast asleep beneath their coverlets of stone.

Slowly, I recovered my appetite — and concurrently, my keen interest in rebellion.

My aunt Patience thought girls ought to be decorative. Indeed, Jane Eyre tucks herself away in a curtained alcove at the beginning of her saga, and thus at least attempts docility.

I was not a fictional orphan but a real one, however. Waking in the full blaze of the May afternoons, I would eat nothing save brown bread and butter for lunch, and the steaming milk soup Agatha made with sweet almonds, eggs, and cinnamon for my tea. My ugly — dare I say French — opinion of Aunt Patience kept her away temporarily, and the rest of the time I spoke low nonsense to the horses or slunk through the woods where the marsh grasses swooned into the embrace of the pond. In the stables, I could allow the stink of manure and clean sweat to calm me as I brushed my last remaining confidants; but in the forest, my musings turned darkly fantastical.

I will set fire to the main house, and then they will be sorry they made Mamma unhappy.

I will run away to Paris, where I will be

*awake only when the stars shine through the
window and the boulevards are empty.*

*I will find my mother's grave and live there
off of dew and nectar.*

True peace did not visit me; but at times,
an edgy calm like falling asleep after a
nightmare descended when I lost myself in
melancholy.

At times, I suspected I was not alone.

As the days passed, my sense of being
watched increased. Agatha gave me free rein
apart from unlocking Mamma's trunk every
evening and packing satchels of apples for
me to carry to the stables; she would never
spy on me, I felt certain. The gardener was
a wizened old thing, and the grooms paid
me as little mind as did the servants at the
main house. Patience Barbary thought the
out-of-doors a treacherous bridge meant to
convey her from one civilised structure to
another.

Still I caught glimpses of another creature
there in the trees, one with round eyes and
a predator's hungry stare; but by the time I
understood that I was the prey, my fate had
already been sealed.

THREE

I was a precocious actress in her eyes: she sincerely looked on me as a compound of virulent passions, mean spirit, and dangerous duplicity.

Invitations to the main house were rebuffed in the rudest manner I could think of: silence. Even adults who are frightened of children come to their senses sooner or later, however, and in early June, I opened a missive demanding I appear before Mrs. Patience Barbary at five o'clock for tea. When I entered the drawing room, I discovered that three people awaited me instead of two.

Aunt Patience presided over the ivory-and-green-striped settee, an expression of foregone success staining her froggish mouth. The fact that her full widow's weeds looked no different after my mother's death (how could they have?) made me long to slit wounds in the taffeta. Edwin, lips already faintly dusted with sugar from the lemon cakes, offered me a polite smile.

In that instant, I knew — as I think I had suspected — that Edwin had been the one spying upon me.

"Jane, this is Mr. Vesalius Munt of Lowan Bridge School. Mr. Munt, this is my niece, Jane."

Doubtless the reader has heard cautionary reports of granite-eyed patriarchs who run schools for profit and, shall we say, misrepresent their amenities? You are partly prepared for what is to come, then. Mr. Munt was clad head to toe in black; his forehead was high, his sable boots neatly polished, and his mien sober. Here Mr. Munt's superficial resemblance to fiction ended.

First, he seemed highly intelligent. He watched those around him closely; this was not a man who ignored the way I settled as far as I could from my aunt, nor who would remark upon it until the observation suited his interests.

Second, Mr. Vesalius Munt was handsome. He was aged somewhere between forty and fifty, but the map of his face — from thoughtful wrinkles to clear grey eyes to slender chin — suggested naturally benevolent inclinations and announced his regret at his self-imposed sternness of character.

Third, he was a tyrant, which returns us to the more familiar literary archetypes. He was a great whopping unrepentant tyrant, and he *enjoyed* the vocation, its artistry — I could see it in his perfectly disarranged black hair and his humbly clasped hands. I thought, with a squirming stomach, that here was a man who would set a snake over hot coals simply to watch it writhe.

"Miss Jane Steele," he greeted me. "You have been orphaned within the month, I am sorry to hear. God's ways are inscrutable, but trust in Him nevertheless brings light to the darkest of valleys."

My aunt primly tucked her chin within her neck. "She is a clever enough girl, only mannerless and stubborn, Mr. Munt. Her intelligence needs moulding into humility and her character into an orderly Christian one."

"Then I won't remind you of my mother any longer?" I hissed.

Aunt Patience whipped out a glint of lacquered wood and began fanning herself with black lace. She wanted *something* between us, even if a scrap of cobwebby cloth.

Mr. Munt's gaze flickered between us like

stage swords, all shine and speed and subtle games. "Your aunt has informed me that your mother was . . . troubled," he said with tremendous care. "It is not unusual for the children of lunatics to —"

"Mamma was *not* a lunatic!" I cried, aghast.

"No *indeed,*" seconded Edwin in a fawning manner which sickened me.

"Her constitution was delicate." My aunt sounded like the teeth were being pried from her head. "Artists are often highly strung."

"Art is a curse," Vesalius Munt agreed, shifting on the hard cane chair. "An infection eating away at godly reserves of abnegation, chastity, and meekness. Show me a contented artist, Mrs. Barbary, and I will show you a dabbler — a pretender, a drudge. True artists belong to a miserable race. Jane, they tell me that your passions are strange ones, and your upbringing . . . eccentric. I run a school, you see, and your aunt thinks you would make an excellent pupil there."

The word *school* provoked the first sensation other than dull misery I had felt since before I could recall. Mamma had been at boarding school as a girl, in the south of France. On holidays they walked to the

47

glimmering seashore, where pebbles clattered under their slippers and the sea spray chased them shrieking with laughter back to the dunes. She learnt both dancing and painting there.

Going to school already seemed adventurous, but my fingers tingled when I realised it would also be imitative of my mother.

Remembering our cottage, however, I was swiftly anchored back to Highgate House; how could I leave everything familiar when I was already so lost? Fear leached the happy nerves away.

Additionally, I was an artful little liar, and what befell artful little liars at school?

"I should rather not go," I whispered.

Aunt Patience snapped her fan.

"To send me away with a stranger —"

"Mr. Munt will make you useful, as orphaned children must —"

"Don't banish me," I pleaded, standing.

"The matter is settled."

"It is not either!" I shouted in most unchildlike fashion.

Aunt Patience thrust her heaving bosom forward. "You horrid puppet, only listen to reason for once. You *must* find a vocation, or —"

"I own Highgate House!" I cried. "Mamma told me so. You're only saying this to me because you *hated her.*"

"I am saying this to you because you must become productive. And if you knew how good I was to your mother after all the suffering she caused, you would drop to your knees and beg my forgiveness."

Is that what I must do, then? My lips were quivering, my guts knotted. *Humiliate myself so I might keep what belongs to me?*

"Is flattery what you're after?" I hissed. "But of course, that's why you loathed poor Mamma so — she was exquisite, and you were never flattered a day in your life."

Sulphurous silence spread throughout the parlour. Mr. Munt studied me so intently he made my neck prickle, and Cousin Edwin gazed in a horrified stupor, his breaths straining his waistcoat buttons. Aunt Patience only smiled, a smile like a gate slamming closed and locking.

"I didn't mean that," I choked out. "Truly. But I want to remain here with . . . with everything I have left of her."

"As well you should. Mummy, you can't send her away!" Edwin protested. "Jane is my only playmate."

Aunt Patience said, in much too babying a tone for a lad of thirteen, "There now, my sweet, soon your tutor will have taught you all he knows and you yourself will go to school and find splendid new companions."

"No," Edwin moaned, burying his face in his hands. "No, I will miss her, you *can't*. It isn't *fair.*"

"Quite touching to see such devotion in young relations." Mr. Munt's stately wrinkles creased approvingly, and he brushed imaginary dust from the knee of his trouser. "It gives me every hope that Jane is indeed redeemable, to have inspired such affection."

Finding none of these observations complimentary and growing steadily more unnerved by Vesalius Munt, whose silvery eyes seemed coins at the bottom of a too-deep pool, I edged towards the door.

"Where do you think you are going, my dear little girl?" Mr. Munt asked, kindness seeping from his tone like blood from a gash.

"I cannot stay for tea." A noose was tightening round my throat.

"Now, Jane," Mr. Munt purred, rising. "You are only proving your dear aunt's point by acting so irrationally. Come here, allow me to examine you, determine your strengths, and perhaps we shall yet find a place for you at Lowan Bridge School."

I was off like a hare; my aunt looked after me in unfeigned alarm, and Edwin gave a small wail.

Mr. Munt, I saw as I glanced behind, meditated on me with his dashing black head cocked: the look of a man who has spied a hill and vowed to crest it, for no reason other than to see what lies upon the other side.

When I returned to Highgate House many years thereafter, I viewed the ravine again, and felt as distant from it as a child does looking at a terrible cave in a picture book. Thus I can describe it as my twenty-four-year-old self perfectly rationally. Our cottage stood at the edge of the woods, with the sweet brown duck pond lying to the west of us. If one passed the pond, the forest which bordered our property gave way to a ridge and thence to a sharp declivity like a small crevasse populated by violet monkshood and sharp wild grasses.

I felt Mr. Munt's eyes searing the back of my skull long after my escape was accomplished, so I repaired to the woods.

My curls stuck to my brow when I reached the trees, glued by means of animal fear to my skin, and I smeared them back. We had pinned two braids like a crown atop my head, but several strands had bolted and I must have looked a malicious dryad there, surrounded by leaf and bracken. Light slanted through the branches as if it possessed physical weight that evening, making prison bars of shadows and penitents' benches of fallen trees. Wandering, I calmed myself.

I should not go to Lowan Bridge with Mr. Munt.

I need not go to Lowan Bridge with Mr. Munt.

I will *not go to Lowan Bridge with Mr. Munt.*

"Are you hurt, Jane?"

Too frightened to shriek, I spun about with my hand clapped over my mouth. Cousin Edwin stood ten feet away from me, a cautious grin pasted over his face, the sort people who are terrible with horses (as I am not) think will calm skittish beasts.

"What do you mean?" I gasped.

Edwin came no closer, but pointed his index finger. His dull hair was half-lit and half-hid in the shade of a crooked branch; he seemed a stitched-together creature from a puppet pageant, the sort in which spouses are beaten within an inch of their lives.

"You're bleeding." He began to walk again.

Looking down, I saw that I had scratched my arm upon a bramble without noticing. A trace of blood wept from the shallow gouge.

"Here," Cousin Edwin said when he had reached me.

He breathed harder as he wound his handkerchief over my arm: round and round, binding the cut, forehead beetling in concentration. Edwin smelled of lemon cake and the faintly *old* aroma he always carried, as if he had been born in a bed of camphor and cheese rinds.

"I won't let them," he announced. "I hate that she thought to send you to school. I am the *man* of this house, and you shall stay here with us, Jane. Don't be afraid."

I watched him tie off the cloth — like a bandage, yes, and like a silken slave's cuff, and like the collar at the end of a leash.

"I'm not afraid."

Edwin glanced up, pale green eyes glowing. "You *were* afraid — of that horrid Mr. Munt. You needn't be. He won't take you away from us."

Edwin plucked a leaf from my hair and placed the memento in his trouser pocket — a habit I had never liked, but never thought quite so pitiful.

"Did you forgive me?" He rocked on his heels. "About the secrets game — we've hardly spoken since. I was only repeating something rude I heard Cook say. Your mother was too beautiful to avoid cruel gossip, don't you think? Shake hands?"

Edwin's pudgy hand thrust before my face. I shook; for an idiot, he was clever to perceive that complimenting my late mother would work miracles.

Instead of letting go my hand, he pulled me closer.

"Do you want to know what my favourite secret is?" he breathed into the space between my eyes.

I swallowed. If I said no, he would rage, pout, fume for days, so I angled my head. He put his rosy mouth to my ear.

"The time in the trap when I *showed* you, and you never screamed. You're every bit as bad as I am. You liked it."

He drew back fractionally. His grip tightened, and whilst I searched for words to tell him that no, opening his trousers had not been a bond between us and that screaming clearly ought to have occurred to me, he chewed his underlip until it was scarlet.

Then he grinned brightly.

"You're not screaming now either."

"Let go of my arm," I ordered.

The breeze sent kindly fingertips through our hair, jays calling from their shadowy canopies, and now I *was* frightened — mortally — of the woods which were leaf curtained and the birds which could not

54

help me with whatever strange sort of trouble this was.

Edwin did not let go. "Let's start a new game."

"Stop it, I tell you. What game?" I demanded.

"I want to know what the inside of your mouth tastes like." Cousin Edwin leant down.

I struck him as hard as I could across the face, and he was startled enough to let go, and I had not known until then what it meant to *run.*

The light shone brighter, and the wind picked up, and I had just burst through the trees in the direction of civilisation when Edwin caught me. We both tumbled to the ground and I swiped at him, shouting his name and *Stop* and he laughed easily and pinned my wrists to the earth at the top of the ravine where the twigs pricked my back and the sky seemed a great billowing, purpling tent above the looming forest.

His lips met my neck; his tongue shoved at my mouth. I kicked and *kicked,* limbs transforming into weapons even as my heart churned pure black fear through my veins. Edwin pinned me with his weight and he had transformed too now, hard where he ground against my thigh, red where my fist had stung his cheek, and *My body isn't working, nothing is working,* I thought, so I used something else.

"I'll tell this time," I spat as I struggled. "I'll tell *everyone.*"

His piggish look of glee dimmed. "No, you won't. You're a knowing little jezebel just like your mother, Mummy always tells me so."

"What do you mean?"

"I mean that you like it."

"I'll tell her we *both* like it," I lied coldly, falling limp. "Then she'll send me away forever. Get *off.*"

Edwin retreated — biting his mouth, straightening his clothing. When he took in my bedraggled state, he grew agitated, reaching into thin air as I brushed myself off with unsteady fingers.

"It was only a game," he offered. "I never meant to — I would never hurt you. I'm sorry, Jane."

My wrists were bruised, my back scraped, my sleeve torn, my heart unbroken but dirtied, as if he had pulled it through the mud. Walking a few paces away, Edwin retrieved something from the ground. It was his pocket handkerchief, which had fallen from my arm, and he passed it back to me as if giving girls pocket handkerchiefs could atone for any offence under the sun.

"Jane, will you be my friend again?"

Rage poured from scalp to sole at this request.

"We were never friends," I lied, and — preparing to run once more — I shoved his chest as hard as I could.

The rock he staggered back upon was loose under his footing; it set off a tiny slide into the ravine, a hushed skidding of granite and dead bracken. That accidents happen is a universal principle — and perhaps the only universal principle worth mentioning, for it governs an enormous percentage of our daily lives.

That my entire being, every last ounce of *me*, had been put into that violent push, however, is undeniable.

When I peered over the top of the short decline and met Edwin's eyes as he sucked in his last breaths with a broken spine and a look of pure disappointment, I did nothing to aid or comfort him.

I walked away.

FOUR

"Do you know where the wicked go after death?"

"They go to hell," was my ready and orthodox answer. . . .

"What must you do to avoid it?"

I deliberated a moment; my answer, when it did come, was objectionable: "I must keep in good health, and not die."

Edwin is dead, I thought.
Perhaps he only fainted.
You killed *him, you idiot,* I thought next, and giggled, and stumbled under star-scarred skies.
I fell to my knees and would have screamed then had I the air to do so, but all I could manage was gasps through a throat which had shrunk to the breadth of a hay

wisp. My fists clutched the sod as if the planet were trying to buck me off and, after a few harrowing seconds, a whimper escaped and the tears came flooding.

That night, I learnt that horror could not physically *kill* me; wave after wave crashed over my head without my drowning, and yet . . . I think that I would rather die than experience such overwhelming *wrongness* ever again.

Curling onto my side on the lawn — visible peripherally to the cottage but not to the main house — I sobbed for an hour or more. When the torrent was a trickle, I passed a sleeve over my eyes and sat up. The sun had sunk well below the tops of the elms, and whether it would ever rise again, I could not have said. In the mire of my misery and confusion, three thoughts emerged:

You really are as wicked as everyone says.

Shame spread like a pox over my skin.

Mamma isn't here to help you, and now you will be hanged.

Like all children, I had read the *Newgate Calendar* raptly, that ostensibly educational account of gruesome violations enacted by the law upon ne'er-do-wells within Newgate Prison. No one embarks upon a life of mayhem because hanging (or drawing and quartering, or slow death by pressing, come to that) sounds like a pleasant Saturday afternoon lark, but parents in those days still supposed the illustrations highly effective deterrents, and I had devoured Edwin's copy. I cried a little longer. A vague shape I knew to be Agatha floated past amber-lit windowpanes.

You are going to have to lie like the very devil to live through this.

Having no stock of tears left, I plotted my escape with hollow bones and shaking fingers.

"You've said it all out plain once, Miss Jane, so I knows as ye can say it all out plain twice," Agatha declared the next morning. She sat on our burgundy settee, one arm around my waist.

My return to the cottage had been a lighting storm: searing flashes of *you've killed Edwin* interrupted a savage downpour of lies. They poured from my mouth, flooding my throat. When the falsehoods had been exhausted, Agatha had said, pulling the coverlet over my head, *There, there, poor girl. Nothing like this lasts forever, for ye'll ken that time passes whether we will it or nae.*

I had meant to pray for forgiveness the instant Agatha left, but instead a deathly slumber took me. I don't know the term for a child who falls asleep *after* her first murder and *before* confessing her sins, but I suspect it is not an intensely complimentary one.

Now it was ten o'clock in the morning and my head felt filled with hornets. I had been ill the night before into my porcelain pot, sour acid bleaching my throat, and now more lies were required — this time for the benefit of Constable Sam Quillfeather.

Constable Quillfeather, seeing I was numb with dread following Agatha's prompt, pretended a sudden rapturous interest in a decorative pillow.

"Such fine work as I've seldom seen, and the elegance of the lilies — their shape, their exquisite colour? Remarkable! Did the late Mrs. Steele create this masterpiece?"

Dear old Agatha nudged me as if this were a serious inquiry.

"Yes," I managed.

Constable Quillfeather was very tall and very thin — a friendly skeleton, in fact — clad in brown flannel with a red-and-yellow-checked shawl-collared vest and tall leather gaiters. His face boasted a jutting chin, an aggressively hooked nose, deep-set hazel eyes, a looming brow, and a great framing shock of forward-swept hair of a dark brown not unlike mine. Everything about Constable Quillfeather seemed to lurch forward on a parabola; I guessed him to be above middle age, but his lanky limbs were puppyish in their urgency, a propulsive quality matched only by his incessant questions. Though he was far from handsome, he exuded a riveting aura of eager enthusiasm.

"Ha! I thought she must have done?" Constable Quillfeather's soft tenor lilted so much at the ends of his sentences, statements became queries. "Was she fond of sewing?"

"Sometimes." My mother had enjoyed needlework, but not as much as she relished throwing new projects across the room.

"I never had the pleasure of meeting her but once, in the village, at the stationer's?" The policeman's bright eyes swept to Agatha's. "She was so charming, and . . . I think a little sad? But I presume too much — Miss Steele, may we talk about how you discovered your poor cousin's body?"

Swallowing, I nodded. No speech was forthcoming, however.

Constable Quillfeather clapped his hands to his bony knees. "Miss Steele, do you require water? A sip of wine to strengthen you?"

I shook my head.

"But you shiver — are you cold?"

Helpless to stop myself, I emitted a hysterical trill of laughter.

Frowning, Agatha attempted, "She's been so poorly, she don't know which end is up, left, or 'indmost, Constable."

"Naturally, naturally!" Constable Quillfeather smiled, a warm horizontal spread which failed to check his air of headlong momentum. "Will you tell me the origins of the magnificent work above the mantelpiece?"

The constable's nose crinkled as he gazed at a wild collection of pinks and yellows incidentally suggesting a landscape, one reminiscent of Turner's works when important structures are burning down. He rose to study it — or perhaps to give me the illusion of unfettered space.

"Mamma was a painter," I rasped.

"And a fine one! Now, this is not a picture set in England? Where, then?"

"In the countryside near Paris."

"Ah, just so. Did she like it here?"

"Why?"

Constable Quillfeather's eyes, dappled with green and brown and amber, twinkled compassionately. "Neighbourly curiosity?"

"I don't think so," I admitted. "But we were safe."

Sam Quillfeather returned to his armchair. "Safety and the comforts of home — what more can one ask of life?"

"Longer life?" I returned without thinking.

The constable winced ruefully. "Quite so. Miss Steele, do you grasp how brave you are being? I know of grown women who, after the multiple tragedies you have undergone, would be prostrate! But here you are, so steady and sure. Might we begin again, and you tell me what happened yesterday?"

He was one of the most engaging men I had ever encountered, and anyway there was nothing for it: I set to.

I informed Constable Quillfeather in a voice trembling like a plucked harpsichord string that I had been to tea at my aunt's residence and that there had been a great row over my going to school. Following this dash of truth, I said that Cousin Edwin and I were so upset that we quit the main house. After planning to run away together to London, and planning to build a tree fortress, and planning to live as highwaymen, we had decided to play a game.

"A game?" Constable Quillfeather repeated slowly.

Yes, I told him, a game called Robin Hood.

Constable Quillfeather rubbed his hands as he leant forward, inquiring what this game involved.

"Hunting for deer in Nottingham Forest." My words may have been false, but my tears were true. "We separated so as to meet again and show what we'd killed for supper. But it was all pretend. Then I went to the meeting place — there's two fallen logs crossed like a crooked *X* not far from the cottage — and, and no one was there. Then I thought Edwin must have . . ."

"There, there," Agatha said as a sob escaped. "There, now."

Like a fever dream, I saw Edwin approaching with a hemmed square of cotton he imagined was an apology.

"I thought he must have been playing one of his tricks," I forced out. "But, oh, I was so vexed he'd left me alone in the woods when it was getting dark. I searched everywhere. I thought of the ravine because we collect things down there sometimes."

"What sort?" Constable Quillfeather desired to know.

"Bright rocks, wildflowers, bones. When I found him, dusk was nearly finished, and . . . he wasn't breathing."

"He had already expired?"

I drew a shuddering breath. "His eyes

looked — I can't stand to think of how his eyes looked, don't ask me, please!"

This was the truth: his eyes had looked utterly betrayed before they had glazed to an unseeing shimmer like ice crusting a pool.

"And no one else saw you?"

"No."

"And no one else saw him?"

"No one I know about."

"And then you returned here?"

"Yes. Slowly," I whispered, hedging my bets as to whether Agatha had noticed the gap between twilight and my return. "I felt so weak. This morning, I should have thought it all some horrid dream, except . . . except it's true."

"Miss Jane, that was very complete," Constable Quillfeather complimented. He brushed his hands over his head, and the wiry locks like accusers arrowed towards my face all the surer. "May I ask you a few more questions?"

"I suppose so."

"The courage in this one, the pluck!" Whistling, Constable Quillfeather winked at Agatha. "She's been raised by a paragon of a mother, but that's in addition to a few stout friends, I think?"

"I hope so, but judge for yerself, sir," Agatha answered calmly.

"That I shall, ma'am. Miss Steele, was Edwin in any sort of fight that evening?"

Either the clock which had been ticking stopped, or I went deaf with panic.

"His button was missing?" Constable Quillfeather indicated the top button on his own waistcoat. "Hereabouts? Seemed to have been torn away?"

"We played at highwaymen before Robin Hood, to practise." I glanced up at Agatha. "We staged a fight. Edwin . . . he'd not have wanted Aunt Patience to know about that, she likes everything to be so proper."

The policeman blew out a breath. "It gave me a turn, you understand? Didn't know what to think — signs of a struggle?"

My stomach heaved. As suddenly as he had introduced the subject, however, Constable Quillfeather abandoned it.

"You'll miss your playmate, Miss Steele, and the blow comes too soon on the heels of another, and it hurts me to see it," he averred, shaking his head. "There's an . . . incongruity? About grief in the very young. It doesn't belong on you? Well, I'm for the grieving mother now."

Constable Quillfeather came to stand before me on spindly stork's legs, bending over like a question mark.

"You'll take care of yourself?"

"Yes."

"What's happened to your dress sleeve?"

We looked at my blue-and-grey-patterned dress sleeve and the short tear in it made by Edmund's final game. Agatha's vision was as keen as a whiskered mole's, and she had brushed off my dress the night before without seeing the rip; since I donned the nearest thing I could find that morning, there it was, a grisly cotton wound with a lurid smoke-coloured bruise beneath.

"I — I don't know," I stammered. "It must have been torn when we were playing highwaymen, just like Edwin's button. It's the only explanation."

After a pause, Constable Quillfeather shook my hand and stood tall as a beanpole, gently frowning. "Well, I am in tremendous debt to you, Miss Steele. If that is the only explanation, then I shall never have to seek out another one, shall I?"

Constable Quillfeather settled a brown beaver hat on his head, bowed to us, and set off for the main house — and only when the ridiculously tall pipe shape of his head-gear departing passed our front window did I allow myself the highly literary indulgence of losing consciousness.

■ ■ ■ ■

After recovering my wits that afternoon, I stood before the broad white steps of the main house with Agatha, preparing myself to enter. My aunt wished to see me, a request which could not be refused. Vacillating, I paced, staring miserably at the lofty leaded windows.

"Sooner a thing's started, sooner as it's done," Agatha mentioned.

"I'm frightened."

"That's neither 'ere nor there," she advised, and since this was again inarguable, I made a proud church spire of my spine and walked inside.

No one greeted me; up I went towards my aunt's bedroom. The servants ought to have been bustling, making arrangements for the inevitable condoling relations and dealers in the commerce of death, but Aunt Patience must have sent them off; the only faces I saw were painted ancestors whispering *murderess* from the cages of their carved gilt frames. I felt as if I were going to my doom.

I was perfectly correct — but it was a doom of my own making, not my aunt's. Of this I can at least be proud, if of nothing else.

Following a knock at Patience Barbary's half-opened door, I entered. The light here was dimmer, keeping its distance as if out of respect for the bereaved. My aunt lay on a fainting couch. She beckoned; it was not until I drew within three feet that I could see her plain, and I stiffened.

"You," Aunt Patience spat.

Her careful mourning attire had been abandoned for a capacious black robe fastened with silk ties. Patience Barbary had shed her smug bravado as snakes do skins; everything about her was new, from the swollen pink edges of her eyelids to her raw expression, tender as a cut where the scab has peeled away. Years of trials I did not know about had hardened her, but now here she was — in desperate need of a shell, and stripped of her defences as she had been stripped of her son. Her habitual mourning was an ostentation, I realised, maybe even a dig at my mother's pale Parisian frocks; this was her, bared to the ravages of the whimsical world.

I wanted to be glad of her ruin — but I was only sad in a sweeping, sky-wide way, and sorry for myself despite the unforgivable thing I had done. I wanted Edwin back, and months previous, so that I could scream when I was meant to and none of this would be my fault.

"Tell me," Aunt Patience demanded. "You are the one who found him. I must know all."

Hesitating, I cast my eyes down. My silences were beginning to shift from weapons into shields. Now I have a wide array, a blood-crusted and blow-battered arsenal; but then I was still learning.

"He was already peaceful, Aunt." My throat worked. "I'm so sorry. I don't know anything."

"You know more than I do." Her voice had been ground to sand with weeping.

"Nothing that can *help.*"

We talked — or rather, Aunt Patience questioned, and I lied. The untended fireplace watched us. No, I did not think Edwin had been in any pain. Yes, it must have been an accident. No, he had not been angry with her any longer when we parted ways.

"He loved me very much," Aunt Patience choked, pressing smelling salts to her flat nose. "He loved you too, his only close kin — he was as affectionate a boy as I ever saw. Why did Edwin have to die in such a meaningless way? It ought to have been you."

Numbly, I digested this; and then I understood.

As if a prophecy had been painted in the

carpet's flourishes under my feet, I knew what I must do to survive my cousin's death. I loathed the prospect; but then I pictured my existence with only Agatha for company, and I knew I was right.

What I did not know was that an inexorable force tugged at my torn sleeve.

Scientists believe that the Earth twirls upon a great pole like a spinning top; this rotational point is theoretically located in the Arctic North, where the land is so desolate and lovely that daylight and nighttime cannot bear to give it up, and trade shifts in six-month intervals. These scientists are mistaken about the Arctic North; for I know in my heart that though the Earth does spin, and spin far too quickly for many of us to bear, London is the centre of the axis.

London is the eye of the circle and the heart of the globe, and London would be the saving of me. I did not know then that Highgate House was a mere overnight journey's away; neither did I know that Lowan Bridge School was even closer to its suburbs. What I did know was that if Aunt Patience looked at me for another second, I would scream.

"Perhaps I see too much of your mother staining you," she husked. "But —"

"Aunt Patience," I announced, "I want you to send me away to school with Mr. Munt."

FIVE

Probably, if I had lately left a good home and kind parents, this would have been the hour when I should most keenly have regretted the separation: that wind would then have saddened my heart; this obscure chaos would have disturbed my peace; as it was, I derived from both a strange excitement, and reckless and feverish, I wished the wind to howl more wildly, the gloom to deepen to darkness, and the confusion to rise to clamour.

If the reader has ever prized solitude, you can imagine my revulsion when a vortex of attention formed in the wake of my desiring an education.

"Well, ye knows what's best for yerself," Agatha said doubtfully, laying out my supply of dresses, pinafores, and pantalettes. Her scrunched rabbit's eyes had a wary cast to them, and a hurt one.

"Here there is no scope," said I.

"Well, if that don't beat everything," Agatha muttered, rolling my hair ribbons and tucking them into a muslin bag. "Nature will out, though, sooner or later."

"What do you mean, Nature will out?" I asked, thrilling with fear.

"Why, only that children can't 'elp a-taking after their parents. And if innocent lasses pretend to need *scope* when meaner sorts are driving 'em away, 'arassing and pestering-like, then the world ain't what it ought to be."

I flung myself at Agatha, helpless to check the gush of feeling; my spindly form met her strong arms, and I held her tight. "No one is driving me off. I only . . . I can't stand it any longer."

Agatha pulled me away from her embrace, shifting her hands to my temples so that she could read me like one of her pudding receipts. I lapped up the attention, for when would anyone ever waste sentiment on the likes of me again?

"Penned creatures suffer, but the more so when they imagine a pen what ain't there," Agatha said softly. "Can ye tell me the difference afore ye leave your 'ome behind?"

"I'm not penned — I'm frightened."

"Ye said that before, in front o' the main

75

house. Of what, lass?"

"Of myself."

Agatha set about mending the worst of my stockings. She stole glances at my mother's painting, however, the one like a sunset seen through tears. I easily divined her secret fear, but knew it to be rootless. Edwin Barbary was ugly in life, uglier still in death; but many lovely things died with him, and one was my desire to be exactly like my mother.

I could no longer afford to be like my mother; my heart must be carried not on my sleeve but deep in my breast, where the complete darkness might mask the fact it too was black as pitch.

The day before my departure, Edwin was placed beneath the grass and the buttercups before a very small assembly. Aunt Patience would have sobbed if she could, but only swayed, murmuring; she may have been addressing Edwin, or the droning minister, or the shovel in the gnarled hands of the grave-digger — who could say?

I stood in silence with my head bowed, wondering whom she would talk to at all without me left to hate.

This morose thought followed me home, where a cold meat supper awaited. Directly before sleep finally captured my twitching eyelids, I mused over whether Aunt Patience would rouse herself and march — froglike, determined, hateful, as she used to be — down to the gate and see me off.

She did not . . . only Agatha kissed my cheek as I was helped onto the rickety wooden step of the coach, with my trunk strapped above.

There is no practice more vexing than that of authors describing coach travel for the edification of people who have already travelled in coaches. As I must adhere to form, however, I will simply list a series of phrases for the unlikely reader who has never gone anywhere: thin eggshell dawn-soaked curtains stained with materials unknown to science; rattling fit to grind bones to powder; the ripe stench of horse and driver and bog.

Now I have fulfilled my literary duties, I need only add that other girls travelling to school may not have dwelt quite so avidly upon the angular faces of police constables as I.

We had journeyed for some seven hours, and I had flicked the curtain aside as the towns came thicker along our misty route, blinking into view as faint collections of red roofs and stone chimneys. I tugged at the rope strung above the window. The otherwise empty coach stopped abruptly, nearly throwing me from the hard seat. A few seconds later, the driver's whiskered face appeared in the act of spitting upon the side of the roadway. He gestured at the string tied to his arm as if my signalling him were the final straw in a long list of liberties I had taken with his person.

"Are we stopping at all before we reach Lowan Bridge?" I asked.

"Stopping!" He rubbed as if to wipe the red from his nose. Even had he succeeded, the pistol flask peeping from his lapel pocket would have replaced the stain in short order. "Are ye sick?"

"No."

"Faint?"

"No, but —"

"Hoongry?"

Glancing at the basket Agatha had lovingly filled with bread and pickles and potted rabbit, I shook my head. "I only need some air."

"Air!" repeated the driver. He shook his head as if from this day forward, no offence would ever be met with surprise. "Ye'll have air enough in half an hour, when we reach yer destination. Ye'll live on the stuff."

"Is the board a frugal one?" I asked, desperate for a hint.

"Ye might say so. Ye might say scraps tossed to pigs are a point of frugality."

"What is your name, sir?"

Rolling his eyes so I could see every feathery red vessel, the man answered, "Nick. What of it?"

"Nick, is life *very* hard at Lowan Bridge? I only want some warning, as Mr. Munt seemed . . . peculiar."

Nick tapped his finger to the side of his ruddy nostril. "Peculiar! Aye, he is that. Ye'll learn a plentiful heap o' facts, if all goes well."

"And how if all goes ill?"

"Then ye'll not need to worry yerself —" he coughed "— as it's prodigious difficult to trouble a corpse."

This intelligence was punctuated by the stomping of boots as the coachman returned to his high post, a friendly cry of "Damn you, Chestnut, you bloody useless sack o' glue!" and we were off again.

Quaking, I ate some pickles and a small piece of bread — however ill I felt, it seemed a prudent precaution. When the carriage ground to a halt, my door opened; Nick tugged the rope line off his sleeve as I stepped down to the road.

We had stopped before a tall iron gate set in a stone wall, a gate with sinister floral embellishments and brutal points like demons' teeth. Half the entrance stood open, a portal to a grim new world; a gravel path drew my eyes into the grounds, which were dotted with weeping trees lamenting my arrival. The building I guessed comprised Lowan Bridge School was grey as a feudal fortress. It possessed three stories, narrow windows excellently suited for a gaol, and a crenellated roof; if it had featured actual cannons thrusting through the stone gaps, it could not have made a clearer impression.

Nick harrumphed, and I turned to see that he had fetched my trunk from the roof and my basket from the coach.

"How can you leave children here to die?" I asked tremulously.

Setting my basket next to the trunk, Nick shrugged. "There's a real education to be had here — that's better than can be said for most o' these governess manufactories. Anyhow, the world is a hard place, and I live in it alone — what's it to me if you do too?"

"Here." I offered the considerable remains of my luncheon. "If they don't want me to have this, they need only take it away. You keep it."

"Keep it! What the devil are ye a-doing of? I've been paid already, ye daft child," Nick said, frowning.

"This is payment for something else."

"What, then?"

"The world is a hard place, and I live in it alone." I swallowed back my tears. "If you don't remember the others, remember me."

Nick studied me; in the end, he merely accepted my basket and shook my hand. Turning, he strode towards the dingy coach and Chestnut, who stood stamping and generally articulating his desire to be rewarded with a bag of hot oats. I could sympathise.

"Straight down the path," he ordered. "Best o' luck to ye, though brains'll be of better use — and mind the headmaster."

"I mean to."

"Good," Nick grunted, clicking his tongue at his weary horse. "Ye'll live longer."

I walked with a palpitating heart, dragging my trunk, up the lane under the brightening glare of midafternoon. The sun had sliced through the cloud bank, leaving an unmendable gash of blue across the sky's face, starkly lighting the battlements before me. Reaching the front entrance, I hesitated and then knocked; the door was of thick wood strapped with iron as if bound in a strait waistcoat. A uniformed servant girl with a pockmarked face answered and beckoned me inside with the instruction, "Mind you wipe your boots. This way."

We marched through corridors lined with carpets of forbidding black and blue, lit with wall-mounted dips rather than gas, featuring art suggesting that a great love of our Lord would be rewarded by the righteous being pelted with rocks. Half having expected a mean hovel lined with manure-seasoned straw, my childish jaw dropped; wherever my aunt had sent me, she had paid a pretty penny to do so, for this was no barnyard masquerading as a school, but rather the castle of a malevolent monarch. Had a dragon inhabited the dungeons, I should not have been in the least surprised. When we reached a smaller side room with books dimly lining the shelves, the servant said merely, "I'll fetch someone," and I was left with my trunk at my feet and mind in turmoil.

About ten minutes later, the door swung open. The woman standing there was quietly dressed in grey, her blond hair parted in the middle and her slender hand lifting a rush-light towards the darkened interior. She had a classically lovely face, features calling to mind a songbird or a sonnet, with a sweet afterthought of a nose and pale blue eyes. I thought her around twenty-five, which seemed a most distinguished achievement and one I felt unlikely to duplicate.

"Are you Jane Steele?"

I nodded.

"Welcome. I am Miss Amy Lilyvale, and I teach music here. If you apply yourself at Lowan Bridge, you will be a valuable addition to any great household in the world. If you are feckless and idle, you will find life hard."

She said these words as if required to deliver them; then she smiled. "You must be weary — you can have a wash before supper, and lie down if you like. Come."

Lifting my little trunk, I followed her light step back into the corridor and up a stately central staircase. We had not halfway climbed it when a bell clanged loudly enough to summon the dead, and the sound of pattering feet from all directions met our ears.

Girls poured into the murky corridors, books clutched to flat bosoms and full ones, for they seemed to range in age from as young as I was to as old as eighteen. They were all dressed in navy blue stuff frocks — coarse material which must have chafed —

with quaint white aprons, and a queer cloth cap fastened over their hair. I must have glanced down at my trunk, for Miss Lily-vale touched my elbow gently.

"Your own clothes will still serve you for holidays when you return to see your family."

"I have no family," I answered without thinking.

"Surely you must have a provider, or you could not afford to attend Lowan Bridge School."

"Yes, I am very grateful to my aunt," I replied, recovering my wits, "but she is not fond of me. She means to keep me away."

"Oh, Miss Steele . . . and to impart a sound education to you, surely?"

This, I was coming to realise, was un-doubtedly true — for had my absence been Aunt Patience's whole design, I might have landed in a Yorkshire sty and been left to moulder there. Meanwhile, the rush of footsteps and the jostling of elbows all around us unnerved me; most of the girls murmured words I could not catch, as if fixing something in their minds, whilst the few who were silent cast brushing looks at me like the scrape of minnows in a shallow brook.

"Here we are." Having reached the dormitories on the topmost level, Miss Lilyvale pushed a door open.

She revealed a long rectangular room furnished with two rows of double beds, several pine tables with basins and unadorned white pitchers thereon, unlit fireplaces at either end, and a window granting us a view of fragmenting clouds. The ceilings were high and imposing, the air as chill as it ever is within a stone tower, where we were to be kept prisoner like dozens of forlorn princesses. Suddenly weak with fatigue, I clutched the nearest bed frame, all but dropping my poor trunk.

"Goodness! That was a very brave show, but now I see the way of it," Miss Lilyvale tutted as she snatched the luggage from my trembling fingers. "Take off your shoes and lie down for a while. Here is your bed, and later you will meet your bedmate, Sarah Taylor, but for now no one should disturb you until I return to fetch you for supper at half six. Till then, rest quiet, dear, and remember to thank God for your safe arrival."

Miss Lilyvale departed. The bedclothes, though cheap and stiff, were clean, and the bed suitably big for the unknown Sarah to share henceforth. I wondered whether she was a good girl, a bright one, a pretty one; I wondered whether Nick would remember the potted rabbit if I ever required precipitate escape.

Sleep was finally weighing down my lids when I spied a ghost in the stark bedchamber.

Gasping, I tightened my loose grip upon the coverlet.

A lump of sheets had transformed into a child who could not have been above six years old — a blond apparition with a pale, freckled face and a tiny mouth. She regarded me stoically with her head on her palm.

"Miss Lilyvale told you to give prayers of thanks, and you haven't done."

Her voice was high even for her age — queerly so, like the tinkling of a bell.

"Why aren't you at lessons?" I returned.

"Ill." Indeed she looked it, for her skin was nigh transparent and her eyes dull, apart from the green circles of her irids. "You'll own up to it and not be angry with me? You forgot your prayers after Miss Lilyvale reminded you?"

"Yes," I agreed, nettled. "What of it? I'm Jane Steele. Who are you?"

"Rebecca Clarke. Call me Clarke, that's the way of it here. And thank you." She let her pale curls fall back to the pillow. "I couldn't have stood another day of this. I'll tell it as mild as I can, I promise."

"Tell what?"

"Tell Mr. Munt you lied about your prayers."

"But why —"

"You can report me in a week, when I've recovered. Fair is fair, after all."

"Report you where?" I demanded as my sluggish pulse sped.

"At Mr. Munt's daily Reckoning," Clarke chirped before burrowing back under the linens and effectively vanishing once more.

Six

"Madam," he pursued, "I have a Master to serve whose kingdom is not of this world; my mission is to mortify in these girls the lusts of the flesh; to teach them to clothe themselves with shame-facedness and sobriety . . ."

A soft hand on my shoulder woke me, and I dragged sleepy eyes open to view the blurred face of Miss Lilyvale. My slumber had been thin and fitful; rising, I glanced about for the mysterious Rebecca Clarke, but her bed was now neatly made.

"Wash up, Steele, and we'll be off."

The shock of the cold water was reviving, and I used my wet hands to smooth the countless ripples from my hair. When I turned back to Miss Lilyvale, she took my arm companionably and we quit the dormitory for the stairs, muddied evening sunlight trickling through the high, grimy exterior windows. The cracks of blue had retreated whilst I slept, beaten back by regiments of austere cloud banks. I watched a great line of girls emerging from a wing of classrooms, marching in pairs towards the open timber doors we approached.

"The housekeeper will leave two sets of uniforms on your bed this evening," Miss Lilyvale informed me. "For tonight, you need not worry about your dress, but afterwards be sure to keep yourself clean and well presented. Oh!" Miss Lilyvale brightened. "Taylor! Steele, this is your bedmate, Sarah Taylor."

The girl who had broken off from the line was twelve, with a moon face which was so beautiful I had no notion whether she should be congratulated or censured for taking matters a trifle too far. Her lips were rosy, her hair a sleek raven black, and the navy of the Lowan Bridge uniform served only to make her own blue orbs shine the brighter. She reached out with her palm down as if she were a noblewoman accepting obeisance — which was not entirely unfair and then again rather tiresome.

"How do you do?" said I. "I am happy to meet you."

"Yes," said she, in a strangely lazy drawl, "very likely."

This was less than promising, but the queue of schoolgirls had nearly entered the dining hall, so we hastened into the cavern from which the rich aroma of stew emanated. The huge chamber could have been a Viking hall, from bare flagstones to immense rafters. Miss Lilyvale walked to a dais at the end of the room; there the remaining teachers were assembled, including — to my dismay — Vesalius Munt. His staff was otherwise made up of females, a bevy of dull pigeons clad in stone and fawn and charcoal and ash. A great black cauldron was perched on sturdy iron before this assembly, with a matronly cook standing next to it.

When Taylor and I sat, to my astonishment I beheld the mutton stew already ladled into a bowl, and a respectable portion at that. Several platters had been set along the roughhewn table, piled high with rustic bread, and mugs of steaming black coffee sent bittersweet curlicues to the distant ceiling.

"Is . . . is this usual?" I marvelled. Taylor had made no move to lift the pewter spoon, so I folded my hands in my lap.

"What?" she returned peevishly.

"Is the fare always so good? It smells divine."

"Well, *that* of all things doesn't matter in

the *slightest,*" she retorted languidly.

This was peculiar, and likewise was it cause for a pulse of concern that none of the girls appeared happy about the fare; they regarded their bowls with slightly less dismay than I had once levelled at my cousin's genitalia. Before I could ask why, Mr. Munt rose from his chair and raised his hands elegantly skyward as we folded our fingers together.

"For what we are about to receive, may the Lord make us truly thankful," Mr. Munt called out in sonorous tones. "May He create in us humble gratitude for this nourishment, and may this fine meal strengthen our bodies that we may serve our Lord with greater steadfastness every day. Amen."

"Wouldn't that be grand," the girl across from me muttered after we had repeated the closing word of the prayer. She had a thin, sallow face and limp ash-coloured hair.

"Oh, *do* hush, Fox, your efforts at humour are *dreadful,*" Taylor crooned snidely.

"Now!" Mr. Munt exclaimed. "The time has come for our daily Reckoning. I adjure you as I always do to be thorough, and above all truthful, for the narrow path to purity lies solely in confession. First, Miss Werwick reports that the advanced Latin class did miserably poorly on their surprise examination. Let them stand and explain themselves."

A block of twenty or so girls rose, looking as if they had been asked to face the Spanish Inquisition.

"If you will not volunteer further information, it is my honour-bound duty to call upon you," Vesalius Munt said reluctantly. "Please raise your hand if you were the highest scoring student in Miss Werwick's class?"

An awkward older girl with a belly slightly wider than her hips and a queer shoulders-backwards posture lifted what resembled a flipper.

"I scored nineteen points out of twenty, sir," she said tragically.

"And do you think you ought to escape punishment for your triumph, Robinson?" Mr. Munt persisted.

Robinson took a long pause. Her classmates regarded her as one might a crouching lion being sighted down a rifle barrel — frightened, threatened, still dangerous.

"Yes." She set her teeth; the others flinched. "Yes, I think that earning so high a mark means I ought not to be punished."

"Oh no," whispered the lacklustre girl called Fox.

"Well, *that* won't go at *all* well," Taylor

echoed in a singsong fashion, though she sounded more intrigued than appalled.

"What —" I began.

"Enid Robinson," Mr. Munt boomed, his facial creases deepening to holy fissures, "do you think that *vanity* relieves you from the shame of having failed to assist your fellows?"

Robinson jerked, a hare caught in a trap. "No, sir."

"Perhaps you imagine that worldly accomplishments will cause God to overlook the sin of self-satisfaction?"

Perhaps Robinson meant to reply to this last, but she was prevented.

"An example must be made!" Mr. Munt's soldierly command rang through the hall, and his ever-roving grey eyes glinted. "Robinson, please lead the queue of girls being punished for Latin infractions and waste no time about it — in addition, you can replace luncheon with prayer in the chapel for the following fortnight."

Robinson paled but ducked her chin. I watched as the hapless Latin students picked up their bowls and carried them to the cauldron; one by one, they dumped the stew back into the vat. They then strode out of the dining hall.

This, I thought, *is very much worse than I*

supposed.

Suddenly several hands shot into the air, a giddy springtime of sprouting fingers. They seemed to belong to the most peakish of the girls, the ones on whom I would not have laid money should they challenge a dandelion to a duel.

"Clarke," Vesalius Munt called out gladly. "Yes, go on, my dear — lean on Allen there, you seem fatigued, though you deserve no less for having stolen from the poorest of God's servants."

Rebecca Clarke, who only managed to pull herself to a standing position by means of the better-fed Allen, raised her leaf-green eyes. Several teachers (including Miss Werwick) stared on with pleasure as if this were some grotesque circus, whilst others (including Miss Lilyvale) concentrated all their attention upon ceiling beams and bootlaces.

I had not been mistaken in my hazy examination of Clarke — she was no more than seven years old if she was a day, and affecting an uncanny look of forced piety, the one I suppose scientists adopted when strapped to a stake and asked whether or not the Earth was flat.

"What happens if you refuse to throw your supper away?" I whispered, horrified.

"Hsst." Fox shot me a jaundiced glance of

warning.

"Clarke, allow your natural urge towards repentance guide you." Mr. Munt's eyes roved, hither and thither, tinsel glints seeking out his victim's victim; I knew who was to be led to the chopping block and felt a contrary surge of pride.

"Poor little mouse has been on a diet of water and brimstone for *four* entire days now, after the larder raid," Taylor explained, sounding bored.

"The new girl," Clarke's tiny voice called. "Please don't punish her, for I hardly know her name. Steele, I think, and she was very tired, as she only arrived today. Miss Lilyvale told her to say her prayers, and she . . . didn't, sir. She fell asleep."

Dozens upon dozens of eyes swept to me as I stood; Mr. Munt frowned happily, returning his attention to Clarke.

"You have redeemed yourself, my child!" he cried. "Clarke, you may eat."

No wild dog ever set upon any limping deer's frame as assiduously as Clarke attacked her stew. She had been reduced to pearly teeth and pink tongue and soiled fingers; I pitied the sight even as my stomach growled.

Miss Lilyvale, a red flag flying across her cheeks, pressed her palm against her stomach and refused to watch.

"Steele, please step forward. You shall not be punished in the usual way, as you are new," Mr. Munt declared, "but you must learn the value we place here upon obedience."

Stepping over the bench, I advanced towards the teachers' table. *Scuff, scuff, scuff* went my shoes and *thud, thud, thud* went my heart as I advanced to be caned or set on a dunce's stool or adorned with a chalkboard or have my hair shorn off.

Mr. Munt smiled as I approached. He extended his hands; Miss Lilyvale, I noted, turned a striking shade of caterpillar green as Vesalius Munt glanced back at her.

"Miss Lilyvale has of late begged me to embrace forgiveness alongside justice, and I hereby publicly grant her wish," he declared.

Mr. Munt is in love with Miss Lilyvale, I thought feebly as his fingers gripped my still-bruised wrists. *That cannot lead to good.* Mr. Munt tugged me so hard that my knees struck the stone floor in front of him.

"You will not go without supper today, Steele," Mr. Munt announced. "You will lead us in prayer instead, for I surmise that despite your reputation for wrongdoing you intended to mind Miss Lilyvale. Pray say what is in your heart, and your brothers and

96

sisters in Christ shall pray alongside you."

Mr. Munt's eyes bored into me, silver picks illicitly nudging a lock open.

I stared back, thrilling with revulsion.

He is not satisfied unless we are complicit: he likes us responsible for our own abuse.

I recalled Cousin Edwin's features, sweat-slick and satisfied, as he played what he thought was a game.

You're every bit as bad as I am. You liked it.

Meanwhile, Mr. Munt's request that I say what was in my heart was a deliberately humiliating one, for what girl on her knees before an authoritarian feels anything save the pooling of hot shame in her belly, alongside bitter resentment that she should be treated no better than a slave?

I felt these insults, reader, and I collected them, strung them like sand hardened into pearls, and I wore them, invisible; I wear them today.

"Our Father, who art in heaven," I called out clearly with my eyes shut. The flagstone bit further into my knees when Mr. Munt gripped the top of my head as if blessing me. "You delivered me safely to the hands of these godly people, who want to stop the, ah, excesses of my nature. I'm so truly sorry that when Miss Lilyvale told me to pray I did not thank You for, um, her kindness and for Mr. Munt, whose attentions are so . . . thorough, and wise."

The hand on my head like an iron halo shifted, running an approving thumb over the part in my hair before Mr. Munt pressed my brow into the muscle of his thigh; I could smell him, something faintly sweet like candle wax and tarry like cigar smoke. Stifling a revolted choking sound with a cough, I hastened on.

"Please, Lord, will You take pity on this poor sinner, and please will you grant Miss Lilyvale and Mr. Munt patience when dealing with my shortcomings, and, ah, please will You bless all Your beloved children at Lowan Bridge. Amen."

The palm on my crown vanished, and the headmaster stepped back. Looking up, I found Mr. Munt wearing a blended expression: part feigned outward joy, part real inner perplexity, and a final ingredient I think surprised even him — recognition.

I've earned my bowl of supper, I thought, gazing up with a holy smile on my lips and a knife at the back of my teeth. *Try to take it from me.*

"Remarkable!" cried Mr. Munt, easily lifting me to my feet again. "Even the untamed, when moved by the Lord's grace, can inspire an entire congregation with her example. Steele, you may return to your seat."

I kept my head down as I stumbled on battered joints back down the gauntlet, but I stole glances at my classmates from behind the bars of my lashes. Clarke, who sat half-slumped over her empty bowl (by empty I do not mean finished, but rather as clean as if the touch of stew had never kissed this particular vessel), winked at me.

"Well," Taylor huffed when my journey had ended, "I *never.*"

"Didn't you?" I returned, and her pretty eyes narrowed sullenly.

"I never did, no."

"Did you mean a word of that?" Fox whispered.

"Of course," I lied, but I crossed my fingers upon the tabletop, and she granted me a brief smirk.

"That was either spectacular, or else the most *disgraceful* thing I've ever seen," Taylor continued.

Can't it be both? I thought, and I must have been delirious with the strain, for I belted out a laugh I covered with a sneezing fit.

Mr. Munt was calling on other girls now, ones who had been sentenced to diets like Clarke's and were shattering like fine china;

one by one, the Reckoning forced about half of those present to dump our meals.

"How is he *allowed*?" I mouthed.

"If any refuse, it's two hours with him in his private office. God knows what happens inside — Fisher went, and would never speak of it afterwards. Anyway, it's the best school for young ladies within fifty miles of London," Fox muttered glumly. "It isn't just the food; they've dozens of ways to make us mind them. Miss Martin gives you hours' worth of lines to write, Miss James will actually ink your offence on your forehead, Miss Lilyvale is a great one for early bedtime — which sounds harmless but we've too many studies for it not to be awful — and Madame Archambault has a little rattan cane in her desk. A fortnight ago, Harper didn't sit for three days."

"None of *that's* so bad," sighed Taylor, her attention pinned to Mr. Munt, "by comparison."

"No." Fox picked at the skin edging her thumbnail. "It isn't."

"And that concludes our Reckoning for this evening!" Mr. Munt surveyed the room, finding no further quarry which tempted him. "I commend you for your diligence, children. Sit, and partake of God's bounty."

The stew was thick and sweet and savoury,

chunks of carrot and potato and speckles of currants swimming alongside succulent mutton; we set upon it like the beasts Mr. Munt intended us to be.

"Have girls not asked their parents to lobby for Mr. Munt's removal?" I asked Taylor.

She tossed her shapely round chin. "It's *quite* hopeless, I'm afraid. Mr. Munt sells the leftovers at reduced rates to the manufactory men four miles from here, and what's left he gives away at soup kitchens. He's positively *worshipped* from here to London."

"Is that why he said Clarke stole from the poor when she really stole from the larder?"

"Exactly," murmured Fox. "She was the only one caught, caught with her arms full and pockets stuffed after lights-out no less, but they knew more were involved. These four days she's been refusing to give him any names."

"She must be very brave."

Taylor snorted, reaching for another slice of bread. "Very *silly,* you mean. Clarke has never really been punished before; they wanted her for the raid because she could fit through the door for the barn cats. She's new, only six, can memorise anything you put in front of her, perform terribly difficult figures — and from a very queer family. *Literary,* I think, God knows what sort of *horrid* people that entails."

"Your parents are tradesmen," Fox said with visible satisfaction.

"Your parents just sold half their estate, and *you* are a cow," Taylor said sweetly.

"My parents are dead," said I, "so I do hope to be friends with you all."

"Hush this *instant!*" Taylor gasped.

"Thank you, no," Fox mumbled.

"The instant you really detest anyone, by *all* means become friends with her," Taylor sang with studied indifference. "When Mr. Munt sets you against each other, be sure to have picked someone you can outtalk, which I'm confident you can after that . . . *display.* Remember when he forced Abbott to tell him that Dunning had helped her study for the botany project?"

"Don't." Fox shivered dramatically.

"How about when Fiddick and Hooper giggled during Communion?"

"I'm trying to eat," Fox complained, jabbing the air with her spoon.

"Mr. Munt just *adores* friends." A pale blue tinge of melancholy had deepened Taylor's tone. "*Most* of us know better."

We finished the meal in silence. When I rose to depart with Taylor and glanced back at Mr. Munt, I saw that his attention was likewise on me — displaying reluctant approval tinged with the desire to run the new Thoroughbred through its paces.

If Edwin had not been so stupid, I thought as the knot of fear in my chest tightened, *they would have been very much alike.*

Seven

And then my mind made its first earnest
effort to comprehend what had been in-
fused into it concerning heaven and hell:
and for the first time it recoiled, baffled;
and for the first time, glancing behind, on
each side, and before it, it saw all round
an unfathomed gulf: it felt the one point
where it stood — the present; all the rest
was formless cloud and vacant depth; and
it shuddered at the thought of tottering,
and plunging amid that chaos.

Some memoirs explain social hierarchies by
means of illustrative anecdotes, but mine is
about homicide, not ladies' schools.

Four varieties of females attended Lowan
Bridge. First, there were girls from wealthy
untitled families (like Taylor) who were
considered too gauche to deserve their
fortunes and were being educated in hopes
of finding a good position in a household of

a higher class or becoming more easily marriageable. Second, there were girls from poor titled families (like Fox) who were expected to become governesses because their fathers had poured thousands of pounds into the gutter. Third, there were orphaned girls who had incurred the wrath of their moneyed relations (like myself) and were being gifted the privilege of becoming drudges on other people's estates.

Finally, there was Becky Clarke, whose parents wanted her to attend school despite the fact they could afford to keep a tutor and a well-stocked library, and had said nothing to her of being a governess; and I have this anomaly to thank for the lesson that there is no accounting for taste.

"Are you feeling better?" I asked her when the bell rang next morn and the girls began to stir, for I had sensed her pensive eyes upon me since daybreak.

"Much," Clarke chimed.

"I heard what happened and admired that you gave no one away."

"When you're half the size of everyone else, you take care not to offend."

"Yes, but you're very . . . noteworthy, for your age."

"Can't be helped," she said in her high, absent way. "My parents say there's no use in clapping a turtle shell on a parrot or gluing wings to a reptile. So they sent me here. That shan't happen again if I can help it, singling you out at Reckoning."

I thought of Mr. Munt's strong hand on my head, my skin against his trouser leg, and thought, *I'd not have liked that to happen to you in my place either.*

"What I said about you was true, but saying it was dishonourable," Clarke mused lightly, pulling a straw-hued strand of her hair through her fingers. "How beastly. I can't bear dishonourable people."

I was such an inappropriate addressee for this remark that I buried my face in my pillow and laughed heartily.

"Friends," groaned Taylor. She kicked me with feet cold as snow, rolling out of bed. "I *told* you. Don't bother."

Donning my new uniform and pairing with my new bedmate as we walked to classes was of no interest other than the fact I was nearly dizzy with anxiety; a brief account of that first day, however, will fully acquaint the reader with my new life.

My first class was art, headed by Miss Constance Sheffleton, a timid silver-haired rabbit who would not have recognised discipline had it whipped her across the palms. Nevertheless, she knew where her bread was buttered, and proved it when she called tremulously, "Davies, you are here to sketch the bust, not contemplate the maple outside the window. Please inform Mr. Munt that I caught you idling."

"Yes, Miss," said a thin waif, and we winced, for this was clearly worse than any other punishment.

Following art was sewing lessons given by Miss Kitts. Ages were combined during class periods, but thence divided into circles appropriate to our ability; having been separated from Clarke, I asked her in high alarm what the matter was when we rejoined in the hall and I saw her doll's mouth a-tremble.

"I was just feeling better and now I'm to miss luncheon, all over badly embroidering a pansy," she confided, angrily swiping at the tears in her eyes. "I'm useless at stitchwork, my mind wanders so. What are decorative pansies to us, Steele?"

When I arrived at Latin, Miss Werwick briefly quizzed me, found me dismal, and bid me sit with the youngest girls, muttering happy imprecations about the amount of meals I should likely be forced to sacrifice. Never having studied Latin previous, I congratulated myself when at the end of the hour, I was explaining the lesson to the perplexed circumference, and Miss Werwick forgot herself far enough to frown at this development.

Midday dinner was allowed me, though it seemed a mere two thirds of the young ladies initially assembled the night before were present. Not seeing Taylor, I sat across from Fox, who fiddled with a piece of her already-greasy hair before saying, "Anything immediate?"

I swallowed hearty cabbage and pork broth, regarding her questioningly.

"It's what we say," Fox confided. "A code. To find out if anyone is . . . well, really in trouble."

"Oh." I set my spoon down, sobered. "Clarke isn't here — an embroidery mishap."

"I've an apple in my pillowcase," Fox said matter-of-factly. "All's well."

This was the day I learnt that friendship need not be labelled as such in order to be a very similar thing indeed.

A combined history and geography course given by Miss Halifax followed dinner. She was a hatchet-faced woman with animated hands — but there was no harm in her, and her enthusiasm was engaging.

"Why, Steele, though you are not well-read regarding the Ottoman Empire, you ask exceedingly incisive questions," she exclaimed. "You shall sit with the thirteen-year-olds and with Clarke here."

Clarke, whose brilliance on all subjects, save that of rendering decorative flowering plants with thread, was the envy of the entire school, seemed strangely happy when I descended into the hardbacked chair beside her.

"Good, we can go over dates of battles before bedtimes," she decreed lightly, adjusting the strange white cap we wore. "My parents are pacifists, the disgrace of our entire street, and when I arrived, I didn't know a Cossack from a dragoon."

"Of course. Anything immediate?" I asked, a shower of golden sparks prickling my skin as I did something illicit.

"Ha. No," said Clarke, one cheek dimpling. "Thank you, indirectly, for the apple."

Music class ensued immediately afterwards. Remembering Vesalius Munt's opinion that spiritually contented artists were beings not to be found upon this teeming globe, I looked forward to Miss Lilyvale's tutelage with intrigue. Was her virtue so potent it could withstand the moral ravages of even art? A simpler answer proved true: Miss Lilyvale's musical ear was the happy amalgam of a deaf mockingbird's and a colicky newborn's, and thus could not have troubled her character in the smallest degree.

"Class, we have much to do today!" she called. "But first as ever, I will lead us in a hymn. Young ladies, here is our music. As this is a new piece — do think of it as an exercise in sight-reading."

We stood all in a semicircle and sang Horatius Bonar's latest opus. My ignorance of whether the Almighty's glory swelled in the wake of our praise remains profound to this day; I can inform the reader, however, that no gain in sight-reading skills resulted. Taylor was present, and I greeted her afterwards, even as she mumbled *George Louis, George Augustus, George William Frederick, George Augustus Frederick. . . .*

"Taylor," I whispered, "anything immediate?"

"Oh, go *away,* you horrid nosy thing," cried Taylor, her eyes edged in pink. "I've had *nothing* to eat since the porridge, and meanwhile Granville is such a sweet girl, all those golden curls and her family from a simply ancient coffee fortune, and so the *best* sort of people, and she was made to slap herself in the face — *herself,* mind, and hard — after Mr. Munt caught her laughing over a sketch Fiddick did of Miss Hardbottle. Don't touch me, I can't bear *any-one,*" she sobbed, fleeing.

Mathematics followed, and theology, and French (at which I excelled, *naturellement,* and thus forever after avoided the red welts my classmates carried as souvenirs from Madame Archambault), and after we had crammed our heads full of geometry and the Book of John, the inevitable Reckoning followed.

I ate my stew and kept my head as low as any true acolyte.

I reproduce this workaday agenda to il-lustrate that we lived practically in one another's pockets, so that in moments of emergency — which were as frequent as moments of breathing — we might offer help. If we succeeded thanks to cleverness and collaboration, we might fall asleep with a meal or even two, perhaps, rounding the hollows of our bellies. We were not *friends;* but so many others strove to make us wretched that we lacked the energy to turn upon one another save in the extremest necessity.

When I dropped exhaustedly next to Tay-lor at nine o'clock that first night as the sun vanished, I felt the same electric charge I have always gained from thwarting author-ity traversing the narrow ridge of my back.

You haven't missed a meal yet, I thought. *You could be very good at this. And the others might be made better off as well.*

"Steele?" came a piping voice.

"Yes?" I answered Clarke.

"Good night," said she, as Taylor's warning toes jabbed me.

Grief is a strange passenger; it rides on one's shoulder quiet as a guardian angel one moment, then sinks razor talons into one's collarbones the next. No sooner had Clarke offered me this kindness than hot salt tears were soaking my pillow. My mother had once bid me good night, and good morning too; and my mother had loved me, and she had died for no reason I could discern, and was never coming back.

I would cry often for Mamma's loss, as children are wont to do — but I could never have guessed that my own melancholy would lead to discoveries which once more dashed my world from its orbit.

The event which caused me fully to embrace my true nature took place some six months later.

By this time, I had come to know many facets of Lowan Bridge School. I knew that Taylor was secretly terrified not of being a governess but of being married to someone tyrannical, as her mother daily hid fresh bruises under flounces and lace; I knew that the curse of Fiona Fiddick's life was that she was the funniest creature on earth, which meant that she weighed a stone less than she ought to have; I knew that under Fox's dour attitude hid a girl who somehow always had an apple in her pillowcase, and never kept it for herself.

I knew that there were stables, unlocked ones, and horses available for caressing. I knew that the roof above our dormitory was accessible if one crept carefully, and that Clarke's eyes as she mapped the swath of glittering black not obscured by the reek of London to the south of us were mossy pools in the moonlight, and that though she seldom laughed, she laughed at a stolen glimpse of the night sky most blithely of all, and her laugh was like the treble of a silver flute.

Sunday was both beloved and dreaded, for while we had no classes and were allowed to play on the lawn or read in quiet nooks, we were compelled to attend chapel. As we marched towards the elegant stone building on the day my life altered forever, a parade of dull blue soldiers plodding under stony November skies, the casual observer might have supposed we were going to be executed.

Sunday, after all, was the day Mr. Munt performed a *weekly* Reckoning, in order to catch out any sins we might have foolishly neglected to mention.

"Steele, will you help me with the Catullus assignment?" Fox's ungainly form landed beside me in the third pew. "I can't make heads or tails of it, and even if Miss Werwick doesn't have a cane —"

"Of course," I agreed. Censure from Madame Archambault was humiliating and painful, but Miss Werwick of all the teachers relished referring us to Mr. Munt, as if we were chess pieces (or, better still, ninepins).

Clarke sat upon my other side. "Anything immediate, mi'ladies?"

Clarke was wont to trill when she was well fed, as if beginning to compose a folk tune, and I adored her for it. I was about to answer in the negative when Miss Lilyvale advanced to take her seat before the pipe organ and commence our two hours of agony.

"With a true spirit of praise, girls, sing with me!" Miss Lilyvale called out.

A veil of authorial privacy will be drawn here; it would behove neither the reader nor the author to dwell upon musical atrocities which reside wholly in the past and cannot now be remedied.

After the initial three hymns had been sung, Mr. Munt ascended to the pulpit. Vesalius Munt was never more happy than when every student's attention speared in his direction, fixed to him like nails as he stood before the crucifix.

"Happy Sabbath to you, my girls," he announced, beaming, and the *my* stuck in our thorny throats, for it was the truest sentiment he would admit to all morning. "I encourage you to rest peacefully upon this holiest of days, and repose knowing that Christ died to save you from your own ignorance and infamy. Let us proceed with our weekly Reckoning, that we might cleanse our souls."

A hand raised. Mr. Munt devised a demeaning punishment for the accused — and often for the accuser. There were no rules in this jungle, no trails we might tread so as to escape the tiger's tooth. We were paying as much mind as we ever did, Fox and I and Clarke, ears pricked for danger, when I startled at the sound of my name.

"Steele *means* well," my bedmate was drawling exhaustedly from two pews distant. "And she's as clever and helpful as everyone says, and oh, it's *dreadful,* but she . . .

she doesn't mean to, and I *hate* to say it."

I turned to gape at her. Taylor's face was bloodless, a mere illustration: black hair thickly inked, eye and lip hinted at in delicate pen strokes. Her beauty had been marred of late by her uselessness at memorisation, and she had forsaken sleep in favour of struggling alone over data which meant nothing to her; now she embraced the only option guaranteed to merit a hot meal. I did not marvel that it was me — I was a proximal target, even a sensible one, already having earned a reputation for lying my way out of scrapes.

"What is it that Steele did not intend to do, Taylor?" Mr. Munt rested a poised arm against the pulpit.

Taylor's round eyes flew to my queer tilted almond ones. "She dreams."

"What in God's name is Taylor doing?" growled Fox.

"It's my fault," I assured her quietly. "I didn't notice she had got so frail. She has every reason to lie about me."

"She isn't lying," I thought Fox muttered.

"Steele has simply *terrible* nightmares about her mother," Taylor declared. "She doesn't mean to scream, but she won't *stop.*"

My heart stuttered.

Yes, I often awoke covered in sweat and raw-throated as a carrion crow and, yes, I dreamt of my mother; but I did not *scream* for her. Did I? Once or twice had I bitten back cries, but these were rarities, accidents.

Rising, I clasped my hands before my white apron. "I'm sorry for giving any trouble, but my mother died recently."

"Over half a year hence," Mr. Munt corrected.

"Mourning her is only *natural*. But please forgive me for disturbing the peace."

"Natural?" Mr. Munt struck the flat of his hand against the podium as if smiting sin itself. "Let our hearts go out, girls, to this wayward lamb, who meditates on death when in the midst of God's abundance."

I bit the inside of my lip until I could taste all I had left of my mother, which was her blood.

"Steady," Clarke chimed softly.

"Let Steele," intoned Mr. Munt, "come to thank You, Lord, for your grace in orchestrating her removal from her mother's evil influence."

My hands gripping the pew had transformed into bleached bones.

"And let us never give up the hope that she may return one day to honest Christian practices!"

"Steady," Clarke squeaked, gripping my skirt.

"Mourning my mother is not dishonest!" I cried.

I may as well have set off a bomb in the chapel; every eye swept to me in dismay. Contradicting Mr. Munt was tantamount to suicide; unfortunately, I had not yet grasped that suicide was the topic.

"Your mother," Mr. Munt enunciated, relishing every syllable, "was a debauchee who perished deliberately by means of self-administered laudanum. She was thus buried with minimal services by the only minister willing to overlook her Gallic Catholic affiliations and willful self-slaughter, and your sainted aunt spared you the indignity of witnessing such a barren sight. Tell me, why should mourning your mother be praised as any sort of virtue when her tainted spirit so obviously haunts your own immortal soul? Your mother was a disgrace to the natural order — an embodied disaster."

He had known all along, I realised.

There had been no mourners in crepe at my mother's funeral, I understood: only the overripe aroma of earth unwilling to accept yet another unpaid houseguest. Suicide was high treason, for what greater violation existed than thwarting God's will?

My sentence (a week of missing dinner) was announced and Taylor invited to rejoin the ranks of the fed; but the pit of my stomach swelled into a cavern long before hunger descended.

Mr. Munt had won; I had not been prepared for the truth. A small hand interlaced with mine.

"You don't cry out so *very* often," Clarke whispered, wide-eyed and earnest.

"I will now," I managed hoarsely before disengaging myself and opening our prayer book with palsied fingers.

I have learnt since that a great many people are ill intentioned and yet behave well. I might have followed suit — winked into the mirror of a morning and worn a white sheep's coat all the livelong day. Jane Eyre was told to pray to God to take away her heart of stone, that she might be gifted a heart of flesh; but my heart of flesh bled for my mother, my mother whom I would apparently *never see again* if I was good.

The wind howled that November night as if mourning a lost love; and the decision I reached in my hard bed with Taylor's cold toes prodding my calves, sobbing as silently as I could, went as follows:

If I must go to hell to find my mother again,
so be it: I will be another embodied disaster.
But I will be a beautiful disaster.

EIGHT

"I might have been as good as you, —
wiser, — almost as stainless. I envy you
your peace of mind, your clean conscience, your unpolluted memory. Little
girl, a memory without blot or contamina-
tion must be an exquisite treasure — an
inexhaustible source of pure refreshment:
is it not?"

It would have been possible for me to
survive Lowan Bridge for longer than the
bleak seven years I spent there had Mr.
Munt not taken it into his head to kill
Clarke.

Oh, we were subjected to daily indignity,
each Reckoning more creatively vicious than
the last; but small moments of happiness
touched us deeply. In a mansion, blessings
are lost amidst bric-a-brac; in a pit, they
shimmer like the flash of dragonfly wings.

There was Miss Lilyvale's boundless

capacity to ruin even the simplest music. There was Fiona Fiddick's faculties for both humour and sewing, which enabled her to hide the words *FEED ME* in an embroidered nosegay of coral peonies which Miss Sheffleton proudly hung upon the classroom wall. There were horses, and riding lessons, and I learnt to love galloping through the daisy-dotted meadows, pretending I need never return. There were the holidays, when Mr. Munt was out lecturing, and there was Clarke's fierce, small-lipped smile when she arrived back after Christmas with her carpetbag and delivered an impetuous peck to my cheek.

Reader, I had miraculously acquired a companion; Clarke's existence owned me, opened me, left me helpless with stifled giggles at midnight. Becky Clarke was brilliant and ridiculous, an effortless scholar who insisted on honour when honour led only to missed meals; she was three years my junior, so I could shrug her off as an irritating protégée the instant anyone raised an eyebrow; and she responded to both compliments and criticism with the same casual piping responses, as if baffled anyone had noticed she was there at all. Her simplicity was droll, her mind captivating — had anyone asked whether I thought her a genius or an idiot, I should not have had a satisfactory answer.

"Would you like to watch the sun rise?" Clarke would ask when the weather was fine, and madly I would accompany her to the roof, yawning and cracking sluggish joints, and we would sit there quite contented, always gazing at the murky haze of London not so very far away from us, and seeming — as was perfectly true — nearer to its outskirts every year. She would hum soft songs whilst gazing at the firmament, and her head would find its way to my shoulder.

Meanwhile, we all grew longer limbs and harder hearts every year.

Granville passed away during the fever which swept through our school when I was eleven years old. Taylor wept dreadfully, saying that Ettie Granville had been the only person ever to understand her; I raided the charity salvage pile and delivered her monogrammed kerchief to my bedmate, who clutched me about the shoulders for all the world to see.

Influenza claimed Fox when I was thirteen; I orchestrated the theft of a bushel of apples to store in her memory and was caught out during a vengeful Reckoning. Clarke smuggled me broth in a hot-water bottle and watched me guzzle it as we both hid behind the bed frame.

We became adept at grieving, suffering agonies for a day or two, and then returning to our altered orbits. I grew accustomed to the facts of my mother's death more slowly, the horrible truth that she had finally managed the trick she must have attempted long before, which was to die. The others treated me predictably poorly for a spell — who can escape the stigma of a lunatic for a mother — but we all hated Mr. Munt so ferociously, with every red pulse of life, that we had not time to hate one another.

All fell to pieces, however, when I had been at Lowan Bridge for seven years, and Clarke's preoccupation with honour swerved from pleasant foolishness into fatal lunacy.

There we stood before Miss Lilyvale's desk, awaiting instructions.

"Would you girls please study . . . oh, goodness, I'm that scattered . . . the piano part, Steele, and this soprano vocal part, Clarke, for the end-of-year gala? I can think of no one better able to demonstrate our talents. Won't you say yes?"

We glanced at each other; excelling at any course was a coveted position, but evidence suggested that our favourite teacher's praise was not so complimentary as her censure. Meanwhile, Clarke was an outstanding vocalist — her tones were dizzyingly high, hovering mid-air as if a magical harp had been strummed. Students came to a bewildered halt in hallways whenever she practised her scales with that mathematical precision which was so innate in her.

"Of course." Clarke took the small bundle of songs.

Then a strange thing occurred: head folding, Miss Lilyvale leant forward against her desk briefly. Her rosy cheeks had lost their blush during the course of the past two years, as if she had been bid to shoulder a stone up an endless mountainside; every month Miss Lilyvale became more of an automaton with something terribly pleading beneath the waxworks. She drew her fingers along the knob of her drawer, eyes briefly falling shut.

"Do you want something else of us?" Clarke asked.

She answered softly, "I can never have the things I truly want."

"Are you all right, Miss Lilyvale?" I inquired, concerned.

"Oh! Heavens yes, I was only . . . distracted. Thank you for being so obliging," our teacher said, smiling, and the strange moment was shattered.

"It's in the desk," Clarke announced as Miss Lilyvale bustled off to see that some younger girls were given appropriate parts. I was sixteen, Clarke thirteen, and thus as model pupils we were often left to our own devices — save for the inevitable Reckonings.

"What's in the desk?"

"Whatever is haunting Miss Lilyvale." Clarke studied her music. The charm of her distraction lay in the fact it was genuine; Becky Clarke could not lie if her life hung in the balance, and I shall soon cite statistical evidence to this effect. "This is rather high even for me, though I do like G major."

"Never mind music," I whispered as we quit the classroom. "Miss Lilyvale is stretched as tight as the catgut on her violin strings. You really mean to say you know what ails her?"

Clarke lifted the choral part as we walked. The birds outside the gloom-shrouded staircases were dumb that April afternoon, the carpets mute beneath our footsteps. "I went into the music room at half four yesterday because I thought I left my sketchbook, and Miss Lilyvale was reading a letter. When I appeared, she shoved it in the drawer she just touched so sadly."

"And you think her correspondent is making her *ill*?"

"No one can say," Clarke owned, tossing her flaxen curls though they were restrained under her chaste cap. "But if ever it looked as if a letter were strangling someone . . ."

The ensuing silence fairly crawled with questions.

Does Clarke wish me to intervene? I wondered, heart thrumming eagerly.

I had countless times thwarted hunger at Lowan Bridge, taking as much joy in naughtiness as in success; I had forged grades, pilfered supplies, told positively operatic lies. Queerly, Clarke had never minded these untruths, though I supposed that was thanks to her natural compassion, or else her practicality. In any event, I had learnt the principle swiftly: if I lied to Mr. Munt (or anyone else to do with the ultimate act of lying to Mr. Munt), I would be praised; if I lied to Clarke — all of these accidental falsehoods, bred of forgetfulness — I would be shunned until her ire burnt itself to cinders and she nuzzled into my shoulder like a cat seeking company.

So I had lied, and grown still better at it — for myself, and for my fellow prisoners. It only followed, since Miss Lilyvale was our unquestioned ally despite being a teacher, that I ought to ferret out what was wrong with her.

I wonder about the verb *to ferret* now I am grown. If a conjugation of a similar verb, *to snake,* existed, I believe that would have been closer to the truth — for my slithering, slinking capabilities had been honed by age sixteen to a nearly reptilian pitch.

I did not dream of inviting Clarke to raid Miss Lilyvale's office that night, which in hindsight was a monstrous error; had we made the discovery together, we might have talked through what was best to be done.

Quietly, I eased my coarse frock on and skipped the apron, that material being too pale for untrammelled moonlight. I flinched as the door creaked, but no one stirred; if the girls knew one thing, it was that my disobedience tended to benefit the majority. Shutting the door behind me and risking further noise would have tempted Fate, so I stepped into the hallway, leaving a draught of air in my wake.

It had cost me two weeks' practice with a bent nail to pick my first lock at the age of ten, aptitude for larder raids being a highly esteemed skill. As I knelt before Miss Lilyvale's music-room door, however, I felt strangely inept — my fingers were clubs, my ears abuzz with fanciful susurrations. At last, I prised open the lock and was greeted by the predictable midnight sight of an empty room within a sinister stronghold, its shuttered windows and watchful walls.

The desk was also locked. After fiddling with the nail, I substituted a hat pin, which swiftly worked its magic, and I pulled open the drawer.

As Clarke had suggested, a stack of letters rested there.

I lit the lamp with a lucifer from my dress pocket, hid the light under the desk, and sat upon the floor Indian-style. At first glance, I thought the letters must have dated back at least a year or two, for how else could some of the eggshell-coloured paper have deepened to pale yolk in tone? The envelopes were blank save for the addressee, *Miss Amy Lilyvale,* and I frowned in concentration as I slid the thin foolscap out.

Then my lips parted ways as I gazed upon the contents of what seemed the oldest correspondence.

They were *confessions.*

Dear Miss L——

I can suffocate no longer under this mask, nor daily live a falsehood when such misplaced secrecy makes hypocrites out of honest Christians. I do beg your forgiveness for what I am about to say, and indeed, begging your forgiveness ought to have been a duty I performed years previous; if I cannot confess all to you now, however, my integrity is meaningless, and my boundless love nothing finer than a canker eating away at my swollen tongue.

I long to put my mouth upon you; yes, your lips, but I confess to far more fervidly desired locales. I wish that when your eyes met mine, they travelled a slow route to my trouser front. I wish that I could taste you where you must ache for me as I do for you. My mouth upon your sweet flesh, and then my journey back up your body, and your face when I finish the first slow thrust into you, the one I compelled you to beg for; these images soak my dreams until there is nothing left of my free will, and I urge you to answer me: Are you innocent regarding my torment?

My hope is that you will not shun me after these disclosures. I am your employer, after all, and so must promise that your reputation as well as my own rests in my careful palms — safe from the censure of a prurient world, I assure

130

you. I only hope that you can help to absolve me now I have disclosed my desires, and that we may unite forever as one flesh, or else live as forthright and forgiving siblings in Christ.

In brotherly love,
Vesalius

After blinking for what seemed hours, I edged under the desk beside the sour-smelling metal lamp with what I have subsequently learnt was a pile of ripe erotica.

Reading the second letter took me ten minutes, as half my body physically shrank from looking; reading the remaining thirteen took half an hour; I was, in this as in all other vices, a fast learner. I hoped that subsequent missives would deplore his initial one, but they were all of a kind, save that vocabulary like *breast* and *cunny* and *arse* and *rut* liberally seasoned later disclosures.

When I had finished, I scrambled out and leant over the desk, feeling a profoundly strange admixture of nausea and high-pitched excitement like the sensation of dismounting after a hard gallop.

Had this been what Edwin had meant?

You're every bit as bad as I am. You liked it.

I did *not* like this feeling, this unsettled tingling wrongness; I felt it with Clarke sometimes at the edge of the rooftop when I thought, *How easy it would be to simply step off,* and my heartbeat soared, and I flinched away from the edge, unspeaking and ashamed of myself and giddy with quicksilver nerves which fired from scalp to spine and lower.

I did not strictly *dislike* the sensation either, however.

I stole the letters and stole back to our dormitory. Crawling into bed next to Taylor following questionable excursions by now carried no risk, and she snored through my manoeuvres; Clarke, however, was aquiver with attention in the next bed, her eyes dancing over me in the grey not-light as I pulled back the coverlet.

"I was right, wasn't I?" she asked.

At a loss for words, I passed Clarke the letters and curled up with my back to her golden curls.

This was not my first mistake, but would prove to be the most careless — no matter how confused I was by the strange pulse of blood in my groin. Sharing my findings with Clarke seemed the only option; the thought of digesting those letters alone, without her to partake in the disgusting yet exotic meal, revolted me — I girlishly wanted someone else to be as agitated as I was.

And yet, it was more than that. Clarke made me mindlessly, achingly happy. I wanted us to share in everything; I wanted us to sail to faraway China, for us to attend a lavish costume ball, for her to be threatened with a pistol and for me to throw myself in the path of the bullet. Often as I fell asleep I fantasised she had been forced to name me as a murderess in a Reckoning, so that I might be sentenced to starve in a frigid straw-lined aerie, and as I lay dying she would visit and we should watch the stars fading through the window and I should whisper in the shell of her ear with my last breath, *Never mind.*

I forgive you.

I didn't mind.

That never happened, but apparently the worst things I can imagine still fall short of reality.

At the next daily Reckoning, we were witness to an act akin to watching a tree sprouting from the sky, or rains bursting forth from the grounds like perverse fountains. I have never been so shocked; and were you, reader, to suggest greater surprises are in store for me, I should suggest you

133

invest in the purchase of a strait waistcoat without delay.

"I name Mr. Munt," Clarke said soberly.

The remark was so unreal that I laughed, choked, and then planted my palm firmly over my lips.

To say that Clarke turned heads would be an understatement. The announcement slammed into my chest like a physical blow. I have been thrown from a horse, attacked by multiple men, fallen down a flight of stairs; none of these events ever struck me so hard, because none of them so explicitly announced, *this is your fault.*

Mr. Munt initially could not believe his own ears. "Whom do you mean to name, Clarke?" he inquired.

"I already did. You've subjected Miss Lilyvale to unwanted attentions, Mr. Munt. Say you're sorry."

Mr. Munt's handsome face paled. He glanced at Miss Lilyvale, who was not looking at him, because Miss Lilyvale was looking at me. I understood then what I had not before: she had *wanted* us to find the letters. Miss Lilyvale was vacillating and weak, and Clarke and I were neither, and others had noticed. Miss Lilyvale's lake-blue eyes dimmed in shame as the other teachers whispered *oh my* and *but it can't be true, can it?*

"Clarke." Mr. Munt by now seemed outwardly composed save for his throat, which was ropy with rage under his white collar. "Do you truly mean to falsely accuse your headmaster when your own situation here is so precarious?"

"I don't understand," Clarke said, lifting her chin.

"Oh, I should never have troubled you with the information had you not made a mockery of the Reckoning," Vesalius Munt hissed. "Your parents have told you they publish books, I presume? That they are among the literary set?"

Clarke said nothing.

"I believe in the value of education for every child, including even *females,* a position which has garnered me much criticism!" Mr. Munt cried with an arm raised. "And here this beggar at the gates of paradise accuses *me* of misconduct! Her parents print lurid erotic fiction, which it pains me to say in your company, ladies," he added, flushing nicely before the rapt teaching staff. "They donated beyond Clarke's fee to consign their daughter to my care; I accepted, hoping to save the child from heinous influences; and now she — the viper! — tells me that I have made Miss Lilyvale the subject of my *unwanted attentions?*"

"Oh my *God,*" breathed Taylor, morbidly fascinated.

We watched as Miss Lilyvale clutched at her voiceless throat and fled the room. When I think of the anger I felt, I will always recall ice and not fire, the way snow sears into one's flesh.

Clarke's face was rigid save for the tremor in her tiny lips.

"Yes," said she, "that's exactly what I mean to tell you."

"Excellent," said Mr. Munt, enjoying himself again. "You can confine yourself to porridge at breakfast for the foreseeable future. Next confessor?"

NINE

"I am very happy, Jane; and when you hear that I am dead you must be sure and not grieve: there is nothing to grieve about. . . . By dying young I shall escape great sufferings. I had not qualities or talents to make my way very well in the world: I should have been continually at fault."

Within a fortnight, Clarke was a shade haunting hallways where no one saw or spoke to her, carrying such slight weight that the desk seats must have thought her a spring breeze. Her skin grew ashen, her lips cracked, her eyes mirrors.

"I am so ashamed of myself," Miss Lily-vale whispered.

We were in the choir room on a Sunday before the service, only she and I, for I had left a note in her drawer demanding she meet me. Outside, the merry May breezes wanted only blithe girls with ribbons for their dance to be complete, and I pitied Miss Lilyvale for the necessity of my company a little; she had already endured unwanted attentions, veiled threats, and now a scheming schoolgirl. The choir room was neat and orderly, save for a dainty rug under the practice piano which had been gnawed by mice and reminded me of my music teacher.

"What can be done?" I urged, outwardly calm and inwardly frantic. "And what did you think *would* be done, anyhow? You must have wanted us to find them, but I can't imagine what —"

"And I can't either!" she cried, eyes wild, before her mouth pressed into a tormented dash. She hugged her own arms. "You must forgive me. No — no, you mustn't, I've no right to even ask. My father is a country parson, my mother an industrious invalid, and they are happy when they've oxtails for their soup. Their parish is just outside London, but poor and plain for all its proximity. I learnt piano, thinking I could give private lessons. Well, I'm an utter shipwreck at music, and Mr. Munt when visiting our parish lecturing hired me anyhow, I arrived just a year before you did though I was far older, and this position pays — oh, don't look at me, I can't bear it."

"You think you're lucky to have the place." I tentatively touched her forearm.

"I think he wanted me and not my music — who could want my music! He courted me for years without ever proposing before the letters started, and now I'm trapped, for what decent woman would have kept a job of all things with such correspondences plaguing her?" She shuddered. "Last month, he stopped me in a deserted corridor to, to *pray* for me, and he put his palms on my brow and here, over my heart."

I required answers, and so increased the pressure on her arm. "Have you spoken with him since Clarke's Reckoning?"

"Not a word. Did you burn the letters?" Miss Lilyvale whispered. "I thought them proof of his disgusting attentions, but that was unspeakably foolish — they are merely evidence of my complicity. Did you destroy them?"

"Yes," I lied.

It was better than saying *I reread them nightly because I do not understand their effect on me and I am studying it in the cause of science.*

"Thank you. I was . . . terrified, paralysed."

"We've tried everything," said I, implacable. "We've shared, we've stolen, we've foraged spring greens when we were meant to be playing hopscotch. Clarke *will not* survive. What can we do?"

Pressing her sleeve to her eyes, Miss Lilyvale glanced in naked fright at the clock in the corner. "God forgive me. I'm your teacher, I ought to have . . . Yes, there is one thing to be done. Mr. Munt is his own bookkeeper. If you altered his accounts, and then took food on the day of its delivery, he would not know you had done so. Tomorrow the farm will deliver the week's eggs and produce."

The information echoed like the clap of a gong, for Clarke that morning had confessed herself bedridden. Porridge, lawn weeds, and rare stolen roast potatoes would no longer suffice.

"I take it I'm meant to perform this little magic trick," I could not help but mention.

"Oh, Steele —"

"Never mind. I'll do it. Does he keep the ledger in his study?"

Miss Lilyvale nodded, righting her hunched posture. "He invited me there for tea once. I shall never forget that occasion, no matter how I try."

"When girls refuse to return their food,

they're told to visit his study, and no one speaks of it afterwards," I said lowly. "Why?"

"He tells them who he thinks they really are, and what they must sacrifice to save themselves from hellfire," Miss Lilyvale answered against a raw throat. "Sometimes he shows them pictures, suggests things . . . things he accuses them of secretly longing to do. For hours. Can you imagine?"

I could, but the service was about to commence. "I must know why you placed me in this position."

Two feverish blots glared from her cheeks. "Please understand that I never meant for Clarke to —"

"Do the idiotic thing she did. I still deserve an explanation."

Miss Lilyvale was a sweet, toothless, impressionable creature, but she was also an honest one, and finally she looked me straight in the eye.

"I know your past is . . . chequered. I also know that you forgive others more readily than anyone I have ever encountered, and I cherish it — you have a great talent, you know, for accepting people. Have you ever kept a secret," Miss Lilyvale asked me, all the blood in her body seeming to drain straight through the floor, "which was not precisely your fault, but which would — if discovered — ruin you? Have you ever awoken to nothing save dread of daylight?"

"You know I have," I answered, comprehending that she spoke of my mother's bad end.

"Mr. Munt means to destroy me if he cannot have me," Miss Lilyvale murmured. "Please forgive my inexcusable actions. I only . . . I simply couldn't do it anymore."

Watching her, I thought about secrets. One can grow accustomed to carrying unseeable scars, as if the tattoo one wears is inked in flesh tone over flesh tone; but nevertheless one is still covered in *secret*, painted with secret, stained by it. I would have done anything to shed Edwin's dead eyes glazed fish-scale grey.

Solving Miss Lilyvale's problem and saving Clarke at once would have to suffice, however, lest I defy the restful nature of the Sabbath.

"I'll be in Mr. Munt's study during the service." I turned on my heel. "If you might make any excuses necessary which prevent my being looked for? That would be rather the least you could do."

Shadows are curious entities; they are lightless and yet cast a shape into the world, just as I do. As I ventured through the empty hallways, I did not think of myself as *myself* at all but as another Jane, a shadow given form. This curious phenomenon echoed the way I had come to think of my cousin's murder — Edwin was no more, due to regrettable events somehow removed from the Jane Steele who had mastered translating Cato and gliding along with a spine straight as a pikestaff. My mother was also no more, but that was another matter, I thought as I tiptoed, flinching at each creak. I had been wicked, in an impulsive fashion; I had been devious, in minor targeted ones.

This time I would invade a headmaster's private office, forge records, and escape, which would be a sure step on the road to perdition.

The unlocked door to Mr. Munt's study swung open. The shelves were crammed, boasting titles from phrenology to poetry, and the dwindling fire's aroma mingled with book must and tobacco. I had visited the coffer-ceilinged chamber twice — once, I realised to my own horror, as a trusted messenger delivering Vesalius Munt a note from Miss Lilyvale; and once, after our late lamented Fox had insisted upon eating, I was sent there to escort the sobbing girl back to our dormitory.

Fox refused to say what had happened —

143

they all did — but I heard her whimper *I'm not as feckless as I am ugly* in my memory as I stepped over the threshold.

The record lay wantonly open next to an ink pot, pen, blotter, and gleaming letter opener. A silvery charge shot through me, and I dived for the thing; my stomach rose up my gullet as I examined the record of purchases never meant for us to consume:

20 lbs. cod, alive — at 2d. a pound
50 bunches turnips — at penny a bunch
13 pints dried figs for pudding — at 1d. a pint

Biting my lip, I reached for his pen and dipped it in the inkpot. Keeping track of foodstuffs was rightfully the cook's province, but considering the profits Mr. Munt made by selling our strength away, it was unsurprising he sought complete control. Meals were planned a month in advance, with decisive check marks next to the supplies that had already been paid for.

My hands were steady as I hovered over the order to be delivered the next day. It would have been a fatal mistake to cross anything out and rewrite it, so some thought was required; but within three minutes, I had changed *70 bunches cress* to *20 bunches cress, 90 lbs. potatoes* to *80 lbs. potatoes,* and *7 dozen eggs* to *4 dozen eggs.*

Granted, I should have to ascertain how to make off with fifty bunches of cress, ten pounds of potatoes, and three dozen eggs, and then hide these items, and then cook them, but these steep obstacles to me seemed mere irritants. The fire languished, and the smiling moon of the standing clock leered at me. My altered numbers were rather strange, but not so very unlike Mr. Munt's other characters, and I blew upon the page to dry my falsehoods, imagining *a great steaming plate of fried eggs and potato hash and cress salad for —*

"I wonder just what you think you're doing — and then again, I don't."

Dropping the pen as horror gripped me, I sent a bloodlike spatter across the page.

Mr. Munt stood in the doorway, half smiling as if he were greeting a friend in a tea shop. My dismay was quickly buried under an avalanche of frozen rage.

"She meant for me to be caught," I found myself hissing.

"The kindhearted Miss Lilyvale?" Mr. Munt shut the door and approached with even strides as I backed away. "Come now, I'm not going to hurt you. When have I ever hurt any of you? Madame Archambault is a

145

fine French instructor, and her ways are set, but despite the Bible's injunctions to spare not the rod, I confess I find violence crude."

"What are you doing here?" I demanded, too angry to prevaricate. "What about your sermon?"

Mr. Munt placed his Bible reverently upon the desk. "The village prelate is delivering his marvellous message upon original sin. One must grasp the squalorous condition of the unredeemed soul in order to be duly grateful for Christ's intercession. As for your accusation regarding Miss Lilyvale, that is more complicated. I may have mentioned to the cook that I was grateful she was so honest — for were this ledger to be tampered with, I should never know whether our deliveries had arrived intact. Miss Lilyvale may have heard me say so, for she was nearby, though I should never imply she is capable of eavesdropping."

Hatred thrust like a stake through my heart.

"I took advantage of my colleague's visit in order to settle the books. I ought to have locked the door, in retro —"

"You planned all of this!" I cried. "This is another of your cruel games."

"Cruel?" He feigned hurt, his fine features twisting. "Steele, is your heart so hardened

146

that you can invade my private office —"

"You left the door unlocked."

"Falsify my accounts —"

"As you indirectly suggested!" I fairly shrieked.

"Plan to steal food from the mouths of your fellow students —"

"You're killing Clarke." Outrage transformed effortlessly to begging. "Please, even you cannot justify death by starvation."

Mr. Munt walked round his desk, the smug uptilt to his lips intact; I have never seen a man enjoy himself so much. "Heavens! Where on earth would you have stored these items, and how would you have cooked them?"

"I would have found a way," I spat, but the bitterness lay in the fact that he was correct.

This had been a fool's errand, and Miss Lilyvale and I the fools.

Mr. Munt sat before his ledger. He was dressed for Sunday, wearing a grey waistcoat which made his pale eyes gleam, and a high collar; his garb ever hinted at the parsonical whilst still accentuating his Byronic appearance. Running a hand through his black curls, he emitted a sigh.

"You will have to be severely punished for this."

"Do what you like," I snarled, confidence bolstered by loathing. "I'll fight back. Only please," I added as his sad look shifted into annoyance, "don't deprive Clarke anymore. I was the one who read the letters first, not she. You know Clarke is half mad, and anyway she's learnt her lesson."

"Half mad," Mr. Munt reflected, pulling his index finger and thumb along his lower lip. "Do you know, Steele, I don't think the half-mad one is Clarke."

A poisonous silence fell, one which burnt my skin.

"Do not pretend that this is about my mother."

"It is not about your mother. It is about whether you are capable of rational behaviour, or whether the devil works his will through you."

"I'm only here to save one of your own students!"

He laughed, showing straight white teeth. "So you will fight me, you say, and in the next breath you plead the case for the daughter of smut purveyors?" Standing, Mr. Munt strode past me to the opposite wall. "Ah, here we are. *The Garden of Forbidden Delights,* author anonymous, published in serial by Whittleby and Clarke. Borrow it, and then tell me whether you think Clarke's

148

judgement of sincere affections is sound."

A small red volume, unmarked on its cover but bearing the frontispiece *The Garden of Forbidden Delights,* was in my hands an instant later. Mr. Munt raised an eyebrow, stony resolve in his granite eyes, and I queasily slid the object into my dress pocket. I saw many more books like them — I saw an entire shelf, as a matter of fact, enough to be termed a collection.

"Do show that to Clarke when you've finished," he added with a cold smirk.

He's actually insane. His power had flooded his brain, eroding it piecemeal. I recalled the phrases I had studied in such repulsed confusion, *the thought of your mouth against my cock-stand,* and *I would lick my way down your spine and lower until* —

"Miss Lilyvale has seemed most upset since you touched her private things," Vesalius Munt chastised, returning to his desk. "She carelessly left a letter lying out, I take it?"

I drew a quick breath. "I was in the teachers' wing looking for food, and one of your letters caught my eye. I told Clarke about the contents. She never . . . It was all *my doing,* Mr. Munt."

"Perhaps so — I blame myself, you realise. It's clear as day that Anne-Laure Steele's unchecked rebellion, her cunning, her willingness to spit in the face of God Himself, all have been passed down to her only child. Pity. Do you long for death too, Steele? Do you think of the Reaper as you would a suitor, turning away from God's myriad blessings?"

Hours of conversation with Mr. Munt, I thought, was indeed too hard a bargain when set against a single hot meal.

"That is why I am contemplating committing you," Mr. Munt concluded, examining his shirt cuffs.

The words hung before me like a corpse displayed for public view.

"It would sadden me beyond words should one of your classmates fall prey to your wild moods." Mr. Munt's eyes gleamed, a powerful king protecting his realm from embodied disaster — disaster by the name of Jane Steele. "You could hurt someone, Steele; you could destroy someone, I believe."

Vesalius Munt could not possibly have known my secret, but my knees turned to water anyhow; he had seen something in me — a sparking flint where there ought to have been a soul, perhaps. Asylums by all accounts, meanwhile, were handy places to be chained to a bed covered in your own filth, subjected to ice baths and mercury doses and leeches on shorn scalps, and fed rather less than was customary at Lowan Bridge School.

"Don't expel me," I breathed. "I'm, I'm not mad — you know that I am not. I'll behave. Only feed Clarke and I shall do just as you say."

Mr. Munt crooked a finger over his full lips as he cogitated. Most would have seen a headmaster wrestling with a convoluted decision; I saw a despot to whom suffering was as amusing as a penny concert.

"I am moved to be merciful," he concluded, "but Clarke's punishment must stand if you remain at Lowan Bridge. The pair of you are potentially harmful to the others when acting together. If you agree to the asylum, Clarke can return to regular meals. If you prefer to remain and repent, her rations shall remain as they are."

When I opened my mouth, it was empty — save for my heart, which lay aquiver in my throat. He was inclined to be *merciful,* and thus was offering me a choice of my life or Rebecca Clarke's. The seconds elongated, an out-of-tune music box winding ever more slowly to its finish; Mr. Munt, smiling, picked up his pen as if to correct my altered numbers.

I was not inclined to be merciful, however, and thus gripped the letter opener and plunged the sharp point deep into my headmaster's neck.

My earlier metaphor had been wrong, I discovered. The splash of ink from the pen dropping onto the page looked nothing like a spray of blood at all.

TEN

. . . like any other rebel slave, I felt resolved, in my desperation, to go all lengths.

There is a passage in *Jane Eyre: An Autobiography* which puzzles me mightily; and because it only tickles at the edges of my understanding, I cannot help but read it over, sitting with a glass of dark sherry as the sun grows teasing and hides behind the elms:

All said I was wicked, and perhaps I might be so: what thought had I been but just conceiving of starving myself to death? That certainly was a crime: and was I fit to die?

I present to the reader an enigma: my mother rushed the giddy business of dying along and was almost universally reviled for it. Speaking as a woman who has deserved

153

to die since the age of nine and often thinks death a charming notion anyhow, I burn to know: When Miss Eyre demands philosophically, *and was I fit to die?* is she asking whether she is wicked enough to earn capital punishment, or holy enough to merit release from the torments of her browbeaten life?

And if she wanted to die . . . did she deserve to any longer?

Few among us are aware of how much blood the human body contains — surging in thick waves should it chance to be spilt.

I had spilled it, meanwhile, and therefore drastic measures were required.

Mr. Vesalius Munt was felled by a strangely skilful blow — as if I had studied the act, when in fact I had simply decided that he should stop being alive. He gurgled a disbelieving shriek, eyes ablaze with wrath and fear, looking perversely more alive than ever, each muscle taut with severest alarm. He even got halfway to his feet, reaching for me, rich gore soaking the fateful ledger.

Then his lips bubbled crimson, his blazing eyes hardened, and he slumped forward over the desk. His fingers, so graceful in life, twitched like the poisonous insect he was; his back ceased to shudder.

I cocked my head and gauged his condition: dead.

I paused to be medically certain; but as he continued dead, I heaved a breath and looked around me, beginning with the mirror above the fireplace.

The spray of crimson across my school uniform was not inconsiderable, and another plume of blood had feathered my hand; I carefully wiped these drops on Mr. Munt's own sleeve. Using the late Mr. Munt's coat the way one would a handkerchief was an act of sufficient disrespect that I turned away giggling, the giggles followed by a hysterical peal of laughter.

A bottle of amber spirits sat upon the side table. *In for a pound, in for a penny.* I poured. The taste was much harsher than the laudanum I had once pilfered from my mother's dressing table; the sear returned my senses and, after spluttering awkwardly, it occurred to me that I was in a not-insignificant amount of danger.

My heart pattered a rhythm like spring rain upon a roof; according to the tall clock, I had nearly an hour before the close of Sunday services.

I rifled through the secretary as well as any drawers I could open without shifting my latest victim, scattering papers and pens.

When my pockets contained coins in the neighbourhood of five pounds, a dented silver watch tucked away for repair bearing the initials *VOM,* and the almost-forgot volume published by Clarke's family, I shut the door of the study behind me and raced silently down the corridor.

Reader, would you prefer me to have felt remorse in the aftermath of my second slaughter?

Though the brutality of the act sent fearsome tremors through my small frame for days and weeks afterwards, never have I regretted ending the life of my headmaster.

Dressed in a too-large brown travelling suit stolen from Miss Lilyvale's wardrobe as by then I owned nothing save school-issued clothing, having wrapped my bloodied uniform in paper and stuffed it in my trunk, I was raiding the pantry an hour later when Clarke discovered me.

A small cough sounded, and I whirled around.

I stood in the windowless room aghast with a single rushlight flickering, shoving bread and fruit into my trunk, preparing to abandon everything I knew — but caught out.

"I went to his study," Clarke whispered.

A word of advice: do not ever kill for love, or you will find yourself tethered, staked to the ground when your cleanest instincts require you to run for your life without a backwards glance. Killing for love is one of the most tangled acts you can commit, reader, in an already twisted world.

She looked so small, this beautiful friend of mine. Clarke's madcap blond curls hung loose and tangled, her miniature lips chalk white. Inexplicably, she was dressed in her holiday travelling clothes, an emerald woollen suit and a cap appropriate to her age. I blinked dumbly; Clarke was the colour of goose down, so I promptly deposited her onto a stool.

"You discovered Mr. Munt, didn't you?" Her seaweed-green eyes flooded with brine. "I dragged myself to chapel to make a point in front of everyone, but he wasn't there, so I tried to catch him alone. I had meant to beg him, it was shameful, but I found — did I find what you found?"

The silent steel cogs of my mind ticked.

"Yes." I clutched her to me, cherishing her still-warm bones. "Oh, Clarke, I meant to plead with him myself. But there were drawers open and thieves must have — it was horrible. I'm so sorry you saw it too."

Lying had never been easier. Either I

157

informed Clarke that I had shoved a letter opener in Mr. Munt's throat, or I kept my beloved companion for another half an hour; the decision did not trouble me overmuch. She set her head against my shoulder and quaked as she cried, whilst I attempted to determine the most efficient way never to set foot upon a scaffold. Swift escape seemed the best option; but swift escape had been delayed by my partner in defiance.

Meanwhile, I reminded myself harshly, Clarke was still dying.

"Here." I tore away from her, hands landing upon some plain bread and shoving it unceremoniously into the white butter pot, tearing her off a portion. "Eat slowly. You know when we don't, it —"

"I know," she answered before devouring the hunk in mouselike bites.

I continued my travel preparations; a paper packet of cheese, a fistful of nuts. For leave I must, and I felt a knife in my own throat when I thought of final separation from Clarke. I wondered why on earth she was wearing ordinary clothing when we were all due at cold Sunday supper in uniform in an hour.

"Where are we going?"

Turning, I regarded my friend, who had

slid off the stool and was reaching for a lone apple in a basket full of onions and braided garlic heads. Her freckles still glared dark as tiny bruises from the pallor of her cheeks, but her voice was stronger.

"Clarke, I haven't anyone to go *to.*" Telling her the truth was always pleasurable, as if I were apologising for the glaring omissions. "My aunt loathes me, and until I'm of age . . . I simply can't go back, not to her. You have a family, you can —"

"They told me they were publishers of poetry and plays." Clarke's eyes glinted hard and gemlike. "The older I grew, the more I thought it odd that they had sent me here. When I was home, they barely entertained or received any callers. For a day it would be splendid, and every hour afterwards I would feel more like a guest, Mother making the rounds at her Bohemian salons, Father at his office and clubs, them glancing at the clock during supper. I would ache to know what *you* were doing — I thought of you whenever they slighted me, whenever they heard my step and seemed almost . . . disappointed. Every visit, I told them we were tormented here, and every time, they said that school was difficult, and how could I move in artistic circles without an education? *Artistic* circles," she repeated in disgust.

"By the time I left after a visit, they could barely contain themselves for joy."

"You can't —"

"They *lied* to me, Jane." The name, after so long without hearing it, stole my breath. She blinked in her oddly deliberate manner, polishing the apple against her sleeve. "They sent me away when I was *six years old.* And now you mean to send me away yourself."

"But I —"

"Please don't leave me behind to survive this school without you, I couldn't bear it. Who knows what sort the replacement headmaster will be? We'll find a new place to live." Doubt pinched the corners of her mouth. "But perhaps you don't want —"

"Of course I do." A weightless feeling soared inside me, a flock of starlings scattering into flight. "I only — I've about five pounds and a silver watch that was my father's, but that won't get us far."

Smiling slowly, Clarke took a bite of the apple. "You'll think of something." Pivoting, she fetched her carpetbag, which I had not even seen previous. "You *always* think of something — you're terribly clever, the cleverest one. It's nearly three — let's be off before the cooks arrive to assemble the cold supper. When they find what's in the head's office," she added with a shudder, "there

160

will be hell to pay."

It may have occurred to the reader that allowing Becky Clarke to flee the scene of a murder — with the murderess, no less — was not my most shining instance of altruism. I was sixteen years old, however, sixteen and nigh berserk to escape, delirious with the old instinct to run which had brought me to Lowan Bridge in the first place. Only this time, I would not be friendless and bereft; this time, I would have someone beside me who wanted, however inexplicably, to be there.

If sixteen-year-olds are accounted selfish generally, then reader, how much greedier was I in the face of freely offered loyalty?

"London," I breathed in Clarke's ear as I took her hand. "Where else would we go save for London?"

We fled on foot to the main road, fearing to look behind lest the hornet's nest had upturned and sent swarms flying after us. The alarm had not yet been raised, however, and the grounds proved as empty as they always were of a Sunday — or had been ever since Granville and Taylor had been caught fleeing years ago and were returned by an obliging seller of trinkets who thought the sight of two unescorted girls demanded his immediate assistance.

The fact that Granville had died soon afterwards, though Taylor had scarcely been punished at all, surely does not require explanation at this late juncture. As for Clarke and me, we scaled the pocky wall next to the black wrought iron gate and tumbled to the ground with no worse consequences than scuffed shoes — or no worse consequences *yet,* unless I acted with miraculous rapidity.

Clarke threw her apple core at Lowan Bridge School, a final gesture of defiance. Half a dozen times, perhaps, we had all visited the village a quarter mile away to inflict Miss Lilyvale's Christmas hymns upon the town square, and only gradually did I realise I was taking us there. London sent out new filaments continually, cast shimmering tendrils like the spread of shattered crystal — we had seen this from the roof every year, when London swelled and burst and swelled and burst again — but it was hardly feasible to walk there. Not with Mr. Munt stiffening over his desk.

"Who do you think it was?" Clarke asked.

Swallowing a spike, I shook my head. "The room looked ransacked. Robbers?"

My friend angled her head, curls twice

gilded with late afternoon sunlight. "Maybe so."

My heart constricted painfully. "Why couldn't it have been?"

"Oh, it could. It's just that . . . possibly someone wanted to find something other than money."

"What sort of something?"

"Well, you never returned Miss Lilyvale's letters. I read them, and then you . . . kept them. As protection, I assumed. But you never returned them."

At the thought of whey-blooded Miss Lilyvale plunging a makeshift dagger into the cords of Vesalius Munt's throat, I laughed so hard that a fox or a badger or some such went crashing away through the bracken.

"All right, she isn't the bravest woman I've ever met," Clarke agreed, half smiling in a way that sent me into further fits. She slapped my arm. "Jane, *stop.*"

"If she was looking for the letters, she took an unnecessary risk in slaying him, for I burnt them," I gasped. This was factual, but Clarke need not know that I had shoved them in the dormitory fireplace after stabbing our headmaster. "In any case, why should I have given them to him?"

"What I mean to say is, we hated Mr. Munt — every student, better than half the teachers, the domestics. Isn't it much more likely that someone he wronged took revenge?"

"He ought to have been at the sermon during that time," I insisted, abruptly no longer amused, "so it would have been the perfect occasion to burgle his sanctum. It was a complete accident that he was present at all. Someone else was there, someone up to no good, and Mr. Munt caught them."

My words skated so close to truth telling that I sliced my eyes to Clarke; shrugging, she nodded.

"You're probably right, but I'm right too — that person could have been any of us."

I pretended to ponder this theory — as if I were upset at the implication that such a monster could hide in the skin of a young girl or a teacher undetected, when in fact I was upset at the fact we could at any moment be dragged back by our hair. The village inn rose before us, half-timbered and sagging at the roof like the shoulders of an ancient farmer, a comfortable pile of lumber emitting a faint aroma of meat pie. Clarke sagged in concert with the building, swallowing audibly in her ravenous state, even as I stiffened.

"What is it?"

"An idea," said I, gazing with impetuous

hope at the vehicle resting on the cobbles. "Come along, we're filling you with a hot meal."

As Vesalius Munt was only my second murder, in the immediate aftermath I imagined that a black reaction would set upon me with razor teeth; such was not the case, however. My mind was piercingly clear, and I recognised the shabby manure-spattered coach which had carried me to purgatory at age nine as soon as I glimpsed it, thinking, *Here — if we are very lucky — perhaps is an ally.*

The instant we entered the tavern, Clarke leaning weakly against my arm, I spied him: Nick, the driver who had conveyed me here so long ago. Swiftly, I ushered us to a table. A cheerful wench wearing an apron which perhaps had been used to muck out the stables previous to dinner service grunted at my order and, upon her departure, I leant across the table to grasp Clarke's frail hands.

"Eat your curry when it arrives, *slowly.* I need to speak with someone."

"Who could you possibly know here?" Clarke asked, but I was already striding towards the coachman.

Nick sat, nursing a pint, staring at grooves carved in the bar by time and dissolution. The same forces had done a workmanlike job with his face, for his mouth was bordered by stark crevasses, and his once-red nose had abandoned its unheeded alarums and subsided to a sulky yellow.

"Nick, I think." I nearly coughed at the ripe cloud surrounding him. His boots were worn, which gave me hope, and his fingernails were cracked. "It's a long time ago we met, but I hope you —"

"I dun't know ye," he slurred, slurping at the beer. "I live on the highway, Lunnon to Manchester, Manchester to Lunnon, picking up fares. Never a respit', never two nights i' the same bloody place. Unless yer a sprite after hauntin' my carriage, and ye *look* a sprite right enough, by Jesus, I dun't —"

"You brought me here when I was a girl. I gave you a potted rabbit luncheon I couldn't eat for nerves."

"Chestnut — he's a horse, mind — knows me better than me own pillow, us having spent considerable more time together, and I've never clapped eye on ye before. I tell ye, I *never stop moving* —"

" 'The world is a hard place, and I live in it alone,' " I whispered.

Flinching, Nick narrowed red-rimmed eyes at me. "By George," he husked at length. "Is that ye in the flesh, then? The

166

wee miss wi' the tragic eyes I dun brought here from Highgate House? Yer alive?"

"And in need of your help."

Nick spat, recalling to my mind his alacrity at this skill. "*Help,* ye say? What daft breed o' thickheaded are —"

"I gave you a basket full of food once. Now I'll pay you six shillings to carry my friend and me to London."

"Stomached enough o' Lowan Bridge, then?" he puzzled, wiping his brow with his wrist.

"You couldn't have chosen a more appropriate phrase."

"And now I'm meant to risk my hide when Vesalius Munt hasn't let a charge disappear in nigh —"

"He's dead." My eyes brimmed — for myself and Clarke, for dread of shackles and scaffolds. "There will be no consequences to you, Nick, upon my honour."

Were I to picture my honour, I imagine it might resemble a less attractive than usual tadpole; Nick owned no inkling of this, however, and his bleary eyes boggled.

"Mr. Munt dead? The shite-arsed bastard what bilks the factory lads from here to three counties hence?"

"Bilks them?"

"Bilks them!" Nick cried, livening at last.

167

"Aye, he never delivers a meal at discount save he's less ten portions promised. Says as benefactors can't give beyond their means or they'd turn paupers themselves! I'd love to see that feller stuck through the —"

"Someone beat you to it. Oh, please, Nick! We can't go back, and you know how hard the world is."

Nick considered, thoughtfully gathering spittle. I thought then that kindness had not deserted him, and I think now that he needed my money, for he did not look well. We are all of us daily decaying, after all; the speed is our only variant.

Nick spat; Nick finished his beer.

"I'll oblige ye, after I've rounded up the other fares what have already paid." He took my coins and dropped them straightaway upon the bar as he nodded to the serving lass. "But if ye thought the world was hard before . . . cor, will Lunnon ever throw ye to the wolves. She were suckled by a wolf mother, they say," he added with a faint flash of his old dire humour.

"At least she was fed," I muttered as Nick called for the bill to be settled.

When he departed, I returned to our table and passed a gentle hand over Clarke's pallid brow, promising to return upon the instant after using the privy and imploring her to be patient as she finished her modest meal. The pressure within my cranium had grown nearly unbearable by then; half-frantic with fear, sidling behind her so that my semi-conscious friend might not see, I bore my trunk to the outhouse, barred the door, and deposited my bloodied uniform therein. It was not a perfect solution — but it was foul enough to serve, and anyhow, I reminded myself grimly, it seemed that most of my solutions to conundrums fell considerably shy of the mark.

By nightfall, Clarke and I were seated together upon the same threadbare object masquerading as a cushion on which I had ridden to Lowan Bridge seven years previous. Across from us sat a lean farmer and full-bosomed girl with a fresh cap and apron who I thought must be seeking domestic employment, as she looked such equal parts terrified and jubilant.

"London," Clarke whispered, resting her head upon my shoulder. The meal had thoroughly drained her, her body flummoxed by bounty; lacing our fingers together, she settled our hands in her lap. "We'll find a new home, a better one. Anyhow, you're home."

Wincing freely since Clarke could not see

169

me with her head tucked under my chin, I squeezed her fingers. I ought to have felt trepidatious, reader; I ought to have felt both culpable and contrite.

I felt thrilled in knowing that upon the morrow, a worthy battle could be fought — even if I, poor leaky vessel of the devil's and never of God's, was chosen as its champion. No less, I felt achingly grateful, and I watched the blue sweeps of blood through Clarke's emaciated wrist for an hour or more. Knowing that home was hateful to us both, I imagined that her calling me by the word meant I was expedient, or sturdy; but if I could only keep her hand in mine, I knew I would give my four limbs and my heart for the privilege, becoming instead four walls and a roof.

ELEVEN

Women are supposed to be very calm generally: but women feel just as men feel; they need exercise for their faculties, and a field for their efforts as much as their brothers do; they suffer from too rigid a restraint, too absolute a stagnation, precisely as men would suffer; and it is narrow-minded in their more privileged fellow-creatures to say that they ought to confine themselves to making puddings and knitting stockings, to playing on the piano and embroidering bags.

Shortly, reader, you shall experience chronological leaps which may startle the timid. *Jane Eyre* contains the delightful passage, *A new chapter in a novel is something like a new scene in a play,* thus I likewise embrace abrupt shifts even as I abhor the imminent subject matter.

We arrived in London, Clarke and I,

homeless and horridly inexperienced, as coral dawn lit the charred air draped over the centre of the British Empire.

"Oh!" Clarke snatched at me as we crossed a deep wheel gouge, further slowing the already painfully lethargic Chestnut.

I steadied my friend, but said nothing; for never had I fathomed such a sight as passed before me like a parade through the coach window.

Some cities bustle, some meander, I have read; London blazes, and it incinerates. London is the wolf's maw. From the instant I arrived there, I loved every smouldering inch of it.

A lad hunched against a shoddy dressmaker's dummy slumbered on, cradled by his faceless companion. The atmosphere was redolent — meat sat piled up to a shop door's limit of some six feet, the butcher sharpening massive knives before his quarry. Yesterday's cabbage was crushed underfoot, and tomorrow's cackling geese were arriving in great crates, ready to kill. So early, the square we passed through ought to have been populated only by spectres. Instead, sounds reverberated from all directions — treble notes from a bamboo flute; the breathy scream of a sardine costermonger; the bass rumble of a carrot vendor, his cart

172

piled with knobby red digits, shouting as his donkey staggered in the slick.

It was not welcoming, but it was galvanising. Arguing with London was useless; she was inexorable, sure as the feral dawn.

"Where *are* we?" Clarke fretted. "This is nowhere near where my parents live."

"I haven't the faintest notion." Bending, I touched my brow to hers. "Are you ready, though?"

Clarke grinned — an easy grin which made me long to buy her hearty sausage and pastry breakfasts. The carriage halted before a dingy public house with a small paved yard. Clarke stumbled out with her carpetbag and I followed, sharp pinpricks running up and down my legs.

"Thank you," I called up. Nick sat like a turtle in his shell on his high plank seat. "I hope that one day —"

"Neither of us hope to see t'other again, ye mad child." He took a long pull from his flask.

"I'm grateful, though. With all my heart, I am."

"Then let it be fer this advice. I've food enough and drink enough to keep what they call a life, but that's all's I can say on the subject. Treat yerself better — keep yerself a good girl, and sleep in a bed wi'out inter-

173

ruptions. Can ye manage that?"

"Yes." I stepped back, passing an arm around Clarke's horridly small waist. "I can, I promise."

Nick had already snapped the jangling reins and pulled away — a man who lived not much better than his horse did. Meanwhile, I knew precisely which vice he was warning me against, and in starker detail than he might have imagined; words like *virtue* and *chastity* and *fallen* were lobbed over our heads like so many shuttlecocks at Lowan Bridge, but I had read Mr. Munt's "love letters," and so understood the mechanics of the practice.

Some form of employment had to be found, and at once, for when I caught Clarke's bright green eye and thought of all which could befall her — rough hands against her freckled shoulders, chapped lips at her slim throat — a swell of disgust rose. Becky Clarke, in a way which had not been true since my mother's sad, soft-edged smile and her cool hand against my cheek, belonged to *me.*

"First, a celebratory breakfast," I decided. "The man across the street with the sign for hot ham sandwiches — doesn't he seem like an expert toaster of cheese and meat?"

"Indeed. And after eating the best ham

sandwiches in all of London?"

I lifted my luggage as the smile faded from my face, willing myself not to say, *I haven't the faintest idea.*

Dark days followed, and far darker nights.

After inquiring after lodgings, all priced too dear, we passed the night in the back room of a public house, Clarke's flaxen hair mingling with the straw strewn across our shared pillow. We passed a night in the spare room of a cottage outside town when we retreated; but we could think of no employment thereabouts and returned to the city. We passed a night hemorrhaging precious funds upon a cheap hotel, knowing we had no means of replacing the currency. We passed a night propped one against the other on an empty crate, dozing fitfully, until a peeler arrived to tidy the red-brick alleyways he imagined belonged to him.

Sssshriiiek! cried his whistle, and off Clarke and I went like arrows from a bow, both knowing that we could not live this way for long.

For five days we wandered, growing steadily, silently despairing, washing our faces with rainwater trapped in old cisterns and weathered statuary. We were not wretched, nor were we rich. We simply did not appear to be trustworthy — we were blue dirt, green clouds — nothing about us made sense. Over and over, we crossed the fat, sombre river seeking new neighbourhoods, but all were either putrid hovels with mutton bones scattered about for the snarling dogs or else brick buildings with maniacally pristine windowpanes, and both frightened us. If approaching a cheery town house with a few cracked vases in the window and a ROOMS TO LET sign, we were turned away for want of references. Should we broach a wreck reeking of sewage and solitude, we would be sent packing on suspicion of thievery (which was, I own, a fair criticism).

"It isn't like I thought," Clarke said.

We had crossed London Bridge again, and I believe now that we were in Southwark, for though the street names blurred feverishly, I recall the thick sparks and steam and soot of the train station and the tooth-jarring clatter of the engines. Having located a squat public house with dull brass fixtures, we had stopped for a pot of tea, and were now loath to leave the place, instead having rested upon an empty wine barrel in the alley behind, the remains of trampled lettuce surrounding us.

"It isn't like I thought either. There's so . . ."

"So much of it," Clarke sighed.

Her skeletal arm slid off my waist when I stood. "You rest here — you look positively done and I've a lucky feeling. I'll be back directly."

Clarke wanted to believe me and did not, which hurt horribly; she watched me quit the corridor.

"Don't leave me." For the first time, she sounded frightened. "You wouldn't, would you?"

"Never," I called back.

I meant it, but which direction was I to take? Clarke and I were educated innocents, a condition resembling stupid clerks or intelligent kitchen slaveys, which is to say useless. Cognisant we would be desperate enough to sell practically anything unless we found regular employment, and terrified of watching the small nest egg I had stolen crack and dribble away, I ploughed through piles of mismatched boots and discarded nut husks, knowing that I had never yet failed to find an opportunity when I set my mind to it and still at age sixteen foolish enough to trust myself.

My stomach was empty, my mind echoing its cavernous snarl. The twisting streets with the brown water trickling between the stones led me farther from Clarke, and it occurred to me then that, were I a good person, I should leave her. Becky Clarke would live better without the hindrances of my demons and my doubts. Surely, were I to vanish, she would return to her parents, and surely being ignored was preferable to being penniless? Kicking through clamshells as I neared the great sluggish foul river, I hesitated.

Do I love Clarke enough to say good-bye to her?

I did not, I realised.

Then I heard a strange voice calling out.

"Most 'orrible and beastly murder done! Most haudacious and black crime committed!"

A man of middle age stood with a sheaf of yellow papers, crying out the latest atrocities. He was bent over — I hesitated to call him hunchbacked, but he flirted with the appellation — a heavy, downward-leaning human whom I could imagine tracking rabbits like a bloodhound. He owned a bloodhound's jaw too, a great slab on either side of his face framing his crooked teeth with fleshy drapery. His hair was russet and his eyes a hard yellowish hazel like petrified wood.

"Murder most 'einous!" he cried. "Murder most hunnatural! Penny a page, miss."

Blinking in astonishment, I reached for the broadside. He growled and I paid him belatedly, walking a few paces away to read:

MOST FOUL AND DELIBERATE MURDER OF A COUNTRY SCHOOLMASTER.

Mr. Vesalius Munt, a most upstanding gentleman of E—— parish, was found stuck like a pig through the gullet and left to die in a pool of his own red gore. The villain what competrated this most perspicable act, an act sufficient to strike thunderific fear into the hearts of even the most auspicillary citizens, remains at large. Many schoolgirls of Lowan Bridge have gone missing; thirty or so have vanished into the idyllious countryside, two hundred more staying under the most dutiful and meritransible guard of their teachers, the rest having returned home.

Mr. Munt was lauded as the most distinguished philanderist, and a knife was shoved so far into his throat that his molars suffered renumerous damages, according to experts. The most authoritive and ingeniable Inspector Sam Quillfeather has been assigned the task of hunting his killer, and the townspeople are most certifitive that his quest will end in the stringing up of the traitorious fiend's neck like the most veriable chicken.

A finger snapped beside my ear.

I had not fainted, but a murky tide swam before my eyes, all grey silt and shrinking terror. The patterer's fleshy face — for he was a patterer of dark deeds, and I had been identifying every way possible to obtain money whilst preventing my legs from parting company — hovered over mine, seeming at once fascinated and annoyed that I had been so affected. He wore funereal black, but had enhanced this theme with a scarlet cravat and trousers to answer, the effect being that one grew fretful over whether he had just been stabbed in the throat and the legs.

"What ails you?" he demanded.

"I went to school there," I murmured, scarcely knowing what I was saying.

Secrets, reader, are tidal — they swell and recede, and my greater misdeeds had forced this lesser intelligence from my lips, a river spilling over its bed; at the unexpected name *Sam Quillfeather,* the constable like an embodied question mark who had peppered me with queries after Edwin's death and apparently been promoted, my spine turned to jelly. The only good news the article contained was that so many had disappeared, for our absence — should it occur to Inspector Quillfeather that a schoolgirl was capable of stabbing her headmaster — would thereby seem much more natural.

"Eh?" he exclaimed. "You were there, ye say?"

"I merely — I was confused. I'll just —"

"A man in my line o' work would pay dear in order to print someone's hinsider perpinion, 'specially if you saw the cold dead corpse, like. Did you?"

He winked, and then I understood — he expected me to lie in order to earn a commission in exchange for the tale.

"Yes," said I, attempting to appear a bad perjurer, which is a bemusing trick and not one I recommend the layman acquire.

The man chuckled, jowls quaking. "Name's Mr. Hugh Grizzlehurst. And yours?"

"Miss Jane Steele."

We shook hands, I and this purveyor of tragedy, as an idea gently hatched in my brain.

"There's another Lowan Bridge girl with me, and we've need of lodgings for the night. I'll exchange my story for our board."

Mr. Grizzlehurst nodded. "If it's an hextraordinary story, I'd not begrudge two nights. Tell Bertha — Bertha's me wife — that 'appy circumstance sent you, and I'll be along when I've hexpleted my stock. The 'ouse is twelve Elephant Lane, Rotherhithe — if you hespy the White Lead Manufactory and the Saltpetre Works, you've gone too far."

Weak with shock and relief, I shook hands. Meeting Mr. Grizzlehurst seemed one of those felicitous coincidences which occur so seldom in fiction — for in fiction, such blessings can scarce be believed, whilst in life they are shared with future generations as thrilling tales of danger averted and luck seized.

I say that it *seemed* just the gift we had been seeking; I have since grown more cautious. Nature's boons are equally plentiful and random, but I have never yet encountered a more capricious mistress — save perhaps for her daughter, madly mercurial London.

Clarke and I, pulses thin with nerves, trudged past warehouses and shipyards, past a harelipped Italian organ boy whose eyes followed us soulfully as he ground his instrument, past earnest geranium boxes tucked under begrimed windows, and finally entered Rotherhithe where it perched upon the edge of the Thames. A whaler, salt in his beard and a blue marine glint in his single eye, directed us to Elephant Lane and trudged away as we knocked at number twelve.

The door creaked open. Mrs. Grizzlehurst stood there, blinking — a dull woman with flat greyish hair and an overbite which rendered her resemblance to a rodent more profound than she might have ideally preferred. Bertha Grizzlehurst's close-set eyes were amiable, however, and her dry lips even spasmed in a theoretical smile.

"I am Miss Rebecca Clarke and this is Miss Jane Steele," Clarke introduced us.

No answer emerged.

"We're looking for Mrs. Bertha Grizzlehurst?" I explained.

The woman who was probably Mrs. Grizzlehurst continued affably saying nothing.

The wind from the Thames scraped across our necks as I glanced worriedly at Clarke; we had made our way from the bridge through market gardens and occasional meadows, rejoicing as the stench of refuse faded and the aromas of maritime saline and humble beds of mint met our nostrils. Rotherhithe was actively being bullied by the metropolis, however; upon nearing the waterfront, the sunlight failed to reach the cobbles as the rickety buildings grew thicker and taller. Huge draught horses lugging wagons of timber passed, making us feel even tinier than we did already. I badly wanted a meal and a bed, and the same for Clarke.

"Your husband asked for our testimony regarding a recent murder," Clarke attempted.

Mrs. Grizzlehurst's smile spread towards her ears; this time she stepped back, and we followed.

The place was shabby, but so impeccably kept that no one could sneer at it; the hearthstone shone like a riverbed, and the irregular panes of glass fitted into the windows had been carefully cut, sparkling in a frenetic rainbow of tonic greens and medicinal ambers and bottle blues. The chimney leaked smoke in a friendly fashion, as if it wanted to join in the conversation, and a misshapen iron pot was just coming to the boil.

"Lodgings." Mrs. Grizzlehurst jerked her head upwards; her voice proved harsh but friendly, like the buzzing of a bee.

"Excuse me?" I replied.

"Low rates, breakfast gratis. He's only been gone these two days, has Mr. Buckle, but I've cleaned it plenty thorough." Mrs. Grizzlehurst waved her knife at a narrow staircase, then dropped a coarsely chopped onion into the pot. A pair of lobsters from a basket followed, flailing against their demise as they were boiled alive.

Clarke and I ascended the staircase, confused but equally curious. There we found a half-height garret room complete with bed, pot, washbasin, and — wonder of wonders — a skylight through which the coral and violet sunset yet gleamed. My friend sucked in a happy breath.

"Might we —"

"I hope so," I agreed instantly.

"But how will —"

"I've a plan," I discovered.

Our hostess, when we returned downstairs, lifted a cleaver as she prepared to make two lobsters do for four bellies. In our absence, a skillet of roasted potatoes had appeared along with a cask of porter, two glasses already poured.

"Day after tomorrow," Mrs. Grizzlehurst concluded, as if she had been conducting a conversation between her ears.

"Beg pardon?" Clarke requested.

"He'll trade two nights for two accounts. You can start paying the day after tomorrow."

Holding up my hands, I said, "We've only modest —"

"The room can't be empty." Gooseflesh sprang to life along Mrs. Grizzlehurst's wiry arms. "You'll pay the day after tomorrow."

I took this to mean that the Grizzlehursts danced upon the lip of penury. My conscientious Clarke had just opened her mouth to explain our own lack of gainful occupation when Mr. Grizzlehurst burst through the door, booming exultations in great volleys.

"If I never see such a day for hexceptional sales, it ain't my fault." Laughing, Hugh Grizzlehurst showed teeth resembling indifferently worn pencils. "This young lady with the fey looks is a good homen, Bertha — a positivical homen, I tell you."

His wife set out potatoes and a modest pat of butter.

"Is this the other heyewitness?" Mr. Grizzlehurst captured Clarke's delicate hand, which I found myself irrationally resenting. "An 'onour, miss."

"Likewise," Clarke managed.

"Mr. Grizzlehurst," I interjected, "I should like to propose that we lodge upstairs; in exchange, rather than pay you directly, I would assist you."

A silence fell; our host's twiglike masses

of eyebrows descended.

" 'Ere now." Mr. Grizzlehurst thrust his face into mine, jowls swinging like pendulums. "True enough Mr. Buckle hasphyxiated down at the granary, but you've habsconded from school by your own hadfession. Now I'm to suffer the keeping o' you?"

Clarke bristled, and I pressed her toe with my boot.

"You write up murders for a living," I reminded him. "Well, I've read the *Newgate Calendar* back to front, and I've been educated by the renowned Mr. Vesalius Munt. I know you didn't believe me, but it's true. I offer stylistic improvements and new material in exchange for room and board."

" 'Eavens above us, hexisely what manner of improvements are you a-thinking of?" Mr. Grizzlehurst growled. "My customers dote on my turn o' phrase."

"Think what fields we could expand into together!" I coaxed. "Gallows ballads, last confessions!"

"They live upstairs and will work for breakfast," Mrs. Grizzlehurst said.

Hugh Grizzlehurst slammed a fist upon the table, still vigorous despite his bowed back and drooping face. "Why them? We've

187

money enough for the room to be hempty a few nights."

"They live upstairs," Bertha Grizzlehurst insisted, though her face paled to match the lobster flesh peeking from the shells.

"I've no need o' hassistance when it comes to my broadsides! My broadsides is known 'ither and yon and every street betwixt!"

"I don't think *positivical* is a word," Clarke observed.

"Can you prove positivically that it hain't?" he shouted in high dudgeon.

"No," I hastily owned, "but wouldn't it be better to employ words which actually exist?"

"Hexistence *nothing.*" He regarded me with an outraged eye. "You lot will hexplicate how Mr. Vesalius Munt came to have his neck spitted like a guinea fowl, and then —"

"The room *can't be empty*!"

The shriek — high but thin, like the feral cry of a shrew — rendered all three of us mute. Following this decree, Mrs. Grizzlehurst, three plates balanced on her left arm and a fourth in her right hand, set the meal upon the table.

When finished, she sat and stared at her husband; a silence of grotesque dimensions ensued.

"We'll sup first," Mr. Grizzlehurst said contritely, "and then — *then,* mind — we can talk about halternatives."

Clarke and I ate as Mr. Grizzlehurst slurped from a lobster shell; Mrs. Grizzlehurst only gazed at her plate, relief softening her ratlike features. After supper had ended, I jotted down an account of Mr. Munt's murder, prudently leaving out my guilt whilst doubling the gore. I did not need to ask whether it would suit; it was a mingling of my memory and imagination, and as such was criminally engaging.

Hugh Grizzlehurst read my work, snorting in approval.

"I decide which crimes deserve hadvertisement," he admonished.

"Of course."

"You get not a cent — just lodgings, that's *hessential.*"

"Absolutely."

"And what'll *she* do, then?" he demanded, pointing at Clarke.

"Teach music lessons," Clarke said dreamily. "All we must do is find a piano, and I shall partner with the owner quick as thinking."

"Well," said Mr. Grizzlehurst. He regarded his spouse as if struck by sudden melancholy. "They live upstairs, then, it's settled."

Smiling, Mrs. Grizzlehurst cleared the plates and uttered not another word that day . . . nor the day after that, nor the day after that, which ought to have set off plentiful warning bells in my ears and did not, more's the pity for everyone involved.

Clarke set out to partner with a pianist upon the morrow. A week later, having failed in many attempts, she disappeared one morning and sent me into a hair-tearing panic — wondering whether she had met with misadventure, wondering whether she had tired of me. She materialised ten minutes after supper ended (which Mrs. Grizzlehurst always served us whether we had paid her the extra fourpence or not) with three shillings, which she pressed into my palm.

"I stood upon the street corner, practicing, before meeting with Mr. Jones, but I needn't bother over using his piano." Her smile engulfed her pretty face despite the small scale of her lips. "I always thought I had a knack for music, though Miss Lilyvale's praise wasn't precisely encouraging."

"You made this much warming up your voice?" I stared stupidly at my hand.

"Imagine what I'll earn when I'm doing it on purpose," she concluded, skipping upstairs to wash.

Thus Clarke settled into an unlikely occupation as a street singer, trilling "Cherry Ripe" and "Poor Old Mam" whilst I penned atrocities; had we not been educated at Lowan Bridge School, learning daily despite our sorrows, I shudder to picture what would have become of us. She was even happy, I think, warbling like a strangely technical songbird, whilst I took heinous tales from my employer and translated them to actual English, with sufficient spilt viscera to please everyone.

These might have been idyllic circumstances, but they were not.

Mr. Hugh Grizzlehurst's behaviour when drunk owned peculiarities which it failed to evince when he was sober; furthermore, these whimsical quirks tended to be visited upon the person of Mrs. Bertha Grizzlehurst. In fairness, Mr. Grizzlehurst only imbibed when he had been unsuccessful, and — as my help and his experience rendered us jointly successful — this was seldom. When every other month, however, the British Empire had been distressingly peaceable, Mr. Grizzlehurst would arrive home with a jug of gin which could either have been imbibed or employed to strip the paint from the chipped green rocking chair.

When Clarke and I had retreated upstairs,

ducking to avoid the low slant of the ceiling beams, we would hear shouting. At times, the shouting would prove the climax, and we should find at dawn Mr. Grizzlehurst snoring upon the knotted rug. At other times, shouting would prove insufficient to Mr. Grizzlehurst's purposes, and the sharp crack of a slap or two would follow, and Clarke's entire body would flinch alongside mine as I set my teeth hard against each other.

"What can we do?" Clarke whispered the third time this happened, shifting up on one elbow to stare at me with her nightgown slipping over her shoulder.

I did not know. Bertha Grizzlehurst was silent for days on end, ugly as her husband, and relentlessly calm; and now that I knew the reason for her insistence upon our lodging there, I suspected we were already doing the task she had planned for whatever tenant occupied the garret: we were witnesses, which went a long ways towards stopping a real crime from ever occurring.

"Nothing," said I. "We are here to prevent things going too far. It isn't our business."

Clarke settled her head between my neck and collarbone, smelling of starlight and lavender as she always did, and murmured, "Then whose business is it?"

Pondering, I sifted her hair through my fingers. I was not, even at age sixteen, foolish enough to suppose that love and marriage always kept company; my mother had loved my father to distraction, but I had never seen it, and as for the union our former music teacher might have enjoyed, the topic was best left unexplored. Theoretically, however, some form of affection was meant to be involved — and though I could only love hungrily, I could not imagine ever striking Clarke if I had been a man and she a woman, no matter what she may have done.

No, it is not my business, I concluded.

But it could be, I thought next, shifting and afterwards falling into a troubled slumber.

Twelve

"Dread remorse when you are tempted to err, Miss Eyre: remorse is the poison of life."

If early reading of the *Newgate Calendar* carved a mark upon my girlish character, I was for two years grateful for the scar.

We were housed thanks to me, kept in ribbons and pub fare thanks to Clarke, and when our presence leashed the mongrel inside Hugh Grizzlehurst, so much the better. Mrs. Grizzlehurst never failed to greet us with buttered porridge or Sunday eggs and herring, so I supposed that her scheme was working, despite occasions when the lilac circle beneath one eye looked darker than the other. Clarke and I hemmed loudly at the occasional nocturnal scuffle, stomping to fetch a glass of water, returning to bed in the widening pool of quiet.

There are households which would have

considered this arrangement paradise — and in retrospect, at times, I did myself.

In the frigid January of the year 1845, Mrs. Grizzlehurst grew thicker about the middle and began to whistle when she was not speaking (which was nearly all the time). Jane Eyre insists, *Human beings never enjoy complete happiness in this world,* and I agree with her — but as Mrs. Grizzlehurst slowly swelled with child, I thought what a lucky chance it was that humans do not often suffer complete unhappiness either.

Mr. Grizzlehurst produced clownish smiles as he bent to kiss her cheek in the morning, his expressions tinged a helpless shade of ash when he went through his account books in the evening. He began to toss me worried glares, meaningless winks and clucks, a pleading slackness hanging heavy in his chops before he whispered:

Miss Steele, hadvantitious as this 'ere week has been, is there nary another penny we might'a misplaced somewhereabouts?

This verse is downright halliterative, Miss Steele, and I happlaud you. . . . Can we not keep it to a single page? Paper is that dear these days, and we don't want to look 'eathenish.

Just before everything fell apart, he handed me this gem:

Most Brutal Stabbing Rips Holes in Nubilous Young Victim —.

Sighing, I dipped my pen; I sat at the rickety table in our garret in the coral glow of a February afternoon, preparing myself to rescue our native tongue from worse than death once more. The chipped yellow vase which I generally filled with weeds — Queen Anne's lace and wild flowering parsley — sat empty in February save for some whimsical thistles Clarke had brought me to cheer my spirits when English had been dealt cruel blows.

We discover a most unforewitted tragedy struck in Church-lane, St. Giles's, shocking even the most hardened of that irascilacious realm. A comely lass of seventeen years was most untimely struck down by a delinquitorious scallywag, a blade thrust twixt her ribs some scores and dozens of times, and left to bleed. Whilst chances the scurrible fiend will be brought to justice are most uncertificable, the humble author prays that he will be left to dangle like the most inconseterial string of garlic.

Since two years previous, "Grizzlehurst's Daily Report of Mayhem and Mischief" had trebled in sales as far afield as Southwark and Deptford, thanks to my style and to Hugh Grizzlehurst's genuine talent for scouting out the rankest misdeeds imaginable; had it occurred to me to be proud of the fact, I should have tried it out. Still — I watched Bertha Grizzlehurst gather up scattered flour from her breadboard as if it were gold dust, listened monthly for the sound of the landlord's hobnailed boots and his rat-a-tat, and understood her husband's wheedling for "Just an extra three days, guv'nor, as yer a charititious Christian." I worked as many hours at the "Daily Report" as he, longer if it sold quickly, and there were four of us in that dear, dingy house, Clarke helping with laundry and mending and mopping, so our hosts never asked us for rent even if they wanted to. At the time, however, I had little notion of what a drinking habit cost, nor did I realise that some landlords considered the worth of their tenants more relevant to pricing than the square footage of their lodgings.

Small wonder, not knowing how hard the world truly was, I sat so peaceably over my paper and nibs in those final hours; small wonder that I lost something when I never knew what I had in the first place.

I felt Clarke's graceful steps entering. Her

feet sounded satisfied, her gentle shutting of the door weary; she had passed a good day in the Rotherhithe marketplace, crooning sweet ballads and the occasional comedic patter song. Her forearms met my collarbone as she rested her chin upon my head; I was ludicrously smaller than she when seated, for where the younger Clarke had grown tall and willowy, I had remained a slight, sparrowlike creature.

"How bad is it?"

I shut my eyes since she could not see me, simply grateful for her; I thought us sisters, partners, the perfect duo save that I was unworthy of her affections. Tapping my pen against the word *irascilacious,* I nuzzled my head against her neck like an overgrown cat. She chuckled into my crown.

"That is almost too inventive to edit out."

"You're an evil temptress and I shun your wiles," I returned in a passable impersonation of the late unlamented Vesalius Munt. It thrilled me to call Clarke evil when the reverse was true — as if every time she laughed, I knew my own secrets remained buried.

Of course, murder was not the only secret I kept from Clarke.

By the time I was eighteen, I had read her father's publication *The Garden of Forbid-*

198

den Delights an indecorous number of times — always in the sleepy midmorning, when Clarke was out singing and I had spent half the night replacing gibberish with words, dependent upon Mr. Grizzlehurst's voluminous lungs to sell our goods each morn. Unlike Mr. Munt's letters, the erotica printed by Clarke's family failed to sicken, only caused a joyous, clamorous sensation I could not help but mistrust, since it meant that Edwin was right about me.

I liked it.

The people in the slim red book thirsted for closeness, unfolded themselves in turgid metaphors like the petals of a spring rose. Everything they did, they did for wild love — women practically scooped out their hearts and passed them to one another, men discovered these Sapphic passions and assisted in their explorations, brothers-in-arms aided one another when the women were exhausted by pleasure. Even quarrels ended in a dizzy swell of bosoms and trouser fronts; I blame my superb memory on the fact that I had memorised entire chapters.

At age sixteen, it had been too much to take in, let alone tell Clarke about; at age eighteen, I had kept the secret for so long that I should no longer be presenting Clarke with a fresh discovery, a tomcat delivering a mouse — I should be informing her that I was perfectly capable of keeping mum. Though I could not be disgusted over their stock in trade, I could understand Clarke's hurt over being snubbed by her parents, and this delicacy led to my complete failure to bring the subject up at all. As the reader has never faced a similar predicament, I warn the tempted: secrets decay, as corpses do, growing ranker over time.

"Mr. Grizzlehurst seemed disturbed," Clarke reported. She passed a glass of port over my shoulder. "What did he print yesterday?"

"Oh." I sipped, leaning into Clarke's — now blessedly filled out — torso. "Tripe about a robber who stole a boat along with its cargo of sardines. None of the people interested in that story can read, but never fear, I'll set it all right tomorrow."

I had never been more mistaken.

That night, rather than the high percussion of slaps, the deep thud of blows met our ears.

Clarke and I both were out of our bed instantly, praying for the sound resembling a rolling pin striking a veiny beefsteak to stop; it did not stop.

"What are we to do?" Clarke whispered.

She dived for her robe, mindless magnanimity surging through her. "I'll go down and —"

"You're not going anywhere!" I captured her elbow.

My throat was tight with *he could so easily harm you* — by mistake, in the braying torrential rage from which some men suffer; but Clarke tore from my grip.

We heard, "Get up, you haudacious piece of baggage!" and luckily we were already tearing down the staircase, for God knows what He might have allowed if we had not done so.

When I reached the ground floor, Clarke stood with her fingers hovering before her own mouth. Mr. Grizzlehurst had wheeled to face her, chest brokenly wheezing and fists knotted. Mrs. Bertha Grizzlehurst lay upon the floor exercising her habitual silence with her arms clutched around her belly and her temple bleeding . . . *but no, not just her temple,* I thought, *for there is so very much —*

"Bertha." Mr. Grizzlehurst looked as if his favourite toy had somehow come to life and bitten him — as if *he* were the one hurt.

Mrs. Grizzlehurst made a sound through her nose, more a whisper than a whimper, which caused a strange calm to descend as if a cannon had fired next to my ear.

My fingers circled Clarke's wrist and I pulled her back, keeping the link between us gentle. The blades in my eyes I saved for Mr. Grizzlehurst and, when I swept them to him, sweat broke out over his shaking jowls.

"Get out," I ordered. "I'll take care of everything, just don't hurt her anymore. Get out."

We bundled an unsteady Hugh Grizzlehurst out the door, Clarke and I; he blubbered a bit, stumbled, groaned as we pushed him into the street.

His wife made not a sound until the heavy bar across the door scraped into place, and we had gathered flannels and hot water and the shallow hip bath, and I had scrubbed the too-solid stain from the floor; then we all wept long and low at the waste the world produces, and the way in which a baby might have been born to a doting mother but was not.

All is colourful flashes when I remember that night — scraps of scarlet emotion, the pale violet sound of soft keening. I think of Mrs. Grizzlehurst's grey head as Clarke cradled it, rocking, and the throbbing sensation that I ought to have been doing more: as if I had been summoned there following a terrible incantation, a spiteful Greek goddess dressed in radiant sapphire and Mrs. Grizzlehurst the supplicant at my altar, offering more blood than I ever wanted to see again for the rest of my life. It was easier to think myself an observer from another realm than merely a parentless child who had just watched something unspeakable take place.

So I scrubbed the floor thrice and made everyone tea with extra brandy and milk, and I soaked rusty linens and watched the sun rise and periodically glared down from our garret window to check for Mr. Grizzlehurst's return, not feeling anything.

When I think of that morning, I remember how I felt, however; I remember that morning very clearly indeed.

People vary widely in their opinions of female usefulness; my aunt Patience, for instance, preferred them to be approximately as useful as antimacassars. I had, in the wake of two murders, no illusions about what I was capable of — and Clarke, when we retreated to our room that dawn after settling Mrs. Grizzlehurst in bed, seemed to be developing dangerous faith in our combined capabilities.

"He's no better than a murderer."

Clarke paced as the moon dissolved like a sugar cube in the spreading sunlight. At fifteen, she was strikingly lovely, with her champagne curls pinned up into a cloud and her freckles grown more populous from singing in the midday square. I watched her, a queer ethereal creature myself, fretting as she stalked from wall to wall with a rose-patterned robe tied over her nightdress. Beyond the horrible fact Bertha Grizzle-hurst's dreams had been shattered, Clarke's vexation pulled at me with the drag of a hundred tiny fishhooks.

"He's . . . a little better than a murderer, Clarke," I corrected, lighting two tapers on my desk.

"He just killed his own baby!" she hissed.

Pondering how easy it was to lose control, I developed an intense interest in retying my grey dressing gown.

"She has to leave him! Jane. Jane, are you listening? She has to get away from here, she'll never be able to look him in the face again without knowing — can you imagine the torment?"

I sat upon the edge of the bed so as to concentrate on the tie, which was proving unexpectedly taxing.

"We have to help her," Clarke decided.

"How?"

"Surely she can seek out a relative — have

you ever heard her speak of parents or siblings?"

Raising an eyebrow, I wordlessly reminded Clarke of the number of sentences we had heard Mrs. Grizzlehurst utter.

"We'll just have to ask — and if she has somewhere to go, we can help her. I have it now!" Clarke exclaimed, clapping her hands.

Diving at the bed we shared, Clarke pulled my trunk from beneath the frame. I recall the exact set of her shoulders, the quizzical turn of her head as she searched, the way I sat watching her, not understanding, until the instant I did understand, and horror clawed at me, and I stupidly gasped, "Wait, don't —" just as Clarke chirped, "Here!" and darted to the brightening window with her prize.

"Don't touch that," I growled in the voice of a cornered beast.

Clarke had already lifted the dinted silver watch to the light, however; at my outburst, she nearly dropped it, but she had seen the initials *VOM* etched onto the metal. Pushing a curlicue of hair away from her eyes, she slowly turned.

"You said you had a silver watch of your father's when we left." Her high voice was considered but flat, as she had sounded when working out algebraic equations, which positively wrecked me. "This . . ." She stopped, her head whipping up. "This is Vesalius Munt's watch, isn't it?"

Desperate, I cast my mind in all directions for a lie which might serve, any lie, every lie, the *right* lie.

"Yes. I . . . I was leaving school, alone I thought, and had hardly any money."

"What else do you have of his?" Clarke's tone had frosted, placid as a winter lake.

Stomach churning, I pulled out *The Garden of Forbidden Delights.* Clarke took the book, pursing her lips in puzzlement. I committed this insane blunder for two reasons which, in my distress, seemed actually sound. First, aware that Clarke possessed zero tolerance for my falsehoods when directed at her, I offered her a secret like a penance; and second, it seemed prudent to remind her that I may have had a lunatic mother and a history of stealing from dead headmasters, but was her own father not also subject to trivial quirks of ethics?

As Clarke flipped through the pages, her grip began to tremble; we had encountered the obscene on London's streets before, but never produced by her own parents. I darted to her, tossed the book away, and took her hands, kissing one and holding the other over where my heart ought to have been.

"It's all right, their business doesn't affect my opinion of you," I breathed. "Oh, please don't look like that! I took the watch thinking I would be friendless and I'm sorry I lied to you, but you're so particular. That book — you should never have seen it. Mr. Munt wanted to turn me against you, but I never loved you any less."

I fell silent as Clarke's eyes grew swollen with dread. She snatched her hands away, staggering back, knocking one of the candles over; wax spattered the floorboards, began to congeal and to harden.

"Wait, I only meant to say that you — you're family to me. Are you hurt? What's come —"

"He gave this to you that day, to spite the pair of us?"

"Yes, but it didn't work, I told —"

"When you found Mr. Munt in his study, you said he was *already dead,* Jane!" she shrieked.

Time seemed to ripple, an eddying effect which left me reeling. Clarke shook her head back and forth, back and forth, like a metronome without any *click, click.*

"It's not what you think," I whispered.

It was, however.

"I never realised," she said hollowly. "I

thought how natural it was that the same thing should happen to both of us, we were always so kindred, but it never entered my mind that . . . you . . . and you scour the papers for crimes every day and they never found his killer, Jane, never found any clue."

This was not precisely true; Sam Quillfeather had released a statement that, thanks to the complete lack of witnesses, his privately held suspicions could never hold up in court, and thus should remain unspoken for the sake of peace and healing. This ambiguous, insinuating news had eradicated my appetite for four days, which I explained to Clarke as a nasty attack of *la grippe.*

"You murdered him." Clarke swayed, pulling at handfuls of her curls.

"Sit down, you'll hurt yourself," I pleaded. "Oh, Clarke —"

"How could I never have worked it out?" She collapsed on the bed with rote obedience.

"Well, it wasn't the likeliest scenario on earth, was it?" I laughed, and she looked at me as if I had turned lupine, as if all my absences during the full moon now made perfect sense.

Kneeling before her, I seized her elbows. "Listen to me. You've always listened to me, and I'm sorry I lied about the watch, and —"

"Being sorry for lying about murdering our headmaster might be more —"

"He was *killing you.*" The tears which had risen were not lies, reader. "He would never have let you eat again, and I went to the study, meaning to alter his food supply records, and he caught me, and I never meant to hurt him."

"By hurt him, do you mean *stab him in the neck with a letter opener?*"

Laughing again did not help my cause. "I'm sorry, that was — I'm so sorry. Please understand, I had to choose between being sent to an asylum or watching you starve. What could I have done?"

"Attempted escape?" she offered hoarsely. "I would have gone with you, you know. Into the woods, the faraway cities. I would have gone with you anywhere."

The past-tense construction of this sentiment spread invisibly around us, graphic as a battlefield.

Disengaging herself, Clarke pulled off her robe and her nightdress; I stayed on the floor, too numb to move as I watched her cover her creamy skin with her underthings and one of her daytime frocks, methodically shoving the others hanging in the wardrobe into her carpetbag. When this horrifying ritual had been completed, she retrieved a few songbooks and snapped the latch on the bag, which sounded to me like a pistol shot.

"Please don't do this," I begged.

Clarke paused, looking down at me almost regretfully. "Do you remember what I just said about Mrs. Grizzlehurst?"

A sob rose in my throat, for I did.

She'll never be able to look him in the face again without knowing — can you imagine the torment?

"I lied at school every day." I sounded angry; but I was not angry, never that, only trying to haul myself out of the rubble. "I lied for you constantly, lied for everyone — and even if you never lied, you stole, and if I would lie for you, and you would steal for me, why . . . why not this too?"

Clarke's eyes had grown dragonfly bright, but there was something else there, an emotion I could not pinpoint, one which looked like shattered glass.

"Because I don't know who you are," she rasped. "You were always so cunning at school, but so gentle, as if you couldn't bear to watch anyone go hungry. Even the beastly ones, like Taylor — yes, she *was*, Taylor was horrid, only you never noticed — and, oh, I so admired you. You have a terribly romantic air about you, you know. And I knew you carried secrets, you've no notion of how sad you look at times, but I thought that if I took enough care, you might trust me one day. I only wanted to know you, the heart of you, for you to *show me.* But . . ."

Trailing off, Clarke glanced at the desk where a stack of half-finished broadsides sat, my odes to every variant of death and damnation.

"I saw that room, after the murder," Clarke said softly. "And I don't know you at all."

She turned to go. At the last moment, she snatched up *The Garden of Forbidden Delights,* hastily shoving it amidst her clothing as if the binding were aflame; then she departed, closing the door behind her.

I did not go to bed; instead I dressed and, at seven in the morning, I brushed a hand over Bertha Grizzlehurst's arm. She seemed alert in a way she had not been the night before, absent-eyed and weeping like a lost soul.

"Has the bleeding stopped?"

She nudged her head against the pillow, indicating it had.

"Have you anyone to go to? Clarke has

received terrible news," I lied. "Her mother is poorly — I intend to offer what solace I can, I'll be quite at home there, and that means we shan't be living in the upstairs room."

Bertha Grizzlehurst absorbed this information. Had she not been quite so mousey or quite so silent, she might have been a friend, I thought, for she took in blows and bitter news with a stoicism her husband entirely lacked.

"What happened last night — that changes everything. Now he has wounded you, who is to say how far he can go?"

She said nothing, but her face grew whiter than the leadworks dust which blew down Elephant Lane.

"This is for you." I pressed the cursed silver watch into her hand, exactly as Clarke had wanted me to do. "No, no! You've been feeding us supper for two years without payment. I ought to have made you take it before now — forgive me. If you pawn this, you should have enough money for travel expenses and some left over to settle elsewhere. After, you'll have to take life as it comes, but we all do, don't we?"

She gave me a thankful blink; I brushed her cheek and she took the watch, tucking it into the bosom of her dress.

"My brother has a farm near Canterbury."
Her voice always grated unexpectedly in my
ears, as if a toast rack had spoken. She sat
with an effort; apart from her other unspeakable injury, her lip was fat as a blood-
worm and her ribs much abused.

"I'll help you sort everything. Come."

"What will Hugh think?" She sounded as
if he were a small boy who needed minding.

"I'll take care of Mr. Grizzlehurst," I
vowed. "You may count upon that."

"You will see Bertha again soon enough.
She needs time to recover," I soothed, pouring two more generous glasses of head-
splitting gin.

Hugh Grizzlehurst had returned to find
me cooking supper, a jug of gin on the table.
He was rheumy-eyed, his jowls hanging like
nooses and the whites of his eyes nearly as
crimson as the puddle I had cleaned. It fell
to me to improve his spirits: thus the gin
and the two beefsteaks and the mashed
turnips with butter and thyme.

"Poor Bertha." He snorted back tears and
mucus; I had set about returning him to
blind drunkenness and was by seven in the
evening approaching success. "I never . . . I
'ate to think of 'urting my girl. It was an
haccident, you savvy?"

I spooned gravy over the plates, seating myself. "Bertha understands. *I* certainly do as well. I only regret that Clarke had to leave so precipitously."

We ate, Mr. Grizzlehurst sniffling into his beefsteak; when we had finished, I placed both my palms upon the table.

"This house is too empty without Clarke and Mrs. Grizzlehurst." I traced the wood with my finger, playful. "Finishing this gin at Elephant Stairs would be just the ticket — the stars are out, and the night is quite clear."

You used to watch the stars through the skylight with Clarke wrapped around you, lazy as a pair of kittens, just as you did back at school on the rooftop, and now you won't feel the weight of her arm over your waist ever again.

Hugh Grizzlehurst hoisted the half-empty gin bottle; he had far outpaced me, and his mouth wore a slack, wet quality. "Gimme 'alf a tick to fetch me coat."

It was a three-minute walk to the waterfront, which was littered with crumbling stairways to the Thames — Princes Stairs, Church Stairs, Rotherhithe Stairs; so late, the streets had cleared and the air lost the graininess of a long day's labour in an ashen metropolis. A single dustman passed us, tip-

214

ping his flat cap, and a vague, chill sweetness overlay the perennial aromas of fish and refuse.

Hugh Grizzlehurst and I sat at Elephant Stairs with the treacly brown water lapping at our feet, and Mr. Grizzlehurst lapping up the gin. He would make it all up to Bertha, he claimed; he would buy her trinkets, take her on holiday to Brighton, compose poems in her honour. His arms swept like scythes, winding down in a jerky, mechanical fashion until he collapsed against the stone step.

"What that woman is, she is *hexceptional.* The habsolute devotion — and after losing two wee ones. Well, never again, Miss Steele, I can hassure you."

"Two?"

Dread crawled up my neck as I recalled her silence following a very important question.

Now he has wounded you, who is to say how far he can go?

Hugh Grizzlehurst returned to the theme, muttering in spasmodic fashion that he would forgive her for running from him.

"And if she tries to stay haway again, well." Mr. Grizzlehurst shook his head regretfully. "Then I'll 'ave to learn the bitch twice over that marriage is a sacramentation. She'll not hescape me, not my Bertha

215

— never you fear for that."

We fell silent. The waves churned and I thought of going to bed that night alone, thought of the many times when I had jolted awake shaking and felt Clarke's soft lips murmuring against my shoulder, remembered the way she would reach up to trace loving patterns on my collarbone until I fell asleep again, and that she never chided me come morning. Then and there I vowed that Clarke should escape me; I should never seek her out, never threaten her fragile freedom, for all that my chest felt as empty as the wide spaces between the stars she so adored.

When my employer lost consciousness, I was not surprised; and when it was discovered by fishermen that Mr. Grizzlehurst had been deep in his cups and fallen into the Thames, drowning, I was not surprised either, for I had pushed him.

VOLUME TWO

Thirteen

"Know, that in the course of your future life you will often find yourself elected the involuntary confidant of your acquaintances' secrets: people will instinctively find out, as I have done, that it is not your forte to talk of yourself, but to listen while others talk of themselves; they will feel, too, that you listen with no malevolent scorn of their indiscretion, but with a kind of innate sympathy. . . ."

A partial veil must be drawn over the subsequent period, reader — not because I wish to conjure a false portrait, but because redundancies are the enemy of narrative, and I rehearsed the same self-annihilating scene long after Clarke's departure.

After killing Hugh Grizzlehurst, for instance, I carried the remainder of the gin home and drank my fill. Upon the morrow, my skull felt as if a horse had kicked it, and my stomach practically leapt into my chamber pot, but *there's more gin where that came from,* I thought, and Clarke was gone, would be gone always, and I only faced what I deserved.

Days followed, then weeks; I had a yellow velvet purse which I had stuffed with spare coin, and the supply rapidly dwindled after I paid our landlord for a further month's rent (with tears in my eyes for poor, unlucky Mr. Grizzlehurst).

Did I mourn him? After a fashion, and this baffled me; where Edwin's demise had devastated me, and Mr. Munt's was a pinprick, I found myself morose over murdering Hugh Grizzlehurst, as if I had smashed a spider which ought to have been shooed out the door. I felt an echo over him of the anguish I once suffered for letting my misbehaving kitten out of doors, and to this day, I sometimes daydream that he approaches me insisting, *Cannivoristic habsolutely is a word, by Jesus, Miss Steele, a genuine word.*

Meanwhile, I concluded: love is a terrible reason for committing murder. I adored Clarke because she was good, and that very goodness had stolen her from me.

Your badness stole her from you.

Sleepless in the hollow hours, I meditated

on her love of the night sky, her wonder at vast, unknowable things; I obsessed over her facility at music, her mathematical precision tied to ethereal tones. I thought to write broadsides, but there was no one to hawk them; I thought to follow my former employer into the Thames.

Instead, I walked the streets, passing the sky-piercing spire of St. Mary the Virgin at a beggarly pace, hoping that I could garner solace outside a church if not inside; this did not work, nor did it assuage the hunger I studiously avoided thinking about. Instead of eating, I supped on gin and melancholy, and watched my shillings disappear.

The day before rent was next due, I struck out for more dismal pastures.

Quoting the fictional Mr. Rochester seems simplest: *In short, I began the process of ruining myself in the received style; like any other spoony.* I slept on mice-gnawed mattresses in public houses, wrote more broadsides, hawked my wares until I sounded like a saw against a board, and then understood what Mr. Grizzlehurst meant when he said, *I've a hunnatural talent for 'awking — not the most dulcedious tones, mind, but I never wear out.*

I did not thank my alma mater for propelling me into the world with expert skills in deportment, Cicero, and decorative needle-

221

work, for I could find no crying need for any of these disciplines along the docksides. In the depths of my melancholy, I fear it did not even occur to me to be equally grateful to Lowan Bridge for its tutelage in thieving, swallowing unpalatable food, and hiding from authority figures, though these proved more useful talents. When I could not sleep in public houses, I slept on the floors of the desperate and the greedy; when I could not hawk, I stole. Discovering that some men pay scant attention to waifs hovering near their pocketbooks, I relieved them of their banknotes. Often these men were cherry cheeked, laughing bright whiskey clouds, and to these men I apologise; others had eyes the colour of scaffolds, muddy and vicious, and to them I simply say thank you.

Through it all I loved Clarke, and wanted her back. When I was caught by a costermonger and he gave chase, clutching at my sleeve and tearing it, I wanted her back; when I took to sleeping rough, half-stupefied with gin and risking the law as I settled under gorse bushes, I wanted her back; when I began to be invisible, strangers' glances sliding off my tangled hair and my veiny eyes, I wanted her back. When I was accosted by leering men, fighting each off with a fury that I think astonished them, I wanted her back.

I ought to have died, reader, but I did not.

" 'Ere, what in Christ's name d'you think you're doing?" Tilly laughed, slapping my forearm as I stole her pipe from her; I inhaled, dark fumes and buzzing light filling my lungs.

"Helping the day along, just as you are," said I, passing it back.

We were at home before my crackling fire, sipping honey-coloured dreams. It was tobacco mixed with scant enough opium to be perfectly respectable, as neither Tilly nor I had any intention of overindulging — or not on that occasion, anyhow.

Reader, we find ourselves six years later, in December of 1851, when I was twenty-four years of age, and you doubtless wonder whether I ignored Nick the coachman's admonishment and was an unfortunate, as we call those not always entirely unfortunate women who pleasure men for frocks and food.

I was not; I was friendly, however, with those who lodged in my building near Covent Garden. Tilly Cate was my favourite, because Tilly was fond of me, the daft sot. Tilly was big bosomed, with yards of wiry dark blond hair, her complexion porous but rosy; and she was motherly, which characteristic made perfect sense when one learnt she had a daughter named Kitty Cate (an appellation which the child, I am thankful to report, did not deserve in the slightest degree).

My bedchamber contained two maroon damask chairs with a bedraggled green ottoman between, a bed beneath a window overlooking Henrietta Street, and a greying basin with funereal lilies edging the bowl. Secondhand books lay piled along the peeling green-papered walls, and my desk with its pen and ink was tucked in the corner.

The desolate period following Clarke's departure ended when a cartman whose pocket I picked, rather than whistling for a bobby and thereby bestowing upon me a stint in Newgate (which I was not fascinated enough by to fancy living there), instead gave me two cracked ribs under a dank archway in Whitechapel. As I recovered from this blessing in disguise, I realised destitution was growing tiresome and — selfishness restored — schemed over how best to earn my bread and cheese. Single pages were all I could afford to print, so I tried my hand at "last confessions," which were the fanciful one-page admissions of the recently executed.

It will surprise no one to learn that I was *marvellous* at them.

Last confessions were quite a different thing from broadsides and from gallows ballads; with our broadsides' contents you are familiar, but as for gallows ballads, here is an excerpt from "Mary May," that you may determine why I did not go in for that line of work:

Before he long the poison took
In agony he cried;
Upon him I in scorn did look, —
At length my brother died.

Since I laughed myself silly over them, I thought it imprudent to write them myself. But oh! — the confessions! The soaring imagination I lent them, the lecherous details, the pathos I could render as if it had been splayed upon a rack before me. I chose my subjects with alacrity and experience; I did not want Samuel Green, who drunkenly bludgeoned a guardsman, but I did want Hezekiah Pepper, a new father who strangled a maiden on the outskirts of St. Giles. The stories were all that mattered — how dark the deed, how deep the despair. Writing them required two to three hours of ink rippling over pages to the tune of my black heartbeats and the street soprano below, who — despite her great rolls of belly fat — reminded me achingly of Clarke.

"Me little one's off raising 'ell, I shouldn't wonder." Tilly ventured to my window to see if she could glimpse Kitty playing amidst the lost violet blooms and the chestnut shells; it was freezing, but Kitty was a reckless, towheaded thing with thick mittens, and no weather could touch her.

I shifted in my chair, wrapped in a brown dressing gown with lace at the collar, sifting through newspapers as the draught of poisoned smoke trickled into my brain.

"You know I'll buy next time," I mentioned, regarding her pipe. "If you're short of chink —"

"Not I, I'm rich as butter." She winked, adjusting a tatty purple shawl over the friendly spillage of her bosoms. "Nay, it's . . . we're nigh out o' hard up, and I've Judge Frost arrivin'."

My friend Tilly's speech was thick with local slang, which made me wish I were more fluent, since I rather adored the dialect of society's underbelly (though I certainly understood *hard up* meant *tobacco*). Meanwhile, most of Tilly's clientele were no more dangerous than horseflies —

pimpled youths with sweaty hands, hawkers who had sold their stock of Barcelona nuts in the market below, sad widowers with silver hair; but Judge Frost was what Tilly liked to call a right scaly customer.

I gasped sharply, and Tilly pivoted. "Lord, Jane, you done give me a turn. What's up, then?"

Folding my lips together, I reread:

WANTED, at Highgate House, ——shire. One young lady to see to a nine-year-old ward. Estate recently taken possession of by Mr. Charles Thornfield, heir of the Barbary family, late of the Sikh Wars, whose household requires the services of a qualified governess. Compensation —————— pounds per annum with room and board, apply care of Mr. S. Singh, with references.

"Ye look like someone just slapped ye in the quim with a fish."

I restored myself to my full senses with a hard shiver. "It's nothing. But . . . I used to live there, you see those words — Highgate House. They want a governess."

The previous August, I read with passionate interest the obituary of Mrs. Patience Barbary, who died abroad; Highgate House had passed into the care of that most universally respected profession, the law. My aunt's death hurt shallowly, like a mishap made peeling potatoes — she had never searched for me, never even advertised, an omission which made me equal parts grateful and furious.

Meanwhile, the thought of Highgate House provoked a queer unease. My mother insisted that it was mine, but died before explaining how or why. I was not unhappy in London; I adored the metropolis, the way I could disappear in it, but approaching a group of gouty men wearing pince-nez had not seemed wise. I was not destitute, but neither was I remotely respectable any longer; I wore jolly frocks with the fronts cut low and slung brightly coloured shawls about my elbows, teased my favourite costermongers with vocabulary that would have quite soured my aunt's digestion. Neither did I have paperwork, nor any means whatsoever of proving I was the Jane Steele who had disappeared so long ago, and thus the idea of knocking up a powder-wigged gentleman to say *How de do, may I have this estate, please?* frankly frightened me. In any case, ought I claim to be Jane Steele when Inspector Sam Quillfeather could be waiting with his ear to the ground, a hunter wise enough to allow his prey to trap herself and save him the bother?

Now, however — the thought of a stranger inhabiting the place smouldered in my stomach. Was the cottage occupied? Was my bedroom? Was Agatha yet living, and would she even know me if she was?

"Lived at a place named Highgate House!" Tilly teased. "Well, I never. Ye was a genuine lady, like, with silks and velvets and a stick up yer arse."

"No velvets. No silks." I folded the paper.

"But the stick?"

"Of course, they equip us with bum sticks from the cradle."

"I'll bet ye had a great bed wi' acres and acres o' white sheets," she surmised dreamily.

"All you ever think about is linens. It's actually impressive."

She shrugged. "Never 'ad naught but a straw tick, so, aye, it occupies me mind."

"Admittedly if I spent as much time in bed as you do . . ." Her face clouded. "Tilly, I'm only joking — you know I'm no better than I should be."

"How *is* Jeremiah, come to that?"

She passed the pipe and I took another slow puff. "I've thrown him over. He snores, and he wasn't much cop at . . . well, anything. He may as well have been winding up his watch."

"Bloody hell, if ye net a guppy, toss 'im back in the river." Tilly giggled.

At my lowest tide of spirits and highest of gin swilling, I had discovered that I enjoyed the practice of lovemaking as much as the theory. My swells were acquaintances from Rotherhithe, mainly — the curly-haired boy from the saltpetre works, the tap man at the Mayflower Pub. By giving the lads some fun, I could at least make a human being happy for a quicksilver moment; and once I had got the knack of pessaries and slow touches and the faint scrape of teeth over hipbones, I enormously enjoyed myself, just as I had imagined I would when gasping alone in my bed with *The Garden of Forbidden Delights*.

"I'll find someone else soon enough," said I.

"Yer doin' it wrong, ye realise," Tilly repeated, shaking her head. "They're meant to pay for the privilege."

Clattering on the stairs interrupted us, and in tumbled Kitty Cate. She had turned twelve in June and moved with that coltish energy of girls who are about to shoot up like fireworks; her great wiry corkscrews of hair were flecked with snow, and she held a

230

golden ribbon.

"Look at what Mr. Frost done give me, mum," she exclaimed, waving it. " 'E said as it would bring out me eyes."

Tilly's mouth wrenched to one side. "Judge Frost done give that to you? In the street, like?"

"Aye." Kitty stroked it, studying the colour. "Won't it look smart, though? I've that green frock, when the weather turns, and —"

"Good afternoon, all," a nasal voice sounded.

Judge Frost stood in the open doorway, belatedly rapping at the wood. Tilly often visited me, "taking the air," and thus I was familiar with her regular customers; I liked Judge Frost so much less than the others that the figure landed in the negative. He was thin and wispy, with dandelion fluff sprouting from his cheeks and neck and ears. Indirectly, he was useful, as he had caused scores of people to be hanged at Newgate and Tyburn; directly, he was petulant and insinuating.

"Well, and do you like your Christmas gift?" He chuckled, rubbing his hands. "Frills and baubles, purses and petticoats, I've a niece myself and she thinks of nothing else. I've chosen well, my pet?"

231

" 'Tis lovely," Kitty said, beaming, and then I noted that Tilly had gone pale.

"That's to the good, then! Now, you'll excuse your mother and me whilst we have a little chat?"

Judge Frost had a voice like chalk squealing, and he was directing all his quivery attention at Kitty, who twisted the ribbon in her fingers as she pelted off downstairs again.

Tilly forced herself to smile. "Shall we pass the time in my room?" she husked, linking arms with the judge and shutting my door behind them.

I was left with an anxious feeling like tiny waves across the sea before a squall. I frowned as I crossed my feet on the ottoman, and my eyes fell back to the advertisement: *Highgate House.* The place seemed like a dream at times, at others a nightmare, but it was *mine,* I thought again with alarming intensity.

Remember when you ran to your aunt Patience with roses and your ears were boxed for ruining the gardener's chances at the flower show.

Remember when you visited the horses with carrots, preferring their company because they wouldn't warn you against hellfire.

Remember when Mamma let you take her

hair down before bedtime and the firelight
painted it red and gold and copper.

I did not want to remember very much of my life — but when I thought of Highgate House, its shape shifted in my memory that day, its stark lines tangling with ivy and sentiment and something disturbingly like fanatical ownership.

The decision that I would apply for the governess position by creating false references, instructing that replies be addressed to pedigreed London post offices to be left until called for, was made as I walked home through Covent Garden three days later. The market was packed to bursting so close to the holiday, donkey barrows edged nose to tail, the mournful-eyed creatures strapped to their carts with everything from knotted handkerchiefs to braided string. The air bit like an errant pup, and I skirted impossible configurations of cabbages and salted fish, smelling the barnyard ripeness of fresh-killed chickens and the sweet sap of the festive pine boughs.

My plan was nearly formed when gaslights began blinking to life under the Pavilion, and by the time I reached Henrietta Street, it was complete; the fact that the solicitors had named Charles Thornfield next of kin (doubtless due to petty machinations set in place long ago by Aunt Patience) would not be a problem if Charles Thornfield was dead. I did not precisely *want* to kill him, mind — thus far I had reserved murder for those I had actually met — but I *could* kill him, and that was a comfort. Meanwhile, my mother left me woefully unprepared; there would be papers to recover, lineage to trace, but the occupation of governess (for which I was eminently qualified) would enable me to spy from within. I had convinced myself that if anyone remained who might recognise me, it would be my own Agatha — and surely I could explain to my old caretaker why I had left, and stayed away, and returned home once more.

After striking the snow and walnut shells off my boots, I ascended the stairs. When I saw no paisley kerchief tied to the knob (our signal she was working), I banged my way into Tilly's rooms and found her alone with a mug of hot whiskey and honey, sitting at the table next to her place of business, its pillows lovingly fluffed.

"Tilly, I know it's sudden but — I'm leaving," I announced breathlessly. "I'm going to try for the job at Highgate House."

Tilly Cate burst into tears.

"Oh, God." I rushed to pull another chair

over, spreading my fingers over her back. "Tilly, I. What —"

"He's going to take her."

"I don't . . ."

Tilly slumped into my side, her heavy chest heaving. "Judge Frost. That filthy cove's been after eyein' my Kitty fer six months and more, askin' if she takes after 'er mum, askin' if she likes 'im. I says to 'im, *Kitty's only a girl,* but he bullied and fussed and finally *no,* I says, and he says smug as a cat, *I'll have ye arrested fer whorin', and then she'll need a friend anyhow, won't she?* Oh, Jane, I 'ave to tell her . . . I 'ave to . . ."

Collapsing, Tilly wept as if her heart had shattered.

"Tilly," I said into her coarse hair. "Shh. No one is going to hurt Kitty. We'll think of something, you and I."

"If she'd turned bad as I did — later, on 'er own, like — I couldn't ha' judged, but this is unnatural cruel, and there's naught to think on. He'll take me and then take her."

I have never longed for children. At times, I suspect this curiosity is due to the fact I have learnt to find Death beautiful — and if I had children, then perhaps I should not think so anymore. The idea of Judge Frost with his pale flesh glowing like a maggot in the light through Tilly's window as he enjoyed a virgin Kitty, however, was not to be endured.

"All right, Tilly." I released a small sigh. "We'll not think of something. You stop fretting; *I'll* think of something."

Fourteen

On a dark, misty, raw morning in January, I had left a hostile roof with a desperate and embittered heart — a sense of out-lawry and almost of reprobation . . . The same hostile roof now again rose before me: my prospects were doubtful yet; and I had yet an aching heart. I still felt as a wanderer on the face of the earth: but I experienced firmer trust in myself and my own powers, and less withering dread of oppression.

When the carriage pulled up the drive before Highgate House and I beheld it again a week later, it was with a wardrobe suited for a governess (staid blacks and greys with high necks and infuriating buttons) and a keepsake in the form of a newspaper (the *Pall Mall*) containing an obituary:

DECEASED, Judge Arthur Polonius Frost,

aged 66 years. Judge Frost was a pillar of the legal community, an advocate for harsher sentencing of those he termed "irredeemables" or that segment of society which makes peaceable living so dangerous for the honest and upright. He died of heart failure following a violent nervous attack in his home in Westminster.

The reader may not be shocked to learn that following Tilly's account, I blackmailed Judge Frost via a street Arab's verbal message, demanding he meet me after giving his servants a half day. When I arrived, he announced his intention to see me hanged. I should have been fidgety over this save for the fact the blackmail was a ruse; I feigned a fainting spell in order to drop arsenic, charmingly known as "inheritance powder," into his half-drunk glass of brandy when he went for help disposing of me.

Did I regret this latest casualty of my nature, reader?

No; I did not regret it at all.

My nerves shrieked like a steam whistle as I alighted from the carriage, however. Highgate House seemed unreal, as if someone had told me a fairy story and I dreamt of the castle that night. The countless windows like eyes, the sinister forest — I could have visited a witch's lair and been more easy. The air numbed my fingers, and my breath came in ghostly gusts.

A man walked out the front door; he was tall and the colour of strong tea, and a tingling in my spine informed me that here was a presence which would somehow influence my life — for better or for worse, I could not say.

"I am Sardar Singh," said he.

Mr. Sardar Singh was strongly but efficiently built — he seemed a whip tensed to crack, all poise and precision. His nose was regal and hooked, his black beard long, and his head was wrapped tightly with a pale blue strip of muslin so that it resembled a beehive; otherwise, he was dressed in quiet English black.

"I am the butler here. You are Miss Jane Stone?"

I nodded, having thought it prudent to conceal the other name. Briefly, I wondered whether I ought to shake hands; but he turned to take my luggage from the coachman, so I simply followed him into the house.

And what an astonishing sight met my eyes! Lips parted, my head slowly revolved. I left behind a staid British manse, all mauve ruffles and china dogs; here were hanging cloths of crimson and gold and indigo, a beautifully carved wooden figure wearing a bronze-painted shawl, an ivory writing box on the hall table, so many potted plants I might have been in a jungle.

Mr. Singh made for the parlour, and I raptly pursued; where once was an open sitting room now a screen stood half blocking the settee, detailed with women carrying water, their hips as curvaceous as their mesmerising eyes. A peculiar smell permeated the place — part clove and part sweet herb, and I soon divined that it emanated from the glowing brass chandelier which hung in the shape of a great starburst above us.

"Welcome to Highgate House, Miss Stone," said Mr. Singh. "Might I bring you anything to refresh your spirits?"

I sat, removing my gloves. "A little wine would be welcome, thank you — the road was long and cold."

"So often the way with roads," said he, crossing to unstop a crystal decanter.

Mr. Singh's voice owned a light lilt, but his diction was crisp and clear. As he poured the claret, I saw that he wore a single steel bracelet, a sort of cuff. Additionally, there was a silver comb wedged into his hair just below the pale blue turban, glinting dangerously.

"Sardar? What on earth are — Oh, but I see she's arrived," a crisp new voice interrupted.

Here I was introduced to Mr. Charles Thornfield. It would be inaccurate to say that my heart skipped — nothing whatsoever happened to that poor excuse for an organ. My breath quickened, however, and my hands fretted, and all other outward manifestations manifested.

Charles Thornfield was neither tall nor short, with a face that seemed almost ferocious in its ruggedness; there was an elegance about the tanned cheekbones, however, and a refinement to the chiselled jaw and straight nose, which suggested diplomacy. He bowed infinitesimally, the effect as much ironic as polite. Like his foreign butler, he wore a metal ring about his right arm, and his hair had not been shorn in quite some time — far more remarkable, it was white as snow, though he looked no older than five and thirty, and he wore it tied behind with a short black ribbon. His attire was sedately rich: a navy frock coat with a grey cravat and trousers, grey gloves, and he was shod in a pair of well-worn riding boots, which endeared him to me immediately. His brows were sable and sharply arched at their outer edges, his eyes an oceanic blue, and they glimmered as they took me in.

"This is Miss Jane Stone, I hope," said he. "Charles Thornfield, at your service, supposing ever I can be. I've so looked forward to greeting young Sahjara's governess, I can hardly express my enthusiasm."

My rival's voice was a baritone with all the complexity and smoke of a good whiskey; yet it was not sombre — the sardonic edge I had seen in his bow likewise seasoned his greeting, and I fought an inappropriate smile.

If I were to kill this very intriguing man, I wonder how difficult he would make the task?

"Is my charge's name Sahjara, then? I am pleased to meet you, and shall be still more pleased to meet your daughter."

"You shan't, actually." Mr. Thornfield corrected. "Sahjara is her name and you may even be pleased to meet her, nothing is impossible, but the sprite is my ward. Frankly, there were irregularities about your application which drew me to you."

My heart gave several futile thumps as I took the glass of wine from Mr. Singh.

"I'm afraid I don't —"

"You see, I could not recognise any of the references you gave, though all returned my correspondence with the highest praises. My

242

hope was that you worked in other . . . eccentric households. Capital, here she is! Sahjara, this is your new governess, Miss Jane Stone."

A honey-skinned, poised little girl entered the room, led by a woman of an age and complexion close to Mr. Singh's; this matron wore a drab dress after the manner of housekeepers, and thus might have been unremarkable — save for a white scar which blazed across her brow like a line dashed through text. At the sight of her, my crackling nerves settled a little. This seemed an entirely new household to the previous — and if they had retained any of my aunt's staff, they were highly unlikely to be people who had ever paid me the slightest attention.

My charge, meanwhile, was attired in ivory muslin perfectly suited to her own golden complexion, wherein I divined the reason for Mr. Thornfield's choosing me: she must have been half-born of foreign parentage. Sahjara's eyes were black and darting, and her thick black hair had been braided into a queue — upon closer inspection, I thought her closer to eight than ten. I felt immediate relief that I should not have to manage anyone who fit more neatly into society than I did.

"I am Miss Stone," I introduced myself, rising.

"Sahjara Kaur," said she, curtseying.

"Miss Stone, may I present the Young Marvel," said Mr. Thornfield dryly, pouring himself a whiskey. To my surprise, he did not remove his close-fitting gloves, an egregious breach of etiquette.

"What sort of horse do you ride?" Sahjara asked next.

"Actually," I replied, stopping there.

"Behold the first spectacular feat of the Young Marvel!" Charles Thornfield leant against the sideboard. "She can take any topic — or no topic whatsoever, working from merest air — and shift the conversation to horses."

"Because you see," the child continued doggedly, "I've nearly outgrown my pony, and Charles says that if I'm *very* cautious, I might try a small mare."

"Brava!" Mr. Thornfield set his drink down to clap neatly gloved hands. "A pitch-perfect performance, and unasked for, as all the best are." Though he was clearly the most sardonic creature alive, perversely his gaze twinkled with affection.

I sat, taking her hands; I had thought long over whom I should model myself after, and tried to say as warmly as Miss Lilyvale

244

would have, "I've never owned a horse, though I love them and used to visit the stables at Lowan Bridge School whenever I could."

And the ones just off your own east wing, come to that.

Sahjara's jaw plummeted in horror. "No! But how horrid. Don't you ride, then? You can have one of our horses, save Charles's stallion."

Mr. Thornfield chuckled. "In astonishing succession, Miss Stone, with such dexterity the mind reels, you have just witnessed the second remarkable facility of the Young Marvel."

"Which is?"

"Giving away my property to whomever she pleases, whenever she pleases."

Sahjara tossed her head; I noted with fascination another ornamental silver comb, this one flowery and delicate, and as she set a hand to her hip in a most un-English gesture I found delightful, a silver bracelet flashed in the firelight.

"Tedious *bhisti*,"* she accused her guardian, but there was no heat, merely warmth.

"Tiresome changeling," Mr. Thornfield

* Water-carrier, a lowly menial occupation on the battlefield.

245

returned, winking at her.

This harmless exchange so perversely reminded me of being spitefully called *vermin* and *scavenger* in the same room that a small knot rose in my throat; I hastened to change the subject. "What is your third great skill, Sahjara?"

"Oh, I haven't really any others," the girl demurred, though her gaze found Mr. Thornfield's through her winglike eyelashes.

"Blatant fibs are considered unfashionable in British *chico*s,* so don't tell 'em." The master of the house dropped a mock-gallant kiss inches above her hand, as if she were royalty. "She can ride as if she were born in the saddle — always could do, from before she could walk, and I promise you, Miss Stone, it is damned infuriating."

As Sahjara blushed dusky rose, Mr. Singh returned. "All is in readiness, Mr. Thornfield, with your baggage packed and Falstaff saddled."

"Thank you, Sardar. Please explain to the new governess the limits placed upon her movements within the house."

"Of course, sir."

Whether my hackles rose faster than my curiosity, I could not say.

* Children.

246

What limits should be imposed upon my movements, when I am to this very manor born?

"Miss Stone, I hope you shall be happy here, though happiness is hardly typical of governesses, I take it, and we no more fashionable a household than the nearest costermonger's — consider any hope of glimpsing society maidens at lavish balls hosted here crushed." Draining his spirits, Mr. Thornfield offered me his hand, yet sheathed in expensive kid.

Astonished, I rose and took it, he observing my discomfiture. "You'll pardon the necessity of my going gloved, I hope? Or are you the severe breed of Englishwoman, the sort who abhor vice and irregularity equally and shall devote your night to prayers on behalf of my immortal soul?"

Englishwoman? I thought, for what else should I have been?

I replied truthfully, "The journey was a trying one, sir, and I am fatigued — I've no intention of praying for you at all."

Mr. Thornfield took half a step closer, eyes narrowing. Though he was not tall, I was diminutive, and he peered down his straight nose with one side of his mouth twitching — whether into a frown or a smile I could not tell. His manner was so rudely scrutinising, I at last extricated my hand.

"You're oddly honest, for a schoolgirl turned domestic dependent," he asserted.

As is so often the case at the worst possible times, I laughed. Quickly subduing myself, I amended, "Merely weary, sir — I've no wish to offend."

"Possibly not," he mused, stepping back again. "You'll do, Miss Stone — supposing you can keep up with the wild beast in your charge. *Idderao,*★ Sahjara." His ward threw her arms around him. "I'll return in a few days' time."

"Sooner," she protested, half-muffled by his coat.

"Will you listen to her?" He sighed. "Is there anything else I can do for you, small tyrant? Should you like a war elephant? The moon, perhaps?"

"Sooner," she insisted, pouting.

"If I can, darling." He pulled away, straightening his waistcoat and glancing at the standing clock, one of the few familiar objects in this bewildering sea of opulence. When next he spoke, his soft tone had regained its bite. "Sardar, bring Falstaff round to the gate."

"Of course, sir."

★ Come here.

248

Sweeping up a tall hat from the piano bench, he tipped it to the pair of us.

"Do not burn down the house," he commanded sternly as he swung up an accusing index finger, lending me yet another shock.

Sahjara took my elbow. "I was reading late, and some curtains caught fire," she whispered. "I was dreadfully sorry."

"You were merely disappointed at the interruption; had I cut off your hands, you should have been sorry," Charles Thornfield growled — but it was a lion's purr, not its roar. "Until next week, then! Good riddance to the pair of you. I can tell I'll have twice the devil-try to reckon with now."

Too true, I thought as he disappeared; but when Sahjara turned her teeth up to flash me a grin, I confess I could not sense a scrap of wickedness — in her, at least — at all.

Sahjara wished to sit up late talking of riding (and of foaling, breeding, racing, and the horse species in the abstract). What ought to have been an annoyance felt a balm; I liked hearing her earnest chatter; I liked the bizarre dishes served alongside our tea — buttered sandwiches, yes, but also a curry-scented bread which drove memories of Aunt Patience's arrogant tiered refreshments straight from my mind.

At nine o'clock, when we were both nodding, I recalled that I was a severe governess, the hired instructor of a rich man's charge, and rang the bell. Sahjara went meekly enough with the scarred woman when I promised to take a full tour of the stables upon the morrow, and I found myself in the company of Mr. Singh, blinking exhaustedly at the indigo tapestries which had replaced the choleric portraits along the staircase.

"Your room has been made ready and your trunk brought up, but do not hesitate to ring," Mr. Singh said as we ascended. I did not have to feign unfamiliarity with my surroundings — the bones of Highgate House remained, but its skin had been shed.

"I expect the coach shall have worn me clean through."

"So often the way with coaches," he intoned.

"Is Sahjara a relation of Mr. Thornfield?"

I imagined slight hesitation before Mr. Singh replied smoothly, "No. Miss Kaur is the daughter of an old friend. As I said, if you need anything, ring for Mrs. Garima Kaur — our housekeeper, whom you saw before — and she will attend you. Though she speaks little English, she will understand

250

you if you make a request."

Pausing, I asked, "Sahjara is . . . her daughter?"

Mr. Singh turned on the landing, his candle illuminating the edge of his tall turban and the hollow crescent of a smile. "Ah, no indeed. Sikh men take the name Singh, as I do, and Sikh women the name Kaur. It is our custom."

"Are all the domestics Sikhs, then?" I asked innocently, my heart tensing for his answer.

"Indeed we are, Miss Stone. I hope that will not prove a problem."

"Oh, of course not," I assured him as I thrilled with satisfaction. "I hope to learn a great deal more."

We continued up the staircase from which the oil portrait of my uncle Richard Barbary had used to stare cunningly. At last, Mr. Singh swung a door open. They had readied Aunt Patience's room for me. It was not Aunt Patience's room any longer, however; the silver lamps gleamed, the corners were full of ferns, the heavy velvet hangings on the bed replaced with magical violet and lilac ones in such dye shades as I had never before seen, and where once a few niggardly coals had gasped for breath, the hearth laughed and crackled.

Wrenching my stupefied gaze from the silent white tiger skin roaring at me from the floor, I turned to thank Mr. Singh.

"Oh, and . . ." I added. He stopped, raising his chin. "Mr. Thornfield spoke of limits regarding where I'm allowed to go within the house?"

Mr. Singh's beard bobbed. "The cellars are under construction, and it is hazardous to explore them. The rest of Highgate House, including the attics should you require storage, is at your disposal — it is only the underground which is kept locked whilst alterations are in progress."

Obviously, the house was much changed; and yet, the back of my brain still prickled at this. When Jane Eyre first tours her new home and hears the tragic laugh she supposes Grace Poole's, the author writes, *but that neither scene nor season favoured fear, I should have been superstitiously afraid.* I was not afraid; but the fierce possessiveness I felt for Highgate House made me long to relearn it from plaster cracks to stone foundation. Being barred from a portion felt galling.

"I shall conduct all remaining introductions in the morning — say, after Sahjara has shown you the stables?" Mr. Singh prompted when I said nothing.

"Yes, of course. Here I stand peppering you with questions which can wait for the morrow — though of course those questions will likely only lead to fresh ones."

"So often the way," said he, and this time I knew it for a subtle jest, "with questions."

A key reposed in the lock and, dizzied at the prospect of experiencing genuine privacy for the first time in my life, I turned it.

Revolving as I crossed the room, drinking in pillows edged with seed pearls and the filigreed birds hanging upon the walls, I suppressed a shudder.

The last time I was here, I requested to be placed in the hands of Mr. Munt.

So much had changed; I now knew myself a thousand times better, as if I were a textbook I had studied, but being at Highgate House conjured everything from the graceful dips above my mother's clavicle to Edwin's damp palms.

One memory at a time would be a welcome diversion: so many together are agonising.

With arms of lead, I tossed some water on my face from the pitcher and braided my erratic waves of hair, donning my nightdress. On an impulse, I went to the window and drew back the sheer amethyst curtains — there was the diagonal line of our cottage's gable in the moonlight, seen through silhouetted trees. Biting my knuckle, I studied it until I knew that I must turn away or else pretend to have caught a head cold come morning.

As my eyes shifted, they snagged upon the drive, a ribbon of heather within the slate, and I thought of Charles Thornfield.

Indeed, once my mind latched upon him, I stood for several more minutes, wondering what business my mortal enemy had that would take him away from his clearly beloved ward; I at last collapsed, worn to a bone shard, upon my deceased aunt Patience's feather bed.

FIFTEEN

It is a very strange sensation to inexperienced youth to feel itself quite alone in the world: cut adrift from every connection; uncertain whether the port to which it is bound can be reached, and prevented by many impediments from returning to that it has quitted.

"I have no doubt but that you will find your way," Mr. Singh assured me, pouring a cup of clove-scented tea at the kitchen table. "We cannot be what you expected to find."

The December morning had been frigid, a pristine lace veil draped bridelike over the grounds. Sahjara had met me before the stables, wearing her riding habit, raven's-feather eyes gleaming. Her enthusiasm for equestrianism was no hardship — I felt pure satisfaction when I tugged back the familiar wooden gate, splinter prone and rust smelling, and entered the stable. After Sahjara gathered that horses were neither averse to me nor I to them, she blithely wondered did I always look so happy when I stood beside a stallion's muzzle, smiling at its single visible eye?

The answer was *yes,* of course, but then Sahjara departed to work with her riding coach, and I rendezvoused with Mr. Singh in the kitchen only to behold the entire domestic staff.

Agatha, I thought, suppressing a fresh gush of panic despite assurances the household was entirely foreign. *She would say nothing, surely — she would never betray my confidence, once she learnt I meant to claim what's mine.*

Agatha, however, was nowhere to be seen.

"I hope meeting us all at once was not too terribly overwhelming." In the satiny winter light of midday, I realised that Mr. Singh was younger than I had supposed; he could not have exceeded Mr. Thornfield's five and thirty. The beard framing his mouth lent the impression he was always mildly smiling or lightly frowning, both somehow solicitous expressions.

"Oh, no." Sipping my tea too soon, I scalded my tongue. "It was lovely."

It was not; I was wholly ignorant of how governesses are expected to behave. We had been groomed for the profession at Lowan Bridge: so was my first step to steal food, tell lies, or thrust a letter opener into someone's gullet?

"They were gratified by your open nature, fearing a traditionalist. You already seem quite at ease with Sahjara. I don't suppose I need tell you she is beloved by us all."

I smiled, shaking my head. I had now formally been introduced to Mrs. Garima Kaur, the housekeeper with the terrible white mark on her brow, who indeed spoke scant English but listened with such care it hardly mattered; Mrs. Jas Kaur, the cook; and eight additional Singhs and Kaurs, the remaining house servants and grooms, all of whom fascinated and overwhelmed in equal measure.

During some confusion I gathered had to do with the cellar workmen, Mrs. Garima Kaur leant into my face as if consulting a mirror and murmured, "Quiet. Afraid?"

"Why would — no," I stammered. "Only anxious."

Garima Kaur was a gaunt woman with severely stark bone structure, her cheeks hollow beneath dark eyes so deeply set one could not help but see the skull beneath. Without the silvery streak across her brow, and with a stone more flesh on her skeleton, she might have been beautiful — as it was, she was only striking. She stared straight into my mind, or so it felt.

She cocked her head, the scar glinting at the same instant as an unreadable smile. "Mr. Sardar Singh — good. Nothing bad. You, how in English?"

I had no notion.

"Safe. Mr. Singh. Do not worry, do not worry," she repeated, using a phrase she must have just learnt.

It might have been dreadfully alarming, save that it was not; butlers have the run of every estate, and to be assured by the housekeeper that ours would not infringe upon my virtue was rather companionable.

"I won't worry," I assured her, touching her sleeve, and I noted she wore no wedding ring. It was common practice for housekeepers to go by *Mrs.* without husbands, however, as a token of respect. "You are unmarried, then, Mrs. Kaur?"

Her lips pursed. "Yes, Miss Stone. You?"

"I can't think of anyone who would marry me," I joked, and Mr. Singh returned to finish the introductions.

Now we sat alone in the kitchen, Mr. Sardar Singh and I. All the hanging copper pans and cast-iron pots remained the replica of my memory's; they were augmented, however, by queer skillets and glazed vessels, and where once only salt and pepper had reposed, a sunset blaze of glass-jarred spices sat next to a heaping bowl of onion, garlic, and gingerroot, all emitting a perfume so overwhelming that I had already sneezed twice. For good measure, I did so again.

"Bless you," my companion said smoothly. "I already informed you last night we must keep away from the cellars, Miss Stone."

Yes, and now I am determined to visit them.

"And now you know everyone here by name."

Would that were true.

"Should you have any further questions, I am your man," he concluded, mouth tipping upwards as he spread his hands.

"Mr. Thornfield is a most . . . peculiar individual," I attempted, feigning interest in my teacup.

"So often the way with individuals."

Chuckling, I added, "He treats Sahjara like a princess."

"Well, she is a princess, so that is quite natural."

My eyes shot up to find that Mr. Singh's were equally mirthful. "You cannot — no, it is impossible."

"Not merely possible but true." Mirroring

259

me, the butler watched the vortex created by his spoon. "We Sikhs call ourselves the pure ones. You were bemused by our names last night — men belonging to the religion are baptised, you would say, with the surname Singh, which means *lion*. Women are baptised with the surname Kaur, or princess."

"Every Sikh female is a princess?"

He took a sip of tea. "You must think us altogether mad."

"No!" I exclaimed so fast that droplets splashed into my saucer. Embarrassed, I set the cup down. "I mean to say, I think I could grow fond of Sahjara, and I intend to do well by her."

"That is gratifying to hear. Mr. Thornfield is not incorrect in calling her the Young Marvel, though he sounds ever in jest — her name means *daybreak,* and she truly does throw the curtains open, doesn't she? You seem too restless for tea, Miss Stone — no, no, I taxed you with social necessities. Might you enjoy a short tour?"

Eagerly, I agreed, and we pushed back our chairs that I might enjoy a tour of my own estate.

"The music room remains relatively intact, but some minor alterations have been made," said Mr. Singh, sliding back a glass-paned door a few minutes later.

The walls were covered with scores of minuscule framed artworks which had been rendered in such fine detail that I imagined I peered through an enchanted telescope. In one set, the same cottage was depicted in high summer, brilliant autumn, blue winter, and lush spring; in another, a saint with a beard and turban stared as if the viewer's soul were being weighed upon his scale; in others, lovers clasped each other with such enthusiasm any governess ought to have been shocked.

I barely remembered to flare my nose in dismay.

"This is Mr. Thornfield's collection of Punjabi miniatures." Mr. Singh either had not noted my pretended disapproval or did not care, for he smiled as he reached my side. "His eye for worth is exceptional, having been raised in Lahore. See this portrait of Maharajah Ranjit Singh, the way the furnishings are patterned so lovingly, but his face most carefully rendered of all?"

"Mr. Thornfield is from Lahore?" I asked, latching on to undeniably the most intriguing word in this statement. "How is that possible, the East India Company only having arrived there some five years ago? Or so I read in the newspapers — I supposed Mr.

Thornfield English."

Again I sensed a tick of the clock before Mr. Singh spoke. "He was born there, to a British entrepreneur, but he studied medicine at the British and Foreign Medical School and then Charing Cross Hospital before he returned to the Punjab. Ah, you would not have known he belongs to the Royal College of Physicians and Surgeons of London, of course. Yes, Mr. Thornfield is a man of medicine. This particular painting is moving for us — Amritsar, the Sikh holy city where our sacred book resides."

It was a gilded palace at the end of a pure white pier surrounded by sapphire waters — an impossible place, a dream breathed from a dawn pillow.

"To have left this behind — you must miss it very much," I mentioned, wisely refraining from commentary regarding homes from which I myself had fled.

"God has his seat everywhere," Mr. Singh returned without inflection, as if quoting a text.

"I thought from the advertisement that Mr. Thornfield had been in the wars?"

An invisible shutter closed over Mr. Sardar Singh's face. "Who has not been in a war? Yes, Mr. Thornfield trained as a doctor but obtained an army commission after military training at Addiscombe."

Mr. Singh strode off and I pursued, anxious lest I had given offence on my second day. We turned left down a corridor, right down another, until I knew we stood before the billiards room, and he rested his fingers upon the door handles.

"Forgive me, I never meant to —"

Air burst into my face as the butler revealed the room; but I could not enter, such was my astonishment at the narrow fraction I beheld.

"After you, Miss Stone," Mr. Singh demurred.

A steel palace, the inside of a diamond — how shall I best describe a billiard room transformed into a war display? Swords — straight, curved, broad, tapered — lined every wall, polished to a sheen echoing the pain of the blade itself. Their handles were inset with ivory carvings, their hilts embellished with golden flourishes, their points angled into queer triangles or hollowed into deadly sickle shapes. Shorter daggers hung above the liquor cabinet, and the hearth was festooned with weapons I could scarce comprehend — tri-pronged silver objects with needlelike points, axes so beautiful I could not fathom using them, bizarre metal circlets which gleamed at us like eyes. I had never viewed such a fascinating collection of murderous devices.

"Oh," I breathed, delighted.

"Do they interest you?" Mr. Singh sounded pleased. "These are the weapons of the Khalsa, and I'm afraid we are all quite adept with them."

"Mr. Thornfield has a cuff like yours," I noted, too alight with inquisitiveness to care whether I was being rude.

"You are observant. Yes — he is a Sikh, just as I am."

"However is that possible?"

"There is no Hindu; there is no Mussulman," he answered, and I again had the impression he quoted scripture. "If there is no Hindu and no Mussulman, and all can form a single brotherhood, then there is no Christian either. I beg your pardon, as that is not a popular opinion in this country."

I could reach only one conclusion: Mr. Charles Thornfield was improbably born in the Punjab, took medical courses, gained a military commission, and at some point embraced an entirely foreign culture. The master of the house (temporarily, anyhow) was the pitied and often despised sort who had allowed his Britishness to fade in the searing desert sun, politeness and gaslight and snobbery leached into the dunes. During my newspaper scoutings, I had often glimpsed accounts of such hapless folk, as we were forever at war with *somebody:* London was pockmarked with men who professed a respect for the Buddha, women who had converted to — horror of horrors — vegetarianism.

"I shock you, Miss Stone."

I laughed. "You don't, on my life you don't. Which of these are you best with?"

Mr. Singh emitted a happy puff through his nostrils, pointing at one of the shining metal circlets. "That is a *chakkar* — a steel throwing ring honed into a blade. Members of the Khalsa used to hurl these at their foes before enemies rode within striking distance. Now experts are almost unheard-of."

"Save yourself."

"I am considered passable," he demurred, but his eyes sparkled.

My attention snagged upon something still more extraordinary, and I approached where it hung above a rack of billiard cues. The object had a rosewood sword grip; where the blade was meant to emerge, however, a metal band was coiled in upon itself and tied with thick black leather, so that it resembled a hilt attached to a lengthy ribbon of steel wound into a tidy ring.

"What on *earth* . . .?" I stretched to the

tips of my toes to look more closely.

"What excellent taste you have in exotic weaponry, Miss Stone." Instantly I relapsed onto my heels, wondering whether it was too late to affect disapproval. "No, no, I cannot fault your appreciation for what may be the most extraordinary collection of Sikh artefacts in England. This is an *aara,* and only highly advanced warriors are trained in them. Essentially, you regard a combination of a whip and a sword — when unrolled, the metal strip divides flesh as if it were butter. I need hardly add that foolhardy fascination with this weapon leads only to missing fingers or worse."

I allowed my pupils to lose their focus in the *aara*'s shining whorls — half recalling all the times in London when a strange man had approached, the jaundiced light of malice in his eyes, and imagining that I could have snapped the blackguard's head off from twelve feet distant.

"Will you show me, sometime, when your schedule permits?"

"I regret I must decline." Mr. Singh held the door open for me, signalling a need to return to his tasks. "I was once considered formidable with the *aara,* I admit, but fell out of practice. For that pleasurable spectacle, you will have to await the return and good humour of Mr. Thornfield."

"I've finished, I *promise.* Now I must see that Dalbir's hoof has been tended properly."

Five days later, Sahjara and I sat in a converted schoolroom which would have elevated most eyebrows — draperies of orange and amber embroidered with flowering trees lined the walls, conjuring an impossible forest when outside all was grey and snow-softened. There were also chalkboards, paper and ink, drawing utensils, plentiful books, and a pianoforte which look neglected and obligatory.

"If you've finished translating the entire passage, I'll correct it — then of course you may check in on Dalbir."

Sahjara's pony, Dalbir, was named "brave soldier," a moniker I should have thought droll for a pony had he not been more along the lines of a petit dragon, dappled-grey and wonderfully irritable with everyone save Sahjara and myself; the unfortunate beast had suffered a badly chipped hoof that morning.

My pupil ambled over with her French essay, handed me the papers, and then unselfconsciously sat upon the luxurious carpet with her head against my knee.

I patted her awkwardly at first, then drew my fingers over glossy braids smelling of the almond oil she used to smooth out the tangles. Sahjara was demonstrative with everyone, adorably so, and it did not mean anything, I told myself; she probably expected a tyrant, but I recalled tyranny and preferred rebellion. Anyhow, I had neatly solved the problem of attention to her lessons by making each and every subject horse themed. She painted horses in watercolours, explored their anatomy, learnt geography specific to legendary cavalry marches, and translated French passages about horses, as she was doing now.

"We *will* be great friends, won't we?" she mused as I shifted to correct her work.

"I hope so. Did you expect a shrivelled old crone with a cane and a pocket Bible?"

Sahjara shrugged against my calf. "Not precisely. I feared someone who would think me unnatural, though."

This gave me pause, even as I marked an improper conjugation of *avoir:* she was almost exactly the age I had been when I left Highgate House, and Sahjara in five short days had already revealed her character; she was headstrong, impulsive, recklessly affectionate, and had gifted me with thirteen possessions of Mr. Thornfield's to date. What did a murderess four times over care if Sahjara was browner skinned than I, forward in her speech, and was familiar with the housemaids? If surnames were to be taken as given, they could be her aunties for all I knew.

"Would you have seemed unnatural at home — or do you remember?"

"That's a hard question," Sahjara said slowly. "The Punjab comes out all jumbled when I try to remember. I see pictures without any story to them."

"Do any of the pictures stand out?"

"The flap of the tent was ripped by a sword, and I was afraid of who would come through the gap, but it was Charles, and he carried me away and fed me. I was very hungry, I recall. And soon after, I was sent to England for safety's sake. I was five."

Well, there is a remarkable fragment indeed.

I pressed, "Did England improve matters?"

"Oh, yes!" she exclaimed. "Yes, before England, men had always been asking me questions. How was I faring, but also *Where is it?* and I hadn't the faintest, you see, and so kept quiet. Keeping quiet made them very cross."

"I can imagine."

Where is it? is a very specific question.

269

Had Sahjara been caught in the middle of the First Anglo-Sikh War and interrogated at so young an age as five? A startling surge of protectiveness coursed through me. I liked Sahjara and wanted her to erase the other little girl, the one who had wandered these halls suffocating on her aunt's hatred.

"Look, I've scored eighty percent!"

"You have indeed. What were the men looking for?"

"A trunk," said she, taking her translation and glaring at the errors. "It had my dolls in it. Though they couldn't have wanted my dolls, so perhaps they thought something else was inside — there was a terrible row when it went missing, I know. I just wanted my dolls back, as I was only a *chico.*"

"Perfectly natural."

"I was very upset over losing them."

A trunk.

I swear upon my copy of *Jane Eyre* that my interest in Sahjara's tale was based in both fascination and goodwill; I wanted to know more about her, and I badly wanted to know more about Mr. Charles Thornfield, who had callously flouted my poor pupil's request and stayed away longer than a few days.

"What else do you remember?"

Her eyes grew unfocused, as if peering

270

through fogged glass. "Our house in Lahore, its balcony. It smelled like livestock and incense in the streets, which were very busy with all the Afghani horse traders, and the merchants bargaining over oranges and goats, and the fortune-tellers at tables divining from maps of the stars. I remember huge walls with heavy guns, white mosques like turnips." She charmingly screwed her face into a pucker. "It's still an awful muddle. I don't even know what the wars were *for*."

Mindful of my role, I cudgelled my brains and drew embarrassing blanks. The Sikhs' Khalsa army was by all accounts a ferocious one — sharp as a pistol crack, and just as keen to hack our East India Company to bits after the first war ended as they had been at the starting gate. Predictably, they had emerged thirsty for blood two years later, and countless British and Punjabi soldiers had blown one another's pates off before the Sikh Empire went the way of the Roman one. I knew this meant outrageous riches for Her Majesty; when I opened my mouth to unmuddle the situation for my pupil, however, I found I knew nothing whatsoever else.

"Did Mr. Thornfield never recover your trunk?"

"No, though he tried." Sahjara stretched

upon the rug like a lean little cat. "It must be lost forever now."

Voice quite composed, I said, "Sahjara, I know we're strangers, and you needn't speak of your parents, nor the past — but you may if you wish, all right?"

She stood, outlined now against the dimming December sunset, for we had not turned up the lamps. "Oh, were you curious over my parents? Charles says my father was a Company man and my mother a Sikh princess. It's horrid but I can't recall them. There was the sword through the tent flap, and the trunk went missing, and I had horses to tend to, I think — but I don't recall much from the Punjab other than Charles."

Sahjara fetched her warmest cloak from where she had thrown it two hours previous, her governess too slovenly a creature to have noticed.

"Give Dalbir my best," I instructed.

"If Charles returns, send someone to fetch me?"

"Of course."

"Charles likes you," she added as she skipped towards the door. "I've never seen him like anyone so fast. He actually shook your hand."

Following this obscure observation, she

disappeared, and I was left once more to ponder the enigmas of my new household. Then, lacking other occupation and knowing I had an hour till supper, a subtle electric pulse thrumming in my boot soles, I likewise donned my warmest things and quit the main house in the opposite direction, marching silently for my cottage and whatever — whomever — I might find there.

SIXTEEN

It is one of my faults, that though my tongue is sometimes prompt enough at an answer, there are times when it sadly fails me in framing an excuse; and always the lapse occurs at some crisis, when a facile word or plausible pretext is specially wanted to get me out of painful embarrassment.

If you expected to find yourself in a Gothic snowscape, reader, ears tickling with spectral whispers as the plucky protagonist breaks into a cottage haunted by the shades of her past, regrettably you are mistaken.

The door was already unlocked. Opening the panel of the small lantern I had brought, I discovered that my erstwhile home was carpeted in grit and vermin droppings, and furthermore that spiders are the most industrious creatures alive.

Slowly, my ears adjusted; no ticking of

clocks greeted me, no exclamations of alarm. The place had been emptied, and not merely of its few antiques — even the bedding and the better chairs were dispatched. A pang struck me at the thought of faithful, nonsensical Agatha turned out to pasture — or worse, deceased — but I could do her no better service than to press on, so press on I did.

The kitchen was mouldering, the parlour decrepit, my mother's bedroom sacked and empty, which hurt my chest terribly, and still I could not bring myself to quit the place. Creeping up to the garret was a whim; I knew I must be back soon to sit with Sahjara over another brilliantly orange curry, swallowing questions down my gullet.

I will have a peek at the attic space, then be done.

And what did I behold but my mother's old wooden trunk, resting in a corner. I dived for its dust-soft handle and heaved open its lid; an explosion of dry grime and a short stack of letters met my gaze, and my fingers discovered the papers were indeed corporeal. I think I had been half expecting leprechaun gold in that cottage, or at least small, strange men proposing dangerous quests. Instead I held foolscap with ink scrawled over it, ink which might very well tell me what I had inherited and what I might venture to do about it.

To escape with the sole prize I had come seeking, save Agatha herself, seemed altogether too good to be true: but I did, and twenty minutes hence had stowed my treasure under my mattress without a single person knowing I had left the main house at all.

"What became of the original staff?" I asked, sniffing at a plate of heartily spiced potato and cabbage with mustard seeds. "Surely this place was populated by English servants, before."

"I regret to say that they were made to feel rather unwelcome." Mr. Sardar Singh spooned out portions of chicken curry and saffron-scented rice to Sahjara and me; twice before he had dined in our company, and I found myself avidly hoping he would do so again. "We brought with us an unknown master, foreign tastes . . . their defection was natural."

"But never forced?" I questioned, envisioning my elderly Agatha scrubbing floors in some rot-ridden dispensary.

"Of course not — heavens, I hope none of them ever felt so. Some had family they wished to return to, others dreams of travel. They were all of them dismissed with a thousand pounds, after all."

"A thousand . . ." I echoed. It was the sort of money a titled landholder or a City purveyor of stocks might have brought in yearly, and it was a princely figure to a domestic worker.

"Miss Stone, I hope that I haven't overstepped the bounds of English propriety. The figure is irre—"

"Of course it isn't irrelevant — Mr. Thornfield could have got away uncensored distributing bonuses at a hundredth the price."

"The master of the house saw no need to be parsimonious," he returned, but I saw he was pleased.

"Not often the way," I quipped, "with masters. Please do sit down."

Mr. Singh laughed, seating himself several places distant and helping himself to the steaming dishes. "At any rate, there were alterations to be effected, and long-time occupants are always dismayed at usurpers renovating their domain."

Mr. Singh was correct; the cellars, at least, were being subjected to significant changes, and it dismayed me. Workmen arrived before I rose in the morning, greeting me with the distant invisible *clink, clink* of chisels and spades as I walked to the morning room to breakfast with Sahjara; at five in the afternoon when I released her, they filed by me out the servants' entrance, anointed with mineral-smelling mud. Twice had I begun marching down the dank stairs I already knew so well, but a member of the staff always materialised with a cordial *Might I assist you?* and all attempts at reconnaissance rendered thereby impossible.

The work rankled. Our cellars had been inhospitable, the remnants of ancient foundations — neither crypts nor vaults, simply stones and pillars. I did not know what Mr. Thornfield could possibly want with caves not even fit to store wine properly (a failing of which Aunt Patience was surpassingly proud).

"When did the cellar renovations commence?"

"Three months ago," Sahjara replied. "Six months after we moved in and began redecorating — the place was dreadful, all stuffy chintzes."

I smiled, for I agreed with her. "Is the cellar to house a wine collection? Mr. Thornfield seems to own a connoisseur's soul."

"He does indeed," Mr. Singh agreed.

This was less than forthcoming.

"Is it for storage, then? This household —

the exotic spices, the incense — it must be difficult to maintain here in England?"

"Not so difficult as you might imagine. Mrs. Garima Kaur, who is a highly competent individual, travels monthly to London to meet with merchants who import Punjabi essentials. She sees to it that Mrs. Jas Kaur is kept in basmati and dhal and so forth, and the rest we can easily buy from neighbouring farms."

"Then perhaps a Sikh chapel for your rituals?" I ventured next.

"Oh, I'm sure he has plans for the place, Miss Stone." Mr. Singh smiled effortlessly, passing me a dish of what appeared to be yogurt. "I myself shall be contented when these local stonemasons — good men but rather untutored — stop tracking filth through Mrs. Jas Kaur's kitchen. I knew her in the Punjab as a saintly woman, and here in England, she is ready to dissolve into fits."

As am I, I thought, *over lack of headway.*

A few hours later, I washed my face and hung my sober black dress and sat in Aunt Patience's room with the letters from the cottage in my hands, nearly in silent tears already at the prospect of voices from beyond the grave. Wrapping my dressing gown tighter, I edged my chair towards the fireplace. This first missive was written in an older, more palsied version of Agatha's hand:

Dear Missus Jane, supposing ever you return,

Your aunt weren't about to do the job herself, but know that I searched and searched for you. Should you find this, well and good, I've done what I'm meant to. Should you not, I hope no harm to anyone who may come across it.

That school was as awful as awful can be, I'd wager, and I don't fault your quitting the place — send word, and we'll all be just as happy as fish in a lake. I'm to go to —— Court, ——shire to be with my sister, who's always been my elder and thus an old woman now in need of some comfort

This new fellow what owns the estate, Mr. Charles Thornfield, seems both a decent sort and terrible peculiar. He has his winning ways, and his peevish ones, but there's no faulting a soldier for quirks — they catch them abroad, and there's an end to the matter.

Mr. Cyrus Sneeves can explain something of the papers. Write to him should you have any questions, but supposing you want to leave well enough alone, I shouldn't fault you either.

Best of luck always,
Agatha

I examined the rest of the stack. Here were more correspondences between Anne-Laure Steele and Cyrus Sneeves and, like the ones I had read so long ago, they dealt mainly with ensuring our claim to Highgate House; my mother's penmanship appeared next, her faintly accented voice in my ear as I read:

Rue M——,
2nd Arrondissement,
TUESDAY

Dear Mr. Sneeves,
I wish to thank you for having granted me such a thorough understanding of our situation. The difficulty as I see it lies in the honouring of our arrangement in perpetuity. Patience Barbary is dead set against us — and when I imagine myself in her shoes, I cannot bring myself to censure her. *On ne peut rien y faire,* however, and it only remains to discover a trusted party willing to visit consequences upon Mrs. Barbary should

she ever attempt to disinherit my Jane.

Suggestions to this purpose will be met with gratitude; in the meanwhile, please move forward as discussed.

Je vous prie d'agréer,

Mrs. Anne-Laure Steele

The hairs at my nape bristled. My mother had regarded Patience Barbary with as much affection as she held for dung stuck to the sole of a heeled French boot; yet I read a curious reluctance in her wording, regret over the fact Aunt Patience would be angry, which I had never glimpsed in life.

The reply told me little, meanwhile:

Rue du R——,
1st Arrondissement,
WEDNESDAY

Chère Mme. S——

Trust that our regard for Mr. S——'s memory will allow nothing less than perfect diligence regarding this most delicate of subjects. A local agent must be appointed to make real the fact that thwarting our designs will only lead to unpleasantness, and I should be ashamed to suggest anyone of less standing in the firm than my partner, Mr.

Aloysius Swansea. I shall make haste to apprise him of all details, but should you ever require direct contact, he may be found at:
    SNEEVES, SWANSEA, AND TUR-
NER
    No. 29C Lisle Street, Westminster

                                    Humbly,
                        Cyrus Sneeves, Esq.

I think it took me eleven seconds to locate a pen and paper and begin a letter to Mr. Aloysius Swansea:

Highgate House,
December 20, 1851

Dear Mr. Swansea,
    My name is Jane Steele, and I recently came across documents suggesting that you conducted business with my father, Mr. Jonathan Steele, and my mother, Mrs. Anne-Laure Steele. I would be grateful for any information you could give me upon this topic, and should the written form prove too cumbersome, I can travel to London. Letters will reach me here, but I beg that you address them to Miss Jane Stone, as the unfortunate circumstances of my mother's unhappy

end have necessitated caution in revealing my true origins.

Gratefully,
Miss Jane Steele

The remaining correspondence confirmed
what I already knew. I must needs await
further instruction — supposing instruction
would come. Stuffing the papers beneath
my mattress again, I lay down, waiting for
sleep to arrive.

No such guest called, however; ants
seemed to crawl beneath my sheets, and the
dawn greeted a weary soul. Head thinly
humming, I stumbled out of bed and
splashed enough frigid water over my face
to appear human at breakfast.

After all, Mr. Thornfield may have returned.

He had not, though, and I smiled sunnily
at Sahjara across the table, a sealed letter
resting in the pocket of my dress ready to
be posted at my earliest convenience.

Every brittle, branching fork of each bare
tree seemed frost-spangled sculptures worthy of auction at Christie's private parlour
that afternoon. Sahjara had insisted I take
to riding again — in particular a bay mare
far too perceptive for her own good, for she
kept questioning me, and I was not ac-

customed to surrendering the reins to any-one.

The three-year-old bay's name was Nalin, or "lotus," and on the sixth day following Charles Thornfield's departure, she flew over rills and creek beds as if we had crafted a fragile truce. I sincerely hoped so, for I was remembering the beauty of Nature and questioning why I had abandoned it for the narrow streets of a soiled city. Having a horse beneath me again made me feel as if the wide world and myself were more akin than separate, and that as much as I re-mained a poisonous creature, I was related to the contrary being under my legs. Admit-tedly I had no proper riding habit, which vexed me only marginally less than it vexed Sahjara; still, my plain grey governess's disguise, when topped with a cape-backed cloak and a cloth cap, suited well enough for the countryside.

I had given Sahjara a Sunday holiday, so I never thought of returning to Highgate House until my letter had been posted and the sun sagged and the skies — of a wool-len complexion all day — began dusting me with powdery motes of ice. These were not the fat snowflakes one so loves to see in wintertime but the ground glass which stings one's skin, and thus I cut across a familiar clearing to take the road home rather than risking the half-obscured thickets.

The daylight was nigh expired, but the moon had risen, and the lane to Highgate House was scarce ever used save by the occupants — so I never considered how foolhardy it was to steer Nalin into a leap over a stunted hedgerow until it was too late.

We landed, a shadow materialised, and Nalin reared as she emitted a shrill neigh.

My own sharp cry echoed hers as I fought to regain control; but when she bucked the second time, I flew through the air and landed with a heavy thud upon the frozen dirt.

Bloody hell, I thought, and then yelled it aloud, and then enunciated several more expressions learnt in London.

Crunch, crunch, crunch.

The shadow approached me; its steps blended with the mocking trill of the last birds left awake in the thickets.

Had I possessed a superstitious spirit, I should have been terrified to look, lest the traveller prove a goblin or a ghoul. One of the advantages to being a cold-blooded killer, however, was that I thought nothing in the woods much more dangerous than I was, so I heaved myself onto one elbow, panting with shock and exertion.

"Stay back!" As if lightning had illuminated my peril, I realised the footfalls were a man's, and I incapable of flight. "I've no money, and a knife in my skirts!"

Happily, this was nothing save God's truth; a pause ensued, but the menacing steps resumed with greater speed.

Wrenching myself fully up on one arm, I had the blade aimed at the stranger two seconds later; there are commodities some men want on deserted pathways which have nothing to do with currency.

"By all means, come closer, you whoreson bastard," I shouted. "I'll cut you to ribbons and laugh at your funeral!"

"Miss Stone, we haven't been long acquainted, but I had hoped I inspired in you a fonder spirit of camaraderie than *that,*" came a deep, pleasantly grainy voice.

My heart lurched. I forced myself to breathe, replacing my knife in the pocket obscured by the pleat near my waist.

As Mr. Charles Thornfield approached, still snow-obscured save his broad shoulders and the white gleam of his hair beneath his hat brim, I debated whether instantly switching personas would be canny or dense. I had cursed, threatened, and brandished a weapon when I could simply have screamed.

You never scream when you're meant to, you dunce.

"I think I'm hurt." Indeed, my ankle seemed to have burst into flames. "Forgive me, please, I couldn't see you properly. Is Nalin all right? Are *you* all right, sir?"

The muffled clop of hooves sounded, and I glimpsed Mr. Thornfield quickly tethering Nalin's reins to a thick hedgerow branch. Once the mare was secured, his silhouette turned to face me with the moon rising behind him.

"If you never speak to me again, it'll prove difficult to sack me." I rolled to my hands and knees and a bolt of brimstone shot up my leg. *"Oh."*

He strode swiftly towards me. "The devil take your impatience!"

Attempting to stand, I insisted, "I only —"

"Wait a moment or you'll make all worse than it need be. Here, please sit down — *sit.* That's right. Heavens, but you're a feral soul at heart, aren't you? No, stretch your legs out straight."

Sitting upon the ground with icy granules accumulating in the folds of my skirts as I sprawled awkwardly, I allowed Mr. Thornfield to clasp me round the torso. The wind cut at my ears, and the stones bit through my petticoats. It had not been the reunion I had anticipated; in fact, I had amused myself by anticipating every possible reunion, from schoolroom tranquillity to defending the house from marauding seekers of mysterious boxes, save this humiliating one. With him at my back, I managed to get my hands round my knees and wrench both limbs to the front, shaking with effort and pain.

"All right, hush now. We'll be fit to conquer the subcontinent in no time."

"Why hush? I didn't say peep."

This earned me a startled chuckle. " 'Pon my life, there's some truth there. No plans on blubbing, or swooning, or stabbing, come to that?"

"Not at present."

"Capital woman," said he. "Now, I saw how you landed, and damned if it weren't a smasher — feel along your legs to the ankle, very carefully, unless you cannot and wish me to do so."

His scruples, for which I ought to have been grateful, seemed merely irritating. "A highly considerate question coming from a sawbones — I heard you were a medical man, sir."

Mr. Thornfield huffed, still bracing my spine. "And I heard you were a governess, but not many of that set can say *bugger* with quite so much purity of conviction."

A fresh wave of embarrassment washed over me. "I am not yet myself, Mr. Thornfield, but I think my legs remain intact."

"Blast, what a shame! I was so looking forward to having 'em off here in the road. Would've been like old times, I can hear the drum and the fife even now. Make certain all is well, please."

My brains were addled, my pride dented, and my ankle probably sprained, but nothing permanent had befallen me; that is, supposing I did not lose my position upon the morrow.

"All my bones are inside. I do beg your pardon, sir — had it been someone other than you there in the roadway, I don't know what I should have done."

"Called some other whoreson bastard a whoreson bastard, I expect."

Fully five seconds must have passed with my neck craned round to look into his eyes before I burst into helpless laughter. I waited for dismay to manifest, but Mr. Thornfield only smiled crookedly, and I wondered what could produce that lopsided mirth again.

"I'd every right to expect the worst of you," I complained as he lifted me easily upright. "Whatever were you doing out here in the middle of an empty dirt path?"

"I requested the local inn to house Falstaff for the night to take a weight off my conscience, for the old fellow was fatigued enough as was, and I trust them, and my mind needed clearing on the route homeward anyhow. My mind, Miss Stone, is now clear as holy water. Shall we see about getting you home?"

I used Mr. Thornfield's support to take a few steps, nearly gasping at the pangs shooting through my ankle. The joint was already swelling — and I left to the mercy of the man I had just threatened with a pocketknife.

"I think I can ride back," I suggested.

"Yes, come to that, what are you doing jumping hedgerows with one of my most expensive mares?"

"Attempting to prove myself to Sahjara — we study nothing save horses in every subject."

For a few lengthy moments, the only sound was the snow crushing under our soles as I limped towards my disappointed steed; Nalin, one of the most intelligent and yet Puritanical horses I have ever met, tapped her right hoof as if to say, *You are a disgrace.*

"Supposing you desire Sahjara's respect, shall I assume you don't want your corpse to be discovered with a snapped neck?" Charles Thornfield asked, regaining his testiness.

By the time we had reached Nalin, my entire body was confused — an ankle ballooning, breath taut and hoarse, rough but kind fingers imprinted upon my torso, roiling anger in my belly at being caught out in such a pathetic state, a strange echoing sweetness in my ears at, *Shall we see about getting you home?*

"I'll lead Nalin," Mr. Thornfield proposed, linking his fingers together and leaning to make a step for me. "Quick, now, before you indulge the urge to faint at last."

This barbed remark proved all that was necessary to effect a complete cure.

Setting the boot of my uninjured foot in Mr. Thornfield's hands, I hoisted myself onto Nalin. My other ankle pulsed bubbling tar, but it would keep; as jauntily as I could, I dipped my head in imitation of his first snide bow and calculated the distance from the hedgerow to Highgate House.

A quarter of a mile, I thought: close enough for me to make it without danger of falling;

close enough for the master to make it on foot.

"I fear this injury should be seen to speedily, Mr. Thornfield," I called down. "I'll send one of the grooms back to fetch you."

With this insane parting jibe, already anticipating my return to London and imminent penury, I set off on my master's horse for my own ancestral house.

Seventeen

I both wished and feared to see Mr. Rochester on the day which followed this sleepless night: I wanted to hear his voice again, yet feared to meet his eye.

I retired straight to my aunt's former room wretchedly humiliated and at once sipped at the laudanum bottle I had packed as a precaution against melancholy or sudden disaster. I awoke to an ankle blazing like a lighthouse beacon, a small breakfast tray of broth and cold green rice, and a folded communiqué written in Sahjara's friendly scrawl:

Dear Miss Stone,
Thank you for seeing to Nalin, as I was ever so worried when I heard there was an accident and the more so for your sake but I was yet glad you returned her to the stables unharmed though you

294

were harmed yourself. Charles has returned! Happy day! He says not to disturb you, but only send you this note and ask that you ring for Mrs. Kaur when you awaken so she might treat your ankle properly and he won't let me see you as he says you must rest but know I am thinking of you every second.

Very sincerely affectionately
and kindly,
Sahjara Kaur

This brought a smile to my face; but, hark — here was another missive below the first, penned on much more masculine paper and in a matching hand:

Dear Miss Stone,

As you refused my offices so far as to flee the scene entirely and barricade yourself against enemy encroachment, I will not crudely offer them again but rather suggest that Mrs. Garima Kaur has a working practical knowledge of the whereabouts of the human ankle and a steady hand, since I've no wish to further alarm you. A repast has been provided, lest your strategy be to remain in your fortifications, but I assure you that should you emerge under the white flag

of truce, the natives — though savage
and frankly even heathen — will greet
you with unparalleled interest.

Your servant,
Charles Thornfield

Groaning aloud did me no tangible good,
reader: and yet, groan aloud I did. I rolled
over with a twofold whimper — half because
it hurt my ankle, half because stupidity
(particularly my own) hurts my heart.

Knock, knock, knock.

"Just a moment," I called.

A glance at the ivory light through the
window told me it was already ten if not
later; duly considerate of my responsibili-
ties, I stepped out of bed and promptly collapsed.

The door flew open to reveal Mrs. Garima Kaur's feet. If feet could be amused, I
have no doubt but that her toes would have
laughed, such was the indignity of my position.

"All right?" she asked, eyes narrowing.

"No," I admitted.

She entered, tension marring the straight
sweep of her scar. After she had got me
safely seated on the rumpled bedclothes,
she searched my face; this was not simple
concern, but rather a critical study — or

perhaps I only thought so because her own physiognomy was so very apparent, her face resembling nothing so much as a handsomely clothed skull. Though she spoke English poorly, Mrs. Kaur's eyes positively radiated intellect, and I wondered what heights of nuance she could achieve in her native tongue.

"Hurt with Mr. Thornfield?" she prodded.

"No, he found me in a ditch." I pushed my posture straight with my fists. "I was hurt *near* Mr. Thornfield. He was unhurt, thank God."

"You . . . not want his help? Do not like him?"

Answering this question truthfully would have been impossible. "I don't like anyone at the moment. Save you, I think, depending on what you have there."

"Poultice." She lifted one hand. "Bandages," she added, raising the other.

"Bless you," I sighed, relief provoking bald sentiment.

"Do not worry," she answered quietly, casting her eyes down.

Some ten minutes later, Mrs. Kaur had gifted me with medical attention, and spiced tea I enjoyed very much, and a crutch I did not in the least appreciate.

"Ready?" she asked when I had fully

297

dressed with her assistance and regained a bit of my colour.

"As I will ever prove," I agreed.

I walked step-thunk, step-thunk, step-thunk down the narrow carpeted strip upon the staircase. I was terrified to meet Mr. Thornfield; when I had not been pathetic the night previous, I had been glib, and when I had not been glib, I had been obstreperous, a truly heady concoction of undesirable traits.

Upon my arrival in the dining room, however, I discovered the household preoccupied; where I imagined my disaster of the night previous would be the sole topic, instead I found master and ward glaring daggers at an unknown person — one who beamed at my arrival and half stood, making an awkward bow.

"Augustus Sack!" he exclaimed, offering a pudgy hand. "Mr. Augustus P. Sack, and this can be no one save Miss Jane Stone. Might I be pardoned for expressing my *absolute* delight that you've rallied valiantly enough to join us for a late breakfast?"

Propping my crutch against the chair's arm, I clasped his clammy fingers. "Pleased to meet you, Mr. Sack." I sat, wincing.

"The captive emerges," Mr. Thornfield drawled. "What can she have been through, this poor prisoner, trapped behind enemy lines after such a daring escape?"

The tone may have been gently needling; but he was up in an instant to fetch me a tasselled footstool, which he deftly slid under the table, where I might take advantage of it.

"Oh, Miss Stone!" Sahjara commiserated. She was clad in sage green with her dark hair hanging loose. "When I imagine what could have happened to you — it's *too* dreadful."

"My dear Young Marvel," Mr. Thornfield put in, seating himself, "what *could* have happened was my trampled corpse, followed by a closed-coffin ceremony."

"Charles, don't!" Tossing her head, Sahjara added under her breath, "He thinks because he served in campaigns in the Punjab, he has the right to be dramatic."

"He does indeed, and correctly so!" Mr. Sack spoke in the style of a compliment; it was received in the manner of an insult, however, for Mr. Thornfield's eyes furiously darted to the pine trees just visible at the top of the windows, and there they remained.

"Well, I feel as terrible about what could have happened to Mr. Thornfield as he does — anyhow, I'm fine, Sahjara." I lifted my napkin as Mrs. Jas Kaur appeared, placing fried breakfast cakes smelling of rose water upon my plate.

"Miss Stone is undoubtedly fine," Mr. Thornfield agreed, "or we should be informed otherwise in highly colourful language."

I promptly redirected attentions. "You arrived this morning, Mr. Sack?"

"You are as observant as you are beautiful, Miss Stone, I state so with absolute conviction."

Hardly a compliment.

Mr. Augustus Sack was a portly fellow — tan as Mr. Thornfield, but budding pink at the crests of his cheeks, the tips of his ears, and the end of his nose. He wore a dark green jacket with a brown velvet waistcoat, accented by an emerald tie, and if he wished to appear more thoroughly English, I honestly have no notion how he would have gone about working the miracle. His face was a plump oval, beaming relentlessly, and this disturbed me, for Mr. Thornfield looked enraged and Sahjara ill.

"Have you some business with Mr. Thornfield, or may I congratulate you upon a trip devoted to pleasure?"

He chuckled, an oily sound. "I fear it is a private matter. Old friends, you understand,

and what with Mr. Thornfield having so recently taken possession of this magnificent estate — I absolutely had to see him, and dear Sahjara as well."

Mr. Thornfield's fingers tensed as if a poisonous insect had appeared, one in need of smashing.

"I thought it had been some nine months since," I observed.

"Correct, as you doubtless always are, Miss Stone. I encountered Thornfield here at my former assistant Mr. John Clements's funeral four days ago; I was *most* distressed that he had not sought me out sooner, as I've been back in London since August."

Mr. Thornfield threw down his napkin. "That's the worst thing about funerals — not only is someone you once liked dead, but there's an indecorous number of people you don't like swarming about."

Augustus Sack only smiled; if a grubworm had smiled, it would have looked similar.

"I should have offered you condolences, had I been aware," I ventured to Mr. Thornfield.

"Are you offering 'em now, or merely filling uncomfortable silences?"

It would have been easy to take offence at this, but the master of the house took no pleasure in the dig himself. His long white hair was neatly tied, his collar and jacket perfect, his slab jaw smooth — but he ought to have been regaling our houseguest over tales of my clumsiness, and instead he appeared almost frightened.

Augustus Sack began to nod as if a profound point had been made. "Miss Stone, Thornfield here values discretion to the point that he errs on the side of secrecy. Mr. John Clements was my assistant, as I mentioned already — he was most instrumental in helping Thornfield regain his health following the Battle of Sobraon. Four of us, in fact, were close as brothers during the first war, serving at the behest of the Director: Thornfield, myself, Clements, and a David Lavell, who was Sahjara's father."

When I turned to her in surprise, Sahjara's face was angled downward. "I don't remember him at all. It's *shameful.*"

"That's the least shameful facet of your character, you magnificent nitwit." Mr. Thornfield rapped his knuckles twice against the table. "Sack, I must suggest that, having conveyed your best greetings, you now —"

"It pains me to think how few of us remain from the small set of British in Lahore before the regime fell." Mr. Sack affected an air of wisdom, but it looked merely as if he were about to sneeze. "Matters were so confused — who was friend, and who foe? Who amongst the Khalsa did not scheme, and who amongst the Company did not plot?"

The master of the house pushed back his chair. "We aren't discussing this here," he said, but it was his teeth speaking, pressed tight with rage.

"Of course, your . . . unusual closeness to Sikh affairs rendered your own judgement so much more *nuanced* than that of the other members of the British regime. I know the Director always thought so."

"Stop talking in riddles, it's nauseating. I don't have what you're after, so what more do you want from me, damn you?" Mr. Thornfield's fist clenched as it struck the table, but a distressed sound from Sahjara caused him to soften a second later.

"Want?" Mr. Sack swivelled his pink countenance, smirking. "Only to reminisce — poor John Clements's death, oh, you'll find it excessively sentimental, but I couldn't bear to think your own call to immortality might come, Thornfield, with so much left unsaid between us."

"Mr. Sack, your carriage has been brought round front."

Mr. Sardar Singh stood at the end of the

dining table with his hands clasped behind him, wearing a sympathetic frown as if he were the bearer of unfortunate news. Sahjara shifted, eyes darting anxiously, whilst Mr. Thornfield's expressive face set in a look of quiet determination.

"Ah, there you are," Mr. Augustus Sack purred. "What's this talk of carriages? No indeed, I've a great deal to discuss with you both."

"Your coachman is under unequivocal instructions to take you wherever you should care to go."

"Of all the — *whose* unequivocal instructions, you scoundrel?" Mr. Sack snarled. "Confound it, you're the entire reason I —"

"Mine, sir."

The already stifling tension twined about our necks. Mr. Sack spluttered, then emitted a laugh which sounded like the yapping of a wild fox.

"Thornfield, any man who once juggled so many export concerns is doubtless most effective at household management, but is this really your idea of a proper butler? His joke is in decidedly poor taste."

"Do you know, Sardar hardly ever jokes," Mr. Thornfield replied, shaking his head sadly. "A deficit in foreign breeding, I've always assumed."

"I am remiss in the arena of humour more than any other." Sardar Singh placed one hand regretfully over his heart.

"That man could run an empire, but when it comes to puns? Satirical drolleries? He's positively dismal."

"After many fruitless attempts at improvement, I have abandoned hope."

"What the hell are you two playing at?" Mr. Sack snarled.

A natural unspoken understanding crackled among Mr. Thornfield and Mr. Singh and Sahjara, fast and ferocious as a thunderstorm, and I felt a surge of irrational jealousy.

"A brick," said Mr. Thornfield, the glimmer of a wicked smile now lurking behind his mouth, "could be on display in the warm glow of the stage footlights and garner more chuckles than Mr. Sardar Singh."

"You will *rue the day* you ever dreamt of mocking me," Mr. Sack growled, lurching up.

"No, no, that's the crux of the thing!" Mr. Thornfield cried. "When Mr. Singh says that your carriage is ready —"

"And that you are about to travel away in it," the butler added, idly examining his fingernails.

"Then it's absolutely inevitable."

It happened so quickly that I must have blinked and missed it — one second, Mr. Augustus Sack's rosy cherub's cheeks were purpling, and the next, all the blood drained from his visage as he beheld the knife in Mr. Singh's hand.

"You pack of bloody infidels!" Mr. Sack cried. "Do you honestly think you can threaten a Company man?"

"Oh, 'pon my word, yes." Mr. Thornfield had risen now, and another knife glinted from his slack, practiced grip.

"Don't test them," Sahjara warned, arm extended, and I saw that what I had always imagined merely a silver hair ornament was also a blade.

"Sahjara!" I threw out a protective forearm.

"Miss Stone has a knife too, Sack," Mr. Thornfield drawled. "It's part of our dress uniform, don't y'know."

"You cannot seriously intend to defy me!" Mr. Sack backed towards the door, soft hands trembling. Strangely, he seemed to address Mr. Singh.

"It's as serious as a Turkish prison," Mr. Thornfield hissed.

"I'll have it out of you one way or another," Mr. Sack spat, jabbing a finger at Sahjara. "That nasty puppet —"

"Get out," Mr. Singh commanded, and now his voice was harder than the metal in his hand. "I'll not ask again."

Mr. Augustus Sack bared his teeth and turned on his heel. For several tightly stretched seconds we waited; then the grind of carriage wheels reached our ears, and I snatched up my crutch and limped to the window, staring with Sahjara under my arm as the neat black coach exited the grounds of Highgate House.

Faintly, I asked, "Do many of your guests depart at knifepoint?"

"Oh, I should not say *very* many." Mr. Singh sat, drawing a pot of porridge near and spooning himself a portion. "But when they do, inevitably I find my appetite improved."

We were all quiet, a quiet as odd and yet as comfortable as any I had ever experienced, before I succumbed to helpless laughter. Mr. Thornfield likewise chuckled, and pressed his glove to Sahjara's temple when she went to him, sliding the silver comb back into her hair.

When his eyes met mine, however, they were grave blue pools — I confess myself likewise sobered, and my ankle began to send invisible darts into my calf.

Mrs. Garima Kaur appeared, short of

breath and eyes flashing. She fired off a rapid series of questions to Mr. Singh in their own language; his replies did not seem to please her, however, for she snarled and gestured at the outer door. Mr. Thornfield interjected in the same tongue, but she would have none of him, aiming another volley at Mr. Singh. When he had reassured her once more, she hissed in frustration and quit the dining room.

"Garima is understandably unsettled — Augustus Sack labours under the delusion we have something of value. A trunk of Sahjara's went missing long ago, and the deuced cur can't cease thinking on it," Mr. Thornfield said to me quietly, causing my ears to prick. "Our friend John Clements's death dredged all this up again — the ghastly affair is long past, but Sack is equal parts cunning and stupidity, a combination peculiar to a certain breed of East India Company executive, damn 'em. I apologise, Miss Stone. Had I not been cowering before the tip of your own blade last night, I should perhaps have worried over offending your notion of a civil breakfast."

"I can't even remember why I don't like him." Sahjara's eyes were wide and wet. "It was all so long ago and far away. I don't like him, though."

"There's the Young Marvel for you — sharp as a bayonet." Mr. Thornfield framed her cheeks with clothed palms.

"Was I awful, though — ought I to like him?"

"You don't like him, darling. You like him as much as you like black pudding. Are you all right?"

"Yes, I think so. Miss Stone's accident, Mr. Sack coming to call — it's too many troubles at once," she lamented, drying her eyes with Mr. Thornfield's kerchief.

"So often the way," Mr. Singh said under his breath, "with troubles."

"Sardar?" Mr. Thornfield said softly.

"Mr. Thornfield."

"Might I speak a word in your ear — say, after supper, in the drawing room?"

"Nothing could please me more." Mr. Singh ducked his frothy beard to us, cleared his small bowl of porridge, placed the remaining soiled china on a tray, and disappeared.

For several seconds, I stood at a complete loss as to how a human being should behave under these specific circumstances; thankfully, Mr. Thornfield spoke.

"Sahjara, I require your absence. Flee, fly, flit. I need to speak with Miss Stone about a few cautions relevant to the new mare you're to begin riding on Monday." Mr. Thornfield smiled, and it struck me that when he was not bored over his own jokes, his smiles were as warm as a fireside.

"Truly? Oh, thank you, *thank* you! That is, if you think me capable."

"What is she playing at?" Mr. Thornfield pressed his fingertips to the bridge of his nose in mock chagrin. "Young Marvel, thank you for defending me against a *bad-mash*.* Now be gone, that I might inform Miss Stone of your new riding regimen."

Sahjara curtsied, so happy her head might have split from her grin, and quit the room.

I went to the window, attempting to calm myself; but hardly had I arrived before I saw the master hesitantly approaching, a stiff-backed reflection in the prophetic windowpane.

"Miss Stone, are you quite well?"

His awkwardness put me at once at my ease. "Very well, sir. How are you?"

"Oh, don't mimic my pretences to English manners, for God's sake, it's hardly sporting." Flashing a grim smile, he continued, "You've questions, no doubt; and I am willing to trade the commodity, for though I did seek an *unusual* governess —"

---

* Villain.

"You hadn't anticipated the scope of my abnormality." I sought the cool of the glass and leant my head against it, as much to mask my fright as in genuine fatigue.

You've scarce had time to dash off a letter to your mother's solicitor and you're already being tossed back into the gutter.

"And therefore I propose you dine with me this evening."

"Of course, I can hardly blame —" I broke off. "You propose what?"

"Dining. You've, ah, heard of the practice? It takes place in the evening hours more generally — at least, north of the Sutlej it does."

"Mr. Thornfield," I announced, "you owe me dinner at the very least over the vast number of weapons displayed just now."

"Of course." A peculiarly endearing crease appeared at the edge of his right eye, encroaching upon his temple. "I've had a blow, Miss Stone. Sack's appearance was entirely unexpected. I should never have wished you to see —"

"I accept your invitation with great enthusiasm, sir."

Mr. Thornfield crossed his arms as I limped towards the hall.

"There have already been multiple moments which cause me to suspect your true self a giant deliberately casting a small shadow," he reflected just as my crutch passed the threshold.

Pausing, I struggled to reply.

"Oh, never fear the ramblings of a former soldier, Miss Stone." He drew a hand over his neck exhaustedly. "We're cracked to a man. Go on, I've business to attend to."

So I shuffled, step-thunk, step-thunk, out of the room and away, reflecting upon the three most immediate tasks before me:

— comfort Sahjara and learn what you can of what threatens this household
— navigate dinner with Mr. Thornfield
— learn to walk silently upon a sprained ankle and thereby perhaps learn a very great deal indeed afterwards

I lay atop my quilt for twenty minutes, taking tiny sips of laudanum, fretting that not only did I understand nothing of the workings of Highgate House but also that I possessed no precedents to guide me.

Are small girls always as formidable as Sahjara? I wondered.

Perhaps they were not; but I had been. The fact that we shared a particular home at a particular age was accidental; how then did I find it so binding, as if she were my responsibility not due to the lie which had brought me here but the truth I was discovering — that I liked these people and wished for them to like me in return?

When is a butler not really a butler?

Gingerly, I flexed my foot. My experience apart from London and Lowan Bridge School, each savage places, was limited to Mamma's midnight picnics beneath the rustling leaves. At the thought of a butler ejecting a guest, however, and all the happy times Sardar Singh had sat with Sahjara and me whilst Mr. Thornfield was gone — something irregular was afoot. And what was Mr. Singh, if he was not the butler?

What has Mr. Augustus Sack to do with a trunk missing from the Punjab?

This seemed a rather more dangerous question, but one which required answering — and to that end, I sat upon the edge of my bed and shifted my weight until I stood fully.

"Bugger," I gasped.

Hobbling as far as my mirror was excruciating; leaning against the edge of the dressing table, I examined myself. At twenty-four, I had not gone far towards matching my mother's undomesticated beauty, and thus I did not often seek my own reflection. My dark hair still undulated irregularly no matter how much care I took in pinning it up, my eyes were as large as a feline's but still the same plain brown, and my face still invited comparisons to the enchanted creatures which left England long ago.

I pinched the colour back into my cheeks, as I had no wish to alarm Sahjara further . . . not when I was so badly in need of answers and she the best purveyor of that precious, perilous commodity. The past, no one knows better than myself, is a silent stalker, and I headed for the schoolroom with the express intention of seeing her pursuer more plain.

EIGHTEEN

"I see, at intervals, the glance of a curious sort of bird through the close-set bars of the cage: a vivid, restless, resolute captive is there; were it but free, it would soar cloud-high."

"Oh, that was so dreadful — and I didn't understand what Charles meant by joking that you had a knife, but I hope you aren't vexed." Sahjara had put on a brave face, but I insisted that we were too rattled for lessons; so we sat in the bow window, pillows stuffed behind our backs, our feet tangled together like schoolmates, gazing at the grounds.

I pulled the small folding blade from my pocket and tossed it once, quickly returning the weapon to its hiding place. "It wasn't a joke — London is dangerous. As for Mr. Sack, he was most insolent to your guardian."

Sahjara rolled her head against the wall tiredly. "He is not Sikh like Mr. Singh and Mr. Thornfield and myself, only an East India Company man."

"I meant to ask whether knives were de rigueur for your people," I teased.

"Oh goodness, yes! The pure ones wear five articles of faith."

"Your comb is a religious symbol? And the metal bracelets as well?"

"Yes, these are the *kanga* and the *kara* — the comb and the wristband. We're also meant to wear a short sword called a *kirpan,* but here in England we find knives more convenient because even though the wars are over, we must remain invisible. And Charles says that if we have to hide in plain sight, then we must make allowances over what will make us look noteworthy to Britons, and fix the symbols to suit us here in England. At first Sardar was a bit uncomfortable over changing tradition, but later he agreed since the *kachera* — those are our knee breeches — would make us look absolutely ridiculous here, Charles says, and God is in the Guru after all, not in outward forms."

We must remain invisible, I thought, wondering at her words. *We have to hide in plain sight.*

316

"You said five?" I asked aloud.

"Oh yes, long hair — *kesh.*"

"It looks more natural on you and Mr. Singh than it does on Mr. Thornfield."

Sahjara regarded me with the eyes of a kitten tracking a string. "I've never seen him without it, so I couldn't say. But I do think Charles handsome — don't you?"

"He's everything a gentleman ought to be, I'm sure." Unsettled, I cast my eyes out at the lingering snowfall, the spun-sugar dust coating the bare limbs of the trees. "Are his gloves also religious, then?"

My charge frowned. "I don't think so."

"Perhaps they could hide burns or marks?"

"Heavens, that would be awful." She shrugged. "I almost forget they're there. They must look awfully peculiar to an Englishwoman."

Englishwoman, I thought warmly; now I knew more of their history, the appellation was magnificently sensible, as they all originated in the Punjab and regarded me as the foreigner.

"Mr. Singh and Mr. Thornfield seem like fast friends."

"Yes, they grew up together!" Sahjara smiled, tapping the edge of her boot against my skirts. "Charles was born in Lahore, you know, and Sardar — well, that isn't his name, but anyhow — Sardar's family traded in indigo and jaggery. They were frightfully rich before the wars."

"Sardar isn't his name?" I repeated, mystified.

"Oh, no." Sahjara hopped out of the window, idly twirling her skirts. "All that rubbish Charles was talking about Sardar being incapable of jokes couldn't be further from the truth. Mr. Thornfield said that for us to live without much remark here in England, he would have to be the butler, and he changed his name not ten seconds later to mean 'high commander.' May I just run downstairs and see whether Dalbir's hoof is any better? Mr. Sack's visit left me so flustered that I might almost have forgot."

"This soup is delicious."

I sat across from Mr. Thornfield in the dining room. After admonishing myself not to gape, I reminded myself *you've never been here before,* and then gaped as I pleased. Every placid English landscape in which the dogs had contemplated the sheep and the sheep contemplated the dogs was replaced with decorative mirrors. There were as many gilt-edged and silver-embossed mirrors as there were days upon a calendar, multiplying us ad infinitum until there were a thousand Jane Steeles and a thousand Charles Thornfields.

"Is it?" he answered.

Mr. Thornfield's voice, I noted, sounded much the richer for what it did not say. It occurred to me that I wanted to know what his favourite summer had been like, whether it happened in England or the Punjab, hot desert sandscapes versus gleaming green afternoons, and then it occurred to me this topic was egregiously far afield from my true mission.

I waited for him to speak; no overtures were forthcoming.

"I think the weather will hold now the snow has stopped — don't you?"

Mr. Thornfield chuckled. He wore a swallowtail coat and a thick rust-coloured cravat — which I thought hardly fair, since my best governess disguise was a drab thing of dove-grey satin striped with a cream pattern and topped with a high lace collar, and it is beastly to be seated across from a bluntly handsome fellow when one looks about as captivating as gravel. Had we been in London, and I my nefarious self, I would have found a secondhand dress of rose silk and filled my hair with tiny yellow tea roses.

"Though of course, your estate is charming covered in white — it looks like a fairy-land."

When again Mr. Thornfield said nothing, I smiled, my heart shivering in my chest; was he wary, even angry? He returned the amiable look, however, and I reached for a second helping of the blistered bread Mr. Singh had left.

"I imagined that you would be more talkative since you seemed eager to speak with me, sir."

"Good Lord, no — that would be dreadful strategy." Mr. Thornfield poured me more claret. "I've a knack for silence. I'll remain quite closemouthed and simply await developments."

"May I ask why?"

"Well, I've two topics on my mind — but if you truly would rather pretend all governesses carry knives, then I admit England would be the livelier for it. And if you won't mention the fact that priggish Company executives aren't often driven out of breakfast rooms with the same weapon, then I choose the topic of soup over snow."

I wished that I could have been Jane Steele and laughed, and flirted; since I was Jane Stone, however, I chose my words with care. "I cannot explain the latter, but I will certainly explain why I carry a knife."

Charles Thornfield's sun-burnished face gave me the sly look of encouragement I have seen many rogues attempt, all having failed miserably by comparison.

I sat forward. "Mr. Thornfield, I am here under false pretences."

The master of the house angled his bull-ish chin at me and took a generous sip of wine.

Lies, honest reader, are organic — they can shift from outright falsehoods into half-truths and even truths, generally when you like the person to whom you are lying, in the way wormlike creatures become but-terflies out of sudden inspiration. I was inspired on that evening by knives and tiny paintings and the fond glances Sahjara and Mr. Thornfield and Mr. Singh all cast at one another.

"To boot, I am probably not fit to be a governess."

Mr. Thornfield snorted sceptically.

"My initial letter to you was correct in every salient particular, of course — I at-tended a school called Lowan Bridge." My heart beat a hornet's-wing tattoo. "But I did not mention that, when I was young, I was accosted in an ungentlemanly manner by my cousin. I think his presumptuousness and later our headmaster's cruelty may have endowed me with a certain fear of men. I go armed due to these experiences. I have been called many things, Mr. Thornfield — pigheaded, wayward, brazen — and yet, no one feels the grievousness of my shortcomings more keenly than I." Unexpectedly raw-voiced, I stopped.

It was hardly a thorough confession; it was a gift, however, a small piece of my saga. If gaining his regard meant I turned over my entire history, I could never oblige the gentleman — but I could proffer a biography with neither shadows nor colours, a vague outline of the person I wanted him to know but did not dare to reveal. Should I expose all, he would surely hate me, and then where would I find myself?

If Mr. Thornfield was mortified, I never saw it; instead, he shifted with a thoughtful finger edging his temple.

"You'll want to know about the swearing as well?" I asked timidly.

Mr. Thornfield laughed — the laugh of a soldier who has brushed the sands of the Sutlej from his trousers, told jokes which should have made any woman blush. "Of course I want to know about the swearing — it was damned expertly done."

My pulse tingled in the tips of my fingers. "When I left school, I went to London because I'd no family who would take me. Have you any experience with distant relations yourself, Mr. Thornfield?" I added slyly, gesturing at our surroundings.

"This place was empty when we took possession, and we should not be here had it been otherwise, Miss Stone." He shrugged, watching his wine swirl gently. "At the risk of sounding a deuced ingrate, it was a stroke of luck not to have made their acquaintance, if y' follow."

"Of course," I hastened to assure him, fearful of pressing. "I quite understand and meant only that penury requires one to live among coarse people, which is the other reason I carry a knife, and the reason I have an atrocious vocabulary — if you worry that I might endanger your ward, Mr. Thornfield, having already endangered your person, I cannot blame you; but I can admit I am not a typical governess and hope that my present candour brings you some mollification."

I awaited judgement as if being sentenced to Newgate.

Mr. Thornfield let his spoon clatter to the dish with a ring of finality. "If you think I'm intimidated by your weaponry, you've clearly not visited the billiards room. And there are practically stars in the Young

Marvel's eyes when she speaks of you, so . . . consider me mollified. You must feel odd being the only knife-brandishing governess outside of London?"

I tipped my glass to him, endlessly thankful he could not see my knees knocking.

"Yes, sir. You must feel odd being the master of a Sikh stronghold in the English countryside."

"Pish — when I feel odd, it's certainly not on that account, as I'm hardly the master of anything. You've ridden Nalin, you know of which I speak. I could threaten to have the whole pack of these lunatics, horse and human alike, sold for glue, and they'd all laugh in my face."

"And how," I ventured, my nerves calming fractionally, "did that strange circumstance come to pass?"

His severely arcing brows tensed below the pristine hair. "Frankly, I find myself a terrible topic for conversation."

"I feel the same about myself, but I'm deeply interested in your household. How did you come to be acquainted with Mr. Singh, for instance?"

The tension in his shoulders melted. "We were practically schoolfellows, before. Shall I be shocking, Miss Stone?"

"Oh, yes, please."

"Where on earth did she come by the cheek? London alone couldn't have managed the feat," Mr. Thornfield muttered. "You are aware from the advertisement I was involved in the Khalsa conflicts. You may know that I was born in Lahore?"

Silence befitted Mr. Thornfield; so I tried it out myself, blankly encouraging.

"Well, how I came to be born there prior to British annexation is brief in telling and rather broad in ripple effect generally, so I'll out with it: my parents were complete scoundrels, Miss Stone."

"Mr. Singh said your father was an entrepreneur?"

"So are pirates, according to the dictionary."

I laughed until I could hardly breathe. Mr. Thornfield rumbled with amusement himself until I had calmed.

"Nathan Thornfield — that's my father, mind you keep up — started life as a merchant in the loosest sense of the word," Mr. Thornfield continued. "Genteel as a baronet, all polished monocles and pinches of snuff. But really, he was what romantics call an adventurer and cynics a rapscallion. Travelled like the pox — Australia, China, even America, the daft old crust. The codger ought to have been locked in a cage lined with pillows, if you take my meaning, but instead he made and lost several fortunes before settling in the Punjab with my mother, née Chastity Goodwill, and if that name don't beat the Dutch, Miss Stone, the Dutch will rule the globe."

Patience Goodwill and Chastity Goodwill. My pulse thumped against my drab grey dress as I recalled my aunt's maiden name. *Sisters — there is the connection.*

"Mum wasn't *quite* mad, by the by," he added wryly. "She must sound so, gallivanting about like that with a complete knave. But the yellow fever had got hold of her altogether, and she was a passionate collector — Chinese vases, Bengali silks. When my father decided that Lahore was absolutely the ticket, I believe he bartered their way into the Punjab with French wine and Turkish opium; the Sikhs were sceptical, and he conducted one or two discussions on the wrong side of a *tulwar.*★ Once he was in, they realised he'd a positive genius for getting them anything they wanted, and the Sikhs ain't Quakers, mind. A hotter hive of lechery and treachery you've not seen since the Vatican."

"It sounds dangerous."

★ Sikh sword.

"So does war." This time his words boxed my ears gently. "But people do it anyhow."

"Were Mr. Singh's family your neighbours, sir?"

"Indeed so. My family was in the import-export line, and Sardar's were trading indigo and suchlike."

"I think he said jaggery?" I lied, for Sahjara had told me.

"Yes! Great brown cakes of sugar and great blue cakes of indigo, and they were so rich they could have used solid gold piss pots if they'd — Oh, I beg your pardon."

"You really needn't, you understand."

Mr. Thornfield coughed, amused. "I am beginning to. Well. We grew up playing at cavalry in the streets of Lahore, daring each other to run beneath the legs of the war elephants when the Khalsa paraded, quarrelling like fishwives over which had to be the villainous Afghan and which the conquering maharajah, manly pursuits of that sort. Sardar would —"

"I've been given to understand that is not his actual name?"

"Oh, a snake in the grass! You've clearly been pumping the Young Marvel for gossip."

I might have quailed, but Mr. Thornfield's tone remained a happy one, a low instrument playing in a major key, as was ever the case when he spoke of his ward.

"She gushes with the substance when the poor girl remembers anything of those days; but in this case, she is entirely correct. Mad as a crate of ferrets, Sardar, and if he was going into domestic work, by gad, he meant to do it in style. What could I do but shrug my shoulders and call the man Commander?"

"Mr. Singh possesses a magnetic presence. He seems a very decent sort."

"He's a saint is what he is, and we were very close as boys, and after I returned to the Punjab, we didn't fancy the notion of parting. Have you ever had a friend, Miss Stone, and thought that if this particular person were absent, you should forever miss a piece of yourself?"

I remembered my quiet, quizzical Clarke and nodded.

"Well, Sardar may not have always called himself Sardar, but he has always been extraordinarily good to me. He took great pains to see the stuffing wasn't thrashed out of me when I was a stripling in Lahore — and he has made certain that Sahjara was safe, always, no matter the circumstance."

"Was it during the wars that Mr. Singh took risks for Sahjara?" I asked with care.

"Yes. We were not at war, however, when he took risks for me." Mr. Thornfield smirked, tapping the tablecloth with gloved hands. "I'm not certain whether fighting or fornicating is the skill Sikhs have mastered the better, but they work terribly hard at both, y'see, and thus as a young *wilayati*,* I had plentiful scuffles to survive."

"Do not Easterners wish to befriend the British in the interests of trade?"

Mr. Thornfield twisted his lips. "Nothing like a friend for a knife in the back."

"Is that true of Mr. Augustus Sack?"

Mr. Thornfield hesitated; but at last he bit the inside of his cheek, shrugging.

"Fair play, Miss Stone — it's only proper etiquette to explain sudden confrontations with knives, as you have so kindly done for me. Mr. Sack and our dead friend Mr. Clements and Sahjara's father, Mr. Lavell, were all Company men when the conflict with the Sikhs broke out. So was I, nominally anyhow. To say the Sikh empire was rich is to say the sun does a jolly decent job at lighting the planet. Mr. Sack figures that some ripe booty which scarpered off God knows where can be found if only he plunders the Young Marvel's head, and I won't

* Foreigner.

329

have it. Neither will Sardar, as you saw. And that's all I have to say on the blasted subject. Oh, look, here's Mrs. Kaur with the roast."

The cover was lifted, the air flooded with cinnamon-spiced mutton, and not another word would Mr. Thornfield speak regarding adventures abroad. Instead he spoke of the new mare, and warned me lest Sahjara knock her head off, and pretended that he had just told me everything I desired to know.

Through it all the gloves remained; and I watched him, riveted.

My instant fascination with Charles Thornfield puzzled no one so profoundly as myself. I had taken enough lovers to know that he was not conventionally handsome, his visage too worn with crags of care to compare with my strapping young working lads. Come to that, he was acerbic and peculiar in equal measure, and he could raise an eyebrow as if raising a middle finger.

I had already borne firsthand witness to his capacity to love, however, thanks to his ease with his ward and the heightened circumstance of Mr. Sack's visit, and as a needy, greedy thing, I was curious as to how one would go about stealing a fraction of it.

"Good night, Miss Stone, and do take

care with your ankles," was his send-off when we had finished. I think courtesy — even his rough version of it — had exhausted him. "Should you ever desire a bigger knife than that hatpin you're carrying, seek out the billiard room."

Smiling, I returned his farewell and made a great racket with my crutch as I went upstairs.

For Mr. Thornfield intended to meet with Mr. Singh after supper; and I knew every inch of Highgate House, the creak of each stair and the groan of each floorboard. If I was going to solve the twin mysteries of the forbidden cellar and the missing trunk, I was going to have to add eavesdropping to my vices.

NINETEEN

"A deal of people, Miss, are for trusting all to Providence; but I say Providence will not dispense with the means, though He often blesses them when they are used discreetly."

My boundless affection for the protagonist of *Jane Eyre* has already been established; and yet, I cannot resist stating that she made the most dismal investigator in the history of literature.

Consider: she discovers Edward Fairfax Rochester practically in flames. Upon the morrow, whom does she meet but Grace Poole, the assumed culprit; and when Jane suspects the vile Grace of sounding her out over bolting her door? Jane, wise woman that she is, proceeds to deliver all her intentions regarding door-bolting to the dour nurse, in detail, upon a silver platter.

Apparently there is nothing like telling

murderous fire-starters exactly what they want to know about locked doors when they ask you — it confuses them, most likely.

After dinner, I made such a purposeful din going up the stairs that Mrs. Garima Kaur's face appeared at the bottom, eyes sharply inquisitive within the enormous bowls of their sockets.

"No, no, I'm all right," I called down, panting. "Nearly there, anyhow!"

"Nothing bad?" she insisted.

"Nothing bad whatsoever. Mrs. Kaur, are you concerned over something in particular?"

"Do not worry," she said, though the quizzical look had not left her eyes.

"Good night, Mrs. Kaur."

"Good night, Miss Stone."

She stood there with face uplifted, watching me until I had turned my back.

When I made it to my room, I locked the door and cast the crutch aside; I was nearly certain my plan would work, but only so long as I could execute it. After a few hobbling circuits, wincing dreadfully, I confirmed that I could walk, provided nearly all my weight was upon my left leg.

Breathless, I sat down and stared at my mantel clock.

Though not well versed in Mr. Thornfield's habits, I did know Mr. Singh's, and we had concluded our dinner during the time the butler checked the doors and windows; I had only to wait for him to finish sealing the house like a crypt, and then rush to the drawing room without my crutch, hoping I had not missed anything.

Schooling myself, I chose a time: eleven twenty-four in the evening. Milksops mewl that sin corrupts the willpower, but I have that in spades — so I sat until the minute exact and set off.

The corridor presented little difficulty, but the fourth step upon the first flight always bellowed as if someone were tormenting a calf: I avoided it. My ankle burnt, but not unbearably so, for I held both hands to the rail and proceeded with a sideways step-hop, step-hop motion. I remembered just in time that the banister squeaked above the second landing: I put my hand against the wall and gingerly set my sprained ankle upon the final step.

Pain lanced through it, and I pressed my free hand over my mouth. I managed, however, jaw screwed tight, and resumed my ludicrous progression to the ground floor.

Once in the hall, I paused, and yes — a

muted glow from the drawing room combined with the muted thrum of male voices told me to hurry, or all would be for nothing. The lights were out, a single pretty bell-shaped lamp of fractured rose glass remaining; by daylight, it was one of my favourite sources of illumination, for it made the drear midwinter light blush charmingly. Now, in the surrounding darkness, all seemed feverish and bruised.

"— thrash the dog from here back to Calcutta, and then good riddance, says I," growled Mr. Thornfield.

My entire frame snapped to alertness.

This was not Mr. Thornfield's usual baritone — it was a voice meant to carry across dunes and canyons, bereft of pretension, barely even English though he possessed no foreign accent. This was who Charles Thornfield actually *was,* or at least had been, when living under vast Eastern skies.

"For heaven's sake, Charles." Mr. Singh sighed. "You always say that first, and it has never been helpful. Not a single time."

I limped close enough to the slightly open door to hear them clearly.

"I haven't another solution," Mr. Thornfield insisted. "Sardar, I need hardly tell you the man is a menace in the extremest degree

— and who knows what *burchas** he has in his employ."

"Which is why I cannot comprehend why you indulged in his request to see Sahjara."

The voice was so stern that my scalp prickled.

"I was wrong to try it," Mr. Thornfield answered instantly. "Pray don't be angry, I've already taken myself to task. But what if meeting Sack again had . . . jostled something loose in what seems to be a fixed state?" A wistful pitch of yearning had crept into Mr. Thornfield's voice and I pictured him as I knew he must look, muscled shoulders taut and dark brows threatening his stately nose. "What if seeing him had made a difference?"

"Charles, Sahjara is not an experiment!" Mr. Singh hissed. Then he sighed once more, and I heard liquor being poured, and I craned my neck further. "That was uncalled-for and yet I delivered it, rather an unforgivable sin in a *khansamah*,† wouldn't you say? Accept my apologies. Tell me your object in letting Sahjara within five miles of Sack, then."

"We will never be safe until a permanent

* Ruffians.
† Butler.

solution is found!" Mr. Thornfield rasped. "When he arrived, shocked as I was, I imagined that if she saw his face again, his own plan might snake round and bite him in the arse. That she might —"

"Ah," Mr. Singh said sadly. "You thought Sahjara might recall everything, maybe even the trunk. Which would allow us to —"

"Grant the vermin king Sack's wishes like simpering djinn —"

"And send him on his way, and then we could live as we please."

"Not that the exquisite scoundrel wouldn't have been practically invited to rob us blind in that case, which would chafe me terribly."

"Yes, Charles, we kept horses and hounds once, but *now* . . ." Mr. Singh trailed off, exasperated.

"It's not about the money!" A pause occurred, and Mr. Thornfield's voice was calmer thereafter. "No, no, this blasted huge draughty *English* house is . . ." I bristled. "This house is wild and weird and cold, bloody cold and wonderful. Sahjara loves it, and I am finding it ever more charming that my bollocks clack against my teeth when I piss."

"Are you? My bollocks have not yet quite got accustomed to making the leap past my kidneys."

"But now Highgate House is ours, you understand that Sack will never stop," Mr. Thornfield ended in a much lower tone. "I told him I inherited it, but he must not have believed me. He must have thought we still have the trunk, that I bought the estate. What else could explain it?"

"I don't know," Mr. Singh confessed. "The fact of his being here was, I agree, the greatest mystery of all."

Briefly, I heard only the crackling of the fire; when Mr. Thornfield spoke next, it was almost too deep and too soft to catch.

"Sardar, if I have arrived at the point where I think experimenting with Sahjara's brains is reasonable, then perhaps it's best if —"

"No," Mr. Singh said calmly.

"No?" Mr. Thornfield's voice grew ever more serrated. "You don't even —"

"No, you are not embarking upon a crazed quest to murder Augustus Sack, who has assured us that the entire scandal will come out via any one of a dozen solicitors if we so much as touch him. Neither are you murdering a dozen solicitors."

"So the scandal comes out? Who is affected?" Mr. Thornfield had risen, for I could hear his boots striking the carpet. "This is a Company affair. Sack dies mysteriously, my shame is aired for all to see, I throw myself upon the mercy of the Director and face some sort of court-martial and five or ten years in gaol, and —"

"And you still miss Sahjara's entire childhood, emerging broken by hard labour with a ruined constitution."

"Is that worse than perennial torment?"

"Yes."

"Why?"

"Because you wouldn't be here, and she needs you." Mr. Singh sounded three shades beyond exhausted. "I need you, for God's sake."

Mr. Thornfield sat, breathing hard.

"Mark me," Mr. Singh said carefully. "That you want to go to gaol for a crime we both committed long ago, simply to save the rest of us, is both typically thickheaded and typically noble. However, you are not thinking this through. Who was your accomplice when you committed the deed?"

"You were," Mr. Thornfield said testily.

"Now. Supposing the Company doesn't actually want to tar and feather you? The white prodigy raised in Lahore who journeyed back on their commission and was rushed through Addiscombe to do so, they were so eager?"

"Well —"

"Why, yes, Charles, I believe the Director would find a scapegoat if he didn't want to sully the papers with ill repute of the Company."

Mr. Thornfield thought this over, shifting in his seat.

"I wonder who might suit."

After a longer pause, Mr. Thornfield admitted, "You *are* rather brown."

"How brown am I, Charles? Take a good long look now."

"Darkish, though a sight short of black."

I did not know what they had done, of course; but my heart gave a rabbity leap at the thought of Sahjara without either of them. As self-sufficient a child as she was, she fed off love as if she were a walking siphon, and both Mr. Thornfield and Mr. Singh quietly, almost without gesture and never with words, delivered the substance to her in staggering quantities.

"All right, throwing myself upon my sword is out," Mr. Thornfield said pettishly. "Your advice is loathsome, Sardar, and it disendears me to you."

"So often the way with advice," Mr. Singh muttered.

"Well, I think it's deuced unfair, really." Mr. Thornfield lightened the tone. "Sack seeing me at the funeral by accident when

340

I'd no idea he was in England at all seems like cheating."

"It is regrettable, though it does not entirely explain his swaggering into our home with such complete confidence. Thankfully we have both been upon our guard —"

"Of course we've been on our guard! But the die is cast. And a sight too soon after arriving here, if you ask me."

"Undoubtedly." I heard the sound of a vesta being struck. "I meant to take up cricket."

Mr. Thornfield snorted, then guffawed, and then the pair of them wheezed together as I leant against the wall, smiling.

"Oh, I don't know what to do." Mr. Thornfield sighed as the laughter faded.

"Fight back," Mr. Singh said. A chair creaked. "The same as we always do."

"And to think that if the good Sam Quill-feather hadn't posted me, we should never have known John Clements had died at all. It's a hard push whether to be grateful or vengeful."

My back was already against the wall, thankfully, or I should have fallen as the fear seized me — Sam Quillfeather, the policeman who questioned me after Edwin's death? Sam Quillfeather, the inspector who had drawn unspoken conclusions over Vesalius Munt's?

"It's a lucky chance," Mr. Singh agreed. "Enough to make me wish to meet him one of these days. Considering your new arrangement, doubtless I'll make his acquaintance quite soon."

My vision swam; I was in a crazily tilting corridor lit the colour of blood.

"You'll like him — he takes more care with his profession than any man I've ever seen. Makes a point of keeping his investigations utterly quiet unless he has the evidence necessary to prove a party's guilt, not like these boorish peelers who bully their way to solutions, pissing on every water pump they see. Certainly of all the lads going in for medicine at Charing Cross, I liked him best, for he'd no business being there and I felt as if neither did I. I was still sweating curry, and here's this mad *chowkdar*★ twenty years my senior taking desultory anatomy lessons. The mind reels, Sardar, that such wonders exist."

"I'd be less shocked at a courteous tax collector."

"Imagine if he had taken the tiger by the tail and joined the Royal College instead of

★ Constable.

merely brushing up on his tibia versus fibula."

"Incredible. A constable who also just happens to be a doctor of medicine."

"Because he thinks it will make him a better police officer."

They were both laughing helplessly again, and a good thing too, for I was struggling noisily for breath. The notion that the Sam Quillfeather I had known would take an anatomy course upon a whim was directly in character — the man was the definition of inquisitive, which is why I felt sick at the mere mention of his name.

"Is it certain, then, Charles?" Mr. Singh's voice had grown grave. "Are you positively certain John Clements was murdered, without question?"

My eyes, which had been shut in terror, flew open again.

"Certain as daybreak." It was a complex tone, layers of sadness and regret. "Poor old Johnny, with that puppyish way he had about him. Remember when he used to sniff around your secretary as if she were Cleopatra?"

"The poor woman must have put him off a thousand times — I asked her if she wanted my help over it, but she said there was no more harm in him than a mule. I've never met a more credulous person."

"True enough. Johnny had sand where his brains ought to have been, but he certainly didn't deserve to be served cyanide with his tea, or however Sack managed it."

"You seem very sure of yourself."

"Consider!" Mr. Thornfield admonished. "Clements and Sack return from the Punjab together to rub elbows with the Company nabobs and kiss their grannies and such before being reassigned. Quillfeather gets called in as a special consultant after Clements expires mysteriously in his rooms, as Quillfeather is madder than a flock of loons but can both solve a murder and keep quiet, and the Director wants to know why they lost Clements. Sardar, you recall the poor blighter — he was tanned same as us, but he weren't never *ruddy,* and his corpse was flushed something awful, not to mention the fact he was in the prime of life and a heart episode seems very unlikely. Cyanide is the military poison of choice, and who save Sack would be coward enough to stir prussic acid in his brandy rather than killing him like a man would do?"

"Yes, but where's the motive? You said Quillfeather called you in initially because of some papers he discovered Clements was working on?"

"Aye, Johnny was looking up David Lavell's record, and naturally there were our names in stark print — reports from his superiors, correspondence, journals. What cause could Johnny possibly have to investigate a scoundrel dead since the first war unless he suspected something amiss?"

"He wanted to know why we did it, perhaps." Sardar said softly. "He knew we were guilty — he wanted to know why."

"And Sack found out he was digging."

"It doesn't quite wash, Charles. Even supposing he discovered Lavell was a blackguard, what difference should that have made?"

"Puts a whole different colour on the affair, don't y' see? It's one thing to harass a pair of footpads, quite another to persecute old friends — Johnny Clements was an intellectual ant, but he was damned decent to the end. The more he knew of Lavell's character, the less easy it would have been for Sack to keep him leashed."

They fell silent. I was breathing easier by this time, yet still hardly myself; I had wanted information, but this variety led only to more questions, and the notion that Mr. Thornfield had an arrangement with Inspector Quillfeather was nothing short of horrifying.

"How was dinner?" Mr. Singh inquired.

My feet sidled closer to the door.

"Very passable. Jas Kaur always did have a way with sheep."

"Charles," Mr. Singh chided.

"Oh, you mean how was the *governess*?" He was smiling, I could hear as much. "She gave me a straightforward explanation without much prompting. Hard living and harder men made her cautious, and the same circumstances led to the saltiest tongue I've ever heard in an English head."

I should not have taken pride in this; and yet, I could not help myself.

"She's a remarkable woman," Mr. Singh replied. "I did my best to take the measure of her whilst you were away, and I confess I did not get far. Miss Stone seems a clear enough pool on the surface, but glimpsing the bottom is another matter."

"I can't put my finger on it either," Mr. Thornfield said quietly. "You ought to have seen her when she was thrown from Nalin. Popped up again like a jack-in-the-box, not even knowing how badly she was hurt. If she weren't so thoroughly British — that pale elven look about her, those lustrous eyes — I'd have thought her raised north of the Sutlej. She doesn't just carry a knife, she knows how to hold it. If I'd meant her any disrespect, I'm fairly sure she'd have made mincemeat of my bollocks."

"She interests you," Mr. Singh mused, and there was a twist to his tone which made me long to have seen his face as he spoke.

"Of course she does, she would interest anyone," Mr. Thornfield retorted. "Not to mention the fact I've had nothing to occupy me all this while, save your company and that of a child whose every third word is *horse*."

"You'll feel better when the dead start speaking to you again."

I had been listening with such rapt interest to the topic of myself that this shocking pronouncement startled me terribly; and further, I realised that the men had risen from their chairs and would find me with my ear to the door in a matter of moments.

"All locked up, then?"

"Snug as a noose," Mr. Singh answered, and I heard the rattling of an iron in the grate.

Whirling towards the staircase, I made as much soundless haste as possible. My ankle felt as if a spike had impaled it, but I forced myself to limp faster.

"I can't bear the feeling there is nothing to be done," came Mr. Thornfield's voice, and now they were at the threshold of the drawing room door.

"We shall consider further. Be at peace in the meanwhile."

"At peace with both eyes open."

"Quite so."

They're coming, I thought in a blind panic, and I had only made it halfway up the first set of stairs, and my ankle was ready to give way under me; getting up a staircase, it seemed, was another matter altogether than getting down. They would see me, they would know. I faced either being caught like a rat fleeing a refuse heap, or . . .

That is a terrible idea, I informed myself.

"Sahjara starts on the new mare tomorrow. She's named it Harbax."

"God's gift," said Mr. Singh as they neared the start of the staircase. "Excellent choice."

"Clever little creature," Mr. Thornfield agreed fondly. "Though *Charles's gift* might have been more appropriate."

"Even you, my friend, are moved by the will of God."

There was nothing for it; I made an about-face, went as limp as I could, and fell down half a flight of stairs.

"What in the name of the devil!" Mr. Thornfield cried.

An inarticulate groan emerged when I had

got my breath back from the wind being knocked out of my lungs. My left side was bruised, my limbs twisted, and my brain rattled into oblivion; beyond this I could not tell where I was hurt, though hurt I knew I must be. Mr. Singh was speaking urgently now, and so was Mr. Thornfield, and there were warm, careful hands on my shoulders. Then one of them shifted and a soft, thin glove with a heartbeat inside it cupped my cheek and drew it away from the carpet.

"Miss Stone! Dear God, Sardar, what has she — Confound it, Miss Stone, look at me."

"She's breathing steadily," Mr. Singh's tense voice added.

"Miss Stone, can you hear me?"

I could; I could feel him as well, feel the pressure of his fingers beneath the glove, and thought for a lunatic instant that apart from having just thrown myself down a staircase, I felt surprisingly happy. I opened my eyes.

"Christ, there you are." Mr. Thornfield blew out the breath he had been holding. " 'Pon my soul, you gave us a fright. Can you move at all? It would greatly endear you to me."

Shifting, I found that I could, but stifled a

cry when I discovered that my knee had been badly wrenched, and this time on my previously uninjured left side.

"Easy, easy now, that's it," he admonished, sliding a hand under my back.

"Oh God, I feel such a fool," I gasped as Mr. Thornfield helped me to sit. "I left my book in the morning room, and I make such a horrid clamour with that crutch — I thought I could manage without."

"You feel a fool because you *are* a fool," Mr. Thornfield growled. "What in hell did you think you were about? You could have woken the whole bloody house with reveille on the trumpet for all we —"

"Mr. Thornfield," put in Mr. Singh, his butler persona back in place, "might I suggest you help Miss Stone back to her bedroom and that you cease swearing at her? Miss Stone, what were you reading?"

"La Rabouilleuse," I lied.

"I shall fetch it up to you with a bit of brandy." Mr. Singh smoothly disappeared.

Mr. Thornfield was still on bended knee, glowering at me as if I had fallen down the stairs on purpose and little knowing I had done exactly that. When I raised my brows, he opened his mouth, shut it again, and composed his features by scrubbing his hand over them.

"May I?" he asked.

"I don't think I can walk," I admitted. "I'm sorry, sir. This grows tedious."

"You find falling from potentially fatal heights tedious?" he returned, but now the tone was less strident, and if I painted it with my own imaginings, it might almost have been called tender.

So Mr. Thornfield effortlessly carried me up the stairs, and when my arms were about his neck, I smelled not only the cigar he had smoked with Mr. Singh but also a faint, clean sandalwood aroma which must have been the man himself, and made me think of steep hills overlooking dry plains, and the sweetness which must surely linger in the air after the monsoons have passed beyond the Sutlej.

TWENTY

I felt at times, as if he were my relation, rather than my master: yet he was imperious sometimes still; but I did not mind that; I saw it was his way. So happy, so gratified did I become with this new interest added to life, that I ceased to pine after kindred: my thin crescent-destiny seemed to enlarge; the blanks of existence were filled up; my bodily health improved; I gathered flesh and strength.

A month passed, reader, before my investigations progressed, partly because for the next fortnight I could not walk.

If you have never lain in bed in your dressing gown, your ankle and knee shrieking as you try to confine yourself to a reasonable amount of laudanum, teaching a bright, babbling girl sitting at the end of your bed by day and fretting by night why the master of the house's spirits will be improved when the dead start to speak, then I am glad for you. I was full of restless energy which could be discharged nowhere, as if I were a kettle coming to boil lacking lid or spout, and if I had exploded, I should not have been the least surprised.

For a week I suffered, uninterrupted by any save Sahjara, a maid bearing meals which included an improbable dish of plum pudding on the day I reasoned must have been Christmas, and Mrs. Garima Kaur, who delivered poultices I suspected came from Mr. Thornfield. These smelt of sage and vinegar and worked wonders for swelling. If I had been an object of wonderment to the housekeeper previously, now I was a nuisance, for she coolly assisted me with an air suggesting my falling down stairs was in poor taste. The fact that the master of the house had not visited chafed terribly, but I supposed it would hardly be proper for him to pass the hours in my bedroom, and he seemed to harbour a horror of making un-English blunders in my presence.

Meanwhile, I wanted him to make certain blunders very much indeed.

By day I taught Sahjara, who brought me unceasing small presents ranging from orange flower cakes to bouquets of jolly red berries; by night, I imagined my employer

353

making the sort of inappropriate advances which would have made most governesses flee the estate forthwith, and in graphic detail, complete with bare thighs and calloused fingers and the diagonal notches which rest so sweetly above the hipbones when a gentleman is in training, as I had no doubt whatsoever Mr. Thornfield was.

Then one morning when I was fidgeting in my sheets, silver sunlight knifing through my curtains, I heard pounding steps hurtling down the corridor which could only have meant Sahjara. A knock preceded her entrance, but she did not wait for me to say "Come in," and the words thus overlapped with her banging open the door.

"Miss Stone!" she cried, her dark eyes alight. "There's a chair!"

I struggled to ascertain the import of this phrase.

"Charles has just brought it back in the carriage. A chair with wheels! He went to the village to get it, I think, and you're to make yourself ready and then you can come down!"

I swiftly dressed in plain governess black with my hair pinned as tidily as my hair ever allows; no sooner had my small charge carefully tied my boots than Charles Thornfield appeared within the open door. Seeing him again after nearly a week without was a disproportionately stirring event, for I should not have cared so much over beholding a man with whom I had passed less than twenty-four hours' time. He crossed his arms and leant against the frame, a sardonic quirk to his lips.

"Hullo, Young Marvel. Behold the Female Prodigy," he announced. "She can tutor the pure ones, wield knives, and fall from dangerous altitudes with equal grace."

I opened my mouth, glanced at Sahjara, and rolled my eyes instead.

"By Jove, is she trying not to swear at me in front of the child?"

He was correct, so I laughed. "Did you really find me a wheelchair, sir?"

Mr. Thornfield straightened, advancing. I have written that he was a man of medium height, not so tall as Sardar Singh, yet it seemed there was not sufficient space for him in this wide room, so great was his effect on me.

"It took rather more reconnaissance than I'd have liked, but the village physician had one in his attic, positively wreathed with cobwebs. One could scare tell it was a chair at all. Mrs. Garima Kaur has dusted it, naturally."

"I'm so glad you'll be downstairs with the

rest of us!" Sahjara exclaimed, throwing her arms round my shoulders.

Blushing is not a habit of mine, but I am unused to raw sentiment being lobbed in my direction. As Mr. Thornfield took in this awkward scene, his ward clinging to me and then unselfconsciously racing away to do whatever Sahjara Kaur does when she isn't on horseback, he looked uncertain whether to be delighted or dismayed, drawing a hand over the back of his neck in what I was learning to be a habitual gesture.

"She's spontaneous," I offered. "It means nothing, I'm well aware."

"It doesn't mean anything like nothing, not to anyone who knows her." Mr. Thornfield shook off whatever uneasy thought plagued him. "I could carry the chair upstairs, but then there remain stairs when we reverse course — should we carry Mahomet to the mountain instead?"

"Whensoever you like," said I.

Again I was lifted — respectfully, more's the pity — by my employer. The journey, reader, was too brief for my liking; but once I had arrived at the ground floor and saw the charming vehicle, all wicker and softly curving wood painted a demure black, with carefully placed cushions, I positively glowed as I was set into it.

"I can't tell you how grateful I am for this." I looked up at Mr. Thornfield, who surveyed the results of his labours with satisfaction.

"Yes, well, do let me know if I should retain possession of it, supposing you decide to fly out the attic window."

"No, I mean . . . thank you. Hardly anyone has ever bothered to take care of me."

I paused to reflect, scarce registering that I had just confided an intimate fact to a near stranger. A list emerged:

— Agatha
— Clarke, when I was not taking care of Clarke

It may seem strange that I did not include my mother; but my mother was a butterfly's wing, too fluttering and fragile to take care of anyone, and though we loved each other . . . she had left me, had she not?

Mr. Thornfield's rough features smoothed into disbelief. "Whatever circumstance you're speaking of, there ought to have been fifty lined up for the job."

I sliced a look at him, unsure if he actually believed such nonsense; but he strode behind me, gripping the handles of the chair. Admittedly I might have wheeled the thing myself, but since Mr. Thornfield pushing me meant Mr. Thornfield a foot distant, I should have been a dunce to defend my independence.

"Where to, Miss Stone? I admit I had not thought so far, only feared that you were like to suffocate if you stayed in the same room any longer."

"May we go to the morning room?"

"Think of this not as your chair but as your chariot, Miss Stone," he proclaimed sarcastically, and I could not help but wonder whether Mr. Thornfield, on occasion, hid truth in falsehoods just as I did.

The master of the house and I forged a pattern when I was not at lessons with Sahjara; in the mornings and evenings, he would carry me downstairs so I could dine with what I was coming to understand was the family — the aforementioned individuals plus Mr. Sardar Singh — and after Sahjara had been led off to bed by Mrs. Garima Kaur, and Mr. Singh had adopted an introspective look and excused himself, the pair of us stayed up later and later and progressively later. I loved these strange sessions, for Mr. Thornfield, despite his prickliness, seemed to love them too, though it was a hard push not to blurt out *What crime did you and Mr. Singh commit in the Punjab?* or *Why should the dead speak to you?*

One night five days into my convalescence, Mr. Thornfield wheeled me into the drawing room after supper, I having confessed that good Scotch and I were not strangers, and when we were both equipped with this lovely commodity, I ventured to ask him a question. We should have been the picture of English domesticity, the firelight in Mr. Thornfield's pale hair and I nestled into my cushions, if only I held a needle in my hand and not a glass of whiskey.

"Is Mr. Singh really the butler?"

Mr. Thornfield's chin shot up. "By the Lord, is she actually interrogating me now?"

"He doesn't sit with the servants at meals," I insisted. "He doesn't count the silver or manage your wine collection or berate the rest of the staff. I should venture to say that his only jobs are answering the door and locking the windows of a night, and those because he likes the control."

Mr. Thornfield frowned. "Are you an inspector, Miss Stone? I shall have to look out over pinching extra kippers at breakfast and telling Sahjara lies about not being able to afford two mares for her instead of one."

"That was a very neat way of not answering my question."

"Oh, what's the use — you've found us out." Mr. Thornfield smiled, and this was an effortless one. "You know that Sardar and I were practically brothers growing up. The rest of the household, other than Sahjara of course, were his own servants in Lahore — we brought them with us, as he'd no wish to sack 'em all and they'd no wish to see the back of him. The man inspires affections left, right, and sideways — it's a foul thing to watch."

"So Mr. Singh is not a butler?" I pressed.

"Of course he is, supposing you want to keep meddling English busybodies out of our hair. But, no, you're quite right — when Sardar vanishes, he is either studying the Guru, taking long constitutionals, or fiddling with Jas Kaur over replicating Punjabi dishes in the kitchen."

I chuckled over my glass. "So though this is your estate, an argument can be made he is the master, since the servants are *his* domestics and not yours."

"We couldn't very well have made off with my parents' household, could we, would've strained relations something frightful. You're near to correct, but one of them — Mrs. Garima Kaur — was Sardar's confidential secretary back in Lahore."

This surprised me. "I thought she knew very little English?"

"Spoken like a true colonialist — didn't matter a fig back then, there were only a pocketful of us. She probably figured it beneath her, never did warm to whites much, come to think of it. She speaks Punjabi, Hindi, Arabic, Farsi, Turkish, and Pashto something spectacular, and that's all Sardar required."

"And now she's a housekeeper."

"Well, what with Sardar a butler and all, she can't be too miffed."

Smiling, I leant my head against the cushion of my chair. "Tell me more."

"More of what, you impudent elf?"

"Anything. Everything. Your parents survived the wars, I take it, since they still needed a staff? And why did you leave them in the first place — why study medicine?"

"Miss Stone," he drawled, "if I did not know better, I would think I intrigued you."

"You do intrigue me."

I said this without a trace of guile. A British chap might have been chagrined over such an open display, but Mr. Thornfield only settled farther back into his armchair.

"Do you know, Miss Stone, that you are exceptional?"

"I have been told so, but never in complimentary light."

Mr. Thornfield's jaw twitched. "That was undeserved on your part, and therefore I will answer you. My parents are still in Lahore, and survived both wars without so much as a scratch. I should be proud of them if it were the done thing to be proud of privateers bleeding Company executives dry; I ought to be delighted, in fact, as it all comes to me in the end and now they have ten times the population of expatriates to drain to the dregs. Pardon, you might mistake me; I cherish my parents, but they are not suitable subjects for small talk."

"Neither are we."

This time he laughed freely. "Quite right, Miss Stone — if misfits cannot converse amongst themselves, then who can? Very well, my parents are brazen criminals and I elected to study medicine because I have always been fascinated by the impermanence of the human body. Does that answer your question?"

I shook my head, waiting for him to continue.

"Becoming a charlatan and a cheat never appealed to me," Mr. Thornfield admitted. "My parents are crafty rather than malicious, but damned if I share their tastes — medicine meant studying mortality, in a

362

sense. The Sikh holy book contains plentiful passages about flesh, and since my parents were about as interested in religion as they were in sobriety, I learnt from Sardar and his family. 'We are vessels of flesh. . . . The soul taketh its abode in flesh. . . . Women, men, kings, and emperors spring from flesh.' Sikhs are very — how shall I put it delicately? — straightforward about flesh. It was a comfort to me that they thought souls separate from lungs and livers, this sack of bones and blood we daily maintain, and I thought there was romance in medicine's efforts to stave off the inevitable. This was when I was young and thick as a marble bust, you understand," he added with a dour expression.

"I adore the macabre," I confessed. "I used to supplement my governess's income by selling last confessions in tea shops and the like."

"Good Lord! Miss Stone, I find it difficult to picture you peddling gallows doggerel."

"No more should you, sir, for it was prose, and I always chose the most poignant subjects, as if by placing hard words upon a page, like so many stones, my own heart would not be so heavy."

Mr. Thornfield ran a finger over his chin. "If your writing was half as good as what you just said, Miss Stone, then I should very much like to read it."

"Oh, they're long gone," I demurred, though my eyes must have shone at the praise. "They harmed no one and interested me — what sort of occupation could be better?"

"Well, there you have it. Medicine was honest work, and I had always wanted to see the place where my parents met, so I fled the Punjab at precisely the wrong time, in order to pursue a career which I've never practised outside of a war."

"Surely you saved lives when you returned?"

He made no reply, his face so fixed that I imagined that I had turned him to stone.

"A few, perhaps," he said at length.

I knew better than to press this point. "What did you think of London?"

Relieved I had shifted topics, Mr. Thornfield answered readily. "It's filthy, and wet, and hides a brutal soul behind majestic walls. Its people are alternately snobbish or base, and if I didn't come from a culture of warriors, I'd say it was the most savage city I'd ever seen. I thought it glorious, of course, from the instant it sullied my boots."

"I loved it as well."

"Yes, and if there are bits of yourself which

you should prefer to toss in the gutter . . ."

"You can shed your skin."

"And no one the wiser."

"Still. It was by far the most crowded place I've ever been lonesome," I added, staring into my glass.

"That ought not to have been the case, Miss Stone," he said quietly. "I know very little about you, but I know you would be absolute rubbish at solitude. Your relish for companionship is clear as print."

Tripping steps sounded, and Sahjara entered the room with her face alight, wearing a dressing gown over her nightdress. Rushing to Mr. Thornfield, she tugged at his sleeve. "Charles, I've had the most *wonderful* idea, and Sardar says he'll only do it if you promise to join him, and of course I will as well though I'm not so good as either of you, but I'll make up for it on horseback I'd wager, and Miss Stone will be so pleased after having been cooped up indoors for so long."

"What is she jabbering about?" Mr. Thornfield asked irritably, swallowing a measure of Scotch. "She speaks English, I know she speaks English, she learnt the tongue in the Punjab from my parents and perfected its nuances here when she was five."

"Charles, don't be dreadful, we're going to put on a demonstration!"

"A demonstration of *what,* you ill-mannered imp?"

"Of everything!" She turned to me, her smooth cheeks flushed with enthusiasm. "Riding, in my case, and perhaps archery. The *chakkar,* the *tulwar,* the *aara* —"

"Has she lost her mind?" Mr. Thornfield exclaimed. "You want to stage a mock fight Khalsa-style in the middle of the British countryside?"

"Yes!" She clapped her hands together decisively. "Yes, the way Sardar says you used to practise outside Lahore's gates, only we'll do it on the grounds, and Miss Stone will *love* it."

"Miss Stone will be entirely put off by our foreign antics and will quit the house in high dudgeon."

I burst out laughing at the transparent falsity of this excuse.

"Have I not given you steeds?" Mr. Thornfield demanded, rubbing his temple. "Have I not given you fine frocks and an English mansion? Have I not given you a governess —"

"Please, Charles." Her smile meant she expected to get her way. "Sardar said yes."

"Sardar spoils you so obscenely it's all I

can do not to throw myself in the nearest river."

"Please?" I interjected, grinning. "It would be so educational."

Mr. Thornfield's glower was fast losing strength; finally he gave a martyred sigh, finished his whiskey with a snap of the wrist, and said, "I'm no match for the pair of you martinets."

"Hurrah!" Sahjara exulted, taking his gloved hand and delivering a peck to it. "Tomorrow?"

"Oh, certainly, supposing you prefer me headless. I've not practised with the *aara* in years."

She swung the hand she still held. "Next week."

"You'll be the death of me yet. Fine."

"It really is a marvellous idea," I said, smiling at her.

"It's a ridiculous idea." Pushing himself to his feet, Mr. Thornfield brushed a wisp of hair off Sahjara's brow. "Go back to bed, darling, and thence to sleep, so that you'll be unable to hatch any fresh schemes to gall me."

"Insufferable gaffer," she said affectionately.

"Impertinent brat."

Sahjara disappeared with a toss of her

367

head. Mr. Thornfield returned our empty glasses to the sideboard, looking contemplative. I had begun to better cherish his silences, for he possessed many shades of stillness and sharing them with me meant he was at ease in my presence; this was a blue quiet, as deep as his eyes.

"I wish that whatever you are thinking, you did not have to dwell upon it," I told him.

"You've a generous nature, Jane." He stopped, turning back to me. "Apologies, I don't know how that slipped, only I've come to think of you . . . Blame it on my upbringing, if you please."

A sting pierced my chest; hearing my actual name was meaningful, as if he had taken my mask off and glimpsed my real face.

"You may call me Jane if you like."

He cocked a brow. "You don't find it overfamiliar?"

"Not from you."

Had he been anyone else, I should have dreaded making so bold a declaration; as it was, my heart thrummed major chords within my ribs as I watched him blink.

"Thank you — as you might gather from the Young Marvel's example, you may call me anything you damn well please." The empty expression he affected did not hide the fact his mouth was pinched at the corners. "Jane, I've apparently a deal of unnecessary physical training to undergo tomorrow — shall we retire?"

Breathlessly, I agreed; but he only carried me up to my room and bid me the usual polite *Good night, then, Jane,* and I pretended the strange sweetness upon my tongue when I bid him the same was due to expensive whiskey. I then assured myself that my symptoms merited a diagnosis of simple lust, and I fell asleep repeating that Charles Thornfield had stolen nothing more serious than my attention.

The air crackled and clawed the afternoon of Sahjara's demonstration; it had snowed again, and an inch of powder lay glimmering upon the grounds, awaiting the performers as the pale January sunlight bent down to kiss the top of the trees. I sat in my wheeled chair wearing my cloak as well as two blankets, hot-water bottles at my lap and feet, upon the terrace at the side of the house; surrounded by Singhs and Kaurs, who spoke excitedly to one another in Punjabi and stamped their feet against the cold, I awaited the performers.

I will not attempt to describe the dexterity

with which Sahjara on Harbax navigated
the jumps the grooms had built and strewn
about the lawn. She was dazzling, and Mr.
Thornfield's face as he watched her mir-
rored Sardar Singh's in a potent combination of glad mouths and strangely anguished
eyes. Neither can I conjure the impassioned
cries of *"Khalsa-ji!"* from the Sikh household
as Mr. Singh, left arm loaded with serrated
metal circles and right forefinger spinning a
disc in the air, threw ten *chakkar*s in rapid
succession, cutting ten distant poles into
splintered halves. His servants screamed
their approval, and I thought I glimpsed a
tear in Mrs. Garima Kaur's eye, reflecting
sunlight just as her scar did.

Should I not at least essay to capture the
spectacle of Mr. Thornfield wielding the
aara outside my childhood home as the sun
sank, however, I should consider this entire
memoir a failure. He joined Mr. Singh on
the lawn with a set of double-tongued metal
whips about five feet in length, both wearing very loose cotton trousers fastened at
the calf and nothing more, bare shoulders
gleaming like cliffsides, and at a nod from
his friend, they began what can only be
called a dance.

They did not merely flick the deadly
tongues at targets, for there were no targets;

370

they leapt from foot to foot, sweeping the flexible steel over and under and above themselves, vicious blades passing within inches of their heads and arms. The snow exploded as they struck it, plumes flying with the sharp snaps of a thousand firecrackers, and the servants and Sahjara screamed encouragement in their native tongue. Faster and faster they whirled, sometimes falling bodily back to catch themselves, sometimes balancing on a palm after throwing themselves forward headlong, and all the while the *aara*s sang and snapped.

Mr. Sardar Singh was the superior; his lightness of foot and the detached technicality with which he performed a madcap dance was unsurpassable.

I could see, however, why he wrongly claimed Charles Thornfield was his better when it came to the *aara*, because he was riveting; he silently snarled as he flayed the ice and mud, surged from foot to foot as if a demon possessed him, and following this onslaught of fury, could flick the tip of the blade to send a scant few snowflakes delicately soaring.

I can assure the reader that I did not do anything so asinine as to fall in love with Mr. Thornfield by watching him demonstrate the *aara;* I had already fallen in love with him, and on that day, a feverish sheen upon my brow despite the winter's chill, I elected to admit it, if only to myself. For the thought of confessing as much could only mean confessing far more about myself, if I truly cared for him, and I could not bear the idea that he should ally himself with evil unawares.

Twenty-One

It had formerly been my endeavour to study all sides of his character: to take the bad with the good; and from the just weighing of both, to form an equitable judgment. Now I saw no bad. The sarcasm that had repelled, the harshness that had startled me once, were only like keen condiments in a choice dish: their presence was pungent, but their absence would be felt as comparatively insipid.

Perhaps the most touching passages in *Jane Eyre* are those after she discovers she loves Mr. Rochester and before she discovers he loves her in return. There is little unwieldy pretension and still less saccharine sentiment; she simply loves him, as I loved Mr. Thornfield, and is woeful because one cannot uproot love any easier than one can force it to flourish.

I wrestled with the identical problem,

although my tactics during this period would have positively curled Miss Eyre's hair.

A week later I was out of the wheelchair with my ankle tightly wrapped, my knee quite healed, limping gamely, and Mr. Thornfield must have supposed himself haunted by a familiar when my mobility was restored. I took his elbow when he asked me if I cared for a walk; I drew my fingertip down the silver cuff he wore; I shone in every way I knew how, and lastly, I told him the truth.

Truth in my case must needs have been partial, but I thrilled at each new self-exposure.

"Sahjara lived with my father's sister in Cornwall when she emigrated, until Sardar and I arrived early this year," he answered my question after a curried fish supper.

"I hated my aunt." My nerves whistled in high alarm, but I soldiered on. "She called me cruel names and snubbed my mother perennially."

Mr. Thornfield scowled around his cigar. "If she had such poor taste as that, failing to hate her should have been shirking, Jane."

Further examples abound; for instance, Mr. Thornfield and I often granted Sahjara's wish that we might all go riding together, precious windswept occasions on which water sprang to my eyes at the keen wind and the joy of galloping over hillsides; and on the first of these rides, I made the acquaintance of Mr. Thornfield's horse — a great rusty-black stallion.

"I just adore him, I can't help it," Sahjara crooned, pressing the flat of her hand up the beast's nose.

"I assume he is called Falstaff because he is so funny and charming?" I asked, smiling.

Mr. Thornfield coughed dryly, his breath clouding in the cold. "He is called Falstaff because given the choice, he would eat oats and sugar until his belly exploded and he was strewn all over Christendom."

I laughed, as did Sahjara, and Mr. Thornfield shot me another of his queer appraising glances, the ones which sent liquid warmth pooling through my torso.

"There were times when the comfort of communing with horses was all I had," I admitted.

"I think the same was true of me, before. I can't remember. Oh, Charles, say you'll give Nalin to Miss Stone — she's better on her than anyone!" Sahjara entreated.

Mr. Thornfield tugged at her cloak's collar until it lay flat. "Young Marvel, ordinarily I should have to box your ears for squandering my assets and forgetting Miss Stone is not in a position to keep her own horses." He glanced at me. "But supposing that I can retain the honour of feeding and sheltering duties, Jane should consider Nalin entirely her own."

Can I be blamed for strewing my secrets like seeds when they blossomed into such kindly responses? A fortnight had been expended on the practise before I began to run dry of tasteful confessions, and then, reader, I invented them like the lying devil I am.

"I should like to read the Guru Granth Sahib," I declared. "It would explain so much about your character." Mr. Thornfield sat writing a letter in his study as I watched him, pretending to be reading Balzac.

"There is neither an adequate explanation for my character, nor a copy of the Guru in the English language." He dipped his pen without raising his head. "Apply to Sardar, he can recite damned impressive heaps of the stuff."

"I shall. I can't give any credence to the Bible because so many villains quote it."

This was not true; I simply wished for something freshly shocking to tell him.

Though the Bible dictated my mother and I would be listening to each other's skin crackling for eternity, and my former headmaster had been cruelty incarnate even as he called upon God's Name, I thought many of its teachings beautiful.

Mr. Thornfield's eyes narrowed in amusement. "Never read the thing, though Sardar has lobbed plentiful passages at me — my parents are more for cheap novels when they can get 'em. Whale blubber and seal pelts and nor'easters. Damsels, you understand." He coughed charmingly. "Heaving bosoms."

"There are plentiful bloody bits, and even some sensuous parts, I suppose," I said idly, passing fingers along my hairline. "Song of Solomon is about a pair of lovers. 'Let him kiss me with the kisses of his mouth!' It's quite salacious material."

"I've heard better. Now kindly shut your head whilst I finish congratulating my father on his latest swindle."

Helpless to stop myself, I tried again the next day, discovering him reorganising books in the library and (predictably enough) offering my assistance.

"Are there any Punjabi books in the house?" I wondered, sorting through several volumes of Medieval spiritual poetry I

377

suspected belonged to Mr. Singh and not Mr. Thornfield.

"Oh, certainly." He craned his thick neck upwards, wearing a frown as he lifted a stack of unbound folios. "But they kept turning up missing, don't y'know, great gaping holes in the collection, and when Sardar found 'em circulating at a jaunty clip in the servants' wing, we installed proper shelves where they were wanted."

"That was good of you."

"Of course it wasn't. I can march over there whenever rereading *Chandi di Var*★ tickles me, can't I? I have legs, and so does Sardar."

Finished, I began sorting through the Renaissance plays. "Your servants are very interesting. They must know you both well, I take it, since they worked for Mr. Singh before? Mrs. Garima Kaur, for example, seems most devoted to him, even for a confidential secretary."

Mr. Thornfield glanced up from where he was kneeling, eyes lit with the wistful shade of earnest. "You know how she came by that extra bit of facial ornament, then?"

"The scar? How should I?"

★ A poem written by Guru Gobind Singh in the classic Punjabi heroic ballad style.

"She saved his life once."

"No!" I exclaimed, kneeling to mirror him. "Oh, do tell me how."

"Nasty business," he owned, frowning. "Sardar was twenty-three, I believe. He was overseeing the delivery of — what was it, indigo or ivory? damned if I can recall, ivory it must have been — across town by the Bright Gate, and he was set upon by thieves. Not your friendly book-borrowing type either, the picking-their-teeth-with-*tulwar*s kind, and Garima was accompanying him to keep records. Sardar is a tiger, but it was five on one, and incapacitating suits his delicate sensibilities better than slaughter. Anyhow, Garima threw herself into the fray and did him a few good turns with the knife she carried before taking that slash over the brow. She'd be dead but for his skill, and he'd be dead but for her help."

He fell silent, sifting through titles.

"I would fight like that, if I cared enough for the person," I confessed with endless devotion in my eyes.

Mr. Thornfield quirked a smile, granting me the merest glance. "*You* would have eaten their hearts in the marketplace afterwards. Just fetch me the magnifying glass on the desk there? Damned if I can make out this inscription."

So it went; day after day he gave me smiles rather than scowls, and at times I tilted my head up at the perfect evening angle when he passed my chair to refill our glasses of Scotch, and still my lips went unkissed and my questions unanswered. Despite these obstacles, I was achingly fulfilled over the simple act of wanting — having passed so much time seeking necessities, a combatant in an arena where to lose is to die, possessing the leisure to lie awake yearning after caresses I did not merit felt like an extravagance in and of itself.

That is, until work upon the cellar was completed a fortnight after Sahjara's weapons demonstration.

The pinging of distant hammers and circular progression of workmen hauling rubble out the back exit had been a torment, and I do not mean in the sense of peace disrupted; I yearned to know what was below; and when one day I came downstairs for breakfast to discover profound silence save the ticking of the standing clock, I quickly inferred that the men had, at last, finished.

"Congratulations." I took the tea Mr. Singh offered me, containing a splash of milk and one lump of sugar, exactly as I liked it.

"Might I ask upon what account, Miss Stone?"

"The completed renovations downstairs."

Mr. Thornfield stirred his coffee, transfixed by the newspaper; Mr. Singh nodded graciously, whilst an uncaring Sahjara yawned over her bowl of spiced porridge.

"The immediate dangers of an unsafe substructure have been seen to, yes," Mr. Singh reported, "but it remains best to consider the place entirely unsafe, ladies. That is, supposing you value your lungs, for the place is yet a haven for mould and damp."

Sahjara's nose wrinkled; Mr. Thornfield made a remark about the weather.

Unsafe, my shapely white arse, I thought.

That night, I heard a tread in the corridor outside my bedroom which was neither Mr. Singh's stately glide nor Sahjara's heedless prance. It was Mr. Thornfield's vigorous stride, at four o'clock in the morning.

A frontal attack seemed best, as the cellar was now kept locked during the day — and should I catch Mr. Thornfield at whatever nocturnal activity he had been indulging in, I could claim to have been frightened of intruders sent by the odious Mr. Sack. At any rate, I did not fear my nominal master's wrath, for he now showed me every cour-

381

tesy, including the caustic teasing I had come to relish. Two days I waited; then a long crate was delivered to Highgate House and quickly spirited away.

Tonight, I determined, and after pleading the excuse of a headache, I lay awake and fully dressed with my ears tinnily ringing, so hard did I listen for the faintest whisper of sound. Midnight chimed, then one o'clock; at last, a bit before two, I heard a man's steady footfalls. As I had done when eavesdropping upon his conversation with Mr. Singh, I waited a few minutes until I knew Mr. Thornfield was fully engaged and then slipped from my bedchamber with a fitfully flickering candle.

When I reached the door to the cellar stairs, again I heard the suggestion of movement below; this was all to the good, however, and — finding it unlatched — I opened it.

Where once only rubble and the columns of the house's foundations stood, here a polished wooden staircase plunged below the earth. Though I glimpsed wall sconces, they were unlit, and the breath seized in my chest at the thought of my taper going out, for the terrain was now an uncharted one.

Step by step I advanced, careful of the faint echoes of my healed injuries, eyes watering as I peered into the gloom. The noises grew louder — what was he doing, this unexpected love of mine, that he waited for the dead of night and hid below the earth's surface?

I reached the bottom and stopped, suddenly fearful; a queer, sweet reek like badly mouldering apples coated my throat. Shaking minutely, I turned the door handle.

Several horrible things happened at once.

There had been a lamp lit, for its amber ribbon had lined the threshold, but upon my opening the portal, the room was subsumed in darkness. This would not have been frightening had I not been pretending false confidence when I threw the door wide, which snuffed out my own flame . . . but not before I had glimpsed an unholy tableau. A muffled male curse pierced the black curtain at the same time I emitted a strangled squeak — nothing so dignified as a scream — and dropped my candle entirely.

All was sable midnight surrounding me, and I shared the room with Mr. Thornfield and a naked corpse.

I clutched the doorframe to orient myself. More curses followed, then slow, confident steps, until an arm wound about my waist and an urgent hand caught my shoulder.

"Jane, please — are you hurt, or only

frightened? Jane . . . I turned down the lamp to prevent your seeing anything you wish not to, but you're quite safe."

When I opened my eyes — for in my insensible startlement I had witlessly shut them — I discerned that I could see after all, as the lamp still held a spark of life, though its ghostly sphere now illuminated only Charles Thornfield's face, the familiar worried line between his brows, and the edge of a great table like a butcher's where a carcass lay supine.

"I'm all right," I managed. "The light gave me a turn when it went out, and . . . the . . ."

The truth was, reader, that — though I had created four corpses — I had never lingered over my accomplishments; this specimen was well past its prime, and the candied egg smell was overwhelming enough to choke me.

"Confound it, Jane, you've no business here!" Mr. Thornfield snapped. "I gave explicit orders —"

"I heard noises. Pray don't be angry, I was thinking of thieves, I —"

"And when you supposed ruthless *bad-mash*es had invaded, rather than wake the menfolk — who are, I will take the liberty of reminding you, deucedly clever when it comes to sharp objects — you marched down here to challenge 'em to a duel with a bloody pocket-knife?"

My mind was a storm cloud, all static and hurtling thoughts. "I was half sleepwalking. I'm sorry." I steadied myself and gripped Mr. Thornfield's forearm, looking down.

This was when I noticed: Charles Thornfield was not wearing his frock coat, and neither was he wearing gloves. My lips parted as I studied his fingers spanning my waist; he retreated now I seemed in no danger of falling, but not before I could see that his hands were positively shocking.

There was not a mark on them. Unscarred wrists, one adorned with a silver cuff, led to subtly veined skin, splitting into slender phalanges with well-shaped knuckles. It felt obscene that I could not drag my gaze from them — as if I had happened upon him naked in a woodland pool and refused to turn my back as he fetched his smallclothes.

"What is it, Jane?"

"Your hands, sir. They're not scarred."

"I never said they were."

I wrenched my eyes up. "You must think me a hateful busybody."

"You haven't the vaguest idea what I think of you."

"Forgive me." My enterprise now seemed detestable. "I'll not broach the subject again, I don't care what you're —"

"Yes, you do!" he exclaimed, shoving a hand over his high brow. "Damn it, I — If we are apologising, then I apologise for accidentally besetting you with waking nightmares. Now, do you wish to see something of my work, or shall I escort you upstairs?"

"Oh, please, if you will have me, I should prefer to . . . to stay."

Mr. Thornfield studied me as the devout study God; then he softened the hard spread of his shoulders.

"I have told you that I've not practised medicine save in two wars?"

Nodding, I straightened my spine.

"I have told you that I've a friend called Sam Quillfeather who is a police inspector?"

Again I inclined my head; Mr. Thornfield stepped back as if testing how much of the view I could manage.

"Behold the Highgate House Mortuary." His voice rang clear as a brook, but I could not discern any pleasure in the telling. "There isn't a single decent deadhouse between here and London, and Inspector Quillfeather is a monomaniac when it comes to collecting evidence. I had him round for dinner not two weeks after arriving here and told him I should require an occupation or else succumb to despair. This morgue, with me as its coroner, was his notion, and the men have been hard at work for three months."

He asked more gently, "If I turn the lamp up, will you swoon?"

"Bugger swooning," I replied, meaning it.

Mr. Thornfield smiled and reached for the tab; the brightening lamp revealed an incongruously lovely sight. The floors had been finished with wood stained quite dark, the walls plastered where before there was only stone. The air made my arms tingle, cool as a cave, and the rough-edged pillars remained; but lining the walls were cabinets and tables, and a set of medical tools was arranged upon a counter. I spied a chemistry apparatus, a formidable hacksaw, and what I would later come to understand was termed a rib spreader.

I forced myself to view the corpse, taking a few steps closer. The stranger was of medium build, with a weak chin and ruddy side-whiskers, aged over forty years, and he lay upon a huge slab of wood with grooves carved along the edges.

"I ought to have had a look at this fellow some two days hence, but was delayed by the family's protests. Chap dropped dead in his barley field, and Quillfeather understands that the bucolic countryside ain't precisely free of murder," Mr. Thornfield observed, watching me carefully. "He and I studied together, so he knew that I always had an uncanny knack for autopsies. It was as if they told me the stories of their final moments — I never once got it wrong."

You'll feel better when the dead start speaking to you again, I recalled Mr. Singh telling him, and could not suppress a shiver.

"Aye, it takes one like that at first." Mr. Thornfield's gloves rested next to a delicate chisel, and he pocketed them as if the sight were too private for sceptical eyes.

"You said that you only used your training when you were at war. Why not start a practice rather than aiding an enthusiastic policeman?"

"Because I touch only the dead, never the living."

Having experienced a fair number of shocks in my time, I gave no outward indication when he said this.

The silence, however, grew around us like a cancer.

"No, not always, not before, I'm not . . . it's a sacrifice," he told me. "For my sins."

"For a period of time, sir?"

"For the rest of my days."

I do not know how it feels when the trap

drops and the noose crushes the windpipe — but though I stood perfectly still, staring at the pained crease thickening above his nose, I imagined the sensation was similar.

"I'll take you on a brief tour, as the facility is modern as possible."

Mr. Thornfield wanted me to attend, and I wanted to settle his spirits; so I listened dumbly to short lectures. Absently he said, *this is a microscope;* absently he said, *this is a bone saw.* The morgue was constructed with an attentive eye for detail — there were grooves in all the tables, drainage, plentiful basins, no white tile even a hairsbreadth out of place. When he was quite through, Mr. Thornfield turned, and the face which ought to have been emblazoned with pride looked near as pale as the body he was about to dissect.

"You are mute, Jane. When we walk out of this place, will we two still be friends?" he asked.

Words formed on my tongue and dissolved like dreams; but I already knew what I wanted to say. Striding towards him, I gripped the bend in his forearms where only shirtsleeves separated us, and his hands lifted to mimic mine as if they were not his own.

"You are either asking me that because

you mistakenly think having a morgue under the house would upset me, which it doesn't, or because you know I seek an explanation for your present distress in your past trials. Mr. Thornfield, I . . . I should prefer to risk all than to inflict further torments on myself. May I ask you three questions?"

"You may ask them, but whether I will answer is another matter."

Shaking my head, I pressed warm skin beneath cool cloth. "Have you ever loved?"

"Yes." The reply was immediate, just as I thought it would be.

"Are you now claimed by anyone who made her pledge in exchange for yours?"

"God, no."

"Do you find me objectionable, sir?"

My feelings were at such a high pitch that he could have said anything and pleased me better than what he did: he released the grip he had on my forearms, pulling himself respectfully away.

"Jane, if anyone ever finds you objectionable, direct me to his house that I might test my crop upon his sorry hide. Please believe that I do not, and forgive me for having befriended you; I ought to have calculated the effect that our conversations might have upon an English —"

"I do not speak this way because I am a confused Englishwoman!" I cried. "You know that I have fallen into past errors and have admitted as much yourself. Despite this, or perhaps because of it — damned if I know whether 'tis one or the other — I understand you, and that understanding led to admiration. We are scoundrels, are we not? Please don't turn your face, I am not through! I should not like you to suppose you were endeared to me because I thought you as deficient as I am, or because your past is chequered: that would be a gross misrepresentation of my sentiments. I care for you wholly, entirely, not piecemeal, therefore I charge you to be honest with me regarding your feelings if not your history. Only tell me whether . . . tell me whether you value me too."

This last was delivered upon the thinnest breath of air, and then truth telling could bring me no further: I had unravelled myself, and had only to await his reply.

"Jane." Reaching, Mr. Thornfield trailed his fingers over my shoulder.

"Don't stand there deciding whilst I watch you." Tears were forming, and I forced them back.

"Such a fragile soul she turns out to be after all," he said softly. "Grievous injury frightens her not, yet my standing here without a yes on my lips quite shatters her. How you look, Jane — don't allow me to hurt you so. I don't deserve the privilege, I might venture to say no one on earth does. For God's sake, be the wild creature I found in the lane, free of ties that will only pull you to pieces."

"I won't be torn apart at all, supposing you stay near, sir." Forcing the words from my swollen throat, I added, "I only want to be closer still. You are unattached, you said as much — where is the harm to anyone in claiming me? Whatever you have done, it cannot be so terrible that you must deny yourself human contact forevermore."

"There you would be surprised."

"No, I honestly wouldn't be!" I cried.

He lightly took me by the shoulders, gazing down with such a look of mingled fondness and misery as I have never witnessed.

"If you knew the immensity of my blunders, if you knew how *culpable* I was, you'd be sore tempted to spit in my eye. But that's neither here nor there — I know, and the knowledge will never cease to haunt me," he hissed. "I took small comfort in the fact you were happier here than whatever bloody hellhole you used to occupy in London, the fact I could keep you fed and safe among people who relish your company, but do you really want a partial man, a grotesque carnival figure? The gloves are only an outward symbol of an inner deformity. Please, darling, I hate to see what harm I've already caused you. It's agonising — say only that we can be friends again."

I could say no such thing; my mind felt full of smoke, my ears muffled with the word *darling,* my veins laced with laudanum though I had taken none. Meanwhile, his eyes could or would not stop roving — from my own, to my lips, to my throat, and back again.

I decided that I would look desperate if I said anything more, and thus my next words were not calculated; they were like slipping off a ravine's treacherous edge.

And as long as you still mark me, I don't care.

"You study me, Mr. Thornfield." I placed a shaking hand over his breast. "Do you find me beautiful?"

Slowly, Charles Thornfield pulled his gloves from his pocket and slid them back on; then, looking as flayed as anyone I have ever seen, he strode for the stairs and disappeared within the house.

Not such a very long period passed between his exit and my lifting myself from the cold floor where I had curled into the hard shape of a shell, my sobs buried in my skirts; soon enough my pride had reared its haughty head, and I dragged myself back to my room to pour the salty confessions into my pillow.

That Mr. Thornfield could not desire me would have been devastating, but a clean cut — that he *would* not desire me was a ragged gash indeed. I imagined that no night would ever prove worse, and thus it came as an unpleasant surprise when the following proved very much more hideous indeed.

TWENTY-TWO

There was nothing to cool or banish love in these circumstances; though much to create despair.

The next morning, I resolved to break through Charles Thornfield's walls as if I were a battering ram; but gently, over the course of years, and in the meanwhile I might see his white head bent over a harness buckle he was adjusting for Sahjara, and hear him casually cursing. This plan greatly improved my spirits, and I set to filling Sahjara's pate with horse-related facts, feeling quite myself again by the time we parted.

I ought to have noted something malevolent in the air, for the skies were heavy as lead. Still favouring my ankle, I went into the hall to sort through the mail and discovered an envelope postmarked from London, addressed to Miss Jane Stone.

The slender ivory packet crackled in my grip, but I made no move to open it; the missive could only be from my solicitors, and if they reported I had no claim on Highgate House, then nothing would change. Alternately, if I did own the property, I already lived here, and the thought of Highgate House without Mr. Thornfield was now as appealing as London sans Clarke.

"Have you a letter, Miss Stone?"

Mr. Singh approached, and his features beneath the wiry sweep of his beard were grave.

"Apparently so. No one ever writes to me, so I'm at a bit of a loss."

"We missed you this morning at breakfast."

"I was a trifle unwell."

"Then I am glad to see you looking hale now. Miss Stone . . ." He hesitated, adjusting the cuff upon his wrist. "Did anything distressing happen last night?"

"I found the mortuary," I owned. "I've no aversion."

Provided I have ample warning every time Sam Quillfeather pays a call.

"Oh, marvellous — we feared distressing you, and if you don't mind failing to mention it to Sahjara, we are unsure how she'll take it. When she is older . . ."

"Of course."

"And nothing else occurred? Mr. Thornfield is not himself today."

"Is he all right?" I felt stricken — if he
were morose, I was culpable. The next
instant I felt glad — if he were affected,
hope was not lost.

"Yes," Mr. Singh replied, but the word was
too lengthy for one syllable.

"He told me about the, um. The penance.
The gloves."

"Ah." A frown formed beneath his nobly
hooked nose. "Did he elaborate upon why
he abstains?"

I shook my head.

"The Guru contains passages about abnegation — fasting, meditation, the renuncia-
tion of wealth, but in my opinion, Miss
Stone . . ." He lowered his voice. "Such a
profound sacrifice is not required by God.
The pair of us made a mistake long ago
which led us into terrible circumstances,
but Charles — I beg your pardon, Mr.
Thornfield —"

"It's all right. I know you're not the butler."

"Do you?" he exclaimed.

"I imagine you're a sight better as a commander," I teased.

"Well." He made a small bow, after which his eyes crinkled in distress once more. "Charles, then, feels so culpable that he denies himself touch as a form of self-mortification. I have not yet directly attempted to prevent him, thinking he needed time more than any other balm — but his heart is wide, and bleeds from many hidden wounds."

"So often the way, with hearts."

Brushing a hand over his beard, Mr. Singh passed me, inscrutable, heading towards the front door. I remembered Mrs. Garima Kaur's early assertion to me that he was good, and was grateful, for I knew no one else in whom I could confide.

"I am for the village to settle our bill with the mortuary workmen. Miss Stone, know that I do not take discussion of Charles's heart lightly, and forgive me if I've overburdened you."

"You haven't. He has mine, you know."

Mr. Sardar Singh lingered even as his hand pulled the ornate brass handle of the door. I could not read his face well in any light, so obscured was it by his beard, but now he was quite masked by the cold glow beyond.

"Yes, I thought he might," he admitted. "I will charge him to guard it, Miss Stone. On my honour."

"The Sikh people seem to me very honourable indeed."

Though wintry gusts pelted us, Mr. Singh paused again, and a look steely as his *chakkar* sharpened his features. Since my initial conversation with Garima Kaur over his character, he had never frightened me; now, however, a chill shot down my spine which had nothing to do with the freezing draught.

"There you are mistaken. Which is worse, Miss Stone, if you will pardon my crudeness — a rapist or a pimp?"

"I . . . I can hardly answer that." Crescendos of arctic air whirled into the house. "I should abhor either one."

"Consider the East India Company the rapists, Miss Stone, and the Sikh ruling class the pimps supplying them." He pulled his collar up. "Forgive me . . . you've no desire for a history lesson. Keep yourself well. Charles and I will not return until tomorrow — he met Inspector Quillfeather at his home some miles distant to raise a glass to the mortuary's completion, and we both plan to pass the night there. Thank you for being so free with yourself, as you have given me much to consider."

The door closed, and I watched as the snowflakes turned into teardrops upon the floorboards. Something about this exchange nagged at me — something which I did not understand but felt like awakening in a lightless room with the fanciful certainty that one is not alone.

Soon, I walked upstairs with the unopened letter; it seemed a breathing creature in my hands, and in a way I have always thought that words are alive a little, for they can whisper sweet nothings and roar dragon flame with equal efficiency. After all that had taken place the previous night, I could not even imagine what I wanted it to say, and when I had closed the door to my room, I placed it on the table and stalked about it in circles as if contemplating a chained beast. If I learnt I was not the true mistress of Highgate House, would I prove so spineless as to simply accept Mr. Thornfield's scruples and live as his lovesick shadow for the rest of my days? If I learnt that I was the rightful heir, would I prove so horribly low as to use my power for leverage against his wishes? Both outcomes made me ill; one or the other must inevitably be contained in the envelope, scratching to escape with malicious claws.

At length, I simply hid the volatile missive in my bedchamber; I did not want it now, could not even look at it calmly, but I could not read my future in my teacup either. The remainder of the day was uneventful, closed by a hesitant spill of Scotch I poured for myself in the spreading silence and an hour spent in my bed over a book of Irish poems.

I ought to have been grateful for the tranquillity; tragedy would not strike upon that night, as it happened, until one o'clock in the morning.

There was no sound at first, merely a sense; I snapped awake, *feeling* him downstairs, my eyes stuffed with sleepy cotton.

Dread crawled over my skin an instant later when an unknown object audibly shattered.

When I remember these swift seconds, I was up almost before the china had finished splintering, knowing that Mr. Singh could never be so clumsy and that if Mr. Thornfield had staggered and fell, then he must be drunk, and it was my responsibility to see he was not hurt, for I must have been the one who hurt him; and even if what I was telling myself was nonsense I still yearned to be near him in every capacity, so I threw my dressing gown on and slipped my small knife into its pocket and flew for the ground floor.

If it sounds foolish to race towards a

clumsy housebreaker, I had ample reason; Mr. Thornfield was all I had thought of for weeks of fever dreams and halfhearted plotting, and even if we were both poorly stitched together creatures made of scar tissue and regrets, I wanted only to find a way to live in his world more fully. So I tumbled into the front hall and came face-to-face with the remains of a vase and a man unlike any I had ever previously met.

I could not tell what race he was, for his eyes were dark and his skin burnished, sidewhiskers bright red in the light of his portable lamp; his trousers boasted a loud check pattern and his secondhand coat was wine-coloured velvet. He swayed, emitting acrid whiskey clouds as he panted like the lousiest Company cur north of Calcutta, as Mr. Thornfield would have put it.

Unfortunately, Mr. Thornfield was not present.

"What are ye?" the ruffian snarled, sounding pleased.

The accent was nigh-impossible to parse, but I thought it might have been the result of a Scottish lilt applied to already-musical Indian intonations.

"The governess."

I considered screaming for once in my life; but Mr. Singh and Mr. Thornfield, who slept on the same floor I did, were from home, and the servants inhabited another wing. Apart from Sahjara three doors down from my bedroom, whom I prayed would *not* come downstairs, I was alone.

"D'ye always keep such midnight hours?" he purred, revealing yellowed teeth.

"Get away from here! I'll call the master of the house."

He slanted a canny look at me. "And why haven't ye already? I suspect he ain't here to come when ye do shout."

Morbidity is not the same as stupidity, so I wheeled and made for the kitchen, intending to shriek my face off for whichever Singh or Kaur could hear me; but I found my throat caught in a vise, hashish-laden breath creeping across my cheekbones.

"I meant t' question the half-bred lass, but ye might be a sight better," the rotting relic of foreign wars spoke in my ear. "Tell me now where the trunk is and ye can sleep sound and safe."

"They don't have it!" I choked. "Let me *go!*"

How long we wrestled in that entryway I cannot recall, though I know I landed a number of ineffective blows. I was once more a being of edges and angles, fighting viciously to preserve not only the little girl upstairs I hoped was not roused by our clamour but the woman downstairs, making it.

"That's the most whoreson lie I've heard since leaving Delhi," his fat lips spoke against my ear.

Howling now, though to no one in particular, I fought to free my hands; he had caught both under one burly sweat-smelling arm.

If I could get to my knife.

I can get to my knife.

I will get to my knife.

Laughing in cruel wheezes like the rasp of a hacksaw, he shoved me facedown over the arm of the sofa in the drawing room after he had dragged me there, filling my nose with sweat and leather and lust, and I knew what happened next, had already faced the prospect. His bones bruised my wrists where they were pinioned, his other hand clumsily jostling at my skirts as he raised them.

"D'ye squeal like cows hereabouts, or just eat 'em?" he asked, rancid teeth brushing my neck.

I heard the approach of measured footsteps on the drive, and the front door opening.

Reader: I screamed, and if I could have

404

screamed loud enough, I would have pierced him clean through.

"Damn ye straight t' hell," he growled.

A scorching pain blazed through my head as my assailant seized me by the follicles and led me into the shadows of the large chamber; the noises from the hall ceased.

"I'll see the whole lot o' ye vipers in hell," my captor hissed.

He pressed pocket-warm metal against my gullet, and I had no choice save to follow as he dragged me by the scalp. When Mr. Thornfield and Mr. Singh burst into the room, I yet supposed the weapon a dull knife, but after the brute brandished the thing, I saw that it was a pistol in his hand.

Upon glimpsing my assailant, both men's faces distorted as if a sword had met their bellies.

"How is it possible you're yet alive?" Mr. Thornfield cried, unsheathing the blade he carried.

"Oh, aye, always so shocked when the rent comes due," crooned the man holding me hostage. "Give me the small one who knows where the bounty is buried — or else the trunk, better still — and we'll argue nae further."

"We don't *have it,*" Mr. Singh protested urgently. "And Miss Stone knows nothing of your monstrous intrigues. Let her loose or —"

"Or what?"

"They aren't lying to you," I croaked, still feeling the phantom clench of a fist round my throat.

"It's nae in the Punjab." He rubbed against my cheek, boar's bristles abrading me. "It's nae in jolly old London town. And ye claim it's nae here, but mayhaps a bullet will jog someone's faculties."

"No!" Mr. Thornfield cried.

"Oh, d'ye prefer this aimed at you, then?"

The scorching grip against my hair blazed into a bonfire even as the *badmash* removed his gun from my neck and swung it in the direction of Charles Thornfield.

Mr. Singh, whose movements were generally so calculated you could have set your watch by them, lifted a futile palm in horrified protest; the master of the house looked endearingly relieved, as if having a pistol aimed at his forehead was preferable to its being aimed at mine. My immediate circumstances branded themselves upon my memory — the setting half-moon, the distant scuffles as the servants were roused, the fact Mr. Thornfield was gazing into my eyes rather than the barrel of the weapon now levelled at him. The sheer horror of the

406

scene nearly finished me.

It did not, however — because the black-guard now had one arm devoted to a gun cocked at Mr. Thornfield and the other to tearing my scalp from its moorings; so I whipped out my knife and stabbed blindly backwards with all the fervour men devote to war.

I do not know whether the casual reader of novels is acquainted with an anatomical curiosity known as the femoral artery; without too much medical meandering, although you might suppose that cutting a man's throat would be the fastest way to slaughter him, a good jab to the thigh will do.

Fainting in front of Mr. Thornfield and Mr. Singh was never my object, but faint indeed I did for the second time in my life. Not due to fright — pain swept me under its carpet. It must have been a brief respite, however, for when I came to, I was tucked deep in the settee with a blanket covering me, and Mr. Thornfield was shouting for towels, hovering over the pitifully whimpering brute. Mrs. Garima Kaur was there, looking haggard, twisting her fingers in violent worriment before running to obey the master of the house.

Walls tilted and furniture swam, and perhaps ten minutes later Mr. Thornfield was not shouting for anything anymore, merely gazing with dark satisfaction at what seemed a corpse and a crimson pond upon our floorboards.

The fact of my fifth murder at first slid off my consciousness like water from a goose feather; but I knew instinctually I could not remain in the same room with the dead man lazing in the pool of blood. Wrenching myself upright, I attempted a graceful exit.

"Wait a moment, Jane!" Mr. Thornfield cried.

"I can't stay here."

"You're reeling from hurt and shock, you'll injure —"

"Don't touch me!"

We stared at each other, I in astonishment I had rebuffed him and he in chagrin he had startled me so. His thin grey gloves were covered with the other man's gore, his shirt and waistcoat too, for he had been practicing his profession automatically, I believe, tending to the injured in spite of everything, and I was ready to splinter into a thousand mirror shards reflecting every memory of my own ugliness. Mr. Singh arrived bearing a mop and a bucket of soapy water and stopped, taking measure of the situation.

"Charles." He passed his friend the cleaning supplies. "Miss Stone, will you let me walk beside you to the morning room?"

I started to speak, but clutched at his elbow rather than continue.

Mr. Singh ducked his cloth-bound head against my throbbing scalp in a glancing touch; Mr. Thornfield spread his arms as if in supplication, but since I could not speak, neither to protest the tainted innocence of accident nor beg forgiveness for guilt, I walked away. Mr. Singh accompanied me and, when we were in the morning room, I crossed to the divan and collapsed.

I could not see the shadow which tangled with mine as Sardar Singh hovered over me; I smelt him, though, warm nutmeg and the clean wintry sweat which accompanies a trek on horseback in January, and I fought not to weep at the strange comfort of it.

"Miss Stone, I am no doctor, but Charles will be here shortly, and in the meanwhile you've nothing whatsoever to fear. Are you injured in any sense we're not aware of?"

"No."

"Thank God for that, then," he said as his footfalls grew fainter. "And thank God we were early in returning — we should have been here around midday tomorrow had we

not been loath to leave the property unpro-
tected."

He knelt on the carpet before me with a
glass of brandy when he returned; I swallowed it, and the searing of my bruised
throat brought me back to myself. When I
could focus, I saw that Mr. Singh regarded
me as he might a casualty of a war he had
started, and I did not think I could bear
that expression.

"All this will pass," said I, unsteadily.

"I am glad you think so."

I wanted to elaborate — in this impossible
future, I would not have just murdered yet
another man, Sahjara would break mighty
stallions, Mr. Thornfield would love me, and
everyone would lose the look we had of folk
waiting for the axe to fall.

"I think about many things that aren't
true, even say them sometimes," I confessed
instead, and his mouth tugged fathoms
deep.

"Miss Stone, there is nothing I can do to
relieve your pain over what just occurred.
But I had a sister once, and in a way — in a
very *English* way," he amended, "you remind
me of her. I don't think that anyone who
reminds me of my sister ought to feel so
melancholy about herself, though I understand you must be in a state of extreme

distress."

You really cannot imagine what sort of state I am in.

"Did I kill him?"

"Yes," said he.

I bit my lip, that sharp hurt dulling the ache in my chest. "Was your sister beautiful?"

Mr. Singh smiled. I have visited many churchyards, both as inspiration for gallows ballads and for perverse pleasure, and it was the smile I had found on the carved angels' faces — peaceful but eroding.

"Indeed she was. Her name was Karman, and do you know, that sealed her fate, I think."

"What does it mean?"

" 'Doer of deeds.' Charles will never tell you this, but I was always a pacifist at heart. Oh, I am a skilled warrior, as is our honour and the will of God. But 'Let compassion be your mosque,' the Guru states, and if you were to discuss compassion with a Khalsa *naik*★ today . . ." He shrugged.

I tucked my arm under my pulsating head. "But your sister was a fighter?"

"The great Maharajah Ranjit Singh would have been hard-pressed to win a battle with

★ Corporal.

my sister," Mr. Singh reflected. "Karman, from the time she was small, was wildly passionate. She loved the Khalsa in the new ways, with sharp swords and fat jewels and daring feats, whilst I loved it in the old ways, with meditation and acceptance. 'Whom should I despise, since the one Lord made us all?' If you were to have asked Karman, she would have spat, 'The British and the Bengali strumpets who service them.' Then she would have laughed and shouted, *'Khalsa-ji!'* and you may have thought it merriment, but there was war in her eyes from the age of five, and later, men adored her for it. I did not blame them. I loved her before they did, after all."

"You were a good brother to her."

"Oh, yes," he scoffed. "I taught her to fight with the *tulwar,* the *chakkar,* just as I did Charles, when I ought to have taught her meditation."

"Did it grieve you, that you were so different?"

"A little — but people cannot help being who they are."

"They can help the things they do because of who they are, however."

"Are you merely shaken, or are you often distressed by who you are?" Mr. Singh inquired gently.

"Either." I laughed. "Both, perhaps. I don't know."

" 'If I say I am perishable, it will not avail me; but if I truly know I am perishable, it will.' Miss Stone, pardon me for asking, but . . . do you ever think about death?"

Only of the many deaths I've caused, and my mother's, and my own, and every day.

When I held my tongue, Mr. Singh pressed my wrist. "You do, I see. Then you are far closer to God than you think you are. I must go help Charles."

"Mr. Singh," I called after him with tears in my eyes, "will you tell me what your name was? Before?"

Hesitating, he replied, "Aazaad was my name. It means 'free of care.' "

"And why did you change it?"

This time, he did not pause.

"Because it did not suit me anymore, Miss Stone," he replied, shutting the door softly as he went.

Rolling onto my stomach, I buried my head in my arms and wept. I have seen, employed as a literary phrase, that characters *wept as though the world were ending;* the world ending, I thought, would be better than continuing to deceive compassionate people, lying from dawn to dusk because to stop lying would mean ceasing to be entangled with them.

When I awoke, I felt perfectly at ease though my pate shrieked with pain, and someone was tenderly cleaning the wound with a damp cloth.

I think Mr. Thornfield sensed my wakefulness due to my stilling rather than stirring. A knee was wedged behind the curve of my lower back, and the quilt covered me from neck to toe. I quickly realised it was impossible for him to work with such delicacy of touch whilst still wearing blood-crusted gloves.

The sea could have parted in the centre and it would not have felt as open as I did then, the whorls of his fingertips parting my already scattered tresses.

"Jane, please speak a word if only to berate me. You've done a damn sight more than I tonight, but grant me this single further favour."

I could think of nothing to say, however.

"Darling? Jane, for heaven's sake, only live and let fly at me with all the abuse you like and you'll make me a happy man."

My lungs produced a frightful sound, and he crossed one arm over my torso diagonally, as if protecting me from falling.

"Will you pardon me for murdering someone in your drawing room?" I breathed.

"Oh, Jane." His voice was wracked, vibrating through me, but I shook for more reasons than I liked to think about.

He handled my hair with bare hands, though he never brushed my skin, and I registered sharp hurts, and glass draughts smelling of herbs and strong spirits against my lips and my head. He dried the tear in my scalp, and washed the blood from my locks in a porcelain bowl, and as dawn approached he lifted a tendril of my hair up to his lips even as I fell asleep in his arms, kissing it as though his heart were breaking.

■ ■ ■ ■

VOLUME THREE

■ ■ ■ ■

TWENTY-THREE

Mr. Rochester did, on a future occasion, explain it.

I did not awaken for many hours, though neither did I sleep; my consciousness thinned into a filmy half-awareness, and when I did feel the slow burn of sunlight drifting across my face, I heard a chair creak.

"Jane?"

"Is there water?"

"Of course."

Mr. Thornfield seemed never to have quit the room. Thirst quenched after the glass had been held to my lips, I discovered I was not as hurt as I had supposed. Yes, I had killed a man in front of two respected friends; yes, I had then acted like an abominable weakling; but, no, my cranium had not cracked, only torn, and I found myself staring glassy-eyed at a haggard Mr. Thornfield.

It would do him discredit to pretend he was unmoved, but I hesitate to set down how distressed he was in fact, his countenance as pale as if he were the one who had been strangled.

"I thought when I saw you with that pepperbox* against your throat . . ." He made an abortive movement. "Jane, I hardly know how to speak to you."

"As the governess would suit." I sighed, shifting my knees.

"No, it bloody well would *not*. As the woman I acted a cad towards in the morgue downstairs, or the woman who saved my skin last night?"

"Please don't, sir. You never acted a cad, and I never saved you."

"You saved me sure as God saved Isaac."

My mind could not seem to light upon important subjects, only trivial ones. "How do you know that story?"

"Sardar could write a book entitled *A Thousand and One Useless Meditations.* He knows all when it comes to retribution and forgiveness."

"Not all, or he'd have taught us both to stop hating ourselves. Who was it I killed?"

"Jane, I am hesitant to —"

* Pistol.

"Don't I deserve to know? Sahjara and I both were at risk, and had you not arrived when you did . . ."

His flinch told me he knew I was right, but he took his time: pouring a pair of neat Scotches, passing me one.

"I am all attention, sir."

Mr. Thornfield's chest gave a small heave, and then he abruptly drew his hand over his mouth and sat down close beside me on the divan.

"Where should I begin?"

"Try the beginning."

"What was the beginning? The wars were years in coming," he said softly. "Believe me or don't, or ask Sardar, but it didn't even occur to the British to conquer the Punjab until the Sikh ruling class started dangling it in their faces as if they were *cunchunees.** It was too well fortified, y'see. The Khalsa army was the best in the world, and they *wanted* to march — on Delhi, on London. Geography was never their top marks, bless 'em, but so long as they stayed in the Punjab, they were unbeatable."

"Yet they were still beaten." I sipped the amber liquid. "Mr. Singh called the Com-

---

* Dancing girls.

pany rapists, and the Sikh royalty their pimps."

Mr. Thornfield nodded as his knuckles met his lips. "I can still see the Khalsa parading on the *doab*★ when I was thirteen: a hundred thousand strong marching in such perfect order a Geneva watch would have dashed itself to pieces forthwith. Sapphire turbans, red feathers thrusting from round steel helms, emerald jackets and scarlet jackets and indigo jackets, every jab of the light infantry's bayonets into the sandbags precise enough to kill a gnat. If you've never seen dozens of war elephants draped in crimson, there ain't a way to describe what happens to your stomach. As for the horses — if you watched their white chargers at parade exercise, you could almost grasp why 'He made intuition his horse, and chastity his saddle' is in the Guru."

"How could the monarchy have wanted to throw away its own empire?"

"They didn't want to throw away their empire, that would have been *ridiculous*," he drawled. "They wanted to keep it — keep

★ Dry land between the five rivers of the Punjab. The word *Punjab* itself translates literally to "five rivers."

the palaces and the stuffed coffers and the all-night debauches with man, woman, and donkey — and throw away their army. You build a fighting force that strong, what do you suppose they're keen to do after breakfast and a spot of coffee?"

"Fight," I realised.

He nodded, staring at his sleeve. "When the royals figured out they'd created an uncontrollable army, they got the trots, and arranged for John Bull to slaughter 'em."

"You cannot mean that is truly what happened?" I exclaimed, horrified.

"I can, I was there. Anyhow. There were too many ghastly betrayals to recount, and when the Director of the Company understood that the area was about as stable as a rocking horse, years before the fighting started, he began to send . . . emissaries."

"Spies," I supplied.

"Oh, Jane," he said warmly, and for a spear-flash moment, he was here with me and not long ago and far away. "Spies, yes. The Company soldiers always rather despised the politicals because the latter gorged over greasy state dinners and the former got shot full of holes, but some of these were good eggs."

"John Clements," I suggested, remembering the half story I had been told regarding the funeral.

"Aye, save he'd the brains of a fly whisk. In any event, Lahore grew a bit thicker with white men, though never so's you'd notice unless you were British yourself." The smile he attempted fell yards short of the mark. "I noticed, though, and my mother and father — didn't *they* fleece the sheep. 'Oh, have you seen the Pearl Mosque yet?' and then, 'If a pipe's in your line, guv'ner, won't you share one with me?' and before long they were rooking the lot. One of these Company interlopers was, as you know, a consummate worm by the name of Augustus Sack. Sack's assistant was John Clements, and the third player in this happy pantomime . . ."

"David Lavell," I supplied. "Sahjara's father."

"Yes." Mr. Thornfield coughed. "Yes, he was that as well. So. David Lavell . . . he was five years older than I when he arrived in Lahore, ostensibly to conduct border discussions, but really to take the measure of every toady he could tattle back to Delhi regarding. My family was brown as a nut by then, and Augustus Sack cut too ridiculous a figure for the Sikh to credit him — and if the superior is absurd, why should they mind John Clements trailing after him like a spaniel? But David Lavell was one of your strapping soldier types. For face furniture, the man was a palace. Adonis's brow, blinding teeth, you see the portrait I'm painting."

As I did not trust myself not to say, *he could never be so handsome as you,* I kept my peace.

"He was also charming." Mr. Thornfield spoke the word as if it cut his lips. "Lavell could talk an elephant in *musth** out of charging and, in a cunning way, there were brains in his head. Witness him flatter the jewels off a *kunwar*† one moment! Gape as he drops a hint and ruins an officer's chances for advancement the next! Two-faced? Whoreson bugger had a hundred of 'em, and you hardly minded when your pockets were empty and your mother cashiered."

"You didn't get on."

"Is she truly teasing me?" He sighed fondly. "No, Jane, we didn't get on, but when he discovered that the Thornfield family was quite close to Sardar's, and that loot flowed down our street like rain down a gutter, he began popping round uninvited."

* A highly aggressive, violent madness which can occur seasonally in male elephants.
† The son of a maharajah.

"That is how you and Mr. Singh and the other two British politicals all became acquainted?"

"Yes, and would the Director had sent the devil himself to Lahore first." Mr. Thornfield's face darkened, as if I could see the spiritual bruise beneath the sun-bronzed features. He shifted, seeming to steel himself, drawing a knee up to rest on the sofa beside me. "Did Sardar ever mention to you he had a sister?"

Oh, I thought, my heart breaking for them.

"Karman Kaur," I replied, proud that I kept my voice steady.

Charles Thornfield's lips wavered, but he did not shrink. "I knew her from the cradle, as she was my closest friend's sibling and was always besting me at sword fighting. Sardar's physiognomy has been hidden under that magnificent bush ever since he was old enough to grow one, that's their custom — but you can guess at it, can't you, and she looked very like him."

"Brown skin, grey eyes, slender nose with a fine crook to it, full lower lip. Yes, I can see her."

"I'm glad, Jane," he said, equally low. "It was laughable how arresting she was. Karman was all fire and fight, and if she had

426

been Maharani instead of Jindan Kaur,[*] tens of thousands of the Khalsa would be alive today, because she would have crushed any army who dared to say boo to her."

"Mr. Singh implied that she was considerably more combative than he."

"Wasn't she just!" A smile died before it reached Mr. Thornfield's lips. "But she had a soft side; deucedly handy with children, not to mention horses — you see where Sahjara caught the itch, at least that's part of it — and a laugh that carried clear to Kandahar. Sardar always preferred studying the Guru to the *chakkar;* he just happens to be damnably talented. Karman, though — the three of us once forded all five rivers of the Punjab on horseback as a dare to ourselves, seeing as Ranjit Singh had managed it. Sardar was half a man by the end, I nearly drowned twice, but Karman? I think the daft girl wanted to do it again."

"You loved her very much."

"Not enough for her to notice," came his answer. "But yes."

A silence followed, one tempered by the whispering of the fire and the knowledge that outside, the sun was rising and the

[*] The regent of the last Maharajah, her son Duleep Singh.

427

wind singing arias to the elms. Mr. Thornfield's sadness must have been excruciating; but mine was strangely sweet for, though it pained me, the mere fact of the melancholy meant that he had taken me into his confidence, and so I wrapped myself in it all the tighter.

When I returned from my reverie, Mr. Thornfield was passing me another large glass of spirits. "To your health, Jane."

"And yours, Mr. Thornfield."

"Where to continue? Ah, David Lavell. The cur took a shine to Karman, because he had eyes in his head, and Karman took an equal shine to Lavell, thanks to that perverse rule of Nature which causes pearls to cast themselves before swine. As a female yourself, can you account for this oddity of science, Jane?"

"In some cases, it's because the pearls know themselves grains of sand at heart, though I cannot imagine that should have been the case for Karman."

Pained laughter escaped Mr. Thornfield's chest. "No, her opinion of herself was middling favourable. Perhaps they shared that in common, and God knows that when it came to flattering the Sikhs, to the point of convincing 'em defeating the Company would only be a matter of three or four cavalry and half an hour's botheration, Lavell was a master. From the moment they took up together, I was an object to be pitied, which is a state I do not care for."

I remembered the cracked cloud cover of a London sky a few months after Clarke left me — brain pulsing fit to leak out my ears, covered in dew, observed by a silent beggar whose legs had been lost at the knees and had likewise slept rough in the park. "I understand."

"It was piss on the wound that it was my own fault." Mr. Thornfield took a hearty swallow. "The three of us had been inseparable — studying, shooting, riding out to the Jupindar rocks to drink French brandy filched from my parents and laugh until we were sick. I had assumed her mine already. I was a dunce, carousing with flighty *houri*s* who meant nothing to me and then smoking *bhang*† with Sardar and Karman — they were family, and I expected it all to remain the same. After three months of pining, I announced to my parents that I meant to take up medicine and packed my bags for London."

"Afterwards you needed a legitimate way

* Beautiful women.
† Indian hemp.

back into the Punjab, though, and so signed up for military training at Addiscombe. What happened in the interim?"

"Sardar's letters had been played plenty close, but I could tell something was rotten," he answered. "He mentioned that Karman and Lavell had actually married; he also said she gave birth to a baby named Sahjara, but I was too melancholy for more detail. After Charing Cross and the Aldersgate Street Dispensary were through and I'd earned a place at the Royal College, I spent a single year at Addiscombe because I knew the Punjab was about to blow like a powder keg, and I'm not puffing myself up but complimenting Sardar's early tutelage when I say that was record time. The Company sent me straight back to Lahore, and when I arrived . . ."

I watched as his face turned to stone.

"Lavell was living it up royally. Relations there aren't the same as in England, the elite have plentiful concubines — even the women take lovers. But Karman's husband was hilt deep in every back-alley cat he could find, and when he wasn't drunk, it was hashish or opium. My parents were appalled and shut him out, but it isn't as if buying double the shite poppy can't sustain the habit. Meanwhile, he was practically setting fire to Karman's money, and the last straw came when Sardar spied one of these sloe-eyed tarts waltzing through the market-place wearing a necklace that belonged to his sister. Karman had the typical Sikh taste in baubles, by which I mean she had a disgusting pile of 'em. It was an emerald choker that got away."

"Did Augustus Sack do nothing about this?"

"Sack wasn't his superior, and anyway he was winning a fortune off Lavell at poker — Karman's fortune. Lavell couldn't sink low enough for Sack's taste."

"I imagine you wanted to thrash the hide off him."

"Oh, I threatened to, Company be damned, but we went to Karman first." Mr. Thornfield's mouth wrenched regretfully. "She wouldn't hear a word against the blackguard. She was drunk when Sardar and I arrived, which wasn't exactly surprising, and she was glad to see us as ever, but she waved it all off, saying when the Khalsa marched to Delhi we would all have twenty fortunes to spend, that he was the father of her child and a man who liked to take his pleasure where he found it, and that she was no better, and that we were a set of old hens."

"What did you do?"

Mr. Thornfield placed his brow in his hand. "We stole her jewellery collection."

This, then, was the terrible crime; perhaps it was the Scotch, I pray so, but I laughed. An instant later, Mr. Thornfield was chuckling in the helpless way people have when it is either that or put a pistol in your mouth.

"I know," he groaned. "Jane, Jane, Jane. We thought we were protecting her, and the war broke out the next day. This was December of eighteen forty-five, and the Khalsa army began their march to Ferozepore. Lavell was still stationed in Lahore at the time, and raised all holy Hades when he discovered his candy dish missing."

"What did Karman have to say about it?"

"That's not a tale worth the telling." His jaw clenched briefly. "Sardar hid the jewellery in a Khalsa military-issue satchel in a secret compartment in his own rooms. Then everything fell apart. The war scattered us, for all it was only three months long. Sardar, bless him, was never part of the Khalsa army and remained in Lahore doing business. Lavell went to Amritsar, the capital, and the Director ordered Sack and Clements to consult with the generals at Ferozepore. After the Company won

Ferozeshah, thanks to the Sikh royals castrating their own military, I was called to Ludhiana to provide my services as a medico and Punjabi translator. Are you following me clearly?"

"Yes," I answered, thinking only, *What terrible fate befell Karman Kaur that you will not speak of?*

"I was involved in the Battle of Sobraon, which was decisive." His voice was brittle as glass, and suddenly I remembered Sack's words, his implication that Mr. Thornfield had been severely hurt in the conflict. "Sack and Clements arrived just as the fighting ended, in an advisory capacity, though I can't speak as to their movements because I had been injured — sweet Jane, don't look like that, it was only a scratch from a *tulwar* across my back and upper shoulder, just here, but the blasted cut was infected and I spent a hellish fortnight hardly aware of myself. Clements was at my side whenever he could be. I never forgot that. It was a kindness."

"Then I am grateful to him," I whispered.

Mr. Thornfield's eyes creased in acknowledgement. "After I recovered, as treaty preparations were finalised, I returned to Lahore. Both Lavell and Karman had been killed in the interim. Lavell played one dirty

433

trick too many and ended up with a sliced throat in Amritsar, and when I have occasion to meditate upon that, Jane, my heart is filled with gladness and song."

"In future, so shall mine be, Mr. Thornfield."

Mr. Thornfield sat forward again. "Lahore was filling with dangerous types in the vacuum naturally caused when a region destabilises. I'm afraid Sardar and I then made a decision still more stupid than stealing his sister's unholy stock of jewels; fearful of the thieves swarming the city, we decided to hide 'em in plain sight, and employed Sahjara's doll trunk. Sardar's mum and my shameless buccaneering parents passed a delightful afternoon stuffing dolls with diamonds we'd pried out of their prongs and decorating their little bodies with precious stones. Sahjara was only five, but she had the finest French doll collection outside Paris, and when they were through, you might not have noticed it was anything but a trunk full of the most opulent *chico*'s toys on Earth."

Raptly, I questioned, "Who did notice?"

"Augustus Sack," Mr. Thornfield snarled. "We had told Sahjara that her trunk was forbidden for the time being, which was a fantastic error — she scarce ever touched those dolls in the first place, but we had reminded her of 'em, you see. When Sack returned to Lahore, the maggot, he went to Sardar's house to pay respects and there she was, playing with a doll covered in rubies. Instead of waiting for Sardar, he asked Sahjara if she would show him the doll's sisters, which she was happy to do. Sack recalled Lavell's hysterics over Karman's missing treasure, he added two and two together, and he decided they spelt blackmail."

"How did he go about it?"

"Ah, there's the clever part, that thrice-damned son of a bitch. He told Clements that Sardar and I must have stolen Karman's jewels before the war broke out, recalled Lavell's lamentations to Clements's mind, and asked Clements, as honourable Company men, what should be done about it considering we were all such close mates? Then Sack suggested that, since Karman and Lavell were both dead, why should they not confront us privately, without bringing the Director into it, seizing the trunk and holding it in trust for Sahjara until she came of age? You can imagine how that would have played out."

"How *did* it play out?"

"Exactly as they wanted it to, save for the

fact the trunk had disappeared!" he exclaimed, slapping his palm against his thigh. "We had been keeping it quite in the open, not knowing Sack had designs on it. It was gone. It remains gone. Some lucky *burcha* came in through the window and is whoring his way through Kashmir to this very day."

"What happened afterwards?"

"Sack thought that between Sardar, myself, and Sahjara, *someone* was playing the crooked cross, and *someone* knew where the trunk was." His voice was full of stones. "He bullied us, threatened us, talked of *chowkdar*s, of driving me out of the Company and Sardar out of Lahore."

"You rebuffed them."

"We thought that best."

"Was it?"

Mr. Thornfield studied his stiff scarlet gloves where they yet lay upon the table, and not once did he look up until he had finished. "Sack ordered Sahjara abducted a week later by a half-caste *badmash* named Jack Ghosh he sometimes used for his dirty work. You not six hours ago killed Jack Ghosh, an act which I assure you deserves a medal and a pension. Sardar and I practically lost our minds when we had word that Ghosh would feed her when we had delivered the trunk to a secret locale. We, I remind you, did not have the trunk."

My lips parted in horror. I thought of Sahjara — her complete candour, her keen black eyes — and could not help but shudder. She had never come downstairs, so I lived in hope that the events of the previous night had not touched her.

"How long did it take you to find her?"

"Four days," he rasped. He pressed his hand over his mouth, then continued. "Clements knew nothing of the scheme, thinking Ghosh had acted alone after hearing of the trunk from Sack, so he was of no use in finding her, though he aided all our efforts — as for Sack, he made certain to be away from Lahore at the time, or I should have knocked her whereabouts straight from his skull. Sahjara was locked in a desert stable when we found her, by which I mean a tent with horses in it, all alone, her captor fled. Ghosh had kept her quiet by having her feed and brush and water the animals, telling her when she was finished, she could eat. She was never quite the same afterwards."

Tears were streaming from my eyes. "Oh, Mr. Thornfield."

"It's not the worst event I've ever caused." He laughed unsteadily. "Enough of this. We retrieved her. Of course we realised who was behind it all, but there was no evidence — only Sack's knowing little smirk when I stormed into his offices raving over the kidnap. The Company was in full force by that time, secretaries and clerks thick as fleas, but Ghosh had fled and I couldn't accuse Sack without exposing the original theft. So I went to my superior officers, begging for Ghosh to be found — they laughed in my face. What was the disappearance of a half-caste villain to the subjugation of an empire?"

"Did they offer you no assistance?"

"The most they would do was provide a guardian to send Sahjara to my paternal aunt's house in Cornwall, for she started at every shadow in Lahore, and I was still in the employ of the Director. Sardar thought of accompanying her, but his mother was ill at the time, and fresh fighting loomed, so we put Sahjara in the frankly doting care of a wounded lieutenant returning to his family. That put Sack off long enough for the second Sikh war to break out, and there you have it. After I inherited this place, I sold my commission, and Sardar and I were bumping across the desert from Suez to Cairo in the back of a wagon to take the steam route here from Alexandria."

I pulled at my hair, wanting the dull ache. "Do you think Sack tired of waiting and sent Ghosh on this occasion as well?"

"Very likely. I'm only glad he's stone dead in the morgue downstairs."

"Did Sahjara ever wake?"

"Yes, but we bundled her off with Garima Kaur, so she's quite snug, thank heaven. If anything should have happened to her here . . . Jane, I am forever in your debt. I've never managed to do as much for her."

"You gave up your home for her, sir. You gave up everything."

"Ridiculous. Christ, if I never see the Punjab again, it'll be too soon. I have her, and Sardar, and this house, and that's a deuced sight more than I merit."

I thought of Clarke long ago, our fleeing to London and her telling me I was *home*, and was so deep in lightless conjectures I nearly missed Mr. Thornfield saying, "And now a true friend in you, Jane."

Suddenly nauseated, I shivered. A wall which has been well constructed with strong stones and good masonry can defend against many a dire circumstance; but put a single crack in that mossy edifice, and a former fortress is as good as a pile of rocks.

They knew me for a killer; Clarke's words regarding Hugh and Bertha Grizzlehurst rang in my ear as if her lips were pressed to the lobe.

She'll never be able to look him in the face again without knowing — can you imagine the torment?

"Jane, wherever you've gone to, please come back to me, or anyway what's left of me at the moment," a rough voice pleaded.

Standing unsteadily, I shook my head. I must have looked a fright, traces of blood on my gown, mermaid hair snaking its brown waves all about my waxen face. I set the glass down and made for the door.

"Let me —"

"I'm fine on my own."

"You most certainly are not."

"Alone, I want to be alone."

"You really do, and for the first time I've ever observed. Is this to be the end of the peculiar smile I see form whensoever you spy me? I can imagine it all too easily — no warm tilt of your head, no spark of light in your eye. Do you think me a blackguard following that terrible account, Jane?" he questioned raggedly, the edge of his sleeve painted ivory by the brightening dawn rays bleeding through the curtains.

"I think you an eyewitness," I gasped before I could stop myself, but he did not know what I meant, he could never ever know what I meant, so I ran from the room and up the stairs and locked the door and did not emerge again that day.

TWENTY-FOUR

He who is taken out to pass through a fair scene to the scaffold, thinks not of the flowers that smile on his road, but of the block and axe-edge; of the disseverment of bone and vein; of the grave gaping at the end: and I thought of drear flight and homeless wandering — and oh! with agony I thought of what I left!

After a sleep which felt more like drowning than rest, tempests tossing me, I awoke to discover it was dark. Silently, I crept to the door, gazing out into the corridor; no one was there, but a tray of bread and cheese and fruit had been left, and a bottle of wine, and I quickly collected these, shutting myself in once more.

Tying my messy hair into a painful braid, I stoked the fire which had burnt down to coals. The sustenance was accompanied by a note:

Dear Jane,

I should have set myself as guardian over your gate forever, save that I cannot know whether I inspire feelings of safety and security in you or dampen them, and immediate arrangements must be made. You shall not be disturbed, I vow, and should you wish to disturb any of us, a bell rung will be answered upon the instant. I cannot help but live in hope I might be called for personally, but already owe you far too great a debt to make any further presumptions.

Sahjara is from home, staying with Mrs. Garima Kaur in the cottage with the grooms rotating watches over them. Whilst investigating last night's siege, we thought it best; should you wish to repair there, arrangements would be made with all haste, and the place has been thoroughly cleaned and heated.

It grows less and less bearable to consider denying you any wishes, come to that, save only those beyond my power — if you can imagine a way I might ease the burden a good woman like yourself should never have had to bear, I beg you to command me.

Your servant,
Charles Thornfield

Laughing at the depth of this miscalculation, I forced myself to eat food which turned to cinders on my tongue, washing all down with half the bottle of wine and a larger dose of laudanum than I had taken since my London days, for my head felt as if a glowing poker had struck it.

It was not, I ought to clarify, troubling to me that Jack Ghosh was no longer numbered among the living; he had hurt a little girl I had grown to love, and in any case, he had not precisely inspired esteem during our brief acquaintance. No, he could rot for all I cared, and he would, too — but he had smashed my dam and now the seawater was up to my neck.

I could live a complete lie, I comprehended as I sorted through the knotted threads of dread in my chest; I could not live a partial one.

Already, falling in love with Charles Thornfield had meant dropping truths in his path like so many bread crumbs, and though he may have approved my stabbing Jack Ghosh, however could I justify four previous killings? The number was outrageous. I could neither lie, nor could I confess; and I could neither pull down his walls without candour nor risk baring my hollowed heart.

When Jane Eyre understands that she must depart from Mr. Rochester or else become his mistress and not his wife, her eyes remain entirely dry, and her former fiancé surmises that her heart must have been weeping blood before he begs her to stay. I admire this passage for a number of reasons — not merely because it is beautiful, but because I can be moved by it even when recalling my own experience of leaving Highgate House, and my reasons for doing so, and want to shake the other Jane's damn fool head off for leaving a gentleman who loved her so, and was remorseful for his error. For I understood that night — not with a dry eye, either — that as much as I had come to adore Sahjara and esteem Mr. Singh, I could not love Mr. Thornfield every livelong day without having him.

I could have lived off my fingers in his white hair, or my brow against his collarbone, or the whole expanse of our bared skin nestled together in sleep, or my lips against his rugged temple. I had done far worse things for love than entwine fingers or kiss the nape of a neck, had I not? The prospect of total famine, however, dying of thirst and nothing betwixt me and the glass of water resting on the table — I cannot imagine that anyone could have done it.

Very well, I determined around midnight, my eyes crimson and my head pounding. *You will live as you used to, and life is a tenuous thing after all, so one day inevitably the hurt will stop.*

There was still the matter of Highgate House, however, so I located the fateful letter from London and opened it with shaking fingers.

SNEEVES, SWANSEA, AND
  TURNER
No. 29C Lisle Street,
Westminster

Dear Miss Steele,

Though you addressed your letter to Mr. Swansea, that gentleman passed away six years hence, necessitating my own return from abroad; thus, know that it is Mr. Cyrus Sneeves who addresses you. If you are able to call upon me at the above address, I believe I can make your position clear to you; in fact, I consider it my duty to do so, as I may have an unexpected opportunity to right a wrong which I had begun to consider permanent.

I regret the loss of my partner but rejoice in the fact your appeal found me.

Forgive my reticence but the matter is of such delicacy that to confide it to ink and paper would be unforgivable. There even exist solicitors who abhor scandal, if you can credit me, and I number myself among them.

Humbly,
Cyrus Sneeves, Esq.

My blood seemed to thin as a weightless excitement filled me.

No longer did I delude myself that I could usurp Highgate House from people I had grown to love; but if the property were clearly mine, perhaps I should not have to pen gallows ballads, or perhaps I could pen them from the relative luxury of a small Chelsea flat. I should not ask Mr. Thornfield for any staff or horses: merely enough of an allowance that I might live well, and my other expenses should be supplied by my writing. Mr. Thornfield had, after all, given a thousand pounds each to the white servants who had left his employ; surely I, a woman for whom he harboured a slight attachment, could request assistance when Highgate House was legally mine?

And think that twice yearly — no, once a month, you might insist upon once a month — a cheque would be delivered to Mr. Sneeves

and perhaps a letter with it! If you had his let-
ters, you could have as much of him as here
at Highgate House.

I dried my eyes. This would not be an ideal life, living with a tiny gouge where my heart had once been; but it would be a possible one, one which would make waiting to die more tolerable.

Since he could not touch me, what was it to him if I was here or in London? I had been accounted a good enough writer to earn my stout and oysters by it; if the endearments I showered him with, all the languidly falling petals of my shaken tree, were written rather than spoken, so much the better — he could read them over whensoever he liked, shove them in a drawer if he preferred, and my love would have some permanence, the way whispers made in the dead of night do not.

I retained his first letter by accident, the one regarding my ankle — I had set it upon the mantelpiece and simply forgot to bin it. Standing, I went to fetch the artefact; for a few seconds, I studied the curve of his *e*'s, and then I carefully refolded this as well as the latest note and placed them in the grey reticule I had bought at a slop shop off Covent Garden, thinking it would suit a governess.

Then I went to the mirror to survey the carnage; my features were so petite that eighty percent of them were blotchy, and my eyes so large that the whites appeared bloody pools. Washing my face in cold water helped a bit, and — when I beheld myself again — I realised that there was a third reason to go to London other than escaping Mr. Thornfield and finding Mr. Sneeves.

If I could settle this dark affair for the residents of Highgate House, would that not be a fine thing?

Resolved, I took a quiet moment to regard Aunt Patience's old room with all its lovely new trappings, the draperies in impossible shades of lavender and plum, the melancholy patina of winter moonlight . . . and then I set to packing.

Getting my things in order was not difficult, and I spent the rest of the night in a downy laudanum haze, only stopping the small doses when I collapsed into bed a mere few hours after quitting it. A brightly scouring sun woke me early, for I had forgot to draw the curtains; this was for the best, however, and I did my hair up carefully but looser than usual. Lifting my trunk, I carried it downstairs and left it in the hall.

The coward in me wanted to avoid Mr.

Thornfield entirely and simply ask one of the Singhs in the stables to drop me in town. When I thought of the crags of his cynical brows, however, I knew I must explain myself or go mad to the tune of hearing, *Do you think me a blackguard following that terrible account, Jane?* So I went to the parlour and dining room and, finding them deserted, approached his study and knocked.

"Enter."

I peered in; Mr. Thornfield was writing a hurried correspondence, but he levered to his feet, rounding the desk. Either his gloves had been cleaned or he owned multiple pairs, for his linens were spotless and his cravat a rich flourish of burgundy; his cheeks below their sharp angles were sunken, however, and his eyes clearly questioned whether he was about to receive a greeting or a curse.

"The heroine emerges." The accompanying smile was a faintly glinting sickle. He approached me. "Oh, Jane, have you been crying all this while?"

"Some."

"God help us, you have every right, only I cannot bear to see it. You are unaware, I think, of the effect your misery has upon me."

"Perhaps so," I owned as another drop escaped.

He brushed it away with an almost reverential touch, then gestured at a chair and abruptly returned behind the desk. "Had you been a precious lamb and I a doting shepherd who found it rent by wolves, I couldn't feel any more harrowed over this — but you are not a lamb, thank Christ for that, you are a lioness and have no need of my bloody incompetent safeguarding. I shall make this all up to you in any way I can, however."

"I wondered . . ." Lowering myself into the chair, I hesitated. "I would appreciate an advance upon my wages."

"Of course." He was already pulling the cheque-book from the drawer. "How much?"

"Whatever you think fair, Mr. Thornfield."

An efficient scratching sounded. "Will a hundred pounds do?"

"You don't owe me a hundred pounds!" I exclaimed.

"Must I listen to her talk utter tripe so early in the morning?" he muttered, gripping the blotter. "Here — payment for initial services rendered, including delivering historical, scientific, deportmental, and elocutionary lessons translated into equine

451

form, not to mention reparations for medical disasters. If you want more, you have only to say."

Swallowing, I placed the cheque in my reticule with the two letters. I did this, reader, because the most idiotic thing that Jane Eyre ever did other than to leave in the first place was to depart without her pearl necklace and half Mr. Rochester's fortune, which he would gladly have given her. If she had been eaten by a bear upon fleeing penniless into the wilderness, I should have shaken that bear's paw.

"How cheerless you look still," he reflected, stormy eyes feathering at their corners. "Come, ask me for something else so that I can say yes, saving only a trunk containing half a million in bauble-draped dolls, for damned if I've got it."

"So much?"

"Yes, blast the cursed thing."

I cleared my throat. "Mr. Thornfield, I came to tell you my things are packed."

He scarcely seemed surprised, and soon I fathomed why. "Do you prefer to take a bite of breakfast with me first, or shall I carry 'em over to the cottage so you can dine with Sahjara? I'll be glad of your company provided you can stomach mine, but you must wish to see her."

I twisted my fingers together in my lap. "Mr. Thornfield, I am quitting Highgate House. I cannot stay here."

Mere seconds had passed since he had called me a lamb he should have dreaded to see injured; even were I to etch the words I am now penning straight into the flesh of my arm, the slices would not cut me so thoroughly as his expression did. Far from protesting, Charles Thornfield froze in surprise, then seemed to crumple, as if taking a blow which was not unexpected.

"No, it isn't that," I pleaded. "It's not your story, nor the distress I was caused — I want to hear all of your woes, and I'd wield a knife for your sake a thousand times over, but you honestly cannot want me to have charge of your ward."

"Why the devil not?" he demanded hoarsely.

"Because . . . because you know me to be a murderer."

"For Christ's sake, Jane, that makes a neatly matched pair of us. We'll set up snug as salt and pepper cellars and Sardar can give sermons to us in the garden of a Sunday."

Mr. Thornfield's shoulders bristled after this statement was hurled at me; but it was all bravado, for he searched my eyes as if all his many missed turnings were mapped in them.

"I . . . But of course, you were in two wars," I stammered. "That isn't the same thing at all."

Charles Thornfield drew a stuttering breath — but instead of speaking, he brushed a hand over his lips, shutting his eyes in despair.

"This is why I cannot stay," I cried. Rushing to the desk, I took both his gloved hands, which shook like the fine tremor in the bow after the arrow has flown. "You could tell me all and never diminish yourself in my estimation, but these half confidences are like Solomon's suggestion of cutting a child in half. I understand what it is to feel so myself, for you *know* I have secrets, and it would never be enough, sharing fractions when I'm the greediest soul in shoe leather. I should blurt it all out, every sordid sin, and want the same of you, be petty and selfish and the most hateful person you've ever known when you deny me."

"That is the most whopping pack of calumnies I have ever heard," he husked, shifting my hands in his and studying them where they sat cradled. "Take 'em back this instant. You could never be hateful. And Sahjara will . . ." He shook his head, still not raising his eyes. "I hardly know what to say to her. Or to Sardar, either."

"Tell them I ruined everything, that I always ruin everything."

"Stop this," he growled. "It was my own wretched fault. You are a young woman — intelligent, beautiful, vibrant. Why should you wish to live with a pair of ruined men in a house full of ghosts?"

"But I never minded that! Only you ought to be free to see ghosts without my demanding to know where the bodies are buried. I've always wanted too much, sir — your not wanting me back doesn't make you culpable."

"I never said I didn't want you."

"You could say it now," I requested, heart hammering.

"No." He glanced up at last. Whatever gnawed him, it had burrowed through to the bone. "I could *not* say that, Jane."

"Heaven help me, this is madness." I leant forward, half-seated on his desk and inches from his weathered features. "The whole truth, is that what you want — *my* truth in exchange for your own? It could quite literally cost me my life, I . . . You know what happened when Ghosh attacked me, and —"

"That was self-defence, you raving —"

"But I'd not care, I wouldn't, not so long as you loved me. I should be the happiest woman on earth if you did. Anyone would be."

"The last one wasn't."

I suspect something else would have happened there in that cosy study, our lips parted and eyes ablaze with both craving and restraint, had we not heard steadily approaching footfalls.

"Jane!" he protested when I pulled away, but I turned my back as he rose, composing myself, and so it was in the mirror above the hearth that I first saw the door swing open following a confident knock and Inspector Sam Quillfeather enter the room.

I did not scream; it was a near thing, however.

"Oh, gracious me, what was I thinking barging in so?"

Teeth set tight as a ship's hull and eyes glued to the mirror, I took in Mr. Quillfeather. He had aged, but not diminished, and the perennial forward sweep of his spine and the exaggerated arches of his nose and chin and brow would already have imparted an impression of relentless momentum without the additional trajectory of his steel-grey shock of hair as he swept off his shabby beaver hat.

"Quillfeather." My employer quickly forced his features into neutrality, but this only left him resembling a tattered shoreline after a squall.

"I'll come back after surveying the cellar?" Mr. Quillfeather proposed, voice retaining the old questioning lilt. "I'm before my time, I see — yes, three full minutes! Won't you forgive me? I'll just —"

"No, no, it's all right." Mr. Thornfield coughed. "Inspector Sam Quillfeather, may I introduce Miss Jane Stone, Sahjara's governess?"

There was nothing for it: I forced my fists to unclench and turned to face the gallows.

He might not recognise you, not after so many years and so much sorrow, I told myself.

Gallantly, he made a neat bow over my hand; and then his eyes met mine, variegated hazel and canny as ever, and a spark flared to life, and I was caught. For Highgate House had been mine before my disappearance and here I was again, and he could not help but know me.

"Mrs. Stone, I take it?" he clarified. "It is very good to see you again in these parts. A country widow and so young?"

"No indeed, she comes to us from London."

Mr. Quillfeather studied me, and then Mr. Thornfield added his curious gaze to the already potent atmosphere, and I was just considering the benefits of throwing myself into the fireplace when the inspector waved his hand in the air.

"Of course, of course, I must have momentarily mistook her? The older I get, the more everything and everyone manages to remind me of, well, of something or someone else entirely? Pleased to meet you, Miss Stone."

"Likewise," I managed.

The floor was opening like a pit beneath me, gravity turned upside down.

"Was Miss Stone affected by these dreadful events?" Mr. Quillfeather asked, politely addressing Mr. Thornfield.

The trail of bodies, oh God, he knows, he must know, first Edwin for certain and then Vesalius Munt in all likelihood, and now there just happens to be another carcass needs burying and here I —

Mr. Thornfield hesitated not a whit. "Miss Stone arrived downstairs first following the crash which alerted us, and suffered injury at Jack Ghosh's hands — but thankfully, he was already bleeding out. I'll show you the window and the glass, naturally, but it's all quite straightforward. Hoisted upon his own petard at last, if you'll pardon my satisfied tone, Quillfeather."

"Nothing to pardon, my good man! You suspect Sack's behind this?"

"I should be a simpleton not to."

"Yes, yes, we'll work it out between us, won't we? How was the young lady injured?"

"Torn scalp. It bled considerably, and she nary made a sound. If you ask me, the blackguard could have died for that alone and I should have said good riddance," Mr. Thornfield droned in his haughtiest tone even as his eyes dared me to contradict him.

"Might I see, Miss Stone?" Sam Quillfeather asked gently.

What could I do? I bent my head, and Mr. Thornfield cupped my nape in a tender touch I did not think planned, and Mr. Quillfeather tutted, "Shameful, Thornfield, simply shameful," and I raised my face after a gentle press to my neck preceded both men stepping back.

"What luck it was only a minor insult?" Again Mr. Quillfeather turned to Mr. Thornfield for confirmation, and the latter nodded curtly. Then the inspector glanced back at me.

"A painful hurt, and a lucky escape," he repeated. "Frankly, it . . . reminds me of something, Miss Stone?"

A torn sleeve and a cousin dead at the bottom of a ravine. My mouth turned instantly dry.

"Jane, why don't you lie down for a little?" Mr. Thornfield suggested, the gash between his brows thickening. "These have been trying times, and for no one more than yourself. Go to the parlour and try the settee — I'll be along after I post Quillfeather here, all right?"

"Just the thing — can you make it unescorted, Miss Stone?" the inspector asked, bending forward solicitously.

"Yes," said I. "Please don't concern yourselves."

"We'll talk further soon," Charles Thornfield said, voice as tight as it was fond. "Sleep if you can, but we shouldn't be more than an hour."

"Take your time. Excuse me, gentlemen."

When I walked into the corridor, I paused for only a second; one glance at the packed trunk persuaded me to leave it behind. It contained nothing I wanted, not without Mr. Thornfield, and I carried the cheque and my collection of letters in my reticule. Walking at first, then sprinting, I raced for the stables and ordered Nalin saddled and after stealing the horse he had given me, I rode hell for leather towards the village.

Twenty-Five

Some say there is enjoyment in looking back to painful experience past; but at this day I can scarcely bear to review the times to which I allude: the moral degradation, blent with the physical suffering, form too distressing a recollection ever to be willingly dwelt on.

I left the spirited mare in the care of the inn, leaving explicit instructions that it should be returned to Highgate House and whatever man they sent would be compensated; this transaction complete, I booked a seat on the next coach with coin collected writing gallows ballads, which stock had not been depleted. Then I bought a penny roll and sat upon a bench outside the inn and began numbly to eat, knowing the miles ahead to be slow and dreary as the Thames.

I had an hour's worth, more or less, of a head start, and the gallop had taken a mere ten minutes. The coach, meanwhile, should leave in half an hour, and *perhaps Mr. Thornfield has not yet been told by Mr. Quillfeather I pushed a child over a cliff and speared a headmaster through the neck, perhaps* —

"Miss Stone?"

Thankfully I had forced the last of the roll down, else I should have suffocated; there stood Mr. Sardar Singh, warmly bundled, a sheaf of papers tucked under his arm, his the only head in the sluggish trickle of pedestrians which had been wrapped in an elaborate configuration of sky blue (which doubtless accounted for the hostile stares). He was accompanied by Mrs. Garima Kaur, who was recording something in a small pocketbook; her gaunt face looked still more stark than usual, her eyes lost in the curves of her skull.

"Oh!" I exclaimed, shrinking. "What are you doing here, Mr. Singh?"

"Picking up blank death certificates for Charles from the village physician — we're not quite outfitted fully, and are to meet with Mr. Sam Quillfeather today."

"Yes, he's there at the house."

I knew I did not sound right; I hated that I did not sound right. Mr. Singh turned to Mrs. Kaur, conferring in Punjabi. She looked at me so oddly, a mingling of inquisitiveness and something I could not identify, that I averted my eyes; thus I only saw in my periphery that, after a muted request, Mrs. Kaur began walking briskly back in the direction of Highgate House.

"We are quite alone, Miss Stone, unless you wish it otherwise," I heard Mr. Singh state.

My vision blurred until I was seeing from the bottom of a lake; then the bench squeaked and a hand was at my elbow.

"What in heaven's name is — Has something else happened, Miss Stone?"

"Nothing to speak of."

"Miss Stone, please know I would hold any confidence from you under eternal lock and key."

"It isn't that I don't trust you."

"Then please assure me that you're all right," he insisted more strongly.

Several seconds passed.

"I'm not all right," I choked at last. "I cannot remain in Mr. Thornfield's company."

Ascertaining what the stuffy, sausage-smelling citizens of that hamlet thought of a Sikh dressed as an Englishman wrapping his arms around a governess as she sobbed soundlessly into his coat would be quite impossible, for I could see nothing whatsoever. However many stares we garnered, the activity served a dual purpose; my heart was breaking, so the simple comfort was appreciated; and if I keened over cruel fate and lost love, I should not have to explain I was also running away to London to escape execution.

"Yes, there . . . that's better," he said as I calmed. "Miss Stone, may I ask what brought matters to this state?"

His grey eyes were bright with compassion when I pulled away. After he had passed me his handkerchief and sat there patiently as the quaking in my shoulders lessened, I found I did indeed wish to speak with him, and still had fifteen minutes before my coach departed.

"Forgive me for making such a scene."

"Not at all."

"It's just . . . the night I killed that scoundrel, Mr. Thornfield told me about your sister and Sahjara's abduction and the trunk, and it's horrible you were dragged into such a nightmare, and I know you both to be honourable, but he says he's a murderer and he won't say how or when, and he won't say he doesn't want me, he won't say anything at all of consequence, nor touch me, nor trust me, and I *cannot bear it* any longer."

"Ah," he said. "Then your sorrow is partly

my doing, and I have been gravely at fault."

"Regarding?"

"Charles's refusal to touch living people."

My mouth must have gaped overlong for, passing his fingertips over his beard, he continued after a brief reflection.

"Charles emulates me, always has done. Even when I have tried to prevent him. But the specific point I am making, Miss Stone," Mr. Singh said, measuring his words, "is that I am both devout and monastic, and I think Charles may well have confused the two. I have never been married. I have no interest in marriage or its accompanying joys."

I stared, yes, but he did not seem ruffled. "You have never loved, then?"

"That is not remotely what I meant," he corrected mildly.

"Oh. You are . . ."

I trailed off, helpless; after he had registered shock, he shook his head.

"No," he answered firmly. "Ah, I see why you — I beg your pardon. Yes, of course I love Charles, but no."

I thought a little longer. "You are like a priest? Devoted to God and to study?"

"There we have it," he approved before the shadow returned to his face. "But you must understand, it is very easy for someone

466

who is not tempted by flesh to be celibate, and I have always been so — content to watch the moon rise, to try a new spice, to practise the *chakkar* but never use it to harm. When I was small, I dreamt of sitting under a tree, waiting for God to possess me with divine knowledge which would incinerate my very soul. If God told me to give up strong coffee, I would feel that loss keenly, and God would thus honour my sacrifice. But I do not actually long for the thing I abstain from — which is not abstinence at all. So I am simply wondering whether, in my own infinite ignorance, I contributed to this great error Charles has made."

"Nothing you've said implies you were gravely at fault in any way."

"Then I have not helped so much as I ought to have done."

"Why should you help me?"

"Why should I not? Help Charles is what I meant, however." He sighed. "His life, his body — I have told you already such sacrifices occur in the Guru, but this is a needlessly raised shield after the battle has already left one bloody."

"You've plenty to fear yet, it seems," I reminded him, feeling Jack Ghosh's fingers crushing my soft throat.

"That is a new battle," he corrected,

frowning. "I never dreamt of the old battle haunting us here save in ways you have already mentioned — our own. It's most peculiar, if you ask me. This trunk business must have an end put to it, for Sahjara's sake if not ours."

And I shall help in any way I can, I vowed to myself.

Mr. Singh's face took on the quality of a death mask. "Did Charles tell you whom he murdered, if neither how nor when?"

I shook my head.

"Do not believe him, then, when he claims to be a murderer," he said hoarsely. "Unless he has been killing other people than the one I am thinking of, he is not to be trusted on the subject."

"I don't know how many subjects he is to be trusted upon — he said he should never miss exile from the Punjab, for instance."

"He and I are agreed." His voice scraped now, a blade being sharpened upon a stone. "I loved Lahore, but to watch an empire sabotage itself so? We were all meant to be lions, but some of us proved unshorn dogs. Why do you suppose we are warriors, Miss Stone? It is because our Gurus have been sat upon red-hot iron plates and covered with scorching sand, sewn into raw hides which shrank and broke their bones, had pegs thrust in their heads and their brains removed when yet alive. My people have been slaughtered like animals, our cities sacked, children's bellies slit, our sacred pool filled with our hacked-apart bodies, and for what? So we might throw away the richest land in all of Asia?" His hands spasmed into fists. "I was not exaggerating when I said my sister should have been maharani — instead, the Company butchered us like cattle. There is too much blood in the sands of the Punjab, Miss Stone."

I did not know what to say. We watched the inching progression of a sweet-faced crone on the arm of her grandson, listened as the church's bell sang salutations to the heavens, marked the stares slitting towards us in charcoal shadows of doubt and disgust.

"Mr. Thornfield implied that as long as you and Sahjara are here, he has all the home he requires."

A smile barely brushed the corners of his lips. "He does us honour, then."

Nodding bleakly, I checked the inn's entrance. The carriage had clattered into the manure-strewn yard and I rose, indicating it to Mr. Singh with my eyes; he stood, looking appalled.

"But — *now*? Where is your trunk, where

469

your farewell to the household, why —"

"I can't." I forced back the tears which newly threatened. "Please tell Sahjara I love her, and ask her forgiveness. If — when I see her again, I'll be glad of it. Mr. Thornfield gave me a hundred pounds. I'll be fine. I still have my knife to protect me from *bad-mashes.*"

I did not achieve a second smile, but the set of his lips did grow a shade less alarmed.

Clasping my hand, he said, "In that case, farewell, Miss Jane Stone, and send us word of your whereabouts at once. Should you ever wish to trade the name Jane Stone for Jane Kaur, however, you should make a wise and courageous Sikh princess, and must return to us immediately. I beg you to consider it — the return, at least, if not the new moniker."

Walking towards the coach was like pulling my own skin off, but Mr. Singh helped by stepping back courteously.

"Keep them safe," I called when I reached the tall step. "Parting from you, from Sahjara, from Mr. Thornfield — well, the poets are liars. It isn't sweet sorrow at all, it's like dying a little."

Mr. Singh turned towards the half-timbered hostelry and Mr. Thornfield's waiting carriage. "So often the way," he agreed sombrely, "with partings."

My journey to London was a clanking, frigid stretch of dull farms and weathered church spires during which none of the other passengers so much as snored in my direction. When I at last arrived in the city, still shaking from the road's vibrations as well as nerves, I knew myself too sensible simply to crawl to a low lodging-house in Drury Lane and forget the sour bedclothes with the help of a pint of rum; so I walked for a few miles, stopping before the door of a seedy theatre for a ham sandwich with mustard and a tin cup of coffee.

Restored, I recalled a guesthouse called the Weathercock in Orchard Street, Westminster, where I had lived for a few weeks high on the hog with the best-paid and best-educated literary patterers. As I was already near Marylebone, travelling there by foot would be easy as blinking, so I thanked the sandwich man and set off.

All was as I remembered it, a pretty white-painted building with gas lamps aglow at either side of the broad front steps, and men of letters guffawing over politics in the lobby. When I rang the bell, the clerk expressed dismay at my lack of luggage; however, as I had the commodities of both tears and money at the ready, pleading railway thieves, I had soon obtained his sympathies, and he vowed to send the boots round for toiletries, laudanum (my pate ached something terrible, as did my heart), and a packet of tooth powder.

The Weathercock had a lending library for the consideration of 1d. per week, to be paid upon Sundays, but I further endeared myself to the establishment by paying for this privilege immediately, made a selection based upon the volume having slipped down against its cohorts in a defeated diagonal posture, and took a glass of hot brandy and lemon to my room.

After a desolate time spent nursing that toddy — though no tears, for the rest of them had taken up residence in Mr. Singh's coat — I had produced a plan of action. This was three-pronged, and intended the following goals be achieved:

— Remove all threat from the lives endangered by Augustus P. Sack
— Ascertain whether you are the heiress of Highgate House
— Escape the clutches of Mr. Sam Quillfeather and avoid the noose

Penning this last, I shivered. Inspector

Quillfeather may well have forgot every-thing, may well have indulged his friend Charles Thornfield, may well even have wanted to see the corpse before leaping to conclusions; but I had witnessed his abso-lute recognition of me, had heard him sug-gest I must have been a widow in a polite effort to explain why he was addressing a Stone and not a Steele. Sam Quillfeather was decorous and might even be kind; Sam Quillfeather was not stupid, however, and he had just examined the body of yet an-other chap slaughtered by my hands.

By my calculation, knowing where I stood upon these matters now that I had vanished would take me no more than a fortnight; resolving them, no more than a few months. I had enough money to live for some two years with only the hundred pounds Mr. Thornfield bestowed, provided I practised economy, and meanwhile the boots had delivered a fresh evening edition to my room with my other requests, and the paper was chock-full of executions. With hard work added to the formula, it would be enough; I might linger here, and so bury myself in projects that no one should see I was transparent by daylight, a ghost with a soul of smoke and secrets.

Once resolved, I picked up the edition I

had selected upon a whim, and began the novel.

> There was no possibility of taking a walk that day. . . .

It will seem peculiar to the reader, doubtless, but I awoke to my exile feeling much refreshed the next morning.

After all, I had a set of purposes; the frenzy of fright I had been driven into by the reappearance of Sam Quillfeather was quite dampened here in the world's greatest cesspool; and the daily agony of seeing Charles Thornfield as if through a glass case in a museum display had ended. Additionally, London crackles and buzzes; it spits and it decays and it shines. I had missed it without knowing, so engrossed had I been by my new companions, but now I felt afresh the energy a metropolis can infuse into its strivers.

The first thing to be done was to purchase new — by which I mean secondhand, but far more opulent — togs, which would further two out of my three schemes.

I obtained a glass of porter and a good penny plate of bread and fried haddock at a pub first, and then took a crowded omnibus towards Aldgate. Far from Highgate House, my abandoned frocks were recalled as spinsterish and depressing rather than merely dull, for I had never dressed so in the city; I had sometimes been destitute and never wealthy, but it must have been my French half insisting upon the richest plaid capes despite their threadbare edges, the daintiest buttoned boots.

Aldgate was a veritable sea of plate glass, a thousand welcoming eyes reflecting happy glints from the gas jets. Even in the wet grey mire of winter, the countless shops were a cheery sight — but I had no intention of making purchases on the main thorough-fare. Instead I veered towards St. Paul's by way of Fenchurch Street, and after travers-ing salt-strewn cobbles for a few blocks, I found the haven I had sought: a nondescript window gleaming citron and edged with holly branches, with no sign posted save for PRIVATE ALTERATIONS UNDERTAKEN. I rang the bell.

So close to Aldgate, secondhand shops kept as demure as middle-class whores, but this was the best of them, and soon I was prattling away with two familiar saleswomen who cooed and clucked over my present drab attire, waltzing about to find something of the sort I had used to like. When I explained money slipped easier through my fingers of late, and that I must dress more like a lady than my previous blithe showiness, our budding friendship was sealed — I suspect they imagined I had a dalliance with the master of the house where I tutored, a hypothesis only vexing because I had failed to do exactly that. I departed the shop with my arms full, promising to return for three more frocks they were altering to my shape.

Next stop after another omnibus ride was the Soho Bazaar, where the rosy-cheeked craftswomen rent stalls inside the row houses at the northwest of Soho Square. By the time I quit this fairyland — equipped with new gloves and a stole and several hats — I was fagged enough to take a hansom back to the Weathercock, drawing a sly but amused stare from my new friend the clerk when he saw me dressed colourfully as a child's top and laden with plunder.

My room, after I had piled my twine-adorned parcels and beribboned hatboxes upon the bed, seemed much the barer for the additions. Mr. Thornfield may not have known my real nature, but he had spoken compass-true when he observed I sought companionship as bees do nectar.

Restlessly, I pulled off my gloves and hung my new powder-blue hooded cloak, and surveyed the afternoon dress I wore in the long glass.

It was the finest dress I had ever owned: dull silk, of a colour as much green as it was brown that made my eyes gleam like mahogany, painted asymmetrically with vines of delicate vermillion roses; along the bosom, the cinched waist, and the fully draped sleeves were barred pairs of emerald stripes. A single cascade of tiny buttons dripped from neck to waist, and it occurred to me, seeing the mischievous tilt to my lips, that I had never looked better.

I am far too vain to even attempt the prevarication this brought me no foolish pleasure; but my eyes soon prickled because there was no one of importance to see me, and I turned hastily away to store my new belongings.

That task accomplished, I sat down to write a pair of letters. The first need not be recounted as it was merely the request for an appointment with Mr. Cyrus Sneeves, eagerly informing him I was now in London; the second had required more imaginative plotting.

Room 26,
the Weathercock,
Orchard Street,
Westminster

Dear Mr. Augustus Sack,

I hope you will remember meeting the governess, one Miss Jane Stone, upon your dramatically terminated visit to Highgate House not two months previous. My note concerns matters confidential in nature, for I gather through your own curtailed speech and hints dropped by the always sinister Messrs. Charles Thornfield and Sardar Singh that acquaintances were renewed at Mr. John Clements's funeral which rekindled old grievances.

I hereby confess that I was so frightened by their display of weaponry that I embarked upon my own private investigation. As a governess, I was in no financial position to quit any master even if he should be a scoundrel — pray exercise your empathy, Mr. Sack, when I tell you I was determined to learn all I could in the interests of my own safety.

Pausing, I poured myself a glass of the claret I had rung for, reading my lies back over. It should not do to lay it on too thick; however, Sack had seemed more of a vicious bully than a master criminal. I dipped my pen once more.

The results of this amateur exploit have been most fruitful — indeed, I may well have learnt the whereabouts of a long-lost object.

Letters to me can be sent to the above address under the name Miss Jane Smith, as bloody deeds were enacted which precipitated my flight from Highgate House. Speak to no one of Miss Stone, if you would be so kind; a Mr. Jack Ghosh, or so I have been told he was identified, broke in during the small hours and died of some misadventure. Singh and Thornfield give out to the police inspector that he cut his thigh upon a piece of window glass when entering, but I cannot believe this account, and when I made the discovery which enabled my departure, the devil himself could not have spirited me away quick enough.

It is this matter of finances of which I wish to speak with you. Do not entertain the idea of coming to my lodgings, for I am not in immediate possession of the item in question; send me a summons for an appointment, however, and we may be able to assist each other.

Expectantly,
Miss Jane S——

I addressed the envelope to Mr. Sack in care of the undersecretary at the Company's headquarters, which was the intentionally imposing East India House in Leandenhall Street. Having passed it before, I realised it suited what I knew of the Company itself: opulent, powerful, and cold as marble.

An equally frigid smile touched my lips at the thought I might soon enter its stone maw, a predator in the guise of a slender young woman.

TWENTY-SIX

The fact is, I was a trifle beside myself; or rather out of myself, as the French would say. . . .

Days of preparation followed, reader, ones which left me in a strange daze of commingled purpose and despair. By now, I thought I might actually expire without Mr. Thornfield, sudden heartaches piercing with the lances of a hundred Khalsa cavalry; at others, I felt haler to know I served him still. I read my borrowed novel twice through, then bought a copy at a quaint bookstall — I have not yet got *out* of the habit of reading *Jane Eyre,* come to that — and idled, and schemed, and awaited answers to my letters.

I had only to wait one day to hear from Mr. Sneeves; he was from home, the message having been forwarded, and so I must wait two more days to meet with him. Hastily agreeing to this via his clerk, I gnawed my thumb and hoped for a missive from Mr. Augustus Sack.

I got one, too, on the very morning I was to meet with my solicitor, and it read as follows:

East India House, Leadenhall Street

My dear Miss Smith,
Of course I recall the pleasure of your company, a boon which rendered bearable an otherwise profoundly distressing journey. I confess that, though I may have an inkling of the matter to which you refer, the less said in written form the better, for this is very much a Company affair, and therefore I propose you visit me in my office. My hours are from eight to seven, but a request from you could find me there at any time.
Very sincerely &etc.,
Mr. Augustus P. Sack

My lips twisted into what resembled a smile, but may have invested the casual observer with more fear than mirth.

Then I donned another of my new frocks in order to properly present myself to Mr. Sneeves. This costume was all of the same patternless fabric, a shimmering fawn colour, but the detailing was exquisite — ten deep pleats, a plain band of the same fabric at the waist, and then it blossomed into fold after fold, like a modern woman's dream of a Renaissance belle.

My eccentric looks did not quite do the workmanship justice; but next I added a calculated finishing touch, a demure but real set of necklace and earrings, the stones of which the jeweller assured me had travelled straight from the Punjab. I had sixty pounds of Mr. Thornfield's advance remaining, and I assured myself that the rest of the money could not possibly have been better spent.

The first sense engaged upon entering Mr. Sneeves's offices was that of smell; the reek of snuff greeted me long before the man himself did, though he was scrupulously prompt. Mr. Sneeves introduced himself in a reedy voice, hastened me into his consulting room, and shut the door.

As soon as we were alone, he lifted a teak snuff box. "You don't mind, I hope?"

"Not at all."

I must waste no time over describing the chamber — the usual maelstrom of ledgers, untidy bookshelves, and the like — for Mr.

Sneeves had my passionate attention. He was a little man with a great round balding dome covered in freckles, as if his shoulders had sprouted a mushroom. Though of fine quality, his black coat was in no way ostentatious, and I realised that — apart from the almost dizzying aroma of snuff — Mr. Sneeves preferred his clients to forget they had ever required his services at all.

"You are most accommodating. Thank you." Mr. Sneeves set the snuff box down and commenced staring at me with pale eyes beneath thistly brows.

An interminable period passed, during which my sweat began to seep forth like morning dew.

"Pardon, Miss Steele, but you stir up old memories," Mr. Sneeves concluded at last, sitting back in his chair. "You resemble your mother, you know, save in colouring — that is entirely upon the paternal side. What should you prefer to drink?"

I sat there, dumb; resembling my adored mother was enough news, leaving me hotly aglow, without the fact that I apparently took after my unremembered father as well. Meanwhile, Mr. Sneeves was already headed for the sideboard with a shuffling gait. I reminded myself of the role Jane Steele was to play today — a moderately interested but well-off woman, that she might get all answers not generally imparted to a beggar at the door.

"Thank you, but I —"

"You must have a taste of something fortifying, Miss Steele, for I fear I may shock you. There are a few solicitors, you will find, who are actually aware their clients possess sensibilities. Sherry?"

"Please," I said rather faintly, "though . . ."

"Brandy, then," he curtly suggested. "Considering your background, it must have been administered as a restorative at one time or another, and once having had brandy, one ought not go backwards."

The man, for all his resemblance to your more affable variety of fungus, was riveting. I drew my soft blue cloak, which I had neglected to shed, closer about my frame as Mr. Cyrus Sneeves planted a brandy snifter before me; he deposited half as much before himself and resumed his place behind the desk.

I soon came to understand from his complete silence that I was expected to make an overture.

"Mr. Sneeves, thank you for seeing me — you must have wondered at my letter's contents."

"Heavens, no." Mr. Sneeves took another

great pinch of snuff, making my own eyes water. "No, Miss Steele, I only wondered who told you about me."

Faltering, I removed my gloves. "My mother left a few letters —"

"May I see them?"

Turning over my mother's letters felt a strangely intimate act, for all that my solicitor would learn nothing he did not already know; I had so little of Mamma left that all my relics were magical, more talismans than mementoes. At last, finished, Mr. Sneeves scrubbed a hand over his mottled pate.

"Miss Steele," he questioned, "do you know more of your legal standing beyond what I have just read?"

When I shook my head, he rapped his desk, as if signalling the start of a race. "I was first recommended to your father in Paris, where Englishmen often preferred to do business with a firm operating upon both sides of the water. His concerns had to do with his status as a landholder. Highgate House was in good repair, but your father desired to settle minor liens and generally ascertain whether keeping the manor was feasible; I am happy to state that he was doing very well indeed in Paris, no less than were his partners in London, and so my advice was, if the property gave him pleasure, to keep it. It was not only matters of his estate upon which he consulted me, however."

Mr. Sneeves waited as my heart pounded a brisk martial beat.

"And these other matters?"

"Were matters to do with your mother." His voice softened, and he smoothed errant grey wisps behind his ears. "Mrs. Anne-Laure Steele was such a woman as you do not meet twice in life, Miss Steele — beautiful, charming, and artistic. Sadly, not long after your first birthday, your father fell prey to an inflammation of the lungs, and your parents wished to know your precise legal standing in Britain should the worst happen. I was tasked with setting measures in place to ensure both you and Mrs. Steele were protected. You remember your aunt, Mrs. Patience Barbary?"

"Naturally."

Mr. Sneeves, dappled head bobbing, made quick work of gathering papers. "She was very strongly against your and your mother's residing at Highgate House — and your father proved to be ill with consumption at an advanced and virulent stage, so your parents were forced to act quickly. Here is the marriage license between Anne-Laure Fortier and Jonathan David Steele; here also

487

is a special contract they devised to be signed by your aunt as a dowager, stating that Highgate House should be your sanctuary for life."

I examined the documents. Rather than clearing the mists, however, the atmosphere thickened — *sanctuary for life* did not mean *inheritance.* For the first time, I examined my mother's statements against the backdrop of what I knew to be true as an adult woman. Unmarried females scarce ever inherited, particularly when wills were disputed; my mother had assured me of my place time and again, but had never explained the whys or wherefores.

Meanwhile, supposing it was mine, why should Mamma and I have lived in the cottage, why not the main house, why should not Aunt Patience and Edwin have lived in —

"Miss Steele, do you know the man in this picture?"

I found myself holding a sketch from a French newspaper describing a series of audacious trades enacted at the Palais de la Bourse.

"Of course — this is my uncle," I answered readily. "Richard Barbary."

"That is your father," Mr. Cyrus Sneeves said, "who for a time — when courting your mother in the guise of a rich gentleman of leisure — went by the name Jonathan Steele."

"No, no." The words emerged before I even had thought them. "That's impossible."

Mr. Sneeves made no answer; I stared at the artist's rendering, all breath ripped from my lungs.

Richard Barbary's portraits had occupied many places of honour at Highgate House before the arrival of Mr. Thornfield, and here he was in starkly inked miniature: a calculating businessman with an air of mischief about him. Effortlessly, I recalled how those portraits had beckoned to me, with their brown eyes like mine, their mocking half smiles, their air of roguish mystery.

I felt as if my bones were curling up inside my body.

"It can't be," I whispered, knowing it true.

Mr. Sneeves took a fortifying pinch of snuff.

"Mr. Richard Barbary was one of our best clients, Miss Steele, and when he informed us of the . . . situation, we strove in every way to accommodate him. Initially, he had only sought an affair with your mother, who was quite destitute save for the odd sou made from her street portraits and work as a cabaret dancer in Montmartre, which I believe is how the pair met. But when Anne-Laure Fortier and Richard Barbary had lived together for over six months and she informed him of her pregnancy, he impetuously determined that her pleas for wedlock be indulged, and he married her under the false name he had given, fearing to reveal all and lose her regard. This was no light task, but your father was a rich man, and so managed the necessary documentation — he avoided mentioning the fact, of course, that he had already left a wife and child behind in England."

Fighting dizziness, I marked him, the words falling as lightly upon my ears as the patter of rain upon a window.

My half brother. Edwin, who tried to rape me, was not my cousin, he was my half —

"Here you are, Miss Steele," a smooth voice intoned.

I drained the brandy Mr. Sneeves had thrust beneath my nose and watched as he poured another, setting it within easy reach. Memories untangled themselves before my eyes, twisting and contorting — Aunt Patience's calling my friendship with her son *family feeling,* my mother's open disgust for Edwin, my aunt's visible loathing of me. Sickened, I tasted the spirits again.

"Tell me," I rasped. "Everything. Please."

Mr. Sneeves sniffed, not unkindly. "I fully intend to. Miss Steele, when your father first fell ill, another event threatened the tranquillity of his, ah, French family life: your mother found a portrait of Patience and Edwin Barbary amongst his belongings. These led to a frenzied quarrel, but your father soon fell into agreement with his illegitimate second spouse: he had no intention of abandoning you, not even in death, for a match begun in the sort of lies wealthy men tell had developed into profound mutual devotion. Mrs. Barbary, I ought to mention, was dealt a bad hand — she was an arrangement made by your paternal grandfather in the interests of money and pedigree, and though your father never loved her, I believe she loved your father, or so Anne-Laure Steele led me to conjecture."

Recalling all the times my aunt begged my mother not to speak of Jonathan Steele, recalling in my mother's own letter to the firm her reluctant, *when I imagine myself in her shoes, I cannot bring myself to censure her,* I felt as if my world had been blasted to shrapnel, and I left clutching the shards with bleeding fingers.

"Why did my father create such a wretched quagmire?"

"As much as in looks you resemble your

mother, Miss Steele, you have your father's direct manner about you, and I find I must battle nostalgia in your presence."

"I cannot begin to imagine whether or not that is a compliment," I rasped. "Please continue."

"Very well, then. Mr. Barbary was the heir to an estate which might once have proven impossible to maintain; he was told to marry Patience Goodwill, whose holdings after her elder sister, Chastity, eloped were considerable. After he proved himself an expert trader here at Capel Court and her wealth proved superfluous, the marriage, already fragile, fizzled despite the birth of a son named Edwin."

"Is that the reason he fled to France?"

"I believe so, though the story given out emphasised the professional benefits of his temporarily relocating. In any case, Mr. Barbary travelled to Paris when offered a liaison with one of la Bourse's officially licensed *agents de change,* and he presented himself to your mother as a gentleman of leisure named Jonathan Steele. You were conceived, your parents were married, your father fell ill, your mother found out his true marital status, and he and your mother threatened Patience Barbary with exposure of all his sins should she refuse to cooperate

— your father blackmailed his wife with his own ill-usage of her, knowing the second marriage illegal."

It fit everything I knew, and it hurt accordingly — from my scalp to my soles, I was altered.

I am not who I thought I was.

Neither had Edwin been — he was my dear, repellent, spoilt brother rather than my dear, repellent, spoilt cousin. What other grotesque errors had I made in my life that I should find myself sitting in an office being told my own father's name?

Meanwhile, my mother — oh, my *mother.* It had been a love match; I had not needed Mr. Sneeves to tell me so. She had been mad with grief over him, and now I understood that Aunt Patience had been similarly afflicted; two women, both in love with a different name, forced to live with revolting insults right before their eyes. It would have been sensible to have hated my aunt Patience all the more now I knew she had kept me in ignorance, to have loathed my father as a philanderer and my mother as a blackmailer; rotten as my own core had proven, all I could do was pity the lot of them.

As for my half brother, I reflected with the cold scrape of an icicle down my spine, *the less contemplation of Edwin the better.* Everything I knew about my blood and bones had been stripped from me, leaving me bare.

"Is my name even Jane Steele?"

"If you like — we've no documentation save that name, so if it suits you better than Jane Fortier . . ."

"It does." I sighed, draining the second brandy. "Mr. Sneeves, supposing as the illegitimate daughter of Richard Barbary I can do nothing whatsoever regarding Highgate House, what is the wrong you meant to put right?"

Mr. Sneeves wheezed in disbelief. "I should have though that was obvious."

"It isn't," said I, with some asperity.

"Miss Steele, I am sorry for what you have learnt today," Mr. Sneeves replied, clasping his fingers together. "But the wrong I meant to right was that you should *know* who you *are*, as I had strong suspicions that no one ever bothered to tell you. You are not without inheritance."

"Oh." It was all I could summon.

"You have an allowance of three hundred a year." Cyrus Sneeves wrote a note to himself, as if that clinched matters. "You do not possess any part of Highgate House, but your independence is assured, as guaranteed by Mr. Richard Barbary. I have your current address here from your last correspondence, I take it? Very good. I shall lose no time in setting up an account for you to draw upon and transferring your yearly allotments there, which after all this time amounts to a tidy nest egg. Lacking your whereabouts but hoping you lived still, I held the funds in trust. Now. Is there anything else I can do for you?"

Dazed, I glanced again at the newspaper sketch of my father. As a child, I had felt about his portraits as I would an imaginary friend; trying to summon greater depth of feeling now, however, I found the task impossible. He was a collection of pen strokes who resembled me vaguely. I ought to have felt grateful to know him at last; instead, I felt grateful for his money.

"Yes," I said quietly. "Burn any evidence of their wrongdoing save documents attending to my stipend, including the letters I brought you from my mother. All of it — and then tell me your fee."

By the time I left my solicitor's office, I was no longer dwelling upon my mother's attempts to escape the cage she had locked herself within, nor my father's inability to ponder future catastrophes of his own making.

No, reader: by then I was mourning the

death of my world entire. I did not even know my own name.

Oh, I knew who I *was* — a scarlet-toothed tigress, one forever burdened by the iron weight of her own black stripes. I was apparently also the illegitimate daughter of a two-faced stockbroker (as if there were any other kind).

Until something has been taken from you, it is difficult to gauge what sort of holes will be left by its absence. Guessing that Clarke's departure would make a yawning cavity would have been obvious, the loss of Charles Thornfield an equally predictable pit; but I hope, reader, that you have never lost something you took entirely for granted, like your name.

Returning to the Weathercock in Orchard Street was a blur of draughty omnibuses and crooked roads, a dreadful numbness settling over me. All I wanted was to call for a hot bath and read Mr. Thornfield's letters. Trudging into the lodging house, I waved a vacant hand to the clerk who had come, however contrarily, to like me.

"No visitors of any kind, please!"

"Wait, Miss Smith!" he called, but after the strangely painful thought *that isn't my name either,* I paid him no mind.

My alias rang out twice more, and urgently

too, but my eyes flooded and I fled — up the stairs, half stumbling in my beautiful new dress, desperate for sanctuary. When I reached my room, I fetched the key from my reticule and was surprised to find the door already unlocked. Hesitant, I felt for the knife in my skirts with one hand and turned the knob with the other.

"Hello, Miss Steele," Inspector Sam Quill-feather said when I discovered him occupying my own room.

Twenty-Seven

Much enjoyment I do not expect in the life opening before me. . . .

Discovering the man who could see me hanged sitting on my striped chaise, smiling peaceably with his hat in his hand, might have been unbearable had I been in a merry humour; I am sure I could never have withstood the shock had I not just learnt I was the bastard child of a philanderer and an extortionist, which had invested me with a certain flexibility.

"Mr. Quillfeather," I whispered.

"You are surprised to see me?" He rose and bowed, gangly limbs folding inward. "But . . . no, I see that you are dismayed? Forgive me, but I was eager to have a discussion with you, a very *frank* discussion, and you quit Highgate House quite precipitously. It was clear that I was the cause, Miss Steele, and I found myself unable to rest until I had located you?"

"How . . ." Swaying, I hid my weakness by leaning on the door as I shut it.

"Only by the most careful searching, Miss Steele! I knew after speaking with Mr. Sardar Singh — interesting man, that, and I'm glad to have made his acquaintance — you had taken the coach to London, and there the trail went quite cold. But doggedness, you will find, works miracles, and I canvassed every respectable guesthouse I could locate where single women of independent temperament might lodge, asking if a woman of your description had recently taken rooms. When I learnt a young lady named Jane Smith had lived here for precisely the right amount of time, could I ignore the possibility it was you?"

Broken in every way imaginable, I turned away from where I had stood with my head bowed before the door.

"Miss Steele!" Mr Quillfeather exclaimed. He crossed quickly to me, hand extended. "Have I already upset you so?"

The ground seemed to heave. For the briefest of moments, I considered a knife to his heart and a mad flight through alleys and over stiles until I had reached another sort of freedom, a true outlaw's comfortless existence — but it was not Sam Quillfeather's fault he was a police inspector, and it was entirely my fault I was a killer.

So I stayed my hand and reached for his instead.

"I know your mind, Miss Steele," he said quietly. "I will share mine with you, and we will reach an understanding after many years of poisonous secrets — does that suit you?"

Such an overwhelming dread possessed me that I thought my faculties must shatter. I opened my mouth, and just as I was about to make an idiot of myself, Mr. Quillfeather urged, "Oh, please, Miss Steele — won't you sit down before you do yourself an injury?"

I obediently sat upon the chaise he had vacated, neck tingling with terror.

"Now, Miss Steele," said he, seating himself upon the chair opposite and leaning forward in his sweeping fashion. "I have some hard words, and want you to understand — I don't wish to say them? But I simply must, and I frankly regret not having said them to you when you were a little girl. I know, you see, why you lied to my friend Thornfield about your name, why you ran without even taking your luggage. You must know . . . I told him nothing? He believes you to be Jane Stone still. But I know the entire contents of your biography, and of your secret fears."

"This is about Edwin, then." My voice was parchment thin.

"Could it be about anything else?" he asked softly.

Yes, I thought, and swallowed what felt like a bullet.

"The fact is that I know . . . everything, Miss Steele, absolutely everything, about the events leading up to your cousin's unfortunate demise."

My eyes fell shut; so I was to lose my name, my claim to Highgate House, and my freedom, all in a single afternoon. In a way, I thought, it was kinder — in a way, it was better than I deserved.

"You were so young then, so . . . vulnerable? I never saw such a sensitive little girl in all my days. Now I have found you, however, and you have grown into such a lovely young woman, could my cowardice *still,* to this *very day* prevent my speaking out?"

A strong wind seemed to blow, a strangely silent one, and I was a leaf floating upon it.

"Oh, Miss Steele, please don't take on so!" To my shock, I opened my eyes to find Sam Quillfeather's beaked nose inches away, his dry, calloused hands grasping mine. "Listen here, my girl — take a few deep breaths, if you can? *Very* good. I must say the words now, and you can hear them bravely, can you not?"

A faint nod was all I could manage at this point.

"I know that your cousin, Edwin, attacked you, and the nature of that attack."

I waited; I continued to wait. When he said nothing further, I heaved a breath as if I had been drowning. Inspector Quillfeather nodded, squeezing my limp fingers. He continued to say nothing of murder, and I continued to gape at him, utterly speechless.

"There, I knew that would be difficult. Shall I go on?"

Shaking my head in disbelief, I managed to husk, "Yes," after which contradictory signals Sam Quillfeather smiled paternally.

"I cannot help but feel that I have done you an . . . injustice? There was evidence, *so much* evidence, but how can one conscience putting a mere child through such trials? Had I to do it over, I think that I should have acted differently? I can only claim misplaced propriety, though I hope you lived the better for my choice, I truly do."

"Evidence," I echoed.

"Oh, evidence in *spades*!" he cried. "The torn button upon your cousin's clothing might have been explained as you suggested, by the idea that you were playing. However! Though I do not claim to be the world's finest policeman, I can assure you that I *aspire* to be, and the tear in your dress sleeve combined with the bruising beneath? Shaped, even what little I could see of it, like a handprint?" Inspector Quillfeather's already clifflike brows surged into bolder protrusions. "Miss Steele, you never got *that* injury playing a game, that was as plain as the nose on my face!"

"Very plain indeed, then," I accidentally said aloud.

"Ha!" exclaimed the policeman. "Oh, may I state how gratified am I that even after such unspeakable liberties being visited upon your person, you retain your sense of humour?"

Pressing my hands a final time, he released them and sat back, though between the hair and the brows and the nose and the chin, this did nothing to diminish the impression that he was a train hurtling towards me. "If you could know the nights I've kept vigil over this affair, would you wish to? No, don't answer that; I think not. But your very attitude that day, Miss Steele — your

503

ramrod posture, your *obvious* terror, your inexplicable distress which, like a puzzle piece which is the right colour but the wrong shape, did not match grief over the death of your cousin . . . The truth was obvious. I asked myself so often, *What can I do?* Such cases of unspeakable violence, particularly against the young, are impossible to prosecute."

"I see." I pressed my still-shaking hands into my skirts.

"Yours would have been, I assure you. And with the perpetrator of the assault, who was likewise the second principle witness, *dead* by tragic accident? Imagine! A nine-year-old girl dragged through the assizes, pointed at, questioned, shamed, her reputation forever soiled, her heart broken, her mind subjected to not merely a single gross indignity but multiple others? *No,* I said — not when the guilty party could not be punished by a mortal court."

"I didn't scream," I blurted out.

"I beg your pardon, Miss Steele?"

"I didn't scream." Suddenly the tears were an ugly waterfall, hot and gushing, and *someone has to know after all this time,* I had to tell *someone.* "He . . . Edwin made a mistake, you see, because I was so shocked that I stayed quiet, which misled him, so it was entirely my fault, you understand, that he . . . that he . . . because I didn't scream."

If a man can look simultaneously exquisitely gentle and boiling with rage, that man is Sam Quillfeather. He pursed his lips and curved towards me.

"You listen to me, Miss Steele, and you listen *ardently,*" he grated. "That a lady's succumbing to shock at exposure to such villainy could ever be considered a black mark against her — put the thought from your mind this very *instant,* do you hear?"

Opening my mouth, I was prevented by a sharply upraised hand.

"Mark me now!" Inspector Quillfeather ordered. "It is a gentleman's greatest privilege to protect the fair sex, and when he abandons that privilege, when he casts it aside in favour of *lechery,* why then he is no longer a gentleman, and therefore the lady in question owes him *nothing,* because he is a coward and a blackguard, and for a lady to doubt her own behaviour in the presence of a coward and a blackguard is *lunacy,* I tell you, from stone silence to violent caterwauling, because she owes him *no interaction whatsoever* from the instant he discards his honour, and I won't have it. Promise me something?"

"Um," I said. He was handing me his

505

pocket handkerchief, I realised, and I took it, though the flow of tears had dried under the blast of his vehemence. "If I can."

"Promise me," he urged, eyes shining, "that you will put this aborted scream from your mind forever?"

"I . . . well . . ."

"You owe your attacker *no debt,* Miss Steele. It is, as I have proven, a logical impossibility? Promise to *try*?

"Yes," I whispered. For the second time in as many hours, I felt as if I had been blown apart and put back together again. "I promise to try."

"I can ask no more of you than that." He stood to his full scarecrow's height, setting his hands against his scrawny hips as if satisfied that a hard task had been seen to. "Well, I think we can both agree I have taxed you enough, yes, Miss Steele? Please forgive me for any harm I may have caused you inadvertently. Now I must return to work, for there are several urgent matters which require my attention, and I have neglected them in favour of finding you. You have eased my mind, Miss Steele."

"Here is your handkerchief," I said, offering it.

"Handkerchiefs should remain where they are needed, don't you agree?"

Weakly, I laughed at this, and Inspector Quillfeather beamed at me as he retrieved his hat and gloves from the table.

"I hope you will trust my complete sincerity in vowing never to reveal your secret to Thornfield?" he pressed. "I ought to say, however, that should you elect to reveal your true name to my friend, I believe he would treat you honourably."

I haven't any true name, I thought in despair, *and he treats me too honourably by half.*

"Forgive me — my words pain you. Here is my card, should you wish to contact me for any reason, great or small? You are looking well, very well indeed, Miss Steele, and I see by your attire that you have no need of governess work. But in any case, don't stay away from Highgate House on my account?" he added kindly.

"I won't." Mr. Thornfield's likeness appeared in my mind's eye, deep-blue eyes and pure-white hair, and I banished the image. "I promise."

He turned to go. We had not finished yet, however — nothing could be this simple. Though the thought of deliberately broaching the subject sent leeches slithering through my belly, I could not allow him to exit without truly mapping the miracle of my safety.

"Mr. Quillfeather, did you know that I was at Lowan Bridge School when . . ." I forced myself to look at him. "When Mr. Vesalius Munt was murdered?"

He lifted his overhanging brows, and the neat set of horizontal lines appeared along his forehead. "Miss Steele, I regret to say that I did, for you were included in the roster of some thirty missing girls? I always wished you well, you know, and I did seek you for a time."

My heart slammed against my rib cage as if attempting escape. "Did you ever suspect anyone in particular?"

"Ah, that would be telling, wouldn't it?" he mused. "But between us, yes, there was a clear suspect."

"You cannot mean it!"

"I must assure you I do."

"For my own peace of mind, then, I beg you to inform me who the culprit was."

"It won't upset you to hear the truth?"

"Not after that . . . other truth," I replied in a hushed tone, and he smiled at me.

"Quite so. Do you recall Miss Amy Lilyvale?"

"Very clearly."

"Yes, she gave me testimony that every single girl without exception had been present at chapel that fateful day, which quite clinched the matter."

"Did it?" I questioned, feeling sick again.

"Oh, I should think decisively?" He began ticking people off on cadaverous fingers. "Miss Rebecca Clarke was not present — ill-usage, I gather, was the cause; you were not present, doubtless comforting your friend; and Miss Davies was laid up with a bad case of the croup. Therefore, Miss Lilyvale was not actually at chapel to check, and wished not to falsely throw any students under suspicion. Other teachers claimed she was there, but the inaccuracy of her attendance report convinced me they were lying in order to shield her." Scowling, Mr. Quillfeather passed his hand forward over his head, a familiar gesture that made him resemble a ruffled bird of prey. "Your headmaster, Miss Steele, was no saint. He kept a diary? Oh, yes, I found it! In it he recorded, in the foulest language, the most disgusting perversions he could conjure, planning to visit all upon Miss Lilyvale. He wrote that he had been sharing such filth with her for years, the villain . . . One is not gladdened by any death, but some touch the heart rather less than others, do they not?"

"Undoubtedly."

"Miss Lilyvale it was, that is certain, but I make a habit of never pursuing an unwinnable case, you see? I cannot find the good in it? And the evidence was *so* circumstantial! Nothing could be done."

"Surely the diary counted for something?"

"Oh, the *diary.*" He made a subtle bow of acknowledgement. "Yes, that would have gone a very long way indeed, but sadly it was lost."

"However did that happen?" I marvelled.

"I fear that *I* lost it, Miss Steele," he declared, eyes twinkling. "In a lit fireplace. Clumsy of me, I know — can you imagine? And they call me a steady policeman!"

So saying, he donned his hat, tipped it, and walked straight out the door.

I had planned to pay a call upon Augustus Sack that evening regardless of the outcome of my meeting with my solicitor; however, the reader will likely empathise when I confess I was too prostrate with nerves following my identity exploding in multiple fashions to infiltrate the East India Company. A message dispatched via the boots conveyed my intention to call upon the morrow. Moving as if in a dream, I unfastened my fine jewellery, brushed and hung my clothing, donned my soft new nightdress, and crawled into bed with a wineglass full of whiskey and *Jane Eyre* within arm's reach.

I was a rich woman now, even without Mr. Thornfield's assistance. Time drifted sluggishly, distorted by the whiskey and the warmth. Everything about me had changed, and yet I could see the slender bend of my wrist at the end of a white forearm, looking the same as it always had, could see the tiny mole between my left thumb and index finger, assuring me that I was still myself.

I was not myself, however. I was a Jane with an imaginary surname, one who apparently was not to blame for failing to scream. It was too mad to comprehend in an instant, or even an hour, so I burrowed farther into the bedclothes to puzzle over it all. My life's sole mission had once been a simple one: to carve out a tiny sliver of human affection, having none of the commodity for myself. For all that I so thoroughly disapproved of my own character, however, Mr. Sneeves and Mr. Quillfeather had proven that day I was capable of grievous errors upon the subject of Jane Steele.

I rolled clumsily onto my belly, reaching, and flipped to a passage from my new copy of my favourite book:

To this crib I always took my doll; human beings must love something, and, in the dearth of worthier objects of affection, I contrived to find a pleasure in loving and cherishing a faded graven image, shabby as a miniature scarecrow. It puzzles me now to remember with what absurd sincerity I doted on this little toy; half-fancying it alive and capable of sensation. I could not sleep unless it was folded in my nightgown; and when it lay there safe and warm, I was comparatively happy, believing it to be happy likewise.

Upon first reading, I had found it bizarre that the adult Jane Eyre regarded this exercise as either puzzling or absurd; upon subsequent readings, I marvel still more at her derision. Lacking interest in dolls, I had once — not unlike my poor, sweet Sahjara — gathered crumbs of pleasure by spoiling horses. This seemed to me neither worship of a false idol nor a quirk of an infantile mind; it did no one any harm if I treated a horse well, and made my days less miserable.

Did I deserve misery for the things I had done?

Yes, of course I did. Even apart from being the tainted bastard offspring of a suicidal mother and a lying father, I was a murderess five times over.

As I seemed incapable of turning myself in, however, would any harm come to the world if for the moment I thought of this newly reborn Jane — Jane without legitimate parentage, Jane without legitimate surname — as a creature worth treating gently?

There was no one else volunteering for the task, after all.

Brisk footfalls outside my bedroom door woke me at eleven the next morning; the anonymous movement dragged me from a weirdly sweet slumber. The sun was high, however, and breakfast long concluded, and the whiskey's solace had left me with an empty belly, so I clambered from bed and washed. Then I donned another of my fashionable frocks, a floral silk with a dramatic shawl collar, all save the white lace sleeves emerging from fabric printed in grey and silver and a blue which reminded me of Mr. Thornfield's eyes.

Today is for you, I thought, *wherever you are and however you fare,* and was seized with such a longing that my breath caught.

My set of modest Punjabi diamonds completed the picture, and I deftly swallowed the remainder of last night's whiskey, fortifying myself as I quit the Weathercock.

Noontide bells rang as my soles struck the cobbles. I had been too disoriented to give Mr. Sack a specific time the day before, so I did not feel rushed. Luncheon was the first order of business, and I knew of a beautiful tearoom Clarke and I had used to frequent mere blocks away from East India House; I was seized with a longing to see it again, its gliding servers and polished brass rails, so I hailed a hansom and directed the driver to the City.

Cox's Tearoom was just as I recalled it when we pulled up before its door, and by the time I had paid the driver, both the wind and my stomach bit sharply. A liveried gentleman led me to a table, where I was soon equipped with Darjeeling and a tower of sandwiches. After a few sips and bites, however, I thought I should be more comfortable with a newspaper; I visited the rack and selected a late-morning edition, glancing at the headlines as I returned to my table. Nearly colliding with a waiter, I looked up, murmuring an apology.

I stopped dead, staring in astonishment.

Rebecca Clarke sat at a table by the window, shafts of illumination waltzing through the golden corkscrews of her pinned-up hair.

Twenty-Eight

But I ought to forgive you, for you knew not what you did: while rending my heartstrings, you thought you were only uprooting my bad propensities.

My heart, so egregiously taxed of late, rung in my breast like a great gong — I thought it must have been audible, so painfully glad was I to see my schoolmate, my companion, nay, my *sister,* again after so long a time.

Once the initial shock had worn off, I ceased marvelling and allowed happiness to spread like a virus through my chest. We had shared the same tastes once, Clarke and I, moved in twin orbits like binary stars. It was not very surprising, therefore, that in this labyrinth of a town I should stumble upon my lost great friend, particularly considering I had sought the place out because it reminded me of her.

Clarke was twenty-one years old, and

where once she had been thin and ethereal, now she was beautiful — as freckled as ever, with the tiny mouth of an inquisitive porcelain doll. So many times had I pictured her starving that the sight of her hale was a gift, the unlooked-for sort which pierce deeper than the expected. Her clothing was fine but eccentric: a long bronze skirt, a close-fitted ivory waistcoat, a dark copper jacket with tails and lapels to it, a golden cravat. This elegant but oddly mannish ensemble was completed by a miniature top hat, and she peered through a pair of half-moon pince-nez at the afternoon edition of the *Times*.

My feet had carried me farther than I realised during this reconnaissance, and I found myself before her, my eager shadow brushing the hem of her skirt.

"Just put it on my account, if you — *oh!*" Clarke exclaimed, her cup clattering into its saucer as she glanced up.

Say something, I thought.

Nothing emerged.

I've missed you terribly and deeply regret the fact you learnt I am a homicidal maniac.

I hesitated.

Not that.

"It's good to . . ." I swallowed, for Clarke had turned as pale as the milk brought for her coffee. "That is — we needn't speak, only I saw you, and . . ." I battled the urge to prove myself the pinnacle of urbanity by throwing myself in her lap and sobbing. "You look well, and I'm glad."

At this juncture, I considered that a sound from Clarke — any sound — would be taken as a boon. Instead, she stared at me with wide green eyes, her hands vibrating hummingbird-fast.

"I'm upsetting you." The admission stung. "I can't tell you what it meant to see you again. I'll just —"

"No." Clarke trapped my wrist with the strength of a steel manacle. "Sit down." She blinked, hard. "I mean, won't you sit down?"

Slowly, she released me.

I sat down.

Clarke folded the newspaper with care; then she took a long breath and sat back, nodding at the silver coffeepot. "Would you like a cup?"

"Please."

A waiter came with an additional service and poured, a civilised piece of pageantry which enabled us both to pretend we were friends meeting for coffee to discuss our summering plans, rather than friends meeting for coffee to discuss whatever we were going to discuss. My teapot and sandwiches appeared, and I gestured for her to help herself; Clarke shook her head, eyes wide under pale lashes, and I looked away.

"You look well too," said she.

"Hmm?" I had been studying my coffee with more interest than that beverage had ever previously inspired.

Clarke smiled — the indulgent one which meant I had journeyed too far into the wilderness of my head. "You look very smart. I'm happy over that, your clearly having plentiful coin. So often I wondered whether —"

"Me too, every single day," I blurted.

When she blushed, she looked more herself again, for her previous pallor had been alarming. Clarke had never blushed often, however, and never lacking a sound purpose, so I wondered at the expression.

"Well." She pretended to polish her pincenez as I pretended to add sugar to my coffee. "I probably did not wonder quite as much as you did, for I used to hear news of you."

"You have the better of me, then," I marvelled. "How?"

Clarke's head found the much-loved angle it adopted when thinking harder than usual; as if remembering something, she spoke.

" 'I always knew my grip upon the thread of time was tenuous, and the harder I clutched, the sooner it would break. Therefore, do not weep for me, my tender sweet love — we must all resign ourselves to the final snapping of that bond between soul and breath, and though it is a present unworthy of your grace and beauty, you must know that I gift my soul to you.' "

Jaw dropping, I laughed. Clarke gave me a faint smile.

"I wrote that!" I exclaimed. "John Jacob Holdworth, hanged at Newgate in eighteen forty-seven."

"Precisely so. When your gallows confessions started selling at newsagents' and tea shops, occasionally I would purchase them, though I never caught a glimpse of you delivering the papers or picking up your earnings."

"But of course my name wasn't on them, only the names of those executed — however did you know it was me?"

"That wasn't very difficult," she said quietly. Brightening, she attempted to adopt a brisk air. "And now what are you doing with yourself? Good Lord, that frock and those jewels — I didn't suppose last confessions brought in ready enough chink for those togs."

I glanced down at my new dress, and my pulse sped, for she was right.

"I had better not say," I confessed softly. "It's complicated."

The set of her shoulders grew brittle after she shrugged. "You always did keep secrets, and everything is complicated these days."

Extraordinary contradiction, I thought, *that she could always condone even the most operatic of my falsehoods, so long as none were directed at her.*

"I'd tell you if it didn't mean betraying another party."

My friend took rapt interest in the traffic outside the window. "It's all one to me."

"Where did you learn slang?" I teased, wanting the light to return to her eyes. "You always spoke so properly, even in Rotherhithe."

"We were speaking with each other mainly, so it was easy to keep pure back then." Surely I imagined the dryness in her tone, having spent too long in Mr. Thornfield's company.

"Oh, *won't* you say what you've been doing?" I begged. "The matter which brought me to London doesn't involve just myself, you see. Pax, please. I'm desperate to know — you never bought that rigging with street-chaunting coin either, and my vocabulary is

521

every bit as disgraceful, and you really must take pity on me. We were so lucky, when we arrived here, to find shelter so quickly, and afterwards when I pictured you . . ." Faltering, I cleared my throat. "If anything had happened to you, it should have been my fault."

Clarke's gaze grew a shade less hard.

"No." She sighed. "I was the one who left, after all."

"But what came next?"

"I continued singing, but finding lodgings was harder than I imagined, since for all those years you'd taken care of me — I was sharp enough at school, but a complete ninny when loosed to the streets. At times, I slept in doss-houses with the dollymops, and it was . . . Don't frown like that, Jane. Most of them were kind, for all that they were filthy and coarse. I could have gone straight back to my parents. I did, for a fortnight," she admitted, wincing. "When they seemed only half relieved to see me, I asked them for a few pounds and struck out again. They claimed what I was doing was 'admirably Bohemian.' "

She sounded so bitter at this last that I hastened to inquire, "How did your fortunes change?"

A wistful look glazed Clarke's eyes. "I was

singing near to Elephant and Castle when a woman — Mrs. Priscilla Pellanora is her name — stopped to speak with me. She asked if I had ever sung in a company before, harmonies and the like, and of course I had at Lowan Bridge, and she offered me a place in the chorus of her production."

"But that's absolutely wonderful!" Laughing, I imagined Clarke in a wooden-walled theatre, her freckles blurred by the faint glow of the footlights, the smell of peanuts and ale thick in the air. "You excelled, of course, which is why now you are so fashionable."

Clarke lifted one shoulder, though she seemed pleased; she had always been peculiarly uninterested in her own talents, the same way she viewed everyone else's attributes and shortcomings as stamped in the stars, inevitable. "Mrs. Pellanora is an excellent tutor."

"Oh! May I come see you? Do please say yes. Are you at the Olympic, or maybe the Delphi?"

Biting her lip, Clarke shook her head.

"The Lyceum, then! I know you must think . . ." I stopped, eyes prickling. "That is, I don't know what you must think of me, but I should so love to hear you sing again."

"I'm not at the Lyceum," she husked strangely.

"Do you sing for penny concerts, then? I'll come to the Surrey side to see you, only tell me which it is. The Victoria? The Bower Saloon?"

"Jane, I sing at Mrs. Pellanora's private club," she snapped.

My ears buzzed in the ensuing silence, drowning out the soft clinking of tableware and the susurration of strangers' voices. A man with a Yorkshire accent was demanding to know where his pudding had got to as the words *private club* echoed in my skull.

"Oh, for God's sake," Clarke groaned, then abruptly lowered her voice. "Surely this cannot be *quite* so surprising as some of your own past revelations. Wipe that expression off your face, if you please — no one touches me, the stage is gorgeously appointed, I've room and board with a set of bang-up girls, I'm petted and toasted all over town, and the costumes are nothing like what you're picturing. They're not far off from what I'm wearing now, come to that, only more . . . theatrical, and with trousers, and apt to get kohl stains."

"I'm sorry," I protested. "I wasn't thinking anything, only that you were always so scrupulous, you see, but now I comprehend it's all quite aboveboard."

"No, it isn't either," she hissed.

"I don't understand."

"It's outrageously bawdy, the content of the programme."

"Oh," was all I could muster.

"That must please you, that I work in a dirty cabaret."

"No! I mean I'm happy — so long as you are."

"You don't *look* happy, Jane."

"I'm delighted for you, only . . . surprised, I suppose. You were always so honourable."

"Well, honour wasn't doing anything for me." The waiter had dropped a salver on the table and she signed her bill with a flourish. "Mrs. Pellanora's establishment does."

"I don't think any the less of you," I said fiercely, panicked at the thought of losing her again so soon — here one heartbeat, gone the next. "I could *never* think less of you."

Wincing, Clarke shook her head. She was so striking in her boyish clothing, the curve of her throat and the flash of her eye beneath the glass half-moons, that save for the skirts and the curls she really did seem a young rake cooing over watch fobs and walking sticks in Regent Street.

"I've an appointment to rehearse with our pianist in half an hour." She tugged on a pair of gloves. "You should know I don't regret seeing you, Jane, and that I don't any longer harbour a . . . Hang it, nothing I say will do any good to anyone. When I think of you, it's altogether fondly."

"Clarke, please don't —"

"Will you say my name at least?" Flushing again, she adjusted her pince-nez. "I don't know why you do that, I never did. Rebecca is my name, Becky what my parents called me, Becca what the four other company girls call me. Take your pick. Why should you want to remind us of Lowan Bridge?"

Because the only shaft of sunshine in all that endless midnight was meeting you.

"Rebecca." The name tasted strange, like salt where sugar was expected. "Let me contact you, please. Have you an address?"

"That would be unwise."

Desperate, I snatched up her bill and stole the pencil from the salver, scribbling my room number at the Weathercock and the street address. I thrust it at her.

After breathing tensely through her nose for a few seconds, she took it. Clarke placed the paper in a pocket beneath her jacket lapel and pressed her lips together.

"I always loved you as a sister." My hand

was so near to hers that taking it was a thoughtless act, the only right one.

My old friend cocked her head at our joined fingers, cogitating; she was a self-made woman, a singer of questionable provenance, and otherwise she had not changed a whit since she was six years old, and I was speaking the truth: I had always loved her.

"I never loved you so," she said.

Clarke freed her hand from my tightening grasp as two tears fell soundlessly from beneath the pince-nez. Had she trussed me up like a slaughtered buck, I might have thought it my just deserts for the web of lies in which I had entangled her — this, though, seemed to exceed the boundaries even of cruelty. When my breath hitched, she rose to depart.

"Do you recall the book you had — the one my father published? *The Garden of Forbidden Delights?*"

My mouth must have worked; but sepulchres cannot produce sound, and I was a monument to wishes ungranted and tenderness left to rot unused.

The whisper of fingertips touched my cheek, and then Clarke was kissing me.

It was only a brief press, but it was neither dry, nor chaste, nor seeking. It was the kiss of a person who has thought about variants of the same kiss for a very long time, as if it were a hundred kisses, all of them passionate and all of them hopeless. I was startled and — in the moment — grateful enough even to reciprocate, did so before even thinking why I should not, and I tasted years in that kiss. I tasted years of dying hope, and the sweet bellyache of longing, and coffee, and Clarke herself, before she pulled away, running her thumb over my open lips.

"That was how I loved you," she told me.

Women often embrace, sisters often kiss, and no one regarded us as she bowed her head, closing her eyes for a fleeting instant, and then turned and walked out of the tea shop.

I floated to the window, following her as she strode into the street. She did not look back, gauging the traffic at the corner with a practised tilt of her head; therefore I was the one turned to salt, and not Rebecca Clarke, when I watched her hand leave the front of her bodice and drop my address to the cobbles, the paper fluttering prettily before it landed in the filth and the straw.

For minutes which stretched before me like miles, I stood at that window, still seeing the ghostly afterimage of her slim back and gleaming hair the instant before I lost her for the second time. Carriages and buses clattered over the bill, no longer visible in the road, but that was for the best — I had never wished Clarke harm in all my days, and if seeing me grieved her, I renewed my vow never to seek her out.

An unexpected peace flooded the air around me.

Some tragedies bind us, as lies do; they are ropes braided of hurt and bitterness, and you cannot ever fully understand how pinioned you are until the ties are loosened.

Other tragedies free us, as Clarke's confession freed me.

You cannot know what it means, reader, to have thought yourself despised for your unworthiness for a period of years — to have supposed your very nature poison, and your friend right to have thus abandoned you — and to learn thereafter that you were loved not too little but too well.

East India House was a fortress; the building loomed over me like a conqueror, the lower two floors absurdly high-ceilinged, and the entrance guarded by six positively enormous Ionic columns. A frail wind whined in my ears, tugging the tailcoats of the men dancing about with their arms full of papers in a chaotically choreographed tribute to wealth. Never had I set eyes on a place which so pungently reeked of power and money, and I hesitated, fearing the consequences should I provoke the lion in its den.

Better you than the residents of Highgate House, I thought. *You have been Jane Stone, Jane Smith, and today you will be Jane Steele — the only woman suited to this task.*

I adopted an aloof air and entered the front hall.

If the shareholders were already assured of the Company's ruthless dominance by the exterior of East India House, the interior hammered the point home; everywhere I looked was marble and crystal and carvings and paintings of faraway lands. Finding Augustus P. Sack's office would have been daunting, but a clerk with waxed grey moustaches escorted me, somehow exuding hauteur and deference simultaneously. A knock produced an instant reply of "Come in!" and the stranger presented me to Sack, making a prompt exit.

"Well, well, Miss Stone," Augustus Sack purred, quitting his desk to drop a kiss above my outstretched hand. "I was very intrigued indeed by your letter."

"Yes, I suppose you must have been."

"Do sit down. Tea or a little wine, perhaps?"

"The latter, if you will join me."

"Miss Stone, a beautiful woman need hardly ask that question — and may I state in addition that your present costume quite takes my breath away?"

It had not escaped my attention that Mr. Sack's shrewd eyes had examined my attire, landing with a spark of lust upon the Punjabi diamonds.

"Governesses are expected to be such drab creatures. It is a life of terrible drudgery even when one is not living in fear of one's employer, Mr. Sack."

"Frightened you, did they, the scoundrels?" Mr. Sack commiserated. "Happily, you are safely under the care of John Company now, Miss Stone."

Mr. Sack poured claret from a decanter on a carved mahogany sideboard; he was just as I remembered him, doughy and pink faced, with gleaming cheeks and fat fingers. Now I saw that his rich attire — a maroon coat on this occasion, with a yellow silk necktie — matched his office, for everywhere I looked were signs of needless expense. From ivory cigar box to silver-chased gasogene, Company executives seemed to display wealth like peacocks spreading their plumage.

He ushered me into a chair, equipped us with wine, and perched on the front of his desk. "First, Miss Stone, let me offer my solemn oath that you may tell me anything in complete confidence — I gather that you departed Highgate House in great anxiety, which I confess does not surprise me, considering the dark history of Thornfield and his shadow, Singh. If we are to be friends, we must trust each other."

So I am already promised immunity for stealing the trunk, I thought, delighted.

"I am yours to command, Mr. Sack, so harrowed was I by my recent experiences."

The sympathetic frown he manufactured was revolting, so sharply did his eyes cut from my necklace to my face and back again. "We speak of desperate men, Miss Stone. Please — tell me everything."

I did not tell him everything, and several of the things I told him were bold-faced lies.

Tremulously, I informed Mr. Sack that after the knives had driven him away at breakfast, I had feared for my life. However, I had determined to wait at least until I was given my first quarterly wages, having no other means of returning to London. In the meanwhile, I had launched a secret investigation of the house's occupants and learnt what Mr. Sack had been doing visiting Highgate House thanks to covert eavesdropping (not untrue); thus had I heard the story of the trunk and its contents.

"The tale sounded to me quite preposterous, but I continued in my quest to discover all I could," I informed him shyly. "There seemed no other choice if I wished to escape their clutches."

"None at all, none in the *world*, Miss Stone — you did quite right," the Company diplomat soothed. "Please go on."

Leaving out the pieces of the story which reflected badly on Sack was simplicity itself. I knew my employer had robbed David Lavell and his wife, Karman Kaur, but said nothing of Sahjara's kidnap; I knew John Clements and Jack Ghosh were both dead, but implied Mr. Thornfield or Mr. Singh were to blame. The Company man's ruddy cheeks creased in sympathy whilst his stare bored into me with all the gentility of a bullet.

"This Jack Ghosh person's death was the final straw," I lamented. "Oh, Mr. Sack, it was so horrid — their claims it was an *accident,* the blood on the floor. I redoubled my search for the trunk, and . . ." I allowed myself to blush.

"And enterprising woman that you are,

you found it, and you took it in order to escape the clutches of these fiends," he said softly.

Pretending a coquettish version of guilt, I said nothing.

"The trunk was hid amongst Mr. Sardar Singh's things, I imagine?"

Dumbfounded, I blinked at him.

"Why do you say so, Mr. Sack?"

"Because it's that posturing heathen who taunted me with word of it upon my arrival back in England. This was before the loss of John Clements, of course — wretched business, that, and I don't know that this Inspector Quillfeather will ever get to the bottom of it, more's the pity. I thought Thornfield to blame at first, and told the Director so, but now I have reached another conclusion."

These assertions sounded nonsensical — that either man would ever stoop to poisoning anyone (as I had once done) was ludicrous, I thought, and the notion that Sardar Singh had made any communication to Augustus P. Sack whatsoever beggared belief.

"I don't understand . . . Mr. Singh seemed so contemptuous of you," I faltered. "You claim he was a correspondent?"

"He did hate me, the swaggering savage,

and wished me to live knowing his crimes would go unpunished. See for yourself."

Going behind his desk, Mr. Sack produced a folded letter. This he passed to me, and upon opening it, it was all I could do not to recoil in horror. Many a time had I watched Mr. Singh as he wrote, and many a time posted letters for him; these were his exact characters, from angular downstrokes to oddly spiked capitals. It read:

Dear Mr. Sack,

As little as I desire ever to see your face again, I can no longer live without informing you that I picture it often upon your making the discovery that you have been thoroughly bested. All subterfuge is futile at this point: we do indeed have the trunk, and should you ever attempt to recover it again, know that I will not hesitate to destroy you utterly.

Your Company has raped my entire culture in systematic fashion; what is in my possession will remain there, and any attempt by you to steal it will result in your bloody death. Highgate House is a fortress, and I its guardian. Lacking any other avenues by which to make you suffer for your arrogance, I send this letter; think upon its contents often, Mr. Sack,

535

for the treasure you seek will never fall into your hands the way our great Empire did.

Charles knows nothing of this and would not believe your lying tongue should you attempt to tell him — it is partly for his sake that I write you, indeed, for you have brought a good man to the brink of mental ruin. Live in discomfort, Mr. Sack, knowing that once, at least, one of the pure ones snatched a bone away from an English cur.

Your enemy, and your better,
Mr. Sardar Singh

My head spun; for it sounded like him, not the usual mellow-tongued Mr. Singh but the warrior whose voice abraded my ears that day in the hall, when he stood in the snow-swept entrance hall and called the Company rapists and the Sikh royals their pimps.

Meanwhile, my entire plan was ruined; I had intended to draw any imminent fire away from Highgate House by proving that the trunk existed and offering it to him myself. The glad news which was to have distracted Sack, bought me time whilst I thought of the perfect way to kill him, was not news after all.

It was not news because apparently Mr. Singh had been lying to us.

"You see how they blame me for their woes." Mr. Sack sighed. "I only wished to see justice done regarding the trunk's recovery, you understand — David Lavell was a Company stalwart, and he would have wanted this fortune to be held in trust by the Company for Sahjara when she comes of age. Had Mr. Singh merely hated me as any guilty party hates the law, he may not have been angry enough to risk such a foolish correspondence; but all is tangled in his mind with Charles Thornfield's subsequent madness, you see, and the pair are quite devoted to each other. It is easier for Singh to blame me for everything than to consider that the fault lies squarely upon their shoulders."

"Madness?" I echoed, stricken. I quickly corrected myself. "Do you mean to say I was living under the authority of a . . . a lunatic?"

"Oh, but then you don't know what happened to Charles Thornfield at the Battle of Sobraon," Mr. Sack crooned. "Clements did, and so do I, you see. We were there."

TWENTY-NINE

The answer was evasive — I should have liked something clearer; but Mrs. Fairfax either could not, or would not, give me more explicit information of the origin and nature of Mr. Rochester's trials. She averred that they were a mystery to herself, and that what she knew was chiefly from conjecture. It was evident, indeed, that she wished me to drop the subject; which I did accordingly.

Reader, I did not drop the subject; and I confess that, greatly as the letter from Mr. Singh had disturbed me, all thought of him was crowded out at the prospect of Charles Thornfield's bloody biography being revealed at last.

I hardly needed to feign my agitation. "Won't you please explain? It would soothe my conscience so to know that I am right in coming to you."

"Let there be no doubt whatsoever about *that*, Miss Stone!" Mr. Sack exclaimed. "David Lavell was a friend, and his treatment at the hands of these reprobates — shocking, simply shocking."

I recalled Mr. Thornfield's account of the same circumstances and gritted my teeth into what I hoped was an encouraging smile.

Sack wasn't his superior, and anyway he was winning a fortune off Lavell at poker — Karman's fortune. Lavell couldn't sink low enough for Sack's taste.

"Oh, do make all clear, I beg — he unnerved me, but I never thought him mad."

Mr. Sack puffed air into his rosy cheeks; he made a show of considering, checking his watch against the richly gilded clock, whilst I channelled my real anxiety into breathless anticipation. Thankfully, I knew I had him, for he was the breed of braggart who enjoys imparting salacious information to delicate-seeming females.

"There really is no putting off a lovely young lady when she makes a fair request of me," he concluded with a sudden air of gallantry.

"Only you can ease my mind, Mr. Sack."

"In that flattering assessment you are correct, Miss Stone," he simpered, and I could see the half-humble, half-preening attitude he took with foreign dignitaries and their wives. "Though I must confess part of my knowledge comes secondhand — my former colleague John Clements helped to nurse Charles Thornfield and was thus the audience to his most ghastly ravings. I am of such a tenderhearted nature myself that I can hardly bear to see anyone suffer, and yet . . . sometimes, I think God visits punishments upon the living as well as the dead, and Charles Thornfield was greatly culpable regarding his own disastrous circumstances."

At least fractionally, this was true, for Mr. Thornfield had told me himself — an infected slash across the back of his shoulder, a long convalescence spent in Clements's company.

"Any man who would rob his closest friend's sister has much to answer for," I agreed.

"Aye, there's the crux of it!" Mr. Sack's ability to swagger whilst stationary cannot be exaggerated. "Between you and me, Miss Stone, Charles Thornfield was desperately in love with Sardar Singh's sister, Karman Kaur. I shock you, I see — forgive me. Jealousy of her husband, David Lavell, caused him to take the crudest measures, and ones which led, as crude measures so often do, to tragedy."

I folded my hands primly. "I gathered that Mr. Thornfield and Mr. Singh preferred to rob their own loved ones than allow them to live as they pleased."

"Precisely so, Miss Stone." Mr. Sack ran a fat finger over the lip of his wineglass, reflecting. "Lavell was a dear friend as well as a colleague — a handsome devil with an adventurer's appetites, and his wife adored him. Oh, we sowed a few wild oats in the Punjab, but you must understand, reputations abroad *shatter* if a gentleman cannot keep pace with the local elite! The Director knows this to be true. What are a few card games, a few harmless flirtations, when failure to carouse with the natives leads to their instant censure?"

Nodding, I twisted my lips into a gracious frown.

"Thornfield couldn't stomach it despite being born and bred there," Mr. Sack huffed. "Pitiful really, how he doted on Karman Kaur when she would have none of him. She was a goddess, Miss Stone, a warrior queen, and all hell broke loose when those miscreants stole what was hers to share with her husband as she pleased. What, allow him to default on his gambling losses? What self-respecting woman would dream of such a thing?"

"Strange that a woman so loyal to the Khalsa should marry an Englishman."

"Not at all! She had grown up with the Thornfields, and Lavell had nothing but praise for the Sikhs — a political of the highest order, he was, and the first man to say that the East India Company didn't stand a chance against the Khalsa on their own ground. These bastards made their own artillery, you understand, based on English designs, and when you've your own foundries, you're your own master. All the better if your army is a hundred thousand strong! As I recall, the line Lavell took was that once the Khalsa had trounced John Company, the world's greatest armies would join forces and rule the territories from Calcutta to St. Petersburg. He was very popular in Lahore, and not just with Karman Kaur."

I swallowed bitter disgust, for this confirmed all my friends had told me — Company spies flattering the Sikhs whilst infiltrating their empire, Sikhs defying the Company whilst their leaders betrayed them.

Small wonder that Sardar Singh longed for vengeance.

"Anyhow, Karman wouldn't have cared a fig about Lavell's politics. It was, how shall

I put this, a *love* match, Miss Stone," Mr. Sack added in a greasy tenor. "Screaming fights, tender reconciliations — they burnt the candle at both ends."

"What did she say when the theft was discovered?"

"Now mind, we never learnt *who* pilfered her treasure until I discovered Sahjara's trunk," Mr. Sack boasted with a hand over his breast. "But we all knew what happened after it went missing — Karman Kaur ordered a Khalsa cavalry uniform altered to fit her, sharpened her *tulwar,* saddled her best horse, and joined the army to seek a new fortune for herself and Lavell."

I forced myself to relax clenched fists.

"She did not consult anyone over this step, I take it."

"Not her!" He chuckled. "Magnificent, she was, Miss Stone, a stunner of the first water. So she had lost a tidy sum — why whinge when the Khalsa were poised to annihilate John Company in the name of the Guru? Lavell was called to Amritsar to negotiate, and Karman was off like a shot to Ferozepore after sending word to her brother to look after his niece. By the time Sardar Singh and Charles Thornfield discovered her plan, she had already joined a Sikh encampment, to the delight of all the men she met there. She distinguished herself in action at Ferozepore as well as at Aliwal and Sobraon."

"The Khalsa did not win the Battle of Sobraon."

"No, they were slaughtered," Mr. Sack returned cheerily.

He moved to refill our wine; by the time he had passed the glass back to me, my spine tingled with horror. It did not matter that Karman Kaur may well have joined the ranks of the Khalsa anyhow; it did not matter that Mr. Singh did not think Mr. Thornfield a murderer. Mr. Thornfield saw every step leading to her decision like paces towards a gallows, saw the fateful instant when the loss of her treasure propelled her into a harrowing war, and he thought himself wholly responsible. It did not matter that I knew any woman would be lucky to be loved by him — would, as I had put it, be the happiest woman in the world.

The last one wasn't, he had told me, for he had set her death in motion.

"The Battle of Sobraon was butchery at its most primitive," the political continued almost gleefully. "It had been pouring rain for days, and the Sutlej River was as bloated as a pagan prince. The Khalsa had been pummelling our Bombay brigades with

544

heavy artillery for hours when the order came to return the bombardment. When that failed, the Bengali troops as well as the King's Light Dragoons launched counterattacks which the Khalsa repelled like true barbarians — hacking down the wounded, finishing the dying as if they were cattle in an abattoir. After confronting them from the west and the south and the east, the Sikh line began to collapse, which is when the true carnage began."

"It sounds sufficiently apocalyptic already, Mr. Sack."

Mr. Sack adopted an introspective look. "All those rains, Miss Stone — the surging of the Sutlej's waters, the vulnerability of their position. One pontoon bridge linked the Khalsa back to the Punjab. Think about it — a single thread of boats leading to the only possible escape after the fords had flooded. The Company may have had . . . friends, let us say, on the Sikh side, friends who understood the value of this bridge. Or they may not, and God Himself may have weakened the moorings linking the line of ships — who can say for certain?"

My stomach turned over.

"Can *you,* Mr. Sack?"

"I, a mere diplomat? You compliment me extremely, Miss Stone."

"Go on," I urged.

"The bridge of boats collapsed and took the Khalsa with it," he mused. "It was never a retreat, for they fought madly every second . . . but it was a reckoning. They had murdered our wounded, and the generals thought it best that an example be made."

"What sort of example?"

Augustus Sack lifted his wineglass, swirling the liquid within as a gentle smile touched his lips. "I did not arrive until the Khalsa had been conquered, but this was the colour of the Sutlej when I saw it after the rout. We fired every weapon we had into that river. Ten thousand Khalsa men and one woman died that day, either drowned or shot whilst in the act of drowning."

"That's horrifying," I breathed because I could not help myself.

"All the more so for Thornfield." Mr. Sack sipped his vintage, clearly unperturbed by its shade. "The woman I refer to is Karman Kaur. Thornfield was in the thick of it and, in his later delirium, it became clear to my man Clements that upon spying Karman in the watery massacre, Thornfield tried to save her. The fool got sliced in the back for his trouble. He nearly drowned in blood and gore before he made it to Karman on a riverbank covered in corpses, but she was so full of holes that only meat remained of her. Head half blown off, body riddled with grapeshot. Pity. She was remarkable. He spent over twenty hours on that beach with her remains amidst the carnage, unable to move from blood loss. Oh. Have I delivered too graphic an account for your taste, Miss Stone? My apologies."

In truth, I did feel faint — with rage, with grief. "Blood has always upset me, and imagining . . ."

"Here, a bit more claret will restore you."

Crimson liquid splashed before me. "Mr. Thornfield was delirious afterwards, you say?"

"He had suffered a large wound which went untreated for a full day after taking a literal bloodbath, so that is hardly surprising." My eyes shot up to the political as I realised Augustus Sack was actually enjoying my distress. "Thornfield was on the brink of death for a fortnight. I was busy planning terms of the treaty with the Director, but Clements was with him for much of it. The illness was an ugly one, Miss Stone. Fever visions, night terrors — often you could hear his screams, before Clements had managed to calm him."

If Mr. Thornfield had been the one to

relate the story, I should not have been able to bear it; seeing his face, his attempts at a wry brow, his guilt like a gouge through his breast, his natural stoicism — all should have conspired to tear me in two. Learning the details from an utter villain, however, one I knew had ordered a child kidnapped and starved, that was a simple matter of endurance. Mr. Sack could smirk knowingly all afternoon, relate any repulsive tragedy which had befallen Mr. Thornfield, and I could sit there, blithely picturing my knife in his guts.

"Tragic, no doubt, and yet I cannot fully sympathise when the man so unnerves me," I owned, downing half the claret. "Thank you. Mr. Sack, I feel much restored."

I had puzzled him, for he beamed in approval whilst his eyes narrowed to cruel slits. "Forgive me — I should never dream of upsetting a lady of your myriad charms intentionally. Where was I?"

"Mr. Thornfield was ill, but . . . I have heard nothing to indicate he was mad?"

"Ah, yes!" The portly diplomat settled himself back in his chair. "I first knew Charles Thornfield as a strapping young medico with a head of hair so black it was nearly as blue as his eyes. After the battle, he was finally brought back to our camp by a Bengali company, and the wretch was so covered in dried gore that an orderly shaved his head. When he could walk again, and speak a little, after three weeks' time, the new growth was white as goose down. The entire camp was unsettled by it — they thought him possessed by a devil. And perhaps it was something to do with the circumstances in which he found his lady love, but he developed the most extraordinary aversion to touch thereafter. Clements clapped Thornfield by the bare arm one afternoon whilst he was shaving and nearly got a razor in his eye. He began wearing gloves soon thereafter, even when the Director demanded his services in the second Sikh conflict. I don't suppose you've ever seen a man performing surgeries whilst wearing gloves, Miss Stone? Madder than a full March moon, and he has never fully recovered."

"Clearly not," I said, half smiling. "Not if he couldn't manage to puzzle out that his closest friend kept the trunk under his nose all that while."

"You most eloquently return us to the topic at hand, Miss Stone." Mr. Sack tapped all ten fingers of his hands together. "I confess to having been testing you — I know it was early days for you at Highgate House when I was present, but nevertheless I could not help but wonder whether a connection formed between you and Charles Thornfield. How foolish would I have been to take into my confidence a confederate of his, sent to sound me out? But now I see that you, like him, are merely a thief."

His words, warm at the outset, deepened to a sickly-sweet growl.

I glanced at the time and then at the window, where scattered snowflakes drifted to their sooty demise. No one, I realised, knew I was here save Sack and the grey-moustached clerk who had shown me in; suddenly I wanted someone else present, anyone else.

Draining my wine, I shrugged. "I am not accustomed to being called names, Mr. Sack, but you can see my dress and the necklace for yourself, so I can hardly contradict you. Anyhow, I have already made my full confession. What do you want from me?"

"I should think that obvious, Miss Stone." Mr. Sack's lips thinned, a predator's expression in a piggish countenance. "I want the trunk. What do you want?"

"A satisfactory recompense for having delivered it to you. And to know all that you do about the circumstances of Clements's and Jack Ghosh's deaths, for I must understand whether forces continue to threaten my welfare. Did you send Ghosh to Highgate House after you were driven off yourself? Mr. Thornfield suspected as much, I overheard."

Augustus Sack snorted in contempt. "Jack Ghosh had his uses, but I should never have sent him *alone,* Miss Stone, not into that household — I should have been a fool for trying. An armed guard of Company officers to search the place whilst the occupants were locked in the cellar, on the other hand? I was organising just such a campaign."

Then I was only just in time.

"Ghosh acted on his own recognisance?"

Mr. Sack tilted his head back and forth, considering. "He has been in this office on many occasions and could easily have found Mr. Singh's correspondence, so that is the most likely explanation. He was a brute and a snoop and the world is well rid of him."

The words were delivered so carelessly that they seemed altogether true. The waters I had dived into were far murkier than I had imagined.

"What about John Clements? You said you no longer suspected Mr. Thornfield of murdering him — why?"

"Poison simply doesn't seem our dear

Charles's style, does it?" The diplomat sighed. "Clements had been looking into the circumstances surrounding David Lavell's unfortunate murder in Amritsar, but my late colleague hadn't the intellect God bestows on sheep. He was low over the project, over his lack of progress. Then he saw an old love of his briefly, and he sank further into melancholy. Honestly, Miss Stone? I believe he took the soldier's way out. Now you will tell me where the trunk is."

The moment of truth could not have come at a worse time.

"I cannot tell you where I have hid the trunk yet, Mr. Sack," I demurred firmly, "not for lack of trust, but because I wish to know what you plan to give me as a finder's fee."

Mr. Sack, far from looking miffed at my insolence, grinned. Rising, he approached me where I sat, rubbing his hands together like a benevolent uncle out of a Dickens novel. An equally avuncular glimmer came into his eyes as his hand rose, seeming about to whisper a caress of fingertips over my hair.

Mr. Sack ripped the necklace from my spine.

I shrieked briefly, but soon mastered

myself. Had I been less frugal and bought a sturdier chain, I might have had my neck snapped — as it was, the metal gave before my bones did, and I was left a shaking huddle on the floor, battling not to whimper as I observed the first red drop of blood trickle from my shoulder onto the creamy carpet.

Mr. Sack squatted, dropping his hand to lift my head. The fiery pain produced when my posture shifted was shocking, and I gasped.

"Miss Stone, I do not think that we quite understood each other when I said this was a *Company* matter," he hissed. "Here is what I propose: I assume the trunk is somewhere nearby. If by midnight tomorrow you supply it, and I find it contains what I am looking for, I will give you a gift. If you do *not* supply it, I warn you that I know every fence and pawnbroker in London, not to mention every ship's captain who might be tempted to sail away carrying a mysterious female passenger. The Company owns this city, Miss Stone, and you have stolen from us — so now I own *you*. Your rooms will be watched, you will be followed, and when you have given me what I seek, my gift to you will be that I shan't rip those earrings from your lobes."

Augustus P. Sack leant forward, close enough to bite me, close enough to kiss, laughing as I scrambled away. He tossed the bloodied necklace in the air, caught it, and put it in his trouser pocket. We stood facing each other, my breath heaving as more jewel-bright liquid seeped into the bodice of my dress.

"Put your cloak on and lift your hood so that no one need glimpse any blood, least of all your own sweet self," Mr. Sack suggested, ringing a bell to see I was escorted out. "Thank you for your visit. And, I assure you, I look forward to our meeting again with the very *greatest* pleasure."

My hooded cloak served his purposes just as neatly as Mr. Sack had imagined, and I arrived at the Weathercock without a single glance of concern darting my way. This is not to suggest that eyes did not follow my progress; shadow-obscured figures trailed after me as I exited East India House, for I saw their doubles in the windowpanes, and when I had reached my lodgings, I peered through the curtains and saw men with hats pulled low, studying newspapers as they idled against the brickwork.

These small impediments served solely to bait me.

I called for linens and hot water. Viciously harsh with the key, I locked my door and pounded a single fist against it, unspeakably vexed both at myself and the *badmash* who had dared to treat me so.

My requested supplies arrived well before an hour had passed, and I barricaded myself in again and stripped all away, sinking into the bath. Gingerly, I cupped my hand and splashed at the line Mr. Sack had torn through my skin, which had already stiffened into a fiercely throbbing counterpart to the tear in my scalp. I then lay back to wash all clean.

Soaking, drifting, I sifted Mr. Sack's fresh details in my mind. Some were valuable wholly in the sense that I loved Charles Thornfield, others in the sense that I wanted him safe. Sack's words could have been false, I told myself, but they had not sounded like any sort of prevarication I had ever encountered — what, therefore, would it mean if they were truths?

Nothing to the good, I thought at first. My feelings upon theorising that Sardar Singh was a liar were, in ascending order: shame, hurt, and dismay. I hesitate to tell you that lies, reader, are a very easily learnt knack, so I did not for an instant marvel over whether he could have retained possession of the precious trunk, crossing oceans with it no less, without confiding in anyone.

Yet I could not reconcile what I knew of Mr. Singh with the fresh sketch which had been inked — and neither could I reconcile his epistolary posturing with his obvious chagrin at Mr. Sack's visiting Highgate House, his love for Sahjara Kaur, and his fury that Mr. Thornfield might have exposed her to evil influences.

At the thought of what Mr. Thornfield must have seen on the battlefield, his childhood love blown apart and swept ashore like so much river flotsam, I was tempted to weep.

No weeping, I thought furiously. *Thinking is more useful than weeping.*

I allowed my mind to drift farther afield; after all, this whole mess had begun in the Punjab.

Who is to say the key to it could not be found in the Punjab?

Lest one mistakenly consider me a close reasoner, I am only a close observer of human nature, my own being defective. On this occasion, however, I had lit upon a valid idea. Streaming bathwater everywhere, I leapt out of the tub, hastily drying myself before throwing a dressing gown over my shoulders. The steam had become soporific, and I needed to wrest nagging hints from the hind of my brain to the front.

After an hour's chaotic sprawl in my bedsheets, I thought I had got somewhere. It was hardly evening, and yet the sunlight had utterly decayed, winter's dreary gleam just visible through my curtains.

Eagerly, I hastened to write a letter to one Inspector Sam Quillfeather.

Solving the murder of Jack Ghosh was irrelevant, for I had killed him; solving the murder of John Clements was impossible at the moment. A grisly trail of blood across the continents, however, had been left behind by those associated with Karman Kaur's vast fortune, and I thought that, all other avenues being barred, I might glean some leavings from an earlier — much earlier — misdeed.

I had to solve the murder of David Lavell — in Amritsar, all those years hence.

It is of the utmost importance that I see the papers regarding Mr. Lavell that Mr. Clements was studying. . . .

This I wrote to Inspector Quillfeather, followed by:

If I am correct in my conclusions, I must

557

confess to you that I have committed a terrible crime, and must be brought at once to justice.

THIRTY

I leaned my arms on a table, and my head dropped on them. And now I thought: till now, I had only heard, seen, moved — followed up and down where I was led or dragged — watched event rush on event, disclosure open beyond disclosure: but *now, I thought.*

"It's a lucky thing I left my card, isn't it, Miss Steele?"

The sun had long since set, the eleventh hour dolefully chimed, and Mr. Quillfeather's bright hazel eyes were creased with fatigue as he passed me paper after paper from a battered black case. Some were written in Punjabi, which I placed in a separate pile. Others were reports from Lavell's superiors, however; some were letters writ in my native tongue; and a few were journals written by Lavell himself, which I snatched up eagerly.

"You were very frank with me, Mr. Quill-feather, and you seem a true friend to Mr. Thornfield, so I must learn to be at ease in your company. Thank you for bringing these so quickly — you've no reason to trust me, after all."

"I have reason to trust myself, Miss Steele, and you have always struck me as a most scrupulous young woman?"

Smiling at this outrageous compliment, I touched the black buttons at the neck of the high-collared coral dress I had donned to hide my fresh battle scar. I had always thought Inspector Quillfeather remarkably affable for a policeman, and it was shocking to realise that speaking with him felt like conversing with an old friend.

"I will thank you for saying so by taking you entirely into my confidence — for I need you, Mr. Quillfeather, both you and your police wagon."

"Yes, you mentioned having committed a crime?" Inspector Quillfeather's prominent brows wriggled in disbelief. "Surely you do not expect me to believe —"

"Let me tell you the story from the beginning. You first called Charles Thornfield to examine the body of John Clements because you knew Clements had been studying Lavell, and that all these men were acquainted in the Punjab?" He nodded. "Would it shock you to learn that Mr. Thornfield has taken me into his confidence regarding that subject?"

"Certainly *not.*" He sniffed. "Forgive my candour, Miss Steele, but may I remark that Thornfield seemed quite, er, *aware* of your presence, very aware indeed?"

My heart leapt skyward at this, but I forced myself to focus. "And you still have no suspects regarding the Clements poisoning?"

"None, though I am convinced that a man in the midst of an investigative effort is very unlikely to commit suicide."

"Then may I ask whether you know the story of the lost trunk?"

"That has rather an air of romance, doesn't it? I fear I do not."

I thought of Mr. Quillfeather losing Vesalius Munt's lust diary in a fireplace, steeled myself, and heaved a great breath.

"If I were to tell you of a mistake that Mr. Thornfield and Mr. Singh made long ago in the Punjab, would you hold it against them? If what they did to protect someone they loved was not . . . entirely legal?"

The tufted brows now swooped like carrion birds towards his nose. "Charles Thornfield is the very *best* of men, and any friend of his, especially for so long a period, must be exceedingly well chosen. Please continue?"

Telling the tale of the trunk took us to the midnight hour. Mr. Quillfeather, positively twitching with interest, paced as I sat painting a crimson picture of a bloody history for him. When I had nearly concluded, after confessing all my prevarications at East India House in an effort to protect my unlikely friends, I began unbuttoning my frock, and he froze in astonishment.

"This is what Augustus Sack did when he saw even a taste of what he thinks is coming to him," I said, revealing the ugly stripe.

"The brute!" he exclaimed.

"We haven't time for outrage," I protested, quickly righting my attire. "Without your help, I am lost, Inspector, and I have an intuition that the trail, though cold now, leads back to Amritsar and David Lavell's demise. You see why I must help you to solve it, and before midnight tomorrow? I've only a day, and the pieces don't fit. Please say you'll assist me."

Mr. Quillfeather flung a long arm out, palm up. "Miss Steele, can a man make a greater blunder than to ignore the intuition of a woman? When our mutual friend has been wronged unspeakably, yourself injured, and a child shamefully abused? I am your man to the marrow!"

"We have only until tomorrow," I breathed, "and if you make an enemy of Mr. Sack, you could —"

"Sleep is for the weak, and what is an East India Company bureaucrat to a seasoned peeler?" He landed in the chair opposite, somehow still conveying the impression he was in motion. "We begin work at *once,* and I shall tell you all about these documents, and we shall see what we can accomplish."

I opened a bottle of claret, Mr. Quillfeather finished emptying the case, and the clock ticked inexorably onward.

So commenced a strange stretch of hours during which I consulted with the man I had once feared as I do the gallows. Inspector Quillfeather saved me time reading by detailing what the officers' reports contained, outlining the contents of the Punjabi documents, and summing up the early diaries. David Lavell, it seemed, was every bit as thoroughgoing a scoundrel as his crony Augustus Sack. His superiors commended his ruthless ability to worm his way into any society he wished whilst revealing, even in their compliments, their distaste at his complete lack of principles. The Company men relied on his insinuating ways as well as his connections to Karman Kaur's family: between them and the Thornfields, the few scattered politicals north of the Sutlej when the fighting broke out were still kept in French wine and aged Scottish whiskey. Lavell's throat had been cut in his own rooms, which led the Company to imagine that one of his many dalliances had grown jealous of Karman, or that a Sikh acquaintance had been fleeced one too many times at the tables.

"The domestic setting means it is extremely unlikely that Lavell should have been killed by a stranger?" Mr. Quillfeather thrust his jutting chin as if to inquire whether I agreed.

I did, and we continued. Lavell had bled out quickly, and there were no witnesses; he was found cold in his bed a week before the Battle of Sobraon.

"Sahjara Kaur inherited, of course," I mused.

"Quite right, but inheritance could not have been the motive, even if the heir had not been a little girl. Despite her mother's assets, her father had amassed considerable gambling debts?"

"Was no one ever suspected?"

Mr. Quillfeather drummed spindly fingers on the tabletop. "I don't believe so? The housekeeper was questioned, and said Lavell had returned, after picking up another delivery of imports and contraband to buy the goodwill of the Amritsar elite."

The clock's hands spun too swiftly, dizzying me. A second bottle of claret became necessary at three in the morning, and at six we called down for toast and kippers. Try as we might, we could find no clue — and if Lavell had died at the hands of an anonymous *badmash,* then I was wrong, and the murder in Amritsar meant nothing, and barring a miracle I would fall into Mr. Sack's clutches upon the morrow.

"We're going about this wrong," I sighed at nine o'clock, squinting balefully at the sunlight shearing through window. "We must consider who *wanted* Lavell dead."

"I fear there are too many options to narrow our choices?"

"Any number of people hated him, but if unrelated to the trunk, they don't help us, so we can discount them anyhow," I answered, shuffling papers. "Mr. Clements could have had nothing to do with it, for he died trying to solve the crime just as we are. Mr. Sack needed him alive if he wanted to keep bleeding Lavell of Karman Kaur's money. Mr. Thornfield had cause, but he was already at war. Mr. Singh . . ."

My eyes flew open again as I gasped aloud. "Miss Steele?"

No, it cannot be. My stomach fluttered weakly with horror.

Yes, it can.

"Lavell picked up a shipment of goods to use for bribes that day, you said. Did any of the officers' letters mention what he employed to curry favour or with whom he did business?"

"He did business with his wife's family, naturally," Mr. Quillfeather said as the colour left his gaunt face. "But by all accounts, Mr. Singh was in Lahore throughout the First Sikh War?"

I thought about Sardar Singh — his history, his noble bearing, his monkish preference for a solitary life of few friends, simple comforts, and quiet study; I thought of his almost casual celibacy. I thought of his distinctive handwriting, the paper Mr. Sack had thrust before my eyes reading, *Your Company has raped my entire culture in systematic fashion; what is in my possession will remain there, and any attempt by you to retrieve it will result in your bloody death,* and swallowed black bile.

"I think I have it," I whispered.

"What is it, then, Miss Steele?" Mr. Quillfeather pressed.

I told him, hoarsely but efficiently, pre-cisely what it was. The policeman's hollow chest leant towards me until I thought he should fall from his chair, and his hand ruffled his hair in appalled disbelief.

"All this time?" he marvelled when I was through.

"All this time." I pressed my hand over my breast, for it ached beyond bearing. "Oh, Mr. Quillfeather, there is only one thing to be done."

"What is that, Miss Steele?"

I held out my wrists. "I'm a hardened criminal — write a note to the nearest sta-tion house and have a police van sent round at once. You've a pair of darbies, about you, I assume?"

Plentiful hay littered the back of the wagon, which clanked as it traversed the ancient streets. There were also blankets and, though they smelled of mildew, I managed awkwardly to wrap one about myself with my hands shackled together, for my lovely blue cloak could not protect me from the freezing draughts gushing through the iron-barred windows. Once bundled, I fell to the straw and rested my head, for by now it was ten o'clock and, for all that I was strung tight as a violin, my eyes kept fluttering closed.

So weary was I, and so overwhelmed, that no blackness resided behind my lids; rather, a kaleidoscope of colours whirled. My scalp ached and my neck throbbed, but these tangible discomforts were as nothing. I knew what must be done and loathed to do it; I knew what must be said, and the words pierced, cold as icicles in my throat.

Oh, Mr. Thornfield, how little do you deserve all that has been done to you.

Nature will have her way, however, and I did sleep for an hour despite being fettered and fretful. The scratch of rough wool and the whispers of the hay were crude lullabies, but comforts nonetheless, for they distracted me from the fear of failure and the near equal fear of success.

"Miss Steele?"

My name brought me back to myself, but it was the scrape of the key in the locked door of the wagon which startled me into full consciousness; shivering, I sat up just as a man's fingers gripped the bars and opened the box I had been penned inside. The blanket slipped from my shoulders as I blew a wisp of hair from my eyes, aware that however unruly it habitually looked, now my coiffure must be positively outrageous.

"Were you warm enough?" Inspector Quillfeather inquired.

"No." I managed to get to my feet with my hands on the nearer bench; my legs prickled, and my limbs felt weak and coltish. "Where are we?"

"Well outside of London — not far from Waltham Abbey?"

I must have tottered on my way to the door, for Mr. Quillfeather gripped my waist with hands that looked absurdly long wrapped round it and swung me to the ground. We were in a stable yard outside a hostelry, and I blinked against the glare as my captor released me from the rust-scented handcuffs.

"I take it the plan worked."

"Never did I doubt it would, but may I admit to some initial anxiety, Miss Steele?" Mr. Quillfeather dropped the darbies into his satchel and swung shut the door. "Happily, my fears were unfounded. You were *most* convincingly distraught as we left the Weathercock, and I observed two men who seemed, as you suggested, to be keeping a watch on the boarding house? They conferred quickly and departed in haste after you were shut in the conveyance."

They will go straight to Sack with news of my arrest, I thought with dark satisfaction.

569

He will search all the London gaols, and when he comes to the division which liaisons with Inspector Quillfeather when they need him in London, the sergeant will confirm my arrest.

I would not, however, be allowed any visitors; I pictured the apoplexed face of the Company diplomat when told by a placid bobby that he could under no circumstances see Miss Jane Stone before she had been thoroughly questioned, and could not help but smile.

"We've bought ourselves a bit of time," I said, "but how long?"

Mr. Quillfeather called for the constable to drive off; gesturing to a much faster one-horse trap, my ally helped me into it.

"Enough, Miss Steele?" he answered gravely. "It does not matter precisely how much time, provided it is enough."

Nodding, I watched the hedgerows blur as we quit the hostelry at twice the speed we had employed upon arrival. We covered our laps with layers of wool nearly as thick as my finger; silently, as if we had long been close companions, we shared bread and cheese from Mr. Quillfeather's satchel. Keeping a fast pace, stopping once to change horses, we could be at Highgate House by dawn.

It only remained to determine whether I

was more frightened of the accursed treasure I would encounter there, or of its
keeper.

As it happened, our trials were to commence before we so much as set foot upon
the property.

Mr. Quillfeather had at first met my suggestion of driving with resistance; but when
I pointed out that a man yawning every ten
seconds surely could not mind the roads
closely, he thanked me, wondered aloud if
there were a finer woman in all of England,
tipped his hat brim over his eyes, and commenced snoring. Our horse was sturdy
country stock which needed little minding,
so I allowed my thoughts to drift; a fox
barked mournfully in the distance, and I
heard the soft hooting of owls, but these
nocturnal companions were as nothing
compared to the friend in my mind's eye.

*You are about to see Charles Thornfield
again.*

How would he look, after these weeks
apart? *Identical to the way he looked before,*
I thought, but then questioned the assumption. Jane Eyre, when leaving her fiancé to
find her own way, writes:

As yet my flight, I was sure, was undiscovered. I could go back and be his comforter — his pride; his redeemer from misery; perhaps from ruin. Oh, that fear of his self-abandonment — far worse than my abandonment — how it goaded me! It was a barbed arrow-head in my breast: it tore me when I tried to extract it; it sickened me when Remembrance thrust it further in.

Charles Thornfield and I had only skimmed the rippling surface of an attachment which went, on my part, deep as the Atlantic; despite his refusals, I could not pretend my departure had affected him not at all. Mr. Singh had begged me to return, and even Mr. Quillfeather had sensed an "awareness" of me on the part of my former master. To this I could add the evidence of my own experience. Mr. Thornfield, upon learning I planned to leave Highgate House, had neither wept nor blustered; he had shrunk, this impossibly large presence curled in on himself as if acknowledging I was right to seek elsewhere for happiness and affection, for loyalty and love.

He had been wrong — but did he know as much? Would the absence of my face at the dinner table cause him to push his plate away? Would he have wasted, would he have

— wonder of wonders — *missed* me?

It will likely make little sense to the reader that seeing my sad, sweet Clarke again had invested me with new hope of winning Mr. Thornfield; but she had transformed me into a creature who, rather than being loved solely by a madwoman, was loved by a mad-woman and a precious friend. I grieved for her, I regretted her sorrows, and yet they inexplicably heartened me. Never had I doubted her devotion prior to her flight, but as to the nature of it — if Clarke could long for the touch of my hand, could not Mr. Thornfield learn to?

Brooding made the time pass more quickly than I should have thought possible, and the birds were chirruping in the yew trees outside of the familiar village when Sam Quillfeather awoke with a punctuating snort. The horizon flamed red-gold, and our second horse, which had given admirable service, snuffled tiredly.

"Nearly there, I believe?"

"Very nearly, Mr. Quillfeather."

"We shall soon get to the bottom of this affair, eh?"

Twenty minutes later, we pulled into the village, and there was the sleepy half-timbered inn, there the post office, there the white steepled church, and there the road leading to Highgate House.

In the next instant, my gaze lit upon something foreign, however, something that emphatically *did not* belong.

"Get down, below the seat," Mr. Quillfeather hissed. "Quickly!"

I threw myself to the floor. A band of half a dozen splendidly uniformed men approached the inn on horseback, presumably seeking eggs and sausages; I had never seen East India Company soldiers in the flesh previous, and yet I should have known one anywhere. These wore white breeches and white waistcoats with gold buttons, black neck stocks with scarlet sashes to match their brilliant blood-red cutaway coats.

"Mr. Sack planned to storm Highgate House for the trunk if he did not have his way," I whispered loudly. "Do you think —"

"I do not know what to think, but we are taking no chances!" Mr. Quillfeather thrust his hawk-nosed face down at me. "Once they are indoors, you shall drive as fast as you can to Highgate House. If you can locate the trunk before giving the alarum, then your story will be strengthened by hard evidence. I fear they may not believe you otherwise, or that the guilty party may fly? I shall learn what these men are planning. Be of good courage!"

Forcing myself to breathe, I nodded. The inspector brought the trap into the yard and swung from it with his stork's legs akimbo, waving away offers from the stable boys to wipe down and water the horse, telling them his niece had need of the vehicle. When Mr. Quillfeather had disappeared into the inn, the lads stared in wonderment as my head popped up like a jack-in-the-box; but I did not linger for conversation, snatching up the reins and setting off at as brisk a clip as the fagged horse could produce.

Mr. Sack's words echoed, their urbanity laced with the tinny sneer of the school yard bully.

The Company owns this city, Miss Stone, and you have stolen from us — so now I own you.

If the Company owned London, its vast power feeding itself like a deadly serpent forever swallowing its own tail, how far did its reach extend? India, of course; China, certainly; the Punjab, without question — but a sleepy hamlet a day's hard ride from the metropolis?

Did Sack mean to wage a literal battle against the warriors of Highgate House? And if so, was he brilliant or simply obsessed?

My joints ached with fatigue when I

pulled up to the gate, tethering the horse to the scrollworked iron. I wanted to treat the poor animal better, but I could not risk my approach being heard, and so caressed its ear and assured it of further attentions directly.

Skirting the main house along the edge of the forest was a simple matter, the dew wetting my boots as I strode round the back. The sun was well up, and my nerves sang so dissonantly with hope and apprehension that I wished only for it to be two hours from now, ten hours from now, when all was settled one way or the other.

I should never have wished such a foolish thing, so in part I blame myself for what took place that morning.

The kitchen door would be unlocked, I knew, for Mrs. Jas Kaur was always up with the dawn, grinding whole spices into blends and rubbing yogurt into cubes of freshly killed sheep. She was there when I appeared like a vision from the mists, pulling the feathers from a chicken, and she gasped out something in Punjabi before smiling at me.

"I'm sorry to have startled you — I'm afraid I wanted my return to have an element of surprise."

Jas Kaur, who spoke no English whatsoever, chuckled and shrugged and waved a down-covered hand at the door, bidding me go about my business.

I did so, stepping into the wider hall of the servants' wing.

The air here was cooler than the kitchen, thin and still; I had walked for perhaps twenty yards before I remembered the night prior to my quitting Highgate House, the terrible attack by Jack Ghosh and what came afterwards, and I knew I was heading in the wrong direction.

The treasure would be close to its possessor, and its possessor had recently moved.

Turning, I ran back the way I came and out the door, provoking another mild exclamation from Jas Kaur.

Sahjara will be having her morning ride, I thought, *and everyone else wide awake and working, and only one guard set to impede you.* I sprinted across the grounds, lungs burning in the cold, cloak flapping about my bright rose skirts. *I will find the treasure, and give it to Mr. Thornfield, and all will be well, though it will hurt terribly.*

When I reached my destination, to my surprise no bearded and turbaned Singh whatsoever awaited me. Having planned simply to wave my way through — as I was known to all the servants despite my terrible facility with their names — I hesitated momentarily. When I realised that Sahjara was the true commodity to be watched over, however, and decided her guard must surely be out riding with her, I gripped the door of the cottage and found it locked.

This, though not precisely surprising, was vexing — until, that is, I remembered my late mother's enormous facility for losing keys, and recalled that Agatha had kept a spare underneath a loose flagstone a few yards from the entrance. It took a few minutes to recognise the right one, but barely a minute had passed before I stood there triumphant, with dirtied fingernails and an eroding key.

It fit, and the door creaked open.

I began the search with the bedrooms, but soon thought better of this and ran for the attic; up, up, up I went to the place where I had read Mamma's letter so long ago. When I reached it, I took in the steep-roofed chamber, all its draped furnishings like censorious guards.

A large wooden crate which had not been there before rested under the round window.

The lid came off easily and revealed paperwork — written in Punjabi, but the neatly lined columns indicated records. I scattered them to the floor, heedless of the mess I was making. I had not tossed many aside before I found a thin piece of wood, and I clawed the false bottom from the crate.

Reader, no dolls rested within.

There were jewels, however — set jewels and loose ones, sapphires wrapped in velvet and topaz tumbling loose, an emerald bracelet which spanned wrist to elbow and a ruby tiara which would have caused the Queen of Sheba to swoon. There were ropes of pearls, golden chains, and the effect was nearly laughable in its opulence: so I did what I always do at inappropriate times, and I laughed.

"I shouldn't celebrate prematurely, Miss Stone."

I turned, electric with fright; there stood Garima Kaur, her once-handsome face set, holding a curved and long-bladed knife in her hand.

THIRTY-ONE

I requested him to shut the door and sit down: I had some questions to ask him. But when he complied, I scarcely knew how to begin; such horror had I of the possible answers.

Her words were free-flowing, practically accentless save for the same familiar lilt Mr. Singh owned, which made my very marrow quiver.

"I had supposed you didn't speak much English?"

This amused the housekeeper, but the twitch of her lips was not even hinted at in her eyes. Where Mr. Quillfeather appeared affably cadaverous, all appendages and hooked nose, Garima Kaur looked as if her flesh had shrunk too tight to fit her, the sleeves of her drab housekeeper's black loose around her pale brown wrists. Save the unsightly scar, one might wonder if she were a shade casting an illusion which only appeared to be human skin.

"Having deceived far better minds than yours, I cannot fault you for thinking so. Do not worry, do not worry," she parroted, and then laughed, her lips stretched over her teeth. "I speak six other languages and worked with Sardar from the time we were both fifteen; he and Charles spoke Punjabi half the time, English the other — I could only have avoided learning your ugly tongue had I stuffed my ears with cotton."

There were things about her I had slowly gleaned, reader, and things I had only just come to understand; I had not, however, expected her capacity for deception to exist on so global a scale, and could not help but admire her.

"And you never let on that you were fluent?"

"Why should I want to deal with every loutish *ferengi*★ Sardar traded with?" she spat. "They only wanted to rob us, as you do now — Charles was raised better, but the exception proves the rule, as you say. Take the knife from your skirts and leave it in the trunk, covering all up again."

★ A derogatory term in India for a Western foreigner.

Of course she knows about the knife, for we had been speaking English as she drifted the corridors all that while, and I never thought twice about it. Peering at her cruelly curved blade, I dropped my paltry weapon in the tangle of treasure at my feet; against a Sikh fighter, it may as well have been a berry spoon.

Lacking even that token means of defending myself, however — every hair on my crown stood on end. I returned the false bottom and the papers to the crate, fitted the lid, and then turned to face my captor.

"Please." I raised my hands in supplication, "I mean you —"

"Surely you are not about to tell me that you *mean me no harm,*" Garima Kaur interjected, and again the shift of her mouth did not affect her cavernous eyes. "Do you really mean to suggest that you intend to leave that fortune in this garret and walk away from Highgate House?"

Deliberately, I exhaled. "There are half a dozen East India Company soldiers in the village sent by Mr. Sack, ready to raid the premises — it's time this was ended."

Conversely, her eyes burst now to life, as if I had turned up a gas lamp.

"Are there?" she said softly.

"Yes, so you see —"

"Then you are correct, Miss Stone. It is time this was ended."

Garima Kaur's voice was a scalpel, and a small wound in the rational world opened; I had assigned many characteristics to her since that morning — brilliant, vengeful, and ruthless all figured prominently.

Not once had I suspected her mad.

"You cannot mean to fight them," I pleaded. "The people you care about will be hurt, maybe even killed, and the wars are over, you cannot bring the battlefield to England and expect —"

"How came you to be here?" she interrupted, swinging the long knife in a lazy, expert circle around her index and middle fingers before palming it again.

"I think you killed David Lavell."

She laughed. "Remarkable. What else do you think?"

"I think that John Clements was in love with you, and when his colleague Mr. Sack received a taunting letter from Sardar Singh, I think . . . I think he suspected you were the one behind it. All those years he trusted you, fed you information without realising that's what you wanted him for. And I think when he concluded you had stolen the trunk, and had finished Lavell, I think he confronted you, and you poisoned him in his rooms in London."

Her mouth worked again, but now pain warped the derision, and she paused before speaking. It was an expression I knew well and, though kissed by madness thanks to my mother, I did not think I lived in its embrace as Garima Kaur did, that obsessive desire to right *the single great wrong* which has swept your life off its course. We could have been sisters otherwise, for our propensities; we could have been friends.

Her silent shock confirmed my suspicions, albeit superfluously — I had only to recall the single thread connecting the dead men to know I was right.

Mr. Sack was the one who had first stimulated my interest, when he had said of John Clements, *He was low over the project, over his lack of progress. Then he saw an old love of his briefly, and he sank further into melancholy. Honestly, Miss Stone? I believe he took the soldier's way out.*

Half a clue is as useless as none at all; but then I recalled a scrap of conversation which illuminated a dark landscape.

Poor old Johnny, with that puppyish way he had about him, Mr. Thornfield had said to Mr. Singh the night I had eavesdropped on them. *Remember when he used to sniff around your secretary as if she were Cleopatra?*

Garima Kaur, of course, was that secretary — a woman loved by a British political she used and despised, a woman capable of copying her employer's penmanship and imitating his voice even in a language she loathed, writing, *Your Company has raped my entire culture in systematic fashion.* Mr. Singh had remained in Lahore throughout the First Sikh War guarding Sahjara, I was certain, for it fit all I knew of him, but his secretary — the loyal princess with the accomplished knife hand — had made at least one delivery to David Lavell in Amritsar, and she had left him with a gash through his neck.

"I think you may have tipped Jack Ghosh as well," I mused, "but I'm not entirely certain of that. Did you?"

"Yes." She had recovered her poise, though the sunken pits of her pupils were glassy. "I contacted him through Clements — he was staying in the village. I waited until Sardar and Charles were guaranteed to be absent, and then I sent him word they were away from home."

"Why?" I demanded.

"To be rid of him. I could have finished him for us. And to be rid of *you.*"

"I don't . . ." I faltered. "God in heaven. Why should —"

"I removed the jewels from Sardar and Charles's keeping, yes, having heartily approved their taking them." Her voice was as smooth as a river stone and twice as cold. "They were keeping it *unguarded,* in a *child's trunk.* I was on my way to meet Sardar when I glimpsed Sack leaving the house in a sort of ecstasy. Sahjara confirmed she had shown him her dolls — I was forced to act quickly. I buried the trunk in the depths of the warehouse the Thornfields shared with Sardar, wedged between cracked jades and silks from poor dye lots, where no one would ever look. When Ghosh took Sahjara . . ." She directed a series of guttural curses in an unidentifiable tongue at the sloped ceiling. "They ran off like puppies, did not tell me what was troubling them, or I could have given them the trunk. Her mind was forever altered, and I love that little girl as if she were mine. How could I *not* vow to kill Jack Ghosh? I waited for years, until the perfect opportunity arose. I meant to do it with my own blade — after he had finished you, of course, but that did not go as planned."

"Yes, but as for myself —"

"I said, *I love that little girl as if she were*

mine!" she screamed.

The air turned to ash between us — thick and hot in our throats, as if a volcano had erupted.

"Oh," I breathed, comprehending.

She laughed miserably, the scar across her brow raised in disbelief. "In an English way, you are quite clever, Miss Stone; but in an English way, you are also very stupid. When Sahjara was sent away, my heart broke — she was all I had left of my friend Karman, and *oh,* Karman was like a shaft of God's light striking earth. Lavell wasn't fit to clean her boots with his spit, and the instant I heard of her demise, I slaughtered him in Amritsar and was back in Lahore before anyone there so much as knew he was dead. He would have alternately ignored and bullied Sahjara, that precious girl."

"Her father would have mistreated her. But not Sardar Singh," I murmured, understanding still more.

"Not Sardar — Sardar is a good man. When she was sent to England, he used to tell me to have patience, tell me that we would all be together again soon. For a while, Miss Stone, I thanked God for my new home here at Highgate House. I was teaching Sahjara Turkish, Pashto, how to sharpen a sword and how to balance accounts. Then Charles hatched a truly foul idea with Sardar — and in English, no less, though they did not know I minded them."

"He wanted an English governess. I'm so sorry."

"No, you aren't," she growled, gesturing with the knife's tip. "You adore the pair of them, and they love you back, they . . . they can *see* you."

A sob escaped her, and she panted, clutching the knife's handle so hard I thought her fingers must break.

"It was bad enough not to work with Sardar any longer — passing the time with him on long journeys, going over inventory, dining with his sister," she seethed. "As his confidential secretary, I negotiated for him, flattered for him, foresaw every difficulty and prevented it happening at all. Here I was sent to the *servants' wing,* none of my efforts with Sahjara were given more than passing praise, Sardar lost all interest in my company, there was no meaningful work to distract me, and then they determined to advertise for a white governess. I wrote to Mr. Sack the next day."

"How could you do such a thing if you truly loved Sahjara?"

"To remind them of *who we really are.*" Her death mask's face tilted up, challenging. "I was wasting away, misery robbing me of flesh by the pound, and they didn't even *notice.* They needed something to fight for, Miss Stone. We all did — it's in our blood. My friend Karman was eighteen years old when she had her first Khalsa cavalry uniform tailored — we were born to fight, destined by God, and she would have despaired at seeing them so emasculated."

This account of Karman's uniform rang like bells; but before I could comprehend why the detail was important, I was being given my marching orders.

"Now, come here, slowly — and walk down the stairs, slowly. If you fail to do exactly as I say, this knife will be in your kidney."

The *slowly* portion was easily managed, for I dreaded accompanying her. My limbs moved stiltedly, as if they belonged to Sahjara's long-lost dolls, but my senses were keenly attuned to the familiar creak of the staircase, the velvety wood of the aged bannister. The only thing to do was to keep her talking — but I could not for my life imagine what to say to a woman who wished I had never been born.

"Why didn't you tell them about Karman's fortune after Sahjara was rescued?" I asked.

"At the start of *another* war?" she sneered from behind me.

"After that war, then?"

"In the midst of transporting an entire household across the continent?"

I stopped, hands visibly limp at my sides, and turned.

"You knew it was wrong," said I. "You don't want to find out what Sardar will think."

"He stole those jewels in the first place, you fool," she spat, but her lip trembled. "Go on, out the back door and head for the forest."

"What are you going to do with me?"

"I haven't decided yet. I am curious, though, how after all you have seen and discovered, that you could dream you mean me no harm."

I stepped outside. The fresh air was like a slap across the cheek; it warned that, unless I was very fortunate, I was about to die. I would not, I had already determined, fall to my knees and allow the guillotine to fall. If this was to be the end, I would fight with tooth and claw at the edge of the woods; but before those methods were employed, I elected to try persuasion.

"We could invent a story," I said, and it was not a lie: it was a *possibility.* "Do you wonder how I came to go armed?"

"No." The tip of her knife caressed the edge of my cloak. "I was listening outside the dining room. Faster now, towards that copse."

The woods loomed before me, the thicket from which Edwin and I had burst, all the starkly bare-limbed beeches and the forbidding pines near to the edge of the ravine, and I did not want to die where Edwin had, could not stop my skin from crawling when I felt his unmoving stare pinned to my face.

"Then you know I have faced hardship," I insisted. "I will tell you more, something I have never deliberately told anyone: I am your equal in infamy. I have murdered — more than once. I can lie for you, only tell me what your reasons were."

"You suppose a false confession will save you?"

This, of all strokes, was surely deliberately arranged by God to needle me.

"It isn't fal—"

"Never mind. I will tell you anyhow what my motives were," Garima Kaur added, and I could sense the gathering snow as the avalanche gained speed, hurtling towards the ravine. "I killed David Lavell because had he never existed, we should all be at peace. I maintained ties with John Clements

591

because thereby I kept my finger on the pulse of the activities of Augustus Sack and Jack Ghosh. I killed John Clements because, imbecile though he was, he knew enough about my movements to grow suspicious after I forged the letter. And I forged the letter because —"

"Garima! And can that possibly be Miss Stone?"

I could have collapsed at the sound of that voice — indeed, I staggered, and Garima Kaur gasped.

We turned as one animal to see Sardar Singh. He seemed puzzled but delighted at the sight of me and said something in Punjabi to Garima Kaur, who had clearly masked the knife in the fold of her skirts upon the instant she heard him call from behind us.

She answered readily enough; but I, much closer to her, could see that her hands shook, and knew that what had previously been a perilous situation was now absolutely a deadly one.

"Miss Stone!" Mr. Singh exclaimed. "What a happy moment I seem to have chosen for a long winter's walk. I have passed many a frank hour in Charles's company since you departed, but had hardly hoped you would return after you sent no forwarding address. Welcome home — or so I hope you think of it."

Garima Kaur aimed a painted puppet's smile at him even as her eyes flooded with tears.

Not long after my mother's death I had a nightmare I actually remembered, the screaming sort which led Taylor to single me out in the Reckoning: a creature came to the doorstep of our cottage, and I knew without seeing, as one does in dreams, that it was a rabbit, and I picked up the small animal thinking to pet its fur. Only after I had lifted it did I realise that it had already been skinned by a hunter, and begun to be butchered as well; deep knife marks were scored along the spine, and only half its head remained, as if the brains had been reserved to tan the pelt. Though it moved as if alive, nuzzling my chest, I knew it must be in unfathomable pain, and I awoke shrieking about needing to kill something because in the dream I had no proper weapon.

I had not thought of that nightmare in years; but Garima Kaur's expression brought it immediately to mind.

"Mr. Singh," said I, stepping two paces away from her.

"Whatever is the matter?" he asked, frowning. "Have I interrupted you?" These questions were followed by what I assumed was the Punjabi equivalent.

Garima Kaur waited to see what I would say, her attention flicking rapidly between us.

For the first time in my life, I decided that truth was preferable.

"She speaks English," I announced. "Very well indeed, and she has the treasure — look in the garret of the cottage, under the false bottom in the crate of records."

Several expressions fought for supremacy on Mr. Singh's face, the winner proving disbelief. "Miss Stone, I cannot imagine —"

"You don't have to; you can find it yourself. She wanted to protect your sister's fortune, but now there are Company soldiers in the village, Mr. Quillfeather is keeping them at bay, and she killed David Lavell in Amritsar all those years ago. I know you won't mourn him, but she's the reason Sack was here — she sent him a letter in your name."

Garima Kaur's fleshless face reacted not at all to my betraying her secrets, but she swayed slightly. I had told only a fraction of what I knew, and only what I thought Mr. Singh and Mr. Thornfield might forgive.

Slanting my gaze, I willed her to understand me.

I will never tell them you killed John Clements, nor that you sent Jack Ghosh — not if you and I can both survive this.

Sardar Singh stood there motionless, taking in my words with eyes wide; I saw the exact moment when he believed me, for he flinched. Then I remembered that — unlike Mr. Thornfield, who seemed to expect trouble to find him magnetically — Mr. Singh had always known that the key to the conundrum lay in how Mr. Sack came to be at Highgate House in the first place.

The fact of his being here was, I agree, the greatest mystery of all.

"Garima, is what Miss Stone says accurate?"

"Yes." The tears spilled down her bony cheeks. "But it was all for you, for *us.* Why should I have told you I speak English? You would talk of your problems to Charles, and I solved them without your ever asking me to — I was your djinn, your secret granter of wishes. You used to need me. How can you think you don't need me any longer?"

"We all of us need one another," he said softly, but she was a rudderless ship close to capsizing.

"Sahjara and I were fine, we were all *fine,*

until *she* came!" Garima Kaur may as well have been brandishing the knife, for her words slashed through the air between us. "So you didn't seek me out any longer, banished me to the servants' quarters, and never thought to visit — none of it mattered whilst I still had our sweet girl to tutor. But you took even that pittance and gave it to *her,* and never noticed I was fading away right in front of you."

Mr. Singh raised his hands, seeming as contrite as he was appalled. "We shall set all this right. Do you hear me, Garima? Please — I am to blame, you are correct, but as to Augustus Sack's coming here — how could you even consider bringing such a plague upon us when he had thought Karman's treasure lost in the Punjab?"

"Because the only time you ever loved me was when I was fighting beside you!" she cried.

A ghastly silence fell. I took in her terrible scar, her posture like prey caught in an iron trap. I did not blame Mr. Singh for being celibate, nor for being stupid, because I am apparently remarkably dim-witted myself where Clarke is concerned. Imagining the eternal desert Garima Kaur had walked through all her life, however — next to the man she loved but never near him — repelled me on her behalf. I had chosen to leave Charles Thornfield, and she had locked herself in a prison with a view of paradise through the window.

Mr. Singh, meanwhile, seemed to have forgot his own mastery of our language — any language — regarding Garima Kaur as if he had never truly set eyes on her previous.

"There were five of them, and they came on us, thirsting for blood and spoils, and you'd no heart to take their wretched lives, but I was there, and so we lived," she said brokenly. "We *survived,* Sardar, and for two terrible, magnificent minutes, I wasn't invisible. And after it was over, after they'd marked me and my chances at marriage to anyone else had vanished, I disappeared again the same way my hopes did. So courteous you were, so distant — I may as well have been your shaving mirror."

Had she whipped the blade from her skirts and slit his belly, I do not think Mr. Singh's expression would have differed.

Then I did something entirely brainless, and thus set a number of dreadful events in motion. What I ought to have done was to bolt whilst her attention was fixed on the object of her affections; I ought to have sprinted to the main house shrieking for

Charles Thornfield, and many ghastly consequences would have been avoided.

Unfortunately, I scarcely ever scream when I am meant to.

"I think we must —"

The instant I opened my lips to offer an unsolicited opinion, Garima Kaur bellowed in rage and swung her knife at my throat.

There was not enough time.

Had there been enough time, I could have evaded her; had there been enough time, Mr. Singh could have drawn a weapon. Had there been enough time, Garima Kaur would not have been almost unhampered in her decision to send me to hell.

I say *almost* unhampered.

Sardar Singh emitted a wordless sound of protest and leapt, using what I only then realised was a final recourse when lacking other shields, and blocked her blade with his metal cuff. The knife slid with a horrid scraping noise down the sheath and then soundlessly sliced off his right hand.

Garima Kaur emitted a despairing groan, dropped her weapon, and ran.

Mr. Singh roared in pain and fell to his knees; I whipped off my cloak, bundled it, and I buried the gushing stump within. The hand with its severed tendons and its white gleam of bone lay to my left, pointing in the direction whence its butcher had fled.

"I'm sorry, I'm so sorry, I — You saved my life."

Mr. Singh's lips were pressed so hard within his mouth that nothing save beard remained; he had not lost enough blood yet to faint, but the shock did battle with his consciousness nevertheless.

"Please, you'll be all right. You have to be. *Please.*"

I think my uselessness roused him, for he ordered, "Help me to stand."

Between the two of us, we managed, though I nearly toppled under his weight; the instant he was upright, he was striding for the main house with his good arm about my shoulders, I pressing the ball of my cloak against his stump.

"Can you make it?"

"I don't know, but I needn't," he gasped. "Not if you fetch Charles to wherever I collapse."

The journey, I am sure, took less than three minutes; if ever three minutes were drenched with horror enough for three lifetimes, it was those. We burst through the front door like marauders, interrupting Charles Thornfield as he came from his study into the hall, dropping several pieces of mail on the table.

"What in the name of the devil —" he began, and then paled. "Is this our Jane returned? Oh my God — Sardar, what has —"

"We'll talk about it later, Charles," Mr. Singh said, breath heaving. "If you could stop me bleeding to death in the meanwhile . . ."

Mr. Thornfield's cry of dismay was the only signal I had that Mr. Singh was about to topple like a felled tree; I was dragged a bit by his bulk, but Mr. Thornfield caught him round the waist and together we made it into the parlour. Mr. Singh landed on the settee and lay back, all his limbs quivering.

"Jane, whatever are you doing here?" the love of my life demanded. "Who dared to lay a finger on —"

Mr. Thornfield tore off the makeshift bandage of my cloak and saw what had been done.

"No." He closed his eyes and shook his head as if the sight could be erased. "For Christ's sake, no. Sardar —"

"No!" I cried, lurching towards the window.

Mr. Singh managed to raise his torso, and the three of us watched as Mrs. Garima Kaur, saddled on Nalin, galloped past the bay window with Sahjara seated between her knees and exited the estate through the gate where my forgotten horse was still tethered with its trap.

Thirty-Two

"I could dare it for the sake of any friend who deserved my adherence; as you, I am sure do."

"What in hell is the meaning of all this?" Mr. Thornfield shouted as he tore off his coat and rolled his sleeves up, dropping to his knees. "Where is Garima off to with Sahjara?"

"Go," Mr. Singh gasped, eyes on me. "Please bring her back. It is unfair to ask it, I know, but —"

I was already running; the last sight which met my eyes before I flew out the parlour door was that of Mr. Thornfield viciously cursing at the spectacle of an arm without a hand attached before tearing off his gloves.

There was no time to think about what that meant as my feet and lungs propelled me towards the stables, my ears burning in the cold. Homelike smells of leather and manure assaulted me as I charged into the refuge of my childhood, my exhalations hanging in the atmosphere like malevolent ghosts.

The Sikh grooms stared at me in astonishment. There might have been some trouble over procuring a mount; but as it happened, Sahjara's new mare was still saddled, having just returned, so I swung myself up onto Harbax, tearing out of the stable as if Satan were at my heels. For the first five minutes of my pursuit, I despaired of catching up to them before we reached the village, for Nalin was the fastest steed in Mr. Thornfield's stables, and young Harbax the most unpractised.

Gift of God. Sahjara named you that, and Mr. Singh supposed it important, though Mr. Thornfield joked about the meaning. Please, please prove to be a gift of God.

I caught sight of them — a silhouette, really, just an outline in the gathering crystalline fog. Recalling with a thrill of hope that Nalin was the least tractable of her species I had ever encountered, I urged the more docile Harbax onward, feeling the mare surge as she sensed my distress.

Garima Kaur heard her pursuer and craned her head to glance behind, her emaciated form looking dangerously fragile atop such a powerful beast. Nothing of Sahjara could be seen save her rhythmically swinging feet; but reader, I loved her then, for she was the victim of blighted hopes and blind circumstance, as so many are, as I am, and Garima Kaur did not have a knife any longer, and I would return Sahjara to the people who quietly, carefully cherished her if it cost me my own right hand — or worse.

Abruptly enough that I feared snapped necks would result, Garima Kaur reined Nalin, and the mare emitted a wild, wary sound; she turned the horse with difficulty, and then it was that I saw Sahjara's lovely face — uncomprehending and panicked.

"Miss Stone!" she gasped. "Where is Charles? Mrs. Kaur says we are to escape to London, that there are Company soldiers making for Highgate House."

"Mrs. Kaur," I cried through the mist, "there is no one more sympathetic to your situation than I. I beg you, however —"

"You will ruin more lives, but you will not ruin mine entirely," Garima Kaur snarled. Nalin's nostrils flared, her hooves agitatedly stamping the ground.

"I seek to ruin no one, I swear to you upon any holy book you like." Harbax, conversely, was an island once halted, perfectly quiet. "Only let me take Sahjara home."

"Sahjara is *mine!*" she cried with the cracking voice of a breaking woman.

At times disaster visits us when we least expect it; and at others, we see the fraying rope and know that the hour of peril is nigh. I did not know what form disaster would take, but I knew then that Garima Kaur would not be returning to Highgate House, knew it with every fibre of my being.

I should have loved to stop the inevitable, but there was nothing whatsoever I could do.

Nalin reared — triumphant, angry, frightened. One never quite knows what a horse is thinking, but I like to imagine that horses are able to sense what people are thinking.

My frantic cry as Garima Kaur was tossed like a flour sack from the fractious horse was not so loud as the hammering of my heart when I saw Sahjara begin to slide after her kidnapper. Dismounting to catch her was impossible, and riding to meet her would cause Nalin to career off until she found the horizon.

Helpless, I flung out an arm.

Falling, Sahjara did the same.

Except she did not mirror me, not quite; she hooked her arms round Nalin's neck, swung a leg over, and tumbled almost grace-fully, a pendulum swinging within a clock. When she dangled from the mare's neck, dropping to the ground a few seconds later, I could have wept for relief; she had Nalin by the reins immediately, thanks only to instinct. Then she viewed the tragically contorted body of Garima Kaur and began to cry.

How long I held her there in the road after dismounting Harbax, I cannot say; how long Garima Kaur took to die I can, however, for she was stone still by the time I had reached Sahjara. Not wanting to leave any erstwhile friend of Sardar's crushed and discarded, I instructed Sahjara to mind both horses and not look at me as I hid the sickeningly light shell of a body under a holly tree.

When I emerged again, I was a wreck and Sahjara similarly blasted. We embraced for a long while, each supporting the other, until I realised that I was freezing to death.

"We must get back to the house," I grated. "Ride Harbax, and I'll take Nalin?"

"Miss Stone," she sobbed. "We can't leave Mrs. Kaur so. What if —"

"There are no more *what ifs* for her, dar-ling," I said, hoping Mr. Thornfield's favour-ite endearment might calm her. "She is sleeping peacefully, and no one can hurt her ever again. Ride back with me — the gentlemen are worried sick over you."

"Because of the Company men?" she asked, touching the knife in her hair.

"Yes," I lied. "We're going home now, as fast as ever we can."

"Miss Stone?" She raised her tearstained face. "You won't tell Charles that I learnt to hang from the neck of a horse —"

"Oh, Sahjara," I gasped, pulling her back to me. "I'll never tell. You're alive, and you've a secret — well and good. Live as long as you can, and have as few secrets as possible. Mr. Thornfield wouldn't last a day without you — remember that, for all our sakes."

When we arrived back at Highgate House, my first task after guiding Sahjara to her bedroom was to take Sam Quillfeather's neglected horse and trap to the stables. The grooms were absent, probably speculating as to what the deuce had happened to Sardar Singh; so I rubbed the beast down and afterwards stood, silently weeping, with my brow against its ribs.

I simply did not wish to face learning that anything disastrous had befallen Charles Thornfield — for he would equally be lost without Sardar Singh, and I had begun to suspect that I might be similarly affected by his absence.

After cursing myself for a weakling, I hurried to the main house, tapping upon doors and tumbling through them as if I had a right to be there. They had made me feel as if I had a right to be there, after all — they had made me feel as if I had a home.

At last I found Charles Thornfield in the kitchen, speaking urgently to Jas Kaur as he washed his bare hands; they were already clean, but his crusted shirtsleeves told a gruesome story, and his white hair was liberally speckled with blood.

"How is he?" I questioned. "Did he tell you . . . did he —"

"Jane!" Mr. Thornfield dived for a cloth, drying his fingers; seeing them naked again was peculiar, as if I ought to turn away and grant him privacy. "Say that you found Sahjara, I beg of you. If she —"

"I'm here," came a small voice, and I saw that the commotion had brought Sahjara out of hiding; she stood in the hall just outside the kitchen, eyes puffy and strained.

I am not proud of many of my actions; most were committed for selfish reasons, and bringing Sahjara back ought to be numbered among these, for I could not bear the thought of losing her. However, the look on Mr. Thornfield's face as he crossed the flagstones in a frantic leap and swept her up into his arms, cradling the shivering child's face against his shoulder without any barrier between them, I thought might be cause for celebration.

"Mr. Singh?" I asked again. "I must know how he fares, and what he told you. Please —"

"He told me, in brief, everything. And he will live, thank God. I was just arranging with Jas here to steep claret with oil, rosemary, and oregano to prevent infection. Supposing that fails us, I'll resort to pine pitch, but Sardar is an accommodating bastard, so I don't suppose he'll put me to the trouble if he can help it. I've knocked the poor fellow cold with laudanum, so now it is merely a matter of vigilance. All right, darling, hush," he spoke against the crown of Sahjara's head. "I was sick with worry over you, but I was busy saving your uncle's life."

"My uncle?" she repeated, dazed.

"Yes, I know you don't remember," he returned tenderly. "Your uncle Sardar he has always been, and ever will be. I didn't quite know how to introduce the topic. Forgive me?"

"Of course," she murmured. "What happened to him?"

"He was hurt." Mr. Thornfield shifted as if to set her down, but she clung to him. "All right, all right, Young Marvel — he'll be fine. Everything is fine now."

"It isn't fine," she choked, clutching his collar. "Garima was thrown from Nalin. Miss Stone dragged her out of the road, but she's . . ."

Charles Thornfield had endured such atrocity in his life that he simply glanced at me and then closed his eyes, nodding after he had seen the answer there. Yes, his jaw tightened painfully, but he gave no other sign. I do not think he meant to be stoic; he had already suffered so deeply, however, and gained so much back in a single hour — Sardar's life, Sahjara's safety, Karman's fortune — that news of Garima's death caused him to bend rather than break.

I shall never forget, however, that after he turned to Jas Kaur and told her the news in Punjabi, she sat at her worktable and split in two — sobbing, palms upwards in helpless anguish before her, her breaths like a death rattle.

It was a lesson, and a welcome one, that one member of the household had not been indifferent to Garima Kaur's existence; it was a lesson that everyone — even myself, I dared to hope — would be mourned by one fellow traveller.

Mr. Thornfield pressed her shoulder warmly and carried Sahjara from the kitchen. As I likewise exited, granting Jas Kaur some privacy in the rawness of her grief, I called, "Mr. Thornfield, there is much which I can explain to you, if you will allow it."

"Allow it?" Despite all which had occurred, a spark of gallows humour entered his eye. "Jane, I think it is safe to say I shall insist."

He was about to take Sahjara upstairs when a forceful knock sounded; instead, he set her down with a quiet, "Stay with Jas, darling," whisking her behind the kitchen door and shutting it firmly.

It is a testament to how well used to this household I had grown that I did not even blink when he pulled a short sword with a carved ivory handle from its place upon the wall. When I snatched up a dagger from farther down the corridor, however, he hissed, "What the devil can you be thinking? That could very well be half a dozen Company soldiers."

"Your point, Mr. Thornfield?"

"For God's sake, Jane, I —"

"Mr. Singh is incapacitated, and if you think I am going to allow you to face *badmashes* alone, you're cracked in the head. Sir."

Mr. Thornfield pronounced several exasperated curses, barked, "Keep *well* back, do you understand me?" and then strode for the entrance, where our visitor was creating still more of a racket than previous.

When he threw wide the door, however, I dropped the blade upon his pile of correspondence there on the table, weak with relief; Sam Quillfeather stood at the top of the steps, his aquiline nose thrusting urgently indoors. Mr. Thornfield gripped his hand even as he turned to cast a concerned eyebrow at me.

"Inspector, I hardly dare inquire as to what happened between you and the Company men — though last I saw you, this pixie vanished seconds later, and that sits poorly enough in my gut. We have much to discuss."

"Yes, upon this very *instant* lest disaster befall you!" Mr. Quillfeather returned. "And Miss Stone will correct me if I am mistaken, but I think she and I have reached an amicable understanding? Good heavens, Thornfield, whose blood is that?"

Mr. Thornfield gripped his neck, rubbing

exhaustedly. "Sardar's, I am sorry to say. He will live, thank heaven, though 'tis a grievous injury. There are tales to be told."

Mr. Quillfeather's fingers clenched around his tall hat. Stepping within, he scuffed his boots upon the rug.

"Then shall we pour a spot of brandy, sit before a fire, and tell them?" he suggested. "Perhaps if we are wise enough, there may be a happy outcome after all?"

"I don't think after all this anyone will accuse me of possessing a speck of wisdom, but I can certainly contribute the brandy and fire." Mr. Thornfield sighed, taking the inspector's place before the door. "Only let me quick march to have men sent for Garima's remains and I'll join you in the parlour."

"Remains?" Mr. Quillfeather asked softly when Mr. Thornfield had vanished. "Oh, Miss Steele, what must you have seen today?"

"Enough," I admitted, drying my eyes. "But far less than some."

We talked much that afternoon, and though I explained that I had schemed to outwit Mr. Sack — much to Mr. Thornfield's belated but vocal dismay — I said nothing yet of my greater history with Inspector Quillfeather, nor did that gentleman press me into broaching the subject. The most difficult moment, therefore, occurred when we had reached an understanding and regarded each other in the pale amber glow of the dying fire, knowing we could postpone the inevitable no longer.

"I shall glance at Mrs. Kaur's remains and fill out the death report, as the task would pain you, Thornfield," Inspector Quillfeather kindly offered. "There is, if all I have heard is true, no need for an autopsy?"

"I should not be offended," I assured them.

"No need." Mr. Thornfield tapped his fist against his brow, the curve of his wide shoulders slack with grief. "I just stitched up what Garima did to Sardar — she could have been in no state to manage Nalin. I only thank Christ you were there, Jane."

Mr. Quillfeather rose. "I shall also get a message to Mr. Sack, and arrange for the village physician to be here by morning. Time this was ended, don't you think?"

"High time," Mr. Thornfield grated, donning his hat and coat as we three exited the parlour.

Mr. Quillfeather headed for the underground mortuary, Mr. Thornfield and I out of doors. The stars were a cold spill of glass shards in the darkening sapphire canopy, sharp and treacherously beautiful; I wondered whether they looked the same in the Punjab, and if Garima Kaur thereby had at least the same sky to wish upon, or if they were hung at another angle in England, and the housekeeper thus entirely alone. Mr. Thornfield, seeming to see me for the first time, shook his head in annoyance.

"You'll catch your death without an overcoat, you mad thing." He passed his own round my shoulders and coughed, abashed. "Your cloak is quite irretrievably ruined, by the by."

"I should think so."

"You'd not have wanted it again in any case, I imagine."

"No, Mr. Thornfield."

"Your new frock suits you much better than governess weeds, though you did 'em better justice than most."

"Thank you, sir."

"Is that what you wanted the advance in wages for — to convince Sack you were a thief?"

"No . . . well, yes, but I've also had an inheritance. I shall tell you about it when we are through."

"Confronting Sack in such an audacious fashion — I hardly know what to make of these extraordinary efforts upon your part."

He gazed upwards as if only the firmament were equally unfathomable. "You could have found a far better recipient for your loyalty, you realise, than a ruffian with a curse upon his house."

"I don't agree," I said, and all my heart was in those words.

"Jane, blast it to pieces, I don't know whether I can do this."

"At least you need not do it alone," I breathed, wanting only to reach out and fold my arms around him.

Charles Thornfield shifted upon the grass, shoved his hands in his trouser pockets, and strode towards the cottage.

I hastened after. We traversed the grounds in lockstep, lit a lantern within the cottage's sitting room, carried it with us as we trotted up the stairs; the door to the garret remained open and Mr. Thornfield made at once for the crate, flinging the lid aside and digging through papers until he arrived at the false bottom and tore it open.

The treasure gleamed with the too-saturated colour of poisonous vipers and venomous toads — a rainbow's spectrum of danger, those jewel tones which Nature employs to warn *keep away.*

"Yes, these are Karman's," Mr. Thornfield said, and it scored my heart to hear his voice breaking. "Oh, Jane, so much suffering, and for this pile of trinkets? You cannot know how I loathe myself, little friend, and the only riddle left to solve is why Sardar doesn't detest me as well."

Then I recalled one of Garima Kaur's last confessions, and why the seemingly trivial detail mattered.

"Garima Kaur said that Karman had her first Khalsa cavalry uniform altered to fit her when she was eighteen."

"What?" Mr. Thornfield's rugged face tilted in confusion.

"She wanted to fight long before her jewels went missing." My entire frame was taut with nerves and desperate hope. "Garima told me so. So now you know it had nothing to do with you — she would have risked all for glory anyhow, can't you see? No object is served by flaying yourself over the circumstances of her departure. War was in her blood and bones, and *doer of deeds* is what Mr. Singh said her name meant, and perhaps you left the Punjab to escape your heartbreak and made mistakes afterwards, but maybe the rest of it — the death, the *loss* — that was only what happens to us after we are born, and not a punishment at all."

"How do you know she died in battle?"

"Mr. Sack told me."

"Damn his eyes." Mr. Thornfield drew a shaking breath. "Jane . . ."

"I learnt in London that there was no subject upon which I was more mistaken than that of myself, sir." Brushing my fingertip over the blood still soaking his sleeve, I met his tearful gaze with my own. "Of you, however, I have made a close study, and I vow that I think no man more deserving of a measure of happiness, and that if I could fetch it for you, I should travel the globe."

"What if my remaining here whilst you travelled the globe would rather hamper my contentment than enhance it?" he answered after weighty pause.

"Then . . . I should stay here," I whispered. "With you."

Mr. Thornfield dashed his fingers over his eyes. "You've had an inheritance, you say."

"Sir?"

"An endowment, a legacy, a *bequest,* you contrary sprite."

"Yes, and a generous one."

"So you've no need of gainful employment any longer? You are an independent woman of means who requires no assistance to make her way in the world. Pressed duck served on fine china, Belgian lace edging your lowliest handkerchief, servants used as ottomans — all this, and without the necessity of drudgery. No longer need you talk horses for six hours daily to earn your bread and cheese."

I saw what troubled him then, and thought to tease him; instead, I laughed, and drew a step closer.

"I like horses," said I, lungs tight with feeling. "I always have done."

"Do you like dreadfully draughty English country houses?"

"I did not always, but I have grown to."

"What about curry?"

"Everyone likes curry, sir."

"Could you like a former Company medic who keeps a morgue in the cellar?" He smiled with such tender sadness that it nearly felled me.

"I don't like him — I love him. You aren't wearing gloves."

"So it would seem. Jane," he said, and then neither of us was speaking, for his mouth was sweetly, reverently pressed to mine, his hands at my nape and on my cheek, and when my lips parted and I tasted all the affection he had kept so long buried, I knew that no words could possibly have served as well as his kiss did.

"You don't know what it did to me."

Breaking away fractionally, he clenched a fold of my skirt in his right hand. "At least before, I could hear your step upstairs, or know you were riding, or catch your laugh when passing my study. One is not always directly regarding the full moon, Jane — but should it disappear, the oceans would rot. I was rotting already when you found me, and then your tide pulled, and you were gone so long. A mere matter of weeks, but still . . . how long till you leave me again?"

Kissing him once more seemed the right answer, but I could manage it only briefly. Realising as one that others' needs should be seen to quicker than ours, we hastened out of the cottage where I grew up, and back to the main house, the sky a faint lavender like a bruise almost forgotten.

The following day, preparations had been made for Charles Thornfield and myself to travel to London with all possible haste; Mr. Quillfeather had made our position clear to us, the village doctor fetched to tend to Sardar Singh in the meanwhile. I breakfasted with Sahjara and Mr. Thornfield, all of us sombre despite our victories. When I laid down my fork, I looked up to discover blue eyes studying me as if I were some sort of miracle, and an irrepressible smile spread over my features.

After the kiss, we had parted, and I believe Mr. Thornfield sat up with Mr. Singh for most of the night. Still — there was a crackling in the air between us now, something electric and wanting.

"May I see Mr. Singh alone?" I asked him. "I feel I cannot leave without thanking him for my continued existence."

"Of course. By extension I owe him my own, for I should have borne the loss of you with very bad grace."

Sahjara looked up curiously, lips curving. "Are you staying, then, Miss Stone?"

"If Mr. Thornfield will keep me after we conduct an important conversation, then yes."

"Naturally I'll keep you, we're all of us deuced keen to keep you — we've considered the benefits of shackles," he huffed. "A conversation on what subject?"

"My name, sir. But first I must see Mr. Singh, and then we must be off, and after all is settled with Mr. Sack, then I must tell you a story."

Charles Thornfield scowled, and shrugged, and said it was all very good if I wanted to play games with him, that I was incapable of changing his mind, and then he swept off to see our carriage was packed.

I kissed Sahjara atop her dark head, and then I hurried upstairs to the bedroom where Sardar Singh lay recovering.

Knocking first, I entered; the injured man was propped upon pillows in his darkened bedchamber, his arm bound in a sling with copious bandaging at the end of it. I could smell herbs and wine from the poultice, incense from a small metal holder in the corner of the room. The walls here — my father's old bedchamber, I realised, thought to be my dead uncle's — had been converted almost entirely into shelves containing score upon score of books, many cracking like so many ancient stone tablets.

"You needn't look like that, Miss Stone." Mr. Singh's voice was rusty but sure. "Charles stitched me up again, and I cannot imagine anyone taking greater care."

"Without gloves, no less."

"A triumph borne of misfortune, yes. He managed on the battlefield with far cruder measures, going so quickly from fallen to fallen."

I perched upon the edge of the bed. Mr. Singh's brow was strained, though not yet feverish, and his head was bare; his long hair glistened faintly, but seemed almost dry, and he smiled at my speechlessness.

"There was blood in it," he rasped.

"Highly dishonourable — it felt almost worse than my arm. One of the servants will be along shortly to tie it up again, for this . . ." He waved at his injured limb.

"Oh, I cannot tell you how sorry I am. Please forgive me," I begged.

"For the loss of my hand?" He shook his head. "There is nothing to forgive — you were the one truly endangered, after all. At last I am able to offer a true sacrifice: a disfigurement upon the altar of justice. Or so I tell myself. Monkishness is second nature to me, but as to my hand — I was quite attached to it."

"So often the way with hands," I agreed, and then we were laughing like overwrought children, wrung to the highest pitch of nerves, and there were tears in my eyes when I added, "I am also sorry for the loss of your friend."

"Yes, Charles told me." He sighed, a devastated look clouding his strong features. "This is on my head, not yours."

"You ought not blame yourself any more than Charles ought to blame himself for your sister's demise."

"I shall have to teach myself that wisdom slowly, Miss Stone, as did he."

I wanted to ask if he had suspected Garima Kaur loved him, but thought the question cruel.

"What does the name Garima mean?" I asked instead.

"There isn't quite an equivalent in English." Shifting, he settled farther back into the nest of pillows. "A crossroads between dignity and pride, perhaps."

"Do people's names always seal their fates, or only in the Sikh culture?"

He smiled again, though it did not erase the lines of suffering etched upon his brow. "I sound superstitious, don't I? I do think that when God gifts a parent with insight, a child's name will reflect their soul. Take Jane Stone, for instance — it suits, does it not?"

"It's the plainest of given names and an adopted surname," I confessed.

"Ah. Is it really? Nevertheless, I believe you mistaken. We are so locked within ourselves, we often lack perspective on these subjects — I take it to mean a rock, an island in the midst of perilous seas, and Jane is from the Hebrew, you know."

I had not known. "What does it mean?"

Mr. Singh's eyes, though laced with red spider's silk, twinkled thoughtfully. "Gift from a gracious God. I have found it, you will pardon me, not unfitting."

Rather than stem my tears, this spurred more. "You are far too kind to me."

"It is a great privilege, to have the opportunity of being kind to anyone. What is your real surname, if you'll pardon my asking?"

"I don't precisely have one — but it used to be Steele. I mean to tell Charles the whole story after Sack is dealt with; I shall give you a full account then, I promise you. Rest well."

"Steele," he mused as I quit his bedside. "Better and better — strength, resistance, a fighting spirit."

"I'll need all I have just to enter East India House again," I said from his threshold. "Mr. Sack is a brute and I shan't relish seeing him again, even with Mr. Thornfield there."

"So that is the meaning of all this bustling." Sardar Singh's eyes narrowed into knife blades. "You are off to London. What do you mean to do there?"

"To give up the treasure," said I, gently shutting the door.

Thirty-Three

"No — no — Jane; you must not go. No — I have touched you, heard you, felt the comfort of your presence — the sweetness of your consolation: I cannot give up these joys."

"Are you mad?" Augustus P. Sack circled his own desk like a jackal.

He was discomfited; I, Charles Thornfield, Sam Quillfeather, and Cyrus Sneeves had descended on him without warning. Freely do I admit that we brought the treasure he sought, and freely did we give it — expecting at any moment the arrival of another guest.

Mr. Sack, for a man who had been seeking a single prize for so many years, did not seem sufficiently glad to have it in view. Soon, I understood this was due to the fact he had loved tormenting Messrs. Thornfield and Singh with that the same glad viciousness which had caused him to tear my necklace from my throat; in addition, he suspected something amiss with the generous overture.

He was perfectly correct.

"Our demands are entirely reasonable, sir," my solicitor droned. To Mr. Sneeves's immense credit, confronting the East India Company sounded as if it were the duller sort of business to conduct on any given Thursday. "You are welcome to this box so long as you never reveal from whence it originated. Mention of the Punjab is acceptable, but this gentleman is to be released from all liability regarding the ownership of these gemstones. To that effect, you shall simply sign this paperwork exonerating Charles Thornfield of any wrongdoing, and I shall have it copied and delivered to any litigators in your employ."

"Surely you will comply, Mr. Sack?" Mr. Quillfeather pressed. "You now have my full report regarding the unsolved murder of John Clements, and the killer is beyond the punishment of mortals. All this, and a fortune in recovered property — what could be a happier circumstance?"

Charles Thornfield, meanwhile, continued to say nothing. When we had learnt the true intentions of the Company soldiers from

Inspector Quillfeather, he had expressed profound relief; the sight of Augustus Sack, however, predictably wreaked havoc with his digestion. He sat expressionless before the political, one finger framing his temple, boring holes into the enemy with his pupils.

"You've forgot your gloves, Thornfield," the Company man hissed.

"Lucky for you, or I would be challenging you to a duel with 'em," Mr. Thornfield drawled. "Are you ready to steal a little girl's property, Auggie, or shall we keep gassing? The box sits before you. You've won. It's the last pound of my flesh and Sardar's you'll be taking."

"And exactly how does *she* come into this, then?" Mr. Sack's full lips curled in a sneer. "Miss Jane Stone, governess, who claimed to have robbed you of the trunk and then was hauled off in a police wagon. What am I to make of it?"

"A profit, I had presumed," said I. Footsteps sounded in the hallway outside. Glancing from Mr. Quillfeather to Mr. Thornfield, I could not suppress a tiny pursed smile.

There was no knock. There was no warning. There was simply a tattoo of approaching footsteps and then the door banged open, revealing a half dozen Company soldiers and the man they all referred to as the Director.

"Oh, thank heaven," Mr. Thornfield sighed, crossing his legs. "I was on the verge of physical violence."

"Sir," spluttered Mr. Sack. "I . . . You are most welcome. To what do I owe the honour — er, pleasure — of this visit?"

The soldiers from the previous day, resplendent in their white and red coats, formed a neat file behind their leader. The Director was a tall man, impeccably dressed in sober black with silver trimmings; he carried a cane but seemed not to require its use, and his face called to mind a dignified greyhound, lean and efficient. He tapped twice with his cane upon the carpet.

"Inspector Quillfeather, I offer you my congratulations." The Director's voice was high but firm. "Charles Thornfield, it has been too long, too long indeed, sir. It is a pleasure to see you in better health."

Mr. Sack sank back into his desk chair like a deflated balloon.

"By the Lord, you're in fine fettle, sir." Mr. Thornfield offered his hand to the head of the Company. "Thank you for meeting us."

"You have made it well worth my while." The Director smiled coldly. "I was informed by Mr. Quillfeather here that you were being . . . how shall I put this . . . meddled with by certain of my staff. I at once launched my own internal investigation, and I have it on good authority that you are a wronged man. Naturally, the happy recovery of the item in question also sparked my keen interest, and I lost no time in sending a small body of troops to your residence after I had discovered the truth. Thankfully, I am told they were not required to defend you and Mr. Singh. Your services to the Crown and your family's favours in the importation line have not been forgot and indeed continue to be valued overseas."

"I'm damned grateful for your memory, sir," Mr. Thornfield replied.

"Do you hold fast to your decision to turn these spoils of war over to the Company?" The Director tapped the crate with his cane, eyes gleaming with avarice.

"If I never see 'em again, I'll die happier than I ever expected to."

"We were just discussing the remaining formalities and awaiting Mr. Sack's signature," Mr. Cyrus Sneeves intoned, taking a large pinch of snuff to fortify himself.

Augustus P. Sack's rosy features had paled during this exchange beyond a shade I had thought possible; he now gaped, fish-mouthed, as the Director stared at him with all the tender affection of a mongoose eyeing a snake. The soldiers at the back of the room stood at parade rest, eyes forward.

"Of course, of course." Suddenly Mr. Sack was scrabbling at the documents on his desk, as if being asked to address them for the first time. "I shall be only too happy to sign."

"See that you are." The Director nodded to the soldiers; two sprang neatly into action, lifting the crate. "Take this directly to my private chambers — I shall be informing the prime minister I require a word with him this afternoon. Inspector Quillfeather, we are grateful for your efforts on behalf of Mr. Clements; Mr. Thornfield, thank you for your cooperation."

"I was only too happy," Mr. Thornfield parroted at Mr. Sack.

"There is one other small matter," said I.

It was, of course, highly unlikely that the Director had ever been detained by a woman within the very walls of East India House, but a man who is a veteran of foreign wars ought to prepare himself for the unexpected, I reasoned. Dumbfounded, the Director tapped his cane against the rug again, frowning darkly, as Mr. Sack's complexion shifted from white to green.

"Mr. Sack was under the mistaken impression that he confiscated a piece of Karman Kaur's treasure from me, when it was in fact my property. I should like the misunderstanding rectified, and the necklace returned immediately."

Mr. Quillfeather hid a smile, and Mr. Thornfield chuckled.

My solicitor's speckled head bobbed dutifully as he suggested Mr. Sack send the item round to his offices.

"Do as she says, Mr. Sack," the Director commanded. "And afterwards, you can clear out your belongings and quit this establishment permanently. You need not expect a reference of any kind from us — I will not tolerate conspiracies fomenting under my very nose. Unless, that is, I am invited to take part in them — trumped-up politicos with delusions of importance have toppled entire empires. I think everyone here knows to which I refer specifically. Deliver Miss Stone what you owe her, and pray to God Charles Thornfield doesn't whip you through the streets like a stray pup. He would certainly, I daresay, have ample cause."

We found ourselves, Charles Thornfield and I, walking slowly down a wide avenue in Westminster after finishing a celebratory

632

repast with Sam Quillfeather. The high-hung moon was as pearly as the oysters we had consumed, and the cold wind whistled along the cobbles. It was the sort of silver-lit midnight which always reminded me of my mother, and made me wish there had been more picnics before she left the cottage and our garden forever.

Not having been sure of the outcome of our adventure, we had made no plans; now we strolled under winter plane trees, their inky fingers grasping at the stars, watching the lights flickering from within the pubs and the parlours. Mr. Thornfield was quiet with the uneasy calm of learning a long ordeal was behind him, as if not quite believing his fortunes had altered; I was equally still, but with apprehension.

My desire to never be parted from him was as ardent as my desire for breath; but I knew, should I fail to broach the subject of my past, I could become a puppet Jane, all wooden limbs and painted smiles. Reader, I do not foolishly suppose any one person can ever achieve perfect eloquence regarding their memories and affections and fears; if I did not take courage, however, I should always be viewing the man I loved through four eyes instead of two, ever cognisant of the monster hid deep in the back of my head.

"You are troubled, Jane."

I looked down in some surprise; his hand had caught mine within the folds of the cloak I had borrowed from Sahjara, as I had never made spectacular achievements in the realm of height and did not care it failed to quite reach my ankles. The fact that we were both gloved against the chill did little to diminish the pulse which surged through me.

"If this — if I — am unwelcome," he attempted, "please tell me so quickly. I recall your feelings as stated with exact clarity, I promise you, but I am overwhelmed. When a chap announces, 'I fancy that star in the sky,' and the star is actually amenable — 'tisn't likely to be true, you see."

"I resemble no star, sir."

"Well, you've clearly never heard of mirrors, then. I'll teach you to use 'em, they're easy as anything."

I gripped his hand harder and stopped us, staring up at him, *because this all might be lost at any moment,* and the idea broke my heart. His roughhewn face was tilted down in concern, his pale hair agleam in the light of the lamp, and he was everything to me, so if I was not to hear his gruff voice in the morning, in all the mornings, I wanted to paint a mental portrait of him on a London street corner with his hand in mine.

"Jane, you look as though you're saying farewell, and it's deuced disconcerting," he said.

"Far from that." I brought the back of his hand to my cheek, and we resumed walking. "Only I said I had to tell you a story, first. Before you kept me."

"It is only the amount of needless secrecy I've subjected you to which prevents my laughing in your lovely face. If shackles won't do it, I've half a mind to try iron bars. Just here," he added, pausing uncertainly before a neat, narrow row house. "I bought this when I first inherited so we should always have a place to keep our heads out of the rain in the city. Garima used to use it . . . well, before. Should you like to come in, and speak with me? If not, I'll find a cab and take you to your lodging house."

My answer was a rather breathless yes, I should very much like to come in, because anxiety and hope were wrapping thick vines about my throat. I found myself in a pleasant sitting room with yellow and green Sikh tapestries upon the walls and a profusion of richly tasselled cushions on the furniture which the neighbours would have found highly disreputable. After carelessly tossing his greatcoat over a chair, Mr. Thornfield poured spirits into crystal glasses for us as he always did — though now we both removed our gloves — and I placed Sahjara's cloak on a tree in the hall.

When I chose the armchair nearest the fire, he endearingly pulled up a footstool directly before me and sat, our heads now near upon a level. Before I knew what I was about, I stroked my fingers over his temple and he smiled with the roguishness of a tomcat. He placed our glasses upon the carpet.

"You invest me with hope you shan't be punishing me for my asinine refusals with your absence." He caught my fingers and wove them with his own. "All other punishments you care to mete out will be met with better bravery. Now. Let's have your secrets. This house was heated and aired this morning, but I ordered all the servants away."

At times, the swiftest cut is the cleanest, so I announced, "The name I gave you is a false one. As a girl, I lived at Highgate House. I am the illegitimate daughter of your aunt Patience Barbary's husband, Richard Barbary, and a French dancer who went mad and took her own life."

Mr. Thornfield's dark brows are dashing

enough to perform great sardonic feats, but I had never before seen them execute such acrobatics. Then his eyes brightened nearly to sapphire and his lips parted. "You don't mean to tell me that you're really Jane *Steele*?" he exclaimed.

"I . . . I do, actually. How —"

He slapped his knee, barking a laugh. "Mum used to mention you from time to time, the French changeling whose mother wormed her into an English estate. Awfully thick situation for Aunt Patience to swallow, but Chastity and Patience Goodwill never got on, you understand — Mum thought it rather a ripe coup d'état. Why didn't you say something?"

Flushing beet red, I replied, "Your inheritance was unexpected. I wanted to live there again, thought that it may have been . . . mine."

"And so it is!" he crowed. "Every brick, every weapon, every bloody blade of grass is as much yours as I am, darling, supposing you'll give me a pallet in the stables and a crust from time to time. Are you *quite* mad?"

"I don't want you to live on a pallet." My tears spilled, and he painted his fingertips over my jaw. "I want you to live in my bones, but how can you not be angry I lied?"

"I'm a scoundrel, Jane. Born of scoundrels, bred of 'em to boot. Not to mention a whoreson bastard, as you yourself once called me, and I remember the occasion with great fondness save for the part where you toppled off a horse."

"Oh, but there's more, there's —"

"Breathe, darling." Running his palms down my arms, he cupped my small hands in his large ones as we had once done in his office. "Please, I'm drowning just looking at you. Have a spot of pity and breathe for me. So you're a scoundrel too, I take it — I'd suggest we make matching uniforms, but that quite sabotages knavery, you see, and should thwart our purposes. What else?"

"I'm a murderess, sir."

"Does she suppose me deaf and blind?" he cried incredulously. "Does she suppose I simply forgot that she —"

"Five times over."

Charles Thornfield began to say something. Then, brushing his thumb under my damp eyes once more, he began to say something else. Finally, after puffing a vexed sigh, he muttered something else entirely, by which time I was prepared to die on the spot. I think my heart must have only commenced beating once more when the wry creases around his brows smoothed into softer seams, as he looked when he spoke with Sahjara or picked up a delicate antique volume from his library — as he looked when he wanted to take especial care. He passed me his kerchief, counting on his left hand.

"The first?" he questioned, and his rough voice had gentled.

"When I was a girl, my half brother tried to rape me and I pushed him," I whispered. "He died. I used to — I no longer think that was entirely my fault; but it was the most important, for it was the first, and made me who I am."

Mr. Thornfield's eyes frosted over entirely. "Oh, my darling Jane. Next?"

"My headmaster gave me the choice of watching my friend starve or being sent to a madhouse. I stabbed him with a letter opener."

He whistled, continuing to count. "Much more impressive. The third?"

"My landlord beat his wife until she lost their unborn child, so I pushed him into the Thames."

"It's not many corpses as can foul the Thames, bless 'em. You accomplished a miracle. Go on?"

"A judge wanted to buy my friend's little girl and turn her into his dollymop. I gave him inheritance powder and he died dread-fully."

"Not so dreadfully as he should have done. And I know Jack Ghosh personally, my darling, so does that make up the full roster?"

"Yes."

Reader, I wanted with every cell in my bloodstream to fly from the room and weep for days, but I was prevented; the grim line above his clear-cut nose appeared, and he pursed his lips sternly.

I waited, frozen in terror.

"I don't think much of your list, y'see," he declared, and though his eyes were warm they were wet as well. "A more sorry lot of rubbish than you've dispatched I've not heard tell of. Why, in battle, Karman killed dozens of strapping British and Bengal gents who'd not have pissed on these dregs if they were on fire. We simply must raise your killing standards, my darling, because I'm frankly ashamed at the quality of chaps you've —"

We were both laughing through tears by the time I had flung myself the short distance into his lap and was kissing him, so warm and so real underneath me. His shoulders under my questing hands were at first as tense with worry as mine, I think, for I had alarmed him; but soon, they calmed, and he cradled me more softly, and dropped his lips against my neck with a breath like a prayer.

"That was egregiously unfair of you," he murmured against my skin. "I thought you were about to confess to fatal consumption, or a fellow whose company you prefer, or the fact you've been called back to faerie, something bloody *important*."

"Do you know that you're entirely insane?" I had pulled the black ribbon from his head and buried my hands in his hair.

"Yes, actually, but this form of madness is far preferable to that of a fortnight since, don't y'agree?"

"God, yes." I calmed myself. "And I never thought that mad, only tragic."

He set his hands softly at my waist, frowning in thought.

I passed quiet fingers over his hairline and waited, wondering whether his torment had been constant or more like owning a heart which had stopped like a broken watch; I wondered whether he knew himself.

"I hated the hands which couldn't help her," he concluded hoarsely. "And all those dead, Jane . . . Even after coming here, when I would walk into a pub or a square, I couldn't look at humans without seeing them as corpses." He shook his white head. "Then I saw you. You are so *alive,* Jane Steele, you make my breath catch, as if a glowing creature from the depths of the forest had lit upon the end of my finger. You had already endeared yourself to me by greeting Sahjara so courteously, as if somehow it were a happy circumstance for you to accidentally enter our madhouse. When I saw you fall from Nalin that night, I knew you were dead, my darling, I knew it with such certainty, because how could anyone I had liked so well from the first survive such an accident? Then you sprang up wielding invective and knives and I adored you. I thought it lunacy that you should take such a frank interest in my history."

"Only insomuch as your history makes you who you are today. I dreaded your knowing mine, sir."

His eyes, so wistful seconds previous, narrowed in amusement. "Had you not better call me Charles?"

Laughing, I pressed my forehead to his. "I love you, Charles Thornfield."

He placed his hand over my heart, and I could not help but wince at the sting; where once he had been about to speak, he stilled in chagrin, and I realised any further intimacy would reveal the injury inflicted by

Mr. Sack. This was distressing. I wanted no words on the subject of the Company to distract us; I wanted fewer articles of clothing between, and ideally a bed, though the nearby sofa would do, or the rug barring that.

"It's nothing, only a scratch."

"A scratch from what manner of animal?" he demanded.

Clearly I was to be thwarted in any attempt to keep the injury secret; I unbuttoned my dress at the neck a few inches, and then several inches more than was necessary, and watched as my love's heated gaze darkened to black. The gash was indeed an ugly one, a crusted purple line.

"Very well, precisely whom am I meant to murder this evening?" he snarled.

"I thought I was the expert on that activity."

"Jane, I demand satisfaction!"

"Might we employ other avenues in our search for satisfaction?" I said in his ear.

"There have been too many outrages upon your person in our brief acquaintance, and it will *not* be tolerated a moment longer, not while I have breath, do you hear me?"

I placed my hands along his stony jaw, set upon having my own way.

"Charles," said I. "While you have breath

in your body is, I hope, a long period of opportunity. Now, if you will forgive me for being coarse, I should like your breath on my body. I am a wicked woman, and I should like for us to go upstairs and wash this blasted scrape, and see that my head is mending well — because that will please you upon a professional level, and because you enjoy being tender with me — and then I should like for you to express that tenderness in positively filthy fashions."

The scowl did not vanish, but now his sculpted mouth and eyes both softened at their corners. "Is that truly how you wish to pass the night?"

"Oh, I do, sir."

"Had I not better ask you to marry me?"

"I don't know. Do you want to?"

Finally, he chuckled and drew me closer, pulling slack lips over the hollow of my throat. "Yes."

I shivered. "I don't see any ministers here, do you?"

"Drat, we seem to have run dry of prelates. Happens at the worst possible times. Jane, we are doing this all out of order."

"Are we?" My nose crinkled in confusion.

"Indeed so." His voice lowered, its warm burr scraping over me softly. "I love you, Jane Steele. I love you. I've loved you since you fell from my horse. I love you, and I'm a damn fool. That should have been said by this time. Now, I've a confession to make." He rose easily to his feet, and I rose with him, for he had slipped his arms round my back and under my legs. "You, my darling, must vow to me on your honour never to fall down another staircase. But you've no idea how cruel it was to have you in my arms like this every night, thinking you should only ever be my friend Jane, so I shall indulge your desire to shift our plans from murder to other sins."

We did exactly so.

At first there was great tenderness, and kissing until our lips were supple and rosy whilst he was still learning for himself that I was all right; and if later there was passion, and muffled cries, and Charles's *No, I want to hear you, please let me hear you,* and expanses of skin being tasted until we were both panting with exertion and simple love, then it is not the polite place of autobiography to address the subject.

When we had more than once exhausted ourselves, however, and Charles in sleep rolled to his belly and I spent long minutes tracing the scar marring the muscles of his back, I thought that this would be the memory I would treasure best, and I was right. As soon as I could leave off stroking his skin, I touched the mark at my own neck and blessed it; for we are doers of deeds, he and I, and as such lose parts of our flesh along the way, and can only pray to meet friends and lovers who can help to stitch us back again, and that we can make them whole in turn.

I did not marry Charles Thornfield until some few years after I began sharing his bed.

I am today Jane Thornfield, née Steele — but I am also, though few outside the household saving Mr. Quillfeather know it, Jane Kaur. Sardar Singh performed the ceremony in June, in the garden at midnight as my mother would have wanted, as Charles and Sahjara looked on proudly. Mr. Singh filled a ceremonial iron bowl with clear water and then poured into it a quantity of sugar; this he stirred with one of the swords from the billiards room, a double-edged one, as he called out in his lion's voice, *Sri Wahe Guruji Ka Khalsa, Sri Wahe Guruji Ki Fateh.*

The passage is a pretty one, even in English: "The Khalsa belong to God, and God's truth will always prevail."

Charles says that he does not care what sort of Jane I am so long as I am his Jane;

Sardar says that he does not care what sort of Jane I am so long as I am my own Jane; Sahjara says that she does not care what sort of Jane I am so long as she is my Sahjara. Thus I am daily three Janes, and so the luckiest of all.

When corpses arrive at Highgate House, they speak to Charles, and he reports to Sam Quillfeather — sometimes they died naturally, but sometimes not, and these occasions are much preferable, for we share adventures, and I cannot imagine a happier circumstance than leading a life spiced with murder and intrigue alongside the man I love.

I hope that the epitaph of the human race when the world ends will be: *Here perished a species which lived to tell stories.*

We tell stories to strangers to ingratiate ourselves, stories to lovers to better adhere us skin to skin, stories in our heads to banish the demons. When we tell the truth, often we are callous; when we tell lies, often we are kind. Through it all, we tell stories, and we own an uncanny knack for the task. In *Jane Eyre,* the wise author writes, "Reserved people often really need the frank discussion of their sentiments and griefs more than the expansive." I have lived this — should we neglect the task of expressing our passions, our species should perish upon the vine, desiccated and desolate.

Mr. Rochester after being married to Miss Eyre announces that their honeymoon "will shine our life long; its beams will only fade over your grave or mine." As I am not a prognosticator, and have been witness to myriad calamities, I can make no such claim regarding my own marriage. Confident I remain, however, and I find myself hopeful as well — if the world is wide enough for me to find someone, who knows what miracles lurk behind each and every closed door? Charles Thornfield and I are far from perfect; but we are perfect for each other, and perhaps in the end, our chains bind us more closely than anyone who has never been a prisoner can imagine.

HISTORICAL AFTERWORD

While *Jane Eyre* needs no introduction, I should mention that Charlotte Brontë's preface to the infamous second edition thrilled me from the instant I first set eyes on the quote, "Conventionality is not morality. Self-righteousness is not religion." While the author continues to lob great Molotov cocktails of scriptural invective at her critics for perhaps a trifle longer than necessary (if Brontë lived today, it wouldn't be impossible to picture her replying to troll tweets and one-star Amazon reviews), the spirit of the thing is marvelous, and to anyone who has read the novel without the preface, know that it was a major inspiration for this satirical riff off the classical Jane.

The position of women in the nineteenth century was notoriously fraught with economic peril and rife with class divisions, and nowhere is this more evident in *Jane Eyre* than when the haughty Blanche Ingram rails against governesses as if they are repulsive insects children have every right to squash ruthlessly. Marriage to a rich man was a respectable way to make a fortune — but to be educated and servile at once, raising the children of others simply due to reduced circumstances, was considered a ghastly fate. Richard Nemesvari, who edited the careful scholarly edition of *Jane Eyre* I myself used, suggests regarding Blanche's tirade announcing "half of them [governesses] detestable and the rest ridiculous" that:

> On one level this is purely a rude attempt to put Jane in her place, but it is also an attempt by Blanche to establish her own place . . . It is absolutely essential for Blanche to despise all governesses, because only in this way can she ensure (in her own mind and others') that there is no connection or potential relationship between them.

Naturally, this made the notion of writing a serial killer governess who was also in all likelihood a wronged heiress cracking good fun, and while Jane Steele is a far more egalitarian soul than Blanche Ingram, she also has no strong objection to pretty frocks, good whiskey, large estates, expensive horses, or marriage to a brooding Byronic hero.

It would be ludicrous to pretend that I could have grasped Sikhism after only six months' research, but a few books in particular were of immense help. First, *The Sikh Religion* by Max Arthur MacAuliffe (1842–1913) was written by an Englishman whose love of the Punjabi religion was roundly ridiculed by his associates within the Indian Civil Service, who really didn't think converting was quite the done thing, by gad. Responsible for producing the first UK translation of the Sikh holy book, the *Guru Granth Sahib,* MacAuliffe continued to pen English-language volumes about Sikh history with the help of Pratap Singh Giani, a brilliant linguist and calligraphist who among other prestigious accomplishments worked as a scripture-reader in Amritsar, the holy city. Second, *The First and Second Sikh Wars* was commissioned by the British Army in 1911, and military historian Reginald George Burton executed his mission with tremendous care and detail — for which I'm grateful, as it's nigh impossible to picture a battle when you've never been in one.

Thirdly, *The Sikhs,* written by political

activist, magazine publisher, and scholarly author Patwant Singh, proved crucial. While Charles Thornfield and Sardar Singh are romanticized versions of nineteenth-century warriors, the bloody battles and corrupt politics were real, and long continued to plague the region. Patwant Singh attempted to intercede for peace during a tragic modern-day confrontation (the 1984 crisis at the Golden Temple, in which three hundred fifty extreme Sikh separatists and seventy Indian soldiers died), and he worked tirelessly to present a faithful and well-rounded picture of a much-misrepresented culture. An entire chapter of *The Sikhs* is titled "Grievous Betrayals, 1839–1849," and describes how gross mismanagement — or more likely, outright treachery — by powerful Sikhs led to the slaughter of the Khalsa, and the eradication of what had once been an opulent empire. Based in personal sacrifice and responsibility, monotheism, pacifism, meditation, but also military prowess, the people who were once massacred for rejecting the inhumanities of the caste system grew into a legendary army, and Patwant Singh did us an incredible service by placing these disparities in vivid context. His books have my highest recommendation, as they are full of what he refers to as the "invasions and inquisitions, triumphs and tragedies, piety and sense of divine purpose, devotion and depravities, loyalties and betrayals, courage and convictions" of his religion.

Finally, it would be disingenuous of me to suggest that this book isn't rather ridiculous, and be it known that its ridiculousness is based in both truth and in fiction. While Mr. Squeers, who "had but one eye, and the popular prejudice runs in favor of two" was not real, the terrible school called Cowan Bridge that Charlotte Brontë claimed took the lives of two of her sisters was. While George MacDonald Fraser's fine novel *Flashman and the Mountain of Light* is almost too deliciously ridiculous to exist, the defeated Sikhs were in fact required to hand over the Kooh-i-Noor diamond to Queen Victoria, which was cut from 186 carats to 105.6 carats and is now part of the Crown Jewels. And while it may appear ridiculous that an accidental avenger should find a home with refugees from Punjabi battlefields, as Nicholas Nickleby mentioned to his friend Smike, "When I speak of home, I speak of the place where — in default of a better — those I love are gathered together; and if that place were a gypsy's tent, or a barn, I should call it by the same good name notwithstanding."

ACKNOWLEDGMENTS

For reasons that are obvious to everyone kind enough to read this book, I dedicated it to Jane Eyre and Nicholas Nickleby, who have given me many hours of literary joy since childhood (and who unfortunately led quite parallel lives of undeserved squalor and questionable headmasters). Jane has often tugged at my heartstrings, however, while Nicholas once caused me to guffaw aloud on the New York subway system, which drew incredulous stares. I'd be remiss if I failed to mention Jonathan Small and the gaunt, devoted Mrs. Danvers to boot; thus, thank you endlessly to Charlotte Brontë and Charles Dickens, as well as to Sir Arthur Conan Doyle and Daphne du Maurier, whose smudgy literary fingerprints are likewise all over this volume.

Thank you to every stunningly fabulous talent at William Morris Endeavor, first and foremost the magnificent Erin Malone, who fixes my mojo when it frequently nosedives. From the moment I first emailed her about Jane Steele years ago, she has been waving magic pom-poms every step of the way. Tracy Fisher and Cathryn Summerhayes, you are splendid midsummer goddesses, as all my foreign publishers (to whom I am also deeply grateful) are well aware. To everyone at WME who has been of such tireless assistance, I am forever grateful.

I had the honor of working with Kerri Kolen on my debut novel, and it feels sublime to have such a fantastic and kindly powerhouse in my corner again. Though she is but little, she is fierce — and brilliant, and I adore her. Thank you as well to Ivan Held, Katie McKee, Alexis Welby, Ashley McClay, and every other person who makes my employment by Putnam and Penguin Random House feel like such a privilege. Grateful thanks to Claire Baldwin and Sherise Hobbs at Headline, whose notes and encouragement were equally appreciated.

My family, as ever, have heaped support on me to the point I'm beginning to resemble an overbuilt skyscraper — but I need it all, and I thank you. My friends deserve a collective vacation to Aruba for talking me down whenever I flounder; to every school chum and coworker and actor and Sherlockian and just plain fellow nerd, thank you from the bottom of my heart. My husband, Gabriel, quietly makes me fish tacos with homemade corn tortillas when the writing is going poorly and I'm being a complete jackass, which is probably the definition of devotion, so I thank him most of all.

Finally, as ever: Reader, I thank you. Your collective existence will forever baffle and delight me.